Aisling wrapped her arms around Zurael's waist . . .

It had to be wrong to lust for a demon. But she couldn't seem to stop herself from wanting him, from yielding a little bit more of herself each time he touched her. "We need to leave," she whispered, almost grateful to be going somewhere where she wouldn't be alone with him.

His hand left her neck and swept down her spine. She moaned softly as he ground himself against her. He made her ache in a way she'd never ached before. He made her fantasize about things that shouldn't be allowed to happen. . . .

She turned her head and kissed his neck.

"Aisling," he said, and the sound made her swell and part in readiness for him. Her hands moved up his sides and around to find his nipples. They were hard points against her palms. She rubbed over them, and thrilled at the way he panted lightly and cupped her buttocks so he could pull her more tightly against him.

"Tell me, Aisling. Can I pass for human?" There was a dark amusement in his voice that made her shiver. . . .

GHOSTLAND

Jory Strong

B

BERKLEY SENSATION, NEW YORK

THE BERKLEY PUBLISHING GROUP
Published by the Penguin Group
Penguin Group (USA) Inc.
375 Hudson Street, New York, New York 10014, USA
Penguin Group (Canada), 90 Eglinton Avenue East, Suite 700, Toronto, Ontario M4P 2Y3, Canada
(a division of Pearson Penguin Canada Inc.)
Penguin Books Ltd., 80 Strand, London WC2R 0RL, England
Penguin Group Ireland, 25 St. Stephen's Green, Dublin 2, Ireland (a division of Penguin Books Ltd.)
Penguin Group (Australia), 250 Camberwell Road, Camberwell, Victoria 3124, Australia
(a division of Pearson Australia Group Pty. Ltd.)
Penguin Books India Pvt. Ltd., 11 Community Centre, Panchsheel Park, New Delhi—110 017, India
Penguin Group (NZ), 67 Apollo Drive, Rosedale, North Shore 0632, New Zealand
(a division of Pearson New Zealand Ltd.)
Penguin Books (South Africa) (Pty.) Ltd., 24 Sturdee Avenue, Rosebank, Johannesburg 2196,
South Africa

Penguin Books Ltd., Registered Offices: 80 Strand, London WC2R 0RL, England

This book is an original publication of The Berkley Publishing Group.

Copyright © 2009 by Valerie Christenson.
Cover art by Tony Mauro.
Cover design by Rita Frangie.
Interior text design by Kristin del Rosario.

PRINTING HISTORY
Berkley Sensation trade paperback edition / April 2009

Library of Congress Cataloging-in-Publication Data
Strong, Jory.
    Ghostland / Jory Strong.—Berkley sensation trade pbk. ed.
        p. cm.
    ISBN 978-0-425-22606-3
    I. Title.

PS3619. T777G56 2009
813'.6—dc22

                                            2008046956

PRINTED IN THE UNITED STATES OF AMERICA

10 9 8 7 6 5 4 3 2 1

ACKNOWLEDGMENTS

Without others, the dream *Ghostland* represents would never have been realized. Thanks to my parents, Neal and Joy Howard, and my husband, Paul, for their unfailing support and encouragement on the long, often-painful road from unpublished author to published one. Thanks to my agent, Ethan Ellenberg, for finding just the right home for *Ghostland*. Thanks to Cindy Hwang, for falling in love with the project and being enthusiastic about a sometimes-grim, post-apocalyptic world. And thanks to Sue-Ellen Gower, who has helped me and challenged me to become a better writer with each story I've crafted.

One

FEAR rolled through the San Joaquin farmland with the rumble of a heavy truck. Children were called in from their chores and women abandoned their laundry without putting it on the lines. Heavy doors and barred windows were closed and locked as prayers were said to whatever gods might still linger in a world altered forever by war-born plague.

A cold knot of dread formed in Aisling McConaughey's stomach as she ran toward the farmhouse. Beyond it she could see some of the others slip into the barn, but she was too far away to make it there and into the well-concealed safe room.

The front door opened. Aisling hurried past Geneva, the woman whose doorstep she'd been left on as an infant.

She raced down the hallway and slipped into the storage closet, then into the small hiding space between it and the kitchen pantry. Her throat closed with dismay when she saw she wasn't the only one who hadn't made it to the barn. One of her youngest sisters sat with her knees hugged to her chest, her eyes dark with fear.

Aisling scooped the girl up in her arms and claimed the spot on the floor. "It'll be okay," she whispered as she hugged the child. "They're probably driving through to make sure the orchards are being taken care of properly. Maybe they're bringing workers. You know the new mayor doesn't let people stay in the city if they can't earn their keep."

The floor in the safe room vibrated as the heavy truck drew closer. Since The Last War and the plague that ended it, only the rich or those on government business had been allowed access to fuel for their vehicles.

Thin arms tightened around Aisling's neck. "What if they want one of us?"

"It hasn't happened yet," Aisling whispered, wanting to soothe her sister's fears with a lie, but giving her the truth instead.

After war and plague killed so much of Earth's population, the supernaturals had emerged from hiding. In the decades since, territories had been carved out. Stockton and the surrounding farmlands were controlled by humans who feared vampires and shapeshifters as well as anyone gifted with supernatural abilities.

The screech of brakes sent a fresh wave of fear rushing through Aisling. The pounding on the door, coupled by a man's voice demanding entry, made her breath grow short.

Shuffling footsteps marked Geneva's slow progress toward compliance. Others, orphans without abilities to mark them as different, scrambled and rustled as they took up positions around the house so everything appeared normal.

"Come in," Geneva said, though the tread of boots telegraphed that their unwelcome visitors were already inside.

Nausea radiated out from the tight knot in Aisling's stomach as the house was searched. She closed her eyes and envisioned the room she shared with several other girls. Her chest tightened just as a voice called, "Captain. In here."

In her mind's eye she followed the heavy footsteps into her bedroom and over to the dresser where the unfinished amulet rested.

The captain's next words sent ice sliding down her spine. "Where's the shamaness?"

Aisling knew then that they'd come for her. The amulet could belong to a witch or an artist. Many of the non-gifted humans hedged their bets by buying talismans and fetishes for protection. But for the guardsmen, the fox carved in abalone was confirmation of what they were looking for.

She hugged her sister again, before extricating herself and moving to the small door that led to a closet seemingly packed with stored clothing. In the room above them the guardsman asked again, "Where's the shamaness, old woman?"

Aisling expected to hear the telltale click of a bullet being chambered or the sound of physical violence. For the rich and well connected, life was much different; freedom and equality were something they took for granted. But for the poor, especially those who didn't own the land they worked, civil rights were something to be found in history books and dreams.

She eased the hidden door open. Some of the tightness left her chest when she encountered nothing but darkness. There'd been only a cursory opening and closing of the closet door when the guardsmen searched the house. She suspected their actions were done for show, to intimidate rather than with the expectation of finding someone.

In the hallway a different voice said, "Ms. McConaughey, we don't want to harm you or any of those in your care. The Church is aware of your good work. Unfortunately, more is at stake here than a woman and her family of orphans. I have been directed to find a shamaness and take her to the Oakland diocese. My search has led me here, to your home. It would be best for everyone concerned if you cooperated."

Aisling closed the hidden door. She took a deep, steadying breath before slipping through the long raincoats and blankets hung to cover the entrance to the hiding place. Her fingers smoothed over the small leather fetish pouch she wore underneath her shirt. There was no choice but to surrender herself.

The guardsmen could kill everyone here and claim they were eradicating disease or defending themselves. As long as the orchards and gardens and livestock weren't destroyed, there would be no protest, no outrage.

She stepped out into the hallway and climbed the stairs of the old wooden farmhouse. When she reached the top, the dark-robed figure of the priest turned. Their eyes met. His flashed with satisfaction and perhaps a hint of relief.

He stepped forward, his body language conveying friendliness. She allowed her hand to be engulfed by his.

Her palms were rough, her fingers callused against the baby-softness of the priest's. Aisling forced herself to relax, to pretend she accepted his overture and didn't view him with suspicion.

"Your name?" the priest asked.

"Aisling."

"Come," the priest said. "Gather what's necessary. Your services are needed."

"I'll be able to return?"

There was just the barest flicker of hesitation before he said, "Of course, but I don't know when. Clothing and food will be provided. There's no need to pack either of those."

Fear tried to claw its way out of Aisling's throat. Panic filled her at the idea of being without her larger fetishes, the ones that remained in the barn safe room except for those times when she traveled deep into the ghostlands and required them for protection.

She couldn't retrieve them, not with the police and the priest here. "I'm ready," she said, unable to keep the shakiness from her voice.

The priest frowned. Creased eyebrows telegraphed his worry. A small flower of hope blossomed in Aisling's chest. He was knowledgeable. Perhaps her lack of stronger protections would make her appear weak to him, unsuitable for whatever task had led him to her.

"You've got everything you need?" he asked. His eyes went to her neck and wrists, to the flat pockets of her working pants and the thin belt that was free of amulets and fetishes.

"I've had no formal training as a shamaness," Aisling said.

It was the truth. What she knew, she had learned on her own or from the spirit guides who aided her.

For the wealthy, or for those living in communities where supernatural gifts were embraced, there were apprenticeships to be had and formal education available. She hadn't benefited from either.

The priest closed his eyes, perhaps in prayer. Or perhaps he looked elsewhere for guidance, though the Church was prone to view such talents in the same way they viewed vampires and shapeshifters, as devil-born or devil-touched.

Aisling's hand closed into a fist. She willed herself to show no emotion. Even so, she felt herself tremble slightly as the small bud of hope was mercilessly crushed when he opened his eyes and said, "If you're ready, then, we'll leave. I want to be back at the diocese before nightfall."

Movement beyond the priest caught her attention. When she saw the black ferret with the golden eyes, a small ray of happiness penetrated the darkness of her fear at being taken away. Aziel meant to go with her or he wouldn't have come out in the presence of these strangers.

"You'll need to take your pet," Geneva said, her expression stoic. "I won't have him here unattended and going after the chickens."

"Come, Aziel," Aisling said, though it was unnecessary. The ferret was already scampering toward her. He made quick work of climbing up her clothing and draping himself around her neck in a living stole.

"You're sure you have everything you need?" the priest asked, his eyes drifting to the ferret briefly before returning to Aisling's face.

She nodded, afraid if she tried to speak the sudden lump in her throat would prevent it.

The walk to the front door and beyond, to the heavy truck favored by police and guardsmen when traveling into the countryside, was a blur. Aisling focused inward. She tried to isolate herself from what was happening.

Unconsciously she sought comfort. Her hand curled around Aziel's luxurious tail and the ferret chirped softly.

Only two guardsmen and the priest had gone into the house, but lounging around the truck were three men carrying machine guns. A fourth stood in the bed, leaning against a machine gun mounted there.

The captain opened the back door and stepped aside; the priest waved Aisling forward. She resisted the urge to look back as she climbed in.

She could feel the eyes of her family members watching her. She could imagine the fear that would cling to them even after the rumble of the truck faded.

The truck doors slammed and the engine roared to life. The guardsmen took up positions on the bed.

"Ready?" yelled the driver.

One of the men in back pounded on the roof in a signal to go.

The priest said nothing and soon they were on the highway. Signs marked the distance to Oakland, to San Francisco and beyond—to worlds both foreign and familiar to Aisling, places she'd never seen except in her imagination and in the books Geneva loved to collect and share.

Fear faded and curiosity grew with each mile they traveled. Aziel repositioned himself to look out the window. Every now and then he chirruped as though he were a tour guide pointing out the various landmarks.

"The ferret is unusual," the priest said, breaking the long silence. "Do you consider him your familiar?"

Aisling turned from the window to look at the man who'd taken her away from her home. He was older than she, with crow's-feet at the corners of his eyes and a mouth that seemed ready to smile.

"He's a pet. I thought familiars were for witches and warlocks to claim. Do shamans have them, too?"

The priest shook his head. "No, not that I've ever encountered."

He tentatively reached a hand toward the ferret, but Aziel turned quickly and hissed a warning.

"He's not friendly with strangers," Aisling said. She didn't want to make an enemy of someone who might prove to be an ally. "Why am I being taken to Oakland?"

The priest tilted his head slightly to indicate the two men in the front seat of the truck. "I'm not at liberty to discuss the matter." His gaze drifted to the ferret that once again had his paws on the window and was looking out. "Where did you get Aziel?"

His continued interest troubled Aisling. She suspected he wouldn't admit to possessing supernatural gifts, at least not to her, but she worried that he'd guessed Aziel was something more, even if she herself wasn't sure exactly what her companion was.

She didn't think of Aziel as her familiar. If she were to label his role it would be spirit guardian. Perhaps a witch's familiar acted in a similar manner. Unfortunately the few witches she knew about were secretive and coven-bound. They were not women to share a confidence with or to ask one of.

When the priest didn't turn away from her, she said, "I found him. I think he was hitching a ride with a trader's caravan. Probably the chickens on the farm tempted him out of one of the vehicles. A day or so after they moved on, I discovered him."

The priest chuckled and let the topic drop. Aisling returned her attention to the rapidly approaching cityscape. "I don't know much about Oakland and who rules it."

"At the moment it has a mayor and a board of supervisors. The Church is represented, as are various human groups. It's safe enough during the day but the night belongs to the predators."

Goose bumps rose on Aisling's arm and spread when they reached the city and were greeted by the burned-out buildings. After the plague had run its course and the supernaturals revealed their presence, anarchy had reigned for a while.

The streets, especially in the big cities, filled with violence and fear, and with the raw need to survive in a place where shelter was plentiful but food and fuel scarce. Eventually the armed services and guardsmen brought order, but the cities were still scarred by their pasts. And though the United States still existed as a nation, it was not the same glorious nation it had once been—if the history books and stories were to be believed.

It all happened well before she was born, and had seemed irrelevant to everyday life until now. She never expected to see any of the big cities. There was no reason to go there and no money to do so. Unless a person was rich or well connected or joined a merchant caravan, travel was expensive and dangerous.

Aisling startled as the men in the back of the truck fired a quick burst from their machine guns. The priest said, "Nothing to worry about. Those are just warning shots."

She studied the scene in front of her: fallen buildings and shattered glass, abandoned automobiles and faded trash. Whether real or imagined, she suddenly felt watched. "Who lives here?" she whispered despite the impossibility of anyone outside the truck hearing her.

"Malcontents. The insane. The unfit and outcast."

"Humans?"

"For the most part, though I imagine it's a hunting ground for the predators."

The blackened, destroyed section slowly gave way to areas where buildings were being reclaimed. Heavily guarded warehouses stood next to abandoned ones. Run-down, darkened tenement houses stood next to buildings with iron bars silhouetted in soft yellow light.

Landscaped medians and planted trees marked the point where poverty and struggle gave way to comfort, though the bars on the windows and doors remained. Armed police and guardsmen patrolled the streets. Men, women and children dressed in bright clothing hurried to get their business accomplished before the daylight faded.

Aisling looked down at her own worn and work-stained clothes. She thought about the priest's hesitation when she'd asked if she would be able to return home.

Fear lodged in her chest and throat again as she wondered if she'd survive this city, this task that had brought armed men and a servant of the Church to the San Joaquin in order to retrieve her.

Aziel turned from the window. His wet nose found her ear in a rooting, affectionate gesture conveying his belief everything would be okay.

She smiled despite the turmoil of her emotions and the sight of the Church that loomed ahead when the truck turned onto a narrow street. They passed through a heavily guarded gate, then slowed to a stop.

"Here we are," the priest said. He smoothed the black material of his cassock as he glanced at the streaks of red marking the impending sunset.

Opulence, wealth, pictures painted by masters who'd been dead hundreds of years before The Last War. Those were the impressions Aisling was left with as she was led through the hallways by a woman in a nun's habit. "Now that I know your size, I'll arrange for fresh clothing," the nun said as she ushered Aisling into a small, comfortably furnished room. "Take a shower. There will be food waiting when you're finished." She glanced at the ferret with curiosity. "Do you need anything for your pet?"

"A litter box."

The nun nodded and shut the door. A lock slid into place with a nearly silent click, trapping Aisling in a room with handwoven rugs and polished wooden floors, furniture that was pleasing to the eye as well as functional. It didn't look like a prison, but even without the locked door, the unfamiliar city and lack of money or allies made it one.

She glanced out into the nearly dark sky and let her thoughts flow to the hot shower and the promised meal. They were all prisoners of the night and the predators waiting in it.

Aisling pulled Aziel from her shoulder and set him on the back edge of a chair before going into the bathroom. She stripped out of her clothing, and shivered with pleasure when she stepped under the hot water. She stayed until a shadow announced the nun's return.

Dismay filled her when she left the shower to find her clothes missing, replaced by a long black dress with a wide skirt. It was a modest garment, meant to conceal the female form.

Aisling didn't want to wear it, but the dress was her only choice other than wrapping herself in a towel or bedsheet. Her eyes widened when she saw a hair dryer next to the sink. It was a luxurious use of electricity she wasn't accustomed to.

In her enjoyment of the hot water, she'd gotten her hair thoroughly soaked. The thick, honey-blond strands curled around her buttocks when unbound and could take hours to dry.

Using the hair dryer was almost as blissful as the shower. She lingered several minutes beyond the point where her hair could be braided and coiled at the back of her head.

Aziel was helping himself to a piece of chicken by the time Aisling emerged from the bathroom. She laughed at his naughtiness. He wouldn't have dared to get on the kitchen table at home, Geneva would have . . .

A lump formed in Aisling's throat. She blinked, suddenly overwhelmed by homesickness and worry.

The ferret looked up from the meat clasped between his paws. He chirped excitedly.

Aisling forced away all thought but appreciation for the food in front of her. She joined Aziel at the table and ate. When it was done she checked the door and found it locked. With no books to read and no one to talk to, she lay down on the bed with Aziel curled on her pillow.

It was getting late when the sound of the door opening woke her. "Come, they're waiting for you," the nun who'd escorted her to the room said.

Aisling slipped from the bed. "I'd like my clothes back."

"They're being washed. When they're clean, they'll be returned."

It was such a small thing, considering everything that had happened and might yet happen, but the knowledge she'd soon be wearing her own clothing lifted Aisling's spirits. "Thank you," she whispered as Aziel reclaimed his perch on her shoulder.

The nun's expression gentled. "Come," she said, her voice warmer. "They're waiting for you. I believe it must be important given the mayor's presence."

Aisling was led to a room. It was cold, as if it wasn't used much and therefore wasn't heated often. Though the nun had said the mayor waited, there were only two men in the room—one was the priest who'd come for her, the other a much older man wearing bloodred robes.

"You've met Father Ursu," the unknown priest said. "I'm Bishop Routledge. Your services are needed. In exchange for a successful performance of them, you'll be granted a license to practice your skills in Oakland. You'll be provided with a residence in the area of town where others with controversial abilities have settled. You'll also receive vouchers for food and transportation as well as a small fee in order to ease your transition."

He started to turn away. Aisling said, "Father Ursu told me I'd be allowed to return home."

The bishop halted. He smiled, though it didn't reach his eyes. "Returning home with a financial reward is a possibility. But first let's see if you succeed tonight."

Aisling tried to appear confident, unafraid. His voice and wording confirmed what she already knew. There was no choice about whether or not she would help them. "What service have I been brought here to perform?"

She asked, and yet she knew there could be only one thing they wanted of her, to enter the spiritlands where the dead waited for judgment or rebirth, where they found heaven or hell, depending on belief. It was a shaman's gift to go into the ghostlands, to walk in the afterlife and bargain for answers and help from the beings found there.

"An important constituent is in need of aid. He asked me to act as a go-between. A woman acquaintance of his has disappeared. The police haven't been able to find out what happened to her. Our constituent wants closure, even if the news is bad. It's not something the Church would typically condone or take part in, but there are extenuating circumstances. We're hoping a shaman or shamaness might be able to locate her, especially if her soul has already departed."

Bishop Routledge retrieved a photograph from a table Aisling hadn't noticed. He handed the picture to her. "The woman's name is Elena Rousseau. I fear time is of the essence. Father Ursu will remain with you. I have other matters to attend to."

The bishop left the room without another word. Father Ursu indicated a chair next to the table. "I've witnessed this kind of thing before. I won't interfere." He picked up a chalice and handed it to her.

Aisling managed to contain her expression and her thoughts when she glanced down to find grains of salt in the silver cup. Aziel chattered happily as he buried his hands in the white granules and threw some of the salt to the floor.

Father Ursu cleared his throat. His face was tense. "It's nearing midnight. The police have discovered several bodies recently. We have reason to believe the victims were all murdered during the witching hour."

Aisling wondered again what abilities he possessed. Fear lurked deep in his eyes, as if he'd seen some of the beings drawn to the dead hours of the night.

She moved to the center of the room and sat on the bare, cold floor. If she'd been at home she would have put Aziel on her lap and enclosed them both in a circle of chalk or ash, or surrounded them with the fetishes she used when she wanted to project her astral self into what most thought of as the ghostlands. Though in truth it was a land of spirits, an ancient place holding much more than human souls. But here, under the watchful eyes of the priest, guided more by intuition than reason, she plucked the ferret from her shoulder and set him away from her.

She dipped her fingers in the salt, uncertain about using it. It was a witch's protection, not hers. She wondered if other shamans used salt to open a doorway into the spirit world.

Tentatively Aisling enclosed herself in a salt circle. Though her eyes were closed, she was aware of Father Ursu watching her. She was aware of another presence as well, of someone nearby and able to witness what happened.

She tried to still the panic deep inside herself, felt caught in a deadly spider's web where to struggle was to become more thoroughly entangled. She focused on breathing, on steadying the rhythm of her heart, on clearing her mind of fear.

There were sigils she usually drew, but once again instinct warned her against revealing the most sacred parts of her ritual. She concentrated instead on visualizing them, on making them real in her mind as she silently called the true names of the ones who offered her protection in the spiritlands.

Her heart rate tripled as the heavy gray clouds of the spirit world rushed toward her. She held herself open and the ghost winds blew through her, seeking resistance, weakness, filling her with the terror of endless death even as they welcomed and claimed her. When they calmed and settled, she looked down and saw her body, there and yet not there, naked as she always appeared in the ghostlands, her hair a curtain down her back.

Without warning a man stepped from the gray mist. His face bore the tattoos of a lawbreaker.

He licked his lips as he glanced at her naked body. His own was covered in clothing that looked expensive. He leaned forward slightly, emphasizing the fact that his hands were bound behind him as they had been in the moment of his death. A metal cable served as a hangman's noose. It twisted around his neck then trailed down his back before disappearing into the mist swirling at their feet.

"I see they've sent a sacrificial lamb," he said in a raspy voice. "Or maybe that's Elena's role." He cocked his head. "Then again, maybe third time's the charm."

Aisling resisted the urge to smooth her hands over nonexistent clothing. "You're here to lead me to Elena?"

"I can find her if I must. Blood calls to blood and all of that." He tilted his head. "And in a few minutes there'll be plenty of blood. You might not need me at all by then."

"What do you want in exchange for your aid?"

"If only it was a matter of what I want. Personally I'd leave Elena to her fate. Once I began collecting the facial artwork, my sister wouldn't have anything to do with me."

He smiled and some of the tattoos cataloging his crimes merged. His eyes reflected a cruel enjoyment. "It was only a matter of time before Elena became disposable. When you make your bed in a nest of vipers, you eventually get bitten. But time's wasting. In exchange for my help you'll agree to take the good bishop's offer. Stay in Oakland." He laughed. "You might as well. They don't intend for you to leave. This is only the beginning act—if you survive it, of course. You realize that, don't you?"

Aisling's heart raced in her chest. His words rang with the same hidden truth she'd heard in the bishop's voice. "Who do you serve?"

"One whose name you're not meant to hear at the moment." He rolled his shoulders, and the cable he'd been hung with shimmered, a long silver leash leading to an unseen master.

Aisling studied him. Good or evil, malicious or beneficial—with no formal training she had only her instinct to rely on when it came to the spirit guides and entities she encountered in the ghostlands. "I will stay in Oakland, for a time."

The man cocked his head as if listening to an unspoken voice. "Good enough," he said before turning and walking deeper into the gray landscape.

There was no sense of time or distance in the spiritlands. They may have traveled for seconds or hours, yards or miles. There was a sense of being watched, but Aisling couldn't be certain which plane it was on given Father Ursu's presence in the room where her body awaited her return. Heat and cold brushed across her ankles; occasionally there was a phantom touch to the back of her hand.

The gray gave way to pink. The pink darkened and became blood-red. Her guide stopped. "End of tour for me unfortunately." He kicked at the red mist at his feet. "Too bad. I wouldn't mind seeing how Elena is faring." He tilted his head. "She's not screaming. Could be a good sign—or a bad one. If she escapes this fate, be sure to tell her that her dear brother John hopes to see her soon." He laughed before taking a step backward and being swallowed by the ghost-lands.

Aisling closed her eyes and let herself sink into the physical world as she remained in her astral self. She was greeted by the sound of chanting, by the thick smell of burning incense mixed with blood. Her breath caught in her throat when she opened her eyes and found herself in a nightmare scene of flickering candles mounted on goat heads, of dark-robed figures surrounding an altar where Elena lay naked and spread-eagled. Sigils were painted on her eyelids and lips, on her palms and on the soles of her feet. The steady rise and fall of her chest was the only indication she was still alive.

The gleam of a blade being raised turned Aisling's attention to a man next to the altar. He wore the headdress of a goat. The chanting stopped when he began to speak in a deep, mesmerizing voice.

The words were unfamiliar to Aisling, but she could guess their meaning, their purpose. Her heartbeat thundered in her ears. She had no true physical presence here. She was only a witness to the events. Even if she left the room and determined where Elena was, by the time she returned to her own body and conveyed the location, it would be too late.

Warm fur brushed against her ankles. She looked down and startled at the sight of Aziel. Always before, he'd touched his physical body to hers and entered the ghostlands with her, or he didn't appear at all.

The flames of the candles flickered and reflected in his yellow eyes as he met Aisling's gaze. Their minds touched in a way they did only when they were both in spirit form. *There is a name you can whisper on the spirit winds, a being you can summon.*

It was her choice. It always was. But there would be a price to pay. *Tell me.*

The ferret climbed to her shoulder. His face pressed to hers as if to ensure the name he yielded would only be heard by her.

Zurael en Caym. Serpent heir. Son of the one who is The Prince.

A shiver streaked down Aisling's spine in soul-deep recognition. There was no time to question the reaction or agonize over her decision. The dark priest's prayer climbed toward a crescendo. When he reached it, the athame in his hand would plunge into Elena's heart.

"Zurael en Caym. Serpent heir. Son of the one who is The Prince. I summon you," Aisling said. "I summon you to me and command you to end this ceremony before the sacrifice is made."

The dark-robed acolytes shrieked as Zurael appeared, black-winged and taloned. With a casual swipe he severed the jugular of the dark priest and sent blood spewing across the altar. In panic the participants tried to escape, only to be grabbed and killed, their bodies tossed casually to the floor as their hearts ceased beating and their souls fled.

Terror and horror filled Aisling at the sight of the demon, at the destruction he wrought with so little effort. His face and naked body were human but his eyes burned like molten gold. When the last of those participating in the black mass was dead, he came to stand before her, coated in blood, his expression promising retribution for being summoned and commanded.

A ring flared to life at her feet, circling her, protecting her. Zurael's eyes slitted as his gaze traveled the length of her and his cock became engorged. "Savor these few moments when you hold me enslaved, child of mud. They will cost your life," he said before disappearing as suddenly as he'd arrived.

Two

ZURAEL shimmered into existence in the exact spot he'd abruptly and involuntarily left moments earlier. The wings and talons were gone, as was the blood, but the rage remained, deadly and focused.

Desert winds streamed through windows hung with a thin, gauzy fabric. Rather than soothe and calm him, the breeze made him think of the woman who'd whispered his name on the spirit winds, who'd dared to summon a Djinn prince and command him.

She would pay with her life. Such magic could not be allowed to rise again.

A knock sounded at the door. It was his father's advisor. Zurael could feel the signature energy. He'd known it wouldn't take long for the knowledge of what had happened to reach The Prince.

Zurael went to the door and opened it. Miizan en Rumjal stepped back, the tilt of his head indicating Zurael was to follow him. His features gave no hint of his thoughts, and Zurael had no intention of asking for them. Though Miizan was bound to the House of the Scorpion and not the House of the Serpent, his loyalty to The Prince was forged in a time thousands of years earlier, when there were no ghostlands, no Kingdom of the Djinn to serve as both paradise and prison, when there was only the place that had been defiled by the humans and stolen from the Djinn by bloody conquest and foul, enslaving magic.

Zurael stepped into the velvety darkness of the night and followed his father's advisor in silence as they moved through courtyards and beneath elegant arches. Pastel window coverings made him think of night-blooming flowers, their color revealed by the soft glow of candlelight. Though they could have taken any number of forms and traveled faster, they walked until Miizan stopped in front of a door few entered. "He waits below."

Zurael's lips curved in a grim smile as he opened the door and began descending the long staircase to the Hall of History. He didn't need to wonder what his father's mood was. It was always at its darkest when The Prince thought of the past.

It was pitch-black, but Zurael navigated the steps with the ease of someone who'd done so for centuries. As was fitting for a people created from fire at the very beginning—when the Earth seethed and boiled, molten rock and unconscious desire to bring forth life— the air around Zurael grew hotter the deeper he went and the closer he came to where his father waited.

At the bottom of the stairs, muted colors began their fight against the blackness in a sardonic metaphor for the history of the Djinn— fire and memory and angel blood. Zurael ducked through an archway and into the Hall itself.

His father stood in front of a mural depicting the first summoning and binding. But unlike the Djinn in the mural, who appeared much as Zurael did—bare-chested and barefooted, a long black braid trailing between his shoulder blades and ending at his hips—The Prince had taken the form of a nightmare, the demon he'd been named when the god cursed him and twisted his shape into something hideous as a lesson to all Djinn.

His fingers were curled talons. Leathery, batlike wings emerged from his back, their edges draped elegantly over his forearms. A snake-like tail coiled around his leg.

The humans believed they were formed in the image of their god. In truth they were formed in the image of the Djinn—not because the Djinn willed it, but because the god who amused himself with an experiment had settled on a form already proven efficient.

"You were summoned," The Prince said. His voice was barely more than a hiss, but it echoed in the hall. It resonated through Zurael's mind like a curse hurtled at the past.

"Yes. I will kill her if you'll grant permission for me to pass through the gates."

The Prince's tongue flicked out, forked in keeping with the image he'd chosen to project, though he'd long since broken the curse that had once trapped him into an abomination of Djinn and beast.

Slowly, demon-red eyes turned to fathomless black. The tail uncoiled, and like the wings and talons, it faded as his father turned to study the mural once again.

Zurael looked at the mural and the depiction of the first Djinn not only summoned but bound to a vessel in order to serve one of the creatures created from mud. Though he would never admit to fear, an icy finger traced down his spine as he viewed Jetrel's fate and flashed to those moments when he himself had been summoned. If the two of them were standing side by side, few would be able to tell the difference between his father's firstborn son and his father's eldest living son, so close was the resemblance.

His father had lost dozens of sons and daughters before he, along with the most powerful of the ancients, had created the Kingdom of the Djinn deep within the ghostlands. Afterward there had been few born to any of their race, even The Prince.

Silence reigned, heavy and full of dark memories in the Hall where The Prince was said to have painted the history of the Djinn using angel blood and the colors of the world that had once been theirs to rule.

His father tilted his head as if listening to voices only he could hear, or perhaps he was glimpsing a sliver of the future, as it was said he could do. "There are few old enough to remember, but this is the moment when even those who belonged to the House of the Dove realized there would be no compromise with the god who came here from a place beyond our understanding and claimed our lands as his own playground. We, who were created of Earth's fire, were ordered to kneel down to the creatures of mud and submit to their will. When we refused, preferring to fight to the death rather than yield, they were given an incantation allowing them to summon and bind us to a vessel so we could be used as unwilling familiars."

The Prince's hand lifted to hover over the image of Jetrel. "This is the moment when we learned what would happen to us if we killed a human who held us enslaved. This is when we learned what it meant to become *ifrit*, soul-tainted, one whose name can no longer be spoken out loud, one whose spirit can't be guided back and re-born into a new life."

His father lowered his hand. Zurael fought the urge to repeat his question, to point out what his father already knew, that he hadn't yet been bound and so he could kill the one who'd summoned him without becoming *ifrit*.

"Though few remember it and those who do won't speak of it," his father said, "before this moment when we knew we must create a separate kingdom for ourselves, there were Djinn who found the humans alluring. The son whose loss is a deep scar on my heart was one of those. Our women were plentiful then and our children easily conceived. Yet he became obsessed with a human woman, refused to give her up when I demanded it. She became his weakness, the bait used to trap him. Her blood was used in the first spell cast to summon and bind a Djinn."

Zurael's spine stiffened at what his father implied. "I have no interest in the human female other than killing her."

"Walk with me," his father said. "Tell me of the summoning."

Zurael's earlier rage returned in a heartbeat. The pictures in the Hall faded from his awareness. "There was no warning," he said, "nothing to hint I was about to be taken. I heard my name and with it a command to end a ceremony before a sacrifice could be made. As we have all been trained to do since childhood, I took the form the humans call demon. There were black-robed figures gathered in a candlelit room and chanting around an altar. Their dark priest had an athame raised and was about to drive it into the heart of a woman. I killed them and would have killed the one who summoned me, but she was protected. When I drew near, a circle flared to life around her and I couldn't cross it. I left before she could command me further or bind me."

"This woman who summoned you, was she naked or clothed?"

Zurael's body tightened as his mind's eye once again traveled over the woman's figure. He turned away in order to hide the sudden erection pressing against the loose flowing trousers. "She was naked," he said, hating that his cock had stiffened in her presence as well.

"Then it was not her physical form that summoned you but her spiritual one. There were sigils in the circle surrounding her?"

"No." Uneasiness slithered down Zurael's spine as he realized he had not seen his full name written in ash or flame as it should have been, nor had she summoned him with the recitation of a spell as she should have done.

His father stopped walking and turned to face him. On either side of them the mural ended.

They were on the cusp of the present. Beyond where they stood the Hall continued in endless darkness, the future not yet captured on its walls.

"A final question and then I will answer the one you asked me. Were you compelled to kill the humans, or did you do so because they deserved it and you desired to do it?"

Zurael closed his eyes and flashed back to the instant when he'd taken form in a world he'd rarely visited, though like most, he monitored it and dreamed of the day when the Djinn would reclaim it. His father's question was a whisper in his thoughts as he relived those moments of ruthless justice when the stench of evil was replaced by the smell of blood. Horror filled him as he realized there was no distinction between his summoner's command and his own free will, but he didn't turn away from the specter of it as he answered his father's question honestly. "I wanted to stop the sacrifice. I killed the humans because I could."

He opened his eyes and saw his father studying him closely, perhaps willing him to say more, to admit it was the female and not the violence that had shaped his cock into a rigid line against the front of his trousers. Zurael said nothing and the silence was like a held breath.

Along the walls, the scenes painted there shimmered with captured emotion. Unwillingly his gaze traveled the distance his feet had covered and stopped on the image of the first son and the first summoning.

Icy dread found its way into Zurael's heart. It was not dispelled when his father said, "Unless summoned, you may leave the Kingdom of the Djinn only once."

AISLING shuddered as she looked at the carnage in front of her. Fear held her trapped in the protective circle. The demon's promise of retribution froze her limbs and withered her courage, even though she knew she needed to find out where she was, so she could return to her physical body with the knowledge.

She closed her eyes and turned her face to bury it in the comfort of Aziel's warm fur. Her heartbeat slowed, though the stench of blood and bowels and scented candles made her queasy.

The desire to be back in her own body swelled up with sudden fierceness, along with an aching need to return to the only family she'd ever known. "Let's get this over with," she whispered to Aziel before she opened her eyes and stepped from the phantom ring.

Elena's chest rose and fell in a regular rhythm. The bloodred sigils painted on her eyelids and mouth, on her palms and the soles of her feet, stirred a memory in Aisling, but she knew it was a shaman's memory and not a personal one.

She climbed the stairs and, moving through the house, stepped out into the darkness in order to look for an address. The night was still, but the presence of the predators who roamed it wasn't hidden from her as it would have been if her spirit and physical body were joined.

Aisling could sense the ice-cold signature of a vampire looking for prey. Farther away a lone Were prowled, its hot energy a beacon though it wasn't close enough for her to determine its animal form.

Inside the other houses on the street she could hear muffled conversation. She could feel the terror the night held for the occupants who sheltered behind barred windows and locked doors.

At the end of the block a bent pole still carried a street sign. Aisling read it and let her awareness of her surroundings fade. The gray of the ghostlands passed with a swiftness that left her dizzy.

When she opened her eyes she found Father Ursu hovering just inches away from the protective circle. "3574 Rhine Street," she said.

Father Ursu took a phone from his pocket and relayed the address, though Aisling knew it was for show. Just as before, she felt another presence, someone else monitoring the room. This time she glanced around and noticed the small mirror on the wall above the table where Elena's picture had been and where Aziel was now curled in apparent sleep.

"You encountered a powerful demon," Father Ursu said, drawing Aisling's attention back to him and making her heart thunder with renewed fear.

"How did you know?" Her voice came out little more than a whisper.

Father Ursu gestured at the blackened ring of salt around her. "What happened?"

Aisling's breath grew short as she stared at the protective circle. She shivered as the demon's beautiful face and deadly words filled her mind.

For a moment terror held her completely in its grip. Impending death covered her with a shroud of certainty. As soon as she broke the protective circle, the demon would come for her.

"What happened, child?" the priest said in a soft voice as he crouched down in front of her.

She tried to find the words and failed. A soft thump sounded as Aziel jumped from the table. He scampered across the room as if sensing her distress and her need of his comfort. Before the priest could grab him, he crossed the circle, brushing the blackened salt away with his feet and tail.

He climbed to his favored position on Aisling's shoulder. He chattered as if he was scolding her, reminding her that *he* was the one who had given her the name Zurael to whisper on the spirit winds.

Aisling shuddered as the terrible fear left her in a sudden rush. She closed her eyes and concentrated on answering the priest's question. "There was a dark mass. They were chanting, but a demon came before they finished the ceremony." She took a harsh, involuntary breath as the events played out in her mind. Guilt tangled with the relief of having saved Elena. She'd wanted the sacrifice stopped, but now the deaths lay on her conscience. She'd commanded Zurael to stop the ceremony and he'd obeyed. She looked at the priest and said, "They're all dead, all except for Elena."

Father Ursu nodded. "Black magic is dangerous." He stood and offered his hand. "Come, child. I'll take you back to your room. You've had a long, difficult day."

Aisling allowed him to help her to her feet and guide her from the room. She was emotionally exhausted, no longer able to worry about whether he was an ally or an enemy.

ZURAEL pushed through the door and out into the night. The gentle breeze and rich scents greeting him did nothing to soothe the turmoil of his thoughts, the conflict of his desires, the unspoken questions raised by his father and left unanswered.

For an instant he was tempted to gather the sand around him in a swirling, seething mass and roar through the desert until his emotions settled. He was tempted to take the form of a falcon and fly until he was too exhausted to think or question. But those were the responses of a child and he hadn't been one in centuries.

Above him the starless, moonless sky was pitch-black. If he were to hunt for the one who summoned him, he would need to do it during the day. The human he was looking for wouldn't go out among the predators of the night.

Zurael retraced the route he'd walked with his father's advisor. He moved with casual grace, barely aware of his surroundings. With each step the urgency to find the one who'd summoned him grew and spread outward like a spider's poisonous bite.

He faltered with the thought, slowed, stopped. He was in a courtyard he rarely delayed in. To his left was an archway he'd seldom found a need to pass through.

For long moments he contemplated what it might cost him. But in the end he turned and took the path leading to the House of the Spider.

A young male Djinn, wearing the simple white trousers of a student, opened the door. He stepped back to usher Zurael in with a sweeping bow. "Welcome, Prince Zurael en Caym of the House of the Serpent. You honor us with your presence. Do you wish to call upon the one who leads our house? Or will another serve you?"

"I will see Malahel en Raum," Zurael said. The payment required of him would be steep, but he didn't want to share the details of his shame, his summoning, with anyone other than the strongest in the House of the Spider.

"As you wish, Prince Zurael." The student bowed again. "If you will follow me, I will take you to the room she favors."

Like the walls of the Hall of History, the walls in the House of the Spider were covered in pictures. The images were captured in the silken weave of tapestries rather than painted in blood. Some of the scenes were reminiscent of the ones his father had created. But where

The Prince's history was filled with war, with small victories and larger defeats, with the theft of the Djinn land, the history found on the walls in the House of the Spider was interwoven with carnal depictions of intertwined humans, angels and Djinn.

Zurael's lips moved in a silent curse as the image of the female who'd summoned him filled his thoughts and his cock hardened in response. He turned his attention away from the twisted silken threads covering the walls and forced himself to think instead of the terror he'd felt in that instant when his name had been whispered on the spirit winds and his body had dematerialized against his will.

Rage returned to fill the place carved out by terror. He thought of the humans and their black mass, their foolish desire to call for those trapped in the hell of the ghostlands. In a blink their deaths passed through his mind, and before he could stop himself he was once again standing in front of the female.

Zurael's penis throbbed. His lips pulled back, a silent snarl in defiance to the heat that rose upward, spiraling through his chest and neck and face. There was no hiding the erection pressed against the front of his trousers.

He nodded stiffly when the student stopped at a doorway and bowed him into a small room. "I will tell the one you seek that you wait here."

The room was bare of influences. The walls were painted the gray of the ghostlands. Three large gray pillows served as seating around a wooden table only inches above the floor. Three teacups waited in a cluster at the table's edge. Nearby, a ceramic teapot sat on a brazier, the glow of hot charcoal a symbol of the Djinn, whose prison kingdom was surrounded by the cold spiritlands.

In four strides Zurael was next to one of the cushions. The smell of jasmine tea teased his nostrils. He contemplated the teacups and felt the stirrings of uneasiness in his chest. He had never been one to frequent this house.

He turned at the sound of the door opening. Malahel en Raum stood in the doorway. She wore the concealing robes of a desert dweller, though like the room, they were gray. In deference to her position Zurael bowed slightly and said, "I thank you for attending me."

"Another would attend you as well," Malahel said, entering the room.

Zurael's pulse spiked at the sight of the Djinn who stepped into the doorway. Like Malahel, Iyar en Batrael of the House of the Raven was dressed in the concealing robes of a desert traveler. His skin was as black as the material covering all of his body and much of his face. Only the gold of his eyes was easily seen.

"Enter," Zurael said, acknowledging Iyar with a bow of equal depth to the one he'd given Malahel.

The three of them seated themselves on the cushions.

"You wish to pour?" Malahel asked, indicating the waiting teacups with a small flick of her fingers and giving Zurael the choice as to whether to lead the conversation or not.

Zurael picked up the teapot and filled the ceramic cups. "I was summoned."

Both Malahel and Iyar freed the lower half of their faces from the concealing material. Iyar's dark fingers stroked the handle of a teacup. "The Prince has given you permission to pass through the gates in order to kill the one who summoned you?"

"Yes."

Iyar nodded and took the teacup to his lips.

Malahel set her teacup down. Her irises were as black as Iyar's skin.

"Tell us about the summoning," she said.

Zurael repeated what he'd told his father, hesitating for an instant but finally including the oddity of the summoner's ability to call him in her astral state with little more than his name. Where his father hadn't shown interest in the humans who'd been killed, Malahel and Iyar leaned forward as he described the black mass and the woman whose sacrifice he'd prevented.

"Where were the sigils written?" Iyar said.

Zurael conjured up the scene, focusing on an aspect that had been insignificant at the time. He'd barely glanced at the woman on the altar, and yet with Iyar's prompting he was able to answer, "Her eyes, mouth, the palms of both hands."

"The soles of her feet?"

"I don't know."

Iyar shrugged. "What you saw was enough."

"Enough for what?" Zurael asked, uneasiness returning with the look that passed between Malahel and Iyar.

Malahel placed her teacup on the low table and settled her hands on her knees. "What is it you wish from the House of the Spider?"

What did he want? What impulse had made him take the path that led here?

Zurael sipped his tea as his thoughts danced from one scene to another, always returning to the female who'd summoned him and the fear that he would be bound in service before he could ensure his freedom by killing her. Divination was one of a Spider's gifts. "I would know what power the human holds over me that she was able to summon me the way she did."

Malahel's head tilted slightly. Zurael's chest tightened as he imagined himself caught in her web. Dark eyes bored into his, unblinking, the thoughts behind them completely hidden.

There was always a price to pay for coming to the House of the Spider. At the moment, his debt was canceled by the information he'd provided about the summoning.

Zurael forced himself to lift the teacup to his lips with a steady hand and drain it of its contents. When he set it on the table, Malahel said, "I will read the stones on your behalf if you will accept a task."

"What task?"

Malahel's eyes flicked to Iyar. Iyar said, "The dark priest you killed was trying to summon an entity from the ghostlands and bind it to a human form. The sigils on the eyes, mouth, the palms and the soles of the feet are meant to give the priest complete control of the being. This is not the first time such a thing has happened in the recent past. There are Djinn lost to us, cursed to wander the human spiritlands because their souls are tainted by the ones they killed, making them *ifrit*. Their names are unspoken, crossed out in the Book of the Djinn. The House of the Raven would not have them summoned again, bound and used again by the humans."

"Nor would I," Zurael said.

"We believe the black mass you interrupted is proof a human is in possession of an ancient stone tablet we thought lost," Malahel said. "Find whoever is in possession of this knowledge and kill them, then bring the tablet to us without delay."

Zurael's eyebrows drew together in consternation and confusion. To accept the task was to remain at risk of being summoned and bound by the human female. "The House of the Scorpion is full of assassins capable of doing what you ask."

Malahel's hands left her knees to float over the table in an all-encompassing gesture. "What you say is true, but none of them were summoned as you were. None of them were brought to the House of the Spider by their destinies."

A bow of his head, a gracious acknowledgment of the tea and the company, and Zurael would be free to escape with his question unanswered. But he couldn't deny the strangeness of finding himself in a place he had rarely visited in centuries of existence.

"We believe the tablet is in Oakland," Iyar said. "The city you were summoned to."

So he would be near the human female, Zurael thought. "I will accept the task," he said.

Malahel clapped her hands. Immediately the door slid open. The male Djinn who'd ushered Zurael into the room stepped through the doorway followed by two females who were also wearing the white clothing that marked a student. Without speaking they doused the charcoal and removed the brazier as well as the table before closing the door behind them.

Zurael leaned forward to study the slab of clear phantom quartz that had been hidden by the table. It shimmered with secrets, ghost crystals trapped in the larger one. The surface was etched with spider lines, their design a spiral of interweaving patterns he found impossible to untangle.

Next to the slab was a ceramic bowl with tiny stones, each one polished and perfectly round, their colors mixed. He could fit a hundred of them in his cupped hand. A second bowl contained larger stones, half the size of his smallest fingernail. They were round and polished as well. It was this bowl Malahel picked up.

She held it out to him. "Choose the stone that will go by your name. When you have found it, place it in the bowl with the ones you will cast."

Zurael dipped his hand into the bowl and let the stones flow through his fingers like water. He recognized many of the stones and knew what they signified in the teachings of his own house, but he didn't make the mistake of thinking they would hold the same meaning in this house. He closed his eyes so the stones would whisper and guide him to the one that would represent him. At the bottom of the bowl he found what he sought and captured it.

He opened his eyes and looked at the obsidian he'd selected. Then he did as he'd been instructed and dropped it into the bowl containing the tiny polished stones.

"Choose the stone that will serve the one who summoned you," Malahel said.

Once again Zurael closed his eyes. Immediately the female's image came to mind and his body tightened, his cock stiffened. His jaw clenched and he shifted position on the cushion in the hopes his physical response wouldn't be noticed.

The female's stone rested close to the top. Misgiving at having delayed his own task filled Zurael when he opened his eyes and saw the blue-and-white angelite with its flecks of red. In the House of the Serpent it was a stone signifying an enemy, one who was angel-touched and dangerous. He placed it next to the obsidian.

Malahel set the bowl with the larger stones aside. She picked up the second bowl and handed it to Zurael. "Mix the stones as you will. Speak your question as you cast them."

Zurael closed his eyes in an effort to center himself. There was no turning away, no escape from the web that held him.

He did as Malahel commanded. When he felt the moment was right he tipped the bowl and said, "I would know what power the human holds over me that she was able to summon me the way she did."

The tiny stones rolled across the phantom quartz of a spider's altar. There were a thousand lines to capture and hold them, but most of the colorful ones fled, rolling into narrow gutters at the edges of the slab. Zurael stared at what was left—the gray shades of the ghostlands and the red clay of the humans, the bloodred of angels and the black of powerful forces, all circling, trapping the obsidian and the angelite together.

Malahel studied the stones for long moments before leaning forward. The tip of her finger hovered above the stones. It traced the curve trapping the obsidian next to the angelite. It silently pointed out that the obsidian stood alone, untouched by any but the angelite, while red, gray and black stones all crowded against the token representing the human who'd summoned him.

"The one who possesses the tablet you seek will be drawn to the one who summoned you," Malahel said. "She is deeply connected to the ghostlands. She was born of them and can call the spirit winds at will. That's how she was able to bring you to her. It's good you already intend to kill her. She is dangerous to us and will be made even more so if she learns what's written on the tablet."

Malahel placed her hands on her knees and Zurael knew she was finished speaking. She had answered his question just as the stones now revealed that in order to accomplish the task he'd agreed to, he would need to find the human who'd summoned him and watch over her until the ancient tablet was recovered and the one who possessed it destroyed.

THE house with the shaman's symbol painted on it appeared worn and tired, haunted by failure and sadness. It was small, old, its door and windows barred like the houses around it.

Father Ursu's hand left the pocket of his robe. "You can do the honors," he said, pressing a key ring into Aisling's palm.

She unlocked the barred door and opened it, then unlocked the wooden door behind it and opened it as well. The house smelled musty, closed up, dead.

Sunlight fought against the darkness of the curtains covering the windows. Small rays of it slipped in to capture dust motes and gloom and tattered furniture. The ferret perched on Aisling's shoulder chattered in excitement over a chance to explore.

"The lodging is yours, and for the moment, in appreciation of your services, you don't have to worry about paying for the electricity," Father Ursu said.

His hand disappeared into his pocket. This time when it emerged it contained a bundle of papers. "Shall we move over to the table?"

Aisling nodded. She left the wooden door open then set the bag containing her new clothing on the floor before detouring to the windows to open them slightly for fresh air and to pull back the curtains rather than turn on the lights. She hadn't failed to notice the priest's exact wording and the warning they held. At the moment she wasn't beholden, but that could change at any time. It was an old game, one in existence even before The Last War and the plague—enslave those who had nothing by letting them build up debt for the cost of food, clothing and shelter.

When she joined Father Ursu at the table, he'd already laid out the papers. "This is the most recent map of Oakland," he said. "Can you read?"

Aisling hesitated, unsure whether to admit to it or not. He took her delay in answering for embarrassment over her ignorance.

"No matter," he said, pushing the map aside. "No doubt you'll make friends here and draw clients quickly enough. They'll help you navigate the city."

Father Ursu reached for a card with a magnetic strip on its back. "This is a transportation pass. There are buses to most areas of the city and to San Francisco. Almost everything you'll require is close enough to reach by foot, but if you need to take a bus, be sure to leave yourself enough time to return home. There is no public transportation beyond sunset or before sunrise and many drivers won't stop to pick up a passenger at dusk. To enter San Francisco requires authorization papers. Come to the church and ask for me if you find yourself needing them. Don't attempt to go there alone. Even in the daytime it's controlled by vampires."

He placed the card on the table and picked up a book of vouchers. He flipped through it quickly for her benefit. There were words on the pages but the pictures served as well. Milk. Meat. Canned fruits. Assorted goods. "When you leave the house, if you go to the right and keep going straight, you'll come to a grocery store. They'll accept these vouchers."

He set the vouchers aside and tapped the final item on the table, a small pile of dollar bills. "Whatever you find in the house is yours to keep or dispose of as you see fit. This is the cash fee promised to you." He hesitated then added, "You should be safe enough here during the day, but be careful. The residents here don't pay for the area to be patrolled by the police."

Aisling studied the assortment of items on the table. Panic threatened to well up inside her. She was alone and there was no one she could trust.

A sharp nip to her earlobe made her smile. The panic subsided as Aziel launched himself off her shoulder and onto the table.

"I need to be going," Father Ursu said.

Aisling walked him to the door and lingered until he got in the chauffeured car and was taken away. Along the street, other cars were parking to dislodge passengers or pulling away from the curb to whisk clients out of the area set aside for those with *controversial* abilities.

Despite the bars, she saw that most of the houses on the street had parted curtains and opened windows or doors, as though the residents in this part of the city didn't fear what might enter in the daytime. Aisling leaned against the doorjamb and closed her eyes. Instantly the image of Zurael's blood-covered body and burning eyes filled her mind, his whispered threat sent a shiver of fear straight to her heart.

There were wards carved in the wood around the door and windows of the shaman's house, but she couldn't be certain they would protect her from the demon she'd summoned. "Let me be safe," she whispered, lifting her face so the sun could caress it.

She willed herself to find the strength to face whatever was to come, to have the courage to meet her fate. Aziel had given her the name Zurael as he'd given her many other names.

She hadn't lied when she told the priest the ferret appeared shortly after a trader's caravan visited the farm. What she hadn't told him was that before the ferret there'd been a crow, and before the crow there'd been a snake, and before the snake, a cat—and they were all Aziel.

Aisling opened her eyes and left the doorway in favor of exploring.

The house was longer than it was wide. The living room and kitchen were a single space separated by a counter. To the right of the front door was another room. Foreboding filled Aisling when she stepped into it and saw the fetishes. They were perched in places where their strengths could be drawn upon. They were positioned to guard and watch.

On a workbench against the wall, stone and crystal lay with shapes unfinished, their creation interrupted. The tools needed to turn rock into something more lay scattered next to them.

A bed of dirt was in the center of the room. It was a poor man's doorway into the ghostlands, so reminiscent of the barn floor where she had started so many journeys that a wave of homesickness assailed her.

Aisling wiped tears from her eyes and turned away, retreating to the living room and kitchen. There were dirty dishes in the sink, their surfaces dusty. The refrigerator held a carton of spoiled milk and a drawer of rotted vegetables. The cabinets were empty except for a small collection of bowls and plates. Rings marked the places where cans of food had been stored.

The bathroom was across from the kitchen. A man's razor rested on the sink. A sliver of soap lay in the bottom of a huge, claw-foot tub that belonged in a past well before The Last War. There was a shower stall as well.

A solid metal door at the end of the hallway opened into the backyard. Aisling peeked outside then locked the door again.

In the bedroom a sparse, threadbare assortment of clothing hung in the closet. The shirts and pants were all made for a man whose bulk explained the size of the tub and shower. Tentatively Aisling reached into the closet and touched a pair of trousers. She knew the man who'd once owned them was dead, not because she felt his ghost or knew his spirit was in the ghostlands, but because the evidence of his passing filled the house.

Unbidden, the image of Elena's brother came to mind. His words held no more comfort now than they'd held when he spoke them in the spiritlands. *I see they've sent a sacrificial lamb. Or maybe that's Elena's role. Then again, maybe third time's the charm.*

Aisling changed the bedding. She returned to the kitchen and disposed of the spoiled milk and rotten vegetables.

A kitchen drawer held burlap shopping bags. She draped those over her arm before picking up the book of food vouchers from the living room table.

Aziel emerged from the shaman's work and ceremony room. He scampered over to meet her at the front door. She let him out and waited for him to take care of his business. But when he would have lingered to explore, Aisling laughed and said, "We'll have a long, hungry night if I don't find the grocery store."

The ferret returned to her side. He rose on his hind legs in readiness for climbing on her shoulder and riding to a new adventure. Aisling shook her head. "Stay here where I know you'll be safe."

His scolding made her smile but she didn't give in to his pleas. Instead she picked him up and brushed a kiss across his forehead. She rubbed her cheek against his soft fur and put him in the house. "I'll be back."

The store was miles away. Normally the distance of the trip and the weight of the groceries wouldn't have made Aisling tired. But the events of the last twenty-four hours, and the sleepless night she'd spent as she worried about the demon Zurael, finally caught up to her. Her footsteps dragged by the time she returned to the shaman's house. Her hands shook with a nervousness brought on by lack of sleep and vestiges of fear.

Aisling fumbled for the key and slipped it into the lock. Her spine tingled with the hyperawareness of someone who knew she was being watched and that she was no match for a predator.

With a click the first lock gave. She opened the barred metal door and found the key for the wooden one. A few seconds later it opened as well.

The musty smell was gone, replaced by an unfamiliar exotic spice. It was her only warning before a hand wrapped around her throat and sharp talons scraped lightly over her jugular.

"Greetings, child of mud."

Three

TERROR held Aisling mute and immobile. Her breath charged in and out of her throat along with small whimpers. Her sole focus was on the sharp tips of Zurael's talons.

Scenes from the night before rushed through her mind, blood-soaked images of those he'd killed with casual strength. The bags of groceries dropped to the floor as she trembled, and like a cat playing with a mouse, Zurael turned her to face him.

Except for the fingernails elongated into claws, he wore a human body dressed in black leather, pants that molded to his skin and a vest left open to expose a bronzed chest. A serpent tattoo curled its way down his forearm and onto his hand, so lifelike that Aisling shivered at having its eyes only inches away from hers.

His hair was pulled back in a long braid, revealing ears studded with obsidian. Fiery rage danced in the center of pupils surrounded by liquid gold, making his face a promise of death.

Zurael clenched his jaw against the sensations bombarding him. Her fear pounded against his palm. It radiated off her, and yet underneath its scent was a heady fragrance that flooded his nostrils and tempted him with dangerous images of coupling with her. He was aroused, not because of her terror, but despite it.

The knowledge she could not only summon him at will, but could make him want her, sent anger burning through his veins. She was weak, fragile, her life span a day in comparison to his own. She was hardly worthy of a Djinn's notice, and yet he found it impossible to look away from her.

She was golden sunshine and angelite eyes, delicate as a fawn and as defenseless as one. It would take nothing to kill her. A flick of his wrist and it would be done.

Slowly he released her. With a thought, the talons shortened and lightened to the clear of fingernails.

"What do you call yourself?" he asked.

She blinked. A small tongue darted out to wet her lips, and his cock responded with a pulse of desire, an escape of arousal through the slitted tip. Zurael's hands curled into fists. "What do you call yourself?" he repeated.

"Aisling."

Her voice was barely a whisper but her name was a roar across his soul. He stepped back involuntarily as it echoed, claimed, reso-nated deep within as if combining with his own name to form a melodious chord that gave her more power over him.

It was why the Djinn never spoke of the *ifrit*, the spirit-cursed. To speak their names out loud was to invite their fate.

The fear left Aisling in a wash of nausea and weakness. She went to her knees and bowed her head, hiding the lack of strength in her legs by gathering the groceries scattered from the burlap bags.

She scanned the room for Aziel. Worry gave way to relief when the ferret slipped from underneath the couch as if sensing her fear for his safety. He chattered at her, his voice reassuring though he remained under the shelter of the coffee table.

From underneath lowered eyelashes, Aisling's attention returned to the demon. He was like a giant, golden cat ready to pounce.

She stood on unsteady legs. Her eyes met the heated gold of Zurael's and she shivered.

He could kill her with ease. The knowledge stood between them like an abyss.

"I need to put the groceries away," she whispered, afraid to take a step for fear he'd strike.

Zurael's gaze dropped to the burlap grocery bags. He nodded, though his eyes promised retribution if she did anything to threaten him.

Aisling was glad the house was small. Only the force of her will got her to the tiny kitchen. Zurael followed as far as the doorway.

Her hands shook as she dealt with the groceries under Zurael's unblinking stare. Her stomach had been cramped with hunger while she walked, but now the thought of food made it tense in rebellion.

Aziel gathered his courage and scurried into the kitchen. He climbed up the leg of her pants and settled on her shoulder, his familiar presence bringing comfort.

Aisling turned her head slightly and closed her eyes. She buried her face in his soft fur and concentrated on the faint beat of his heart and his warmth.

The rumble of his stomach made her smile. She returned to the task of dealing with the items she'd purchased. A package of chicken breasts remained on the counter when she was finished.

Aziel would have been happy to eat his food raw, but she needed to keep her hands and mind busy. She washed a cutting board then cast a nervous glance at the demon before pulling a knife from an oak block. His smile was a savage flash of white in a face worthy of an ancient god.

Her heart fluttered. Heat painted her cheeks and made her look away. She remembered only too well how his eyes had traveled over her naked body, and his penis had grown hard in response. She wondered if the reason he hadn't killed her was because he intended to use her first.

Aziel's tail twitched. His sharp claws dug into her flesh as if he sensed the direction of her thoughts and wanted to derail her fear before it rose to consume her.

Aisling took a deep breath and cut a chicken breast into slices before searching for oil and a skillet. The smell of frying meat stirred her hunger. She added more chicken. Her gaze strayed to the demon and she willed herself to meet his eyes, to reclaim her courage when dealing with him.

His name had been given to her by Aziel. She'd summoned him with a pure heart and commanded him to fight something evil. Those were not things she could undo and she didn't want to.

"Are you hungry?" she asked.

Surprise flickered across Zurael's face. It was followed by a tightening of his features and a stiffening of his spine, as if somehow she'd struck him with her question in a way she couldn't with the knife. "No."

Aisling's attention returned to the chicken. She removed the strips cut for Aziel and set them aside to cool.

While the remaining piece cooked, she opened the cabinet and studied the cans she'd brought home. None of the vouchers covered fresh fruits or vegetables, and the small amount of money she'd been given by Father Ursu would barely have paid for salad. She'd have to plant a garden once she found a way to protect it from human and animal scavengers.

Homesickness stabbed through Aisling's chest. Her hand went to her work pants. She touched the bills folded inside the pocket. At the moment it seemed impossible that she'd ever have enough money to return to the farm. Traveling was a luxury for those who could afford the road tolls and the cost of protection as well as transportation.

She pulled out a can of green beans and opened it, then cleaned a pan and heated the vegetables on the stove. When her meal was finished cooking, she loaded it onto a plate. She put Aziel's dinner on a saucer before setting it on the floor.

There was a table in the corner of the living room but Aisling remained in the kitchen, conscious of Zurael's unwavering stare. Aziel ate greedily, then scampered past the demon to disappear into the shaman's workroom.

Aisling finished her meal slowly. It was difficult to eat with Zurael watching her, but the prospect of finishing her meal and walking past him was equally unnerving. She washed the dishes when she was done with them. Her stomach knotted when Aziel reappeared holding the carved image of a hawk in his mouth.

It was time to pay for the name he'd given her.

The ferret retreated to the shaman's ceremony room. Aisling stiffened her spine and approached Zurael. She tried to concentrate on the narrow space between the edge of the counter and where he leaned on the door frame.

It was impossible to keep her eyes from traveling over the exposed skin, the tightly fitted pants, the tattooed serpent coiled around his arm. Her gaze darted upward when he shifted position. Her eyes met his, but he didn't reach for her or speak as she slipped past him.

ZURAEL was finding it harder and harder to remain aloof. She'd caught him off-guard with her offer to share her meager food supplies.

He'd known life was hard for the humans without wealth or privilege. He'd assumed a female with the ability to summon a Djinn would reek of arrogance and hold a position of power. Instead he found Aisling vulnerable and strangely innocent.

It was an intoxicating combination.

From the moment she'd returned home, he'd been unwillingly aroused. He'd been assaulted by darkly erotic fantasies and the scent of sweet surrender.

Her fear had lessened. Her gaze had strayed to linger over his flesh. Her mind had filled with images that left her lowering her eyelashes and blushing.

He could have her if he wished it. The Djinn weren't promiscuous, but they weren't afraid of the carnal side of their nature either.

Zurael's hands curled into fists. He forced his thoughts to veer from the direction they were taking. He reminded himself that once he'd honored his debt to the House of the Spider then he was free to finish what he'd come here to do—not only for himself, but for his people. Aisling couldn't be allowed to live, not if she was able to summon any of them at will and might one day bind them.

Misgiving slithered through him. He'd thought it would be simple to kill her, but now there was no rush of rage to catapult him into action. There was no satisfaction to be found in bloody images of retribution.

He couldn't pinpoint the moment his resolve had weakened. Was it her offer to share her food? Was it the instant she'd bravely faced him and their eyes met as his talons danced over her jugular and her terror beat against his palm?

He was no longer sure he could kill her, and yet he knew with certainty an assassin from the House of the Scorpion would be sent if he returned to the Kingdom of the Djinn and she remained alive. A human who could summon a Djinn was a threat to all of them.

Zurael rolled his shoulders and shrugged the thoughts aside. There was little point in thinking of the future and his part in it. For the moment Aisling was bait for a more dangerous prey.

His eyes followed her when she gracefully sat on a bed of packed earth at the center of the room. When she folded her legs and ducked her head, he couldn't look away from the delicate curve of her neck.

She pulled on a thin leather string until a small pouch emerged from underneath her shirt. Zurael stepped farther into the fetish-guarded room when she opened the pouch and dumped a dozen tiny carvings into her hand before scattering them onto the dirt.

Bone fetishes gleamed against clay-red soil. The ferret scampered to her side. He dropped the hawk he carried in his mouth a short distance away from the collection of figures on the packed dirt.

Zurael drew closer. Uneasiness settled in his chest as he realized the ferret had been with her when she'd summoned him in her astral state.

He hadn't remembered before. In his mind's eye he hadn't seen the creature, and yet as it picked up the carving of a serpent and placed it in Aisling's hand, Zurael's earlier memories were overlaid with fresh ones, images with Aziel draped over her shoulders as he'd been in the kitchen. He could sense nothing otherworldly about the animal, but now its presence worried him. It raised questions he couldn't answer.

A raven fetish followed the serpent, a spider came next. Zurael's thoughts flashed to his visit with Malahel, where a spider, a raven and a serpent had gathered around a crystalline altar as the stones were cast.

Aziel hesitated. He cocked his head as if he were listening to a voice only he could hear. When his attention returned to the scattered fetishes, he picked up a bear. Once it was placed in Aisling's hand, he scratched the ground until the remaining carvings were in a pile.

Aisling set the four she held in her hand aside and collected the others. She returned them to the leather pouch and dropped it under her shirt.

Another step took Zurael to a wooden strip, one of four trapping the dirt into a square. Aisling's gaze flicked nervously to his face then back to what she was doing.

He crouched but didn't interfere as she selected the raven and stood it on the dirt. The spider followed, to the right and down, east to the raven's north. South was marked by the serpent, west by the bear. She picked up the hawk resting in the center of the other four and set it aside.

Zurael tensed when she drew a small athame from a sheath hidden at her lower back. He cursed himself for not thinking she could be armed, even if it would be nearly impossible for her to kill him.

She connected the four fetishes with arced lines so they were bound in a circle. When she turned her palm up and he saw she intended to drag the knife's blade over it, Zurael reacted without thought.

Fear and rage flooded him. He knocked the athame from her hand and took her to the ground with the swiftness of a pouncing cougar.

"You will not bind me," he said.

The confusion in her face calmed him as quickly as the sight of her getting ready to make a blood offering had spurred him to strike. In place of the rage and fear came awareness, of the softness of her body beneath his, of her scent, of the hardness of his cock where it pressed against the juncture of her thighs.

She licked her lips in a nervous gesture and he wanted to cover her mouth with his own. He wanted to plunge his tongue into her heated depths and taste her essence.

Shock made him scramble off her. For the Djinn, the sharing of breath was the sharing of spirit, and he had no wish to give a piece of his soul to another—especially one of the alien god's creations.

Aisling sat. His words reverberated through her mind. The heat of his body and a fierce awareness of his arousal lingered.

She hesitated only a second before saying, "I have no desire to bind you, and even if I wanted to, I don't know how. I'm not a witch or a sorceress."

Anger flashed in the demon's eyes. She knew he was remembering her summons.

"I wouldn't have called for you if the need wasn't urgent. If there was another name I could have used instead, I would have."

Her admission surprised him. His gaze traveled to the fetishes that had been scattered when he pinned her to the ground. She could see the question forming, but before he could ask it, someone knocked on the front door. The knock was followed by the sound of the door opening and a female voice calling, "Hello. Is anyone home?"

Aisling rose from the dirt and brushed herself off. Aziel darted into the living room ahead of her. Surprise held Aisling in the doorway for a second when she recognized the woman the dark priest and his followers had intended to sacrifice.

"I hope you don't mind me coming here," Elena said.

"I don't mind."

"May I have a seat? Can we talk? Or do you have a client with you?"

"Please, sit down. I can give you water or make hot tea."

"No. I'm fine." Elena took a chair.

Aisling sat on the couch while Aziel curled up on the second chair.

"Luther says you saved my life last night," Elena said.

Aisling didn't think Elena meant Father Ursu or Bishop Routledge. "Luther?"

"Luther Germaine." Elena's eyes widened slightly when Aisling didn't respond. "He's the mayor of Oakland."

"Until yesterday I lived outside Stockton."

Elena smiled. Her gaze traveled around the room. "That explains a lot. Someone with your ability . . ." Her eyes met Aisling's. There was a fevered intensity in them. "I want to hire you to find out what happened to me last night."

Aisling's stomach fluttered nervously. "What do you mean?"

Movement at the corner of Aisling's eye distracted her. Her heart rate spiked when she turned her head and saw the snake moving toward them in a mesmerizing glide of scales over wood. Its likeness to the serpent tattooed on Zurael's arm was unmistakable.

Elena gasped and started to rise from her chair.

"It's all right," Aisling said automatically, though she had no idea whether it was or not. The snake was venomous, the demon as lethal in this form as in any of his others.

Golden eyes gleamed in the dusky room as Zurael closed the distance between them. With ease he found the edge of the couch and followed it with his upper body until he reached the armrest. He dipped his head to allow gravity to work in his favor as he slid down to the cushion and across to Aisling, the rest of his body following in an exotic pattern of black and gold.

Aisling's pulse raced. Her breath shortened as Zurael's upper body rose once again, swaying like a cobra ready to strike.

His face was only inches away from hers but she didn't cower away from him. She refused to cringe each time he tested her.

His tongue flicked out to touch her cheek, to taste her fear and measure it. For an instant she thought she saw approval in the golden depths of his eyes when she didn't flinch.

He coiled himself around her arm and rested his head on the back of her hand in perfect imitation of the tattoo he wore in his human form. His scales were smooth and warm against her skin, his tongue a whisper across her knuckles.

Aisling glanced at the ferret curled on the chair and smiled. If Zurael thought to horrify or terrify her, then he'd failed. Aziel had once taken the body of a huge, heavily banded king snake. She'd spent hours with him draped over her neck or coiled around her waist.

Elena dropped back into her seat. Aisling's attention returned to her guest.

"I want to hire you to find out what happened to me last night," Elena repeated, reaching into the pocket of her jacket and pulling out a change purse with fancy stitching. She tossed it on the coffee table between them.

The sound of it hitting the table was like a gunshot in the still room. Aisling really looked at Elena then. Instead of images of a naked female painted with sigils and lying helpless on an altar, she saw the cut of Elena's clothing, the expensive weave, the jewels she wore on her fingers and wrists, her neck and ears.

"Go ahead and count it," Elena said with a negligible wave of her hand toward the coffee table.

Aisling opened the purse. Her hands shook slightly when she saw the pieces of silver. They were more valuable than the coins and bills created by the Treasury. Even now, long after The Last War and the plague, the distrust of anything other than gems or fine metals as payment lingered.

With enough silver coins she could return home. She could give something back to the woman who'd taken her in as an abandoned infant and raised her with love and acceptance.

Aisling counted the silver pieces. There were ten of them.

"That's half of what I'm willing to pay you," Elena said.

Aisling closed the purse and returned it to the table. Her palms were damp as she rubbed them over her knees. "What do you mean when you say you want to find out what happened to you last night?"

"I want to know how I ended up on that altar. The last thing I remember is being at a club. Then I woke up in a room at the church. A nun was washing the bottom of my feet and Father Ursu was praying over me. They wouldn't let me leave until they were sure I wasn't possessed." She shivered, and for an instant the anticipation glittering in her eyes gave way to a fear.

"Won't the authorities investigate?"

"No. Not now. Luther swallowed his pride when he asked Bishop Routledge for help." Elena's lips twisted in distaste. "Luther's wife is devout and from an extremely influential family. She's been confessing her sins to the bishop since she was a child. I'm sure he's heard an earful about Luther's affair with me. I doubt the good bishop would have helped if Luther wasn't the mayor and married to one of his important constituents."

Elena leaned forward with the intensity of a predator. "Father Ursu told me you were there when something went wrong during the ceremony. He said a powerful demon slaughtered them all."

"I was there in an astral state."

"Can you find their souls? Can you ask them why I was picked as a sacrifice?" Elena slid forward, to the edge of her seat. "The police won't investigate because the dark priest was Anthony Tiernan. His family is wealthy and powerful. His followers were from similar families. Luther won't push because all of the families involved want to keep what happened quiet. The Church wants the matter closed, too, because of the demon. Everyone I've gone to thinks justice was served, everyone but me."

Aisling shivered. Even for a purse of silver she wasn't sure she wanted to seek out the dark priest or his followers in the ghostlands. There were malevolent beings that collected human souls just for the song of their terrified cries and the pleasure of hearing their tortured screams. There were dark places that required a heavy toll to enter and an even heavier one to exit. There was knowledge that could shatter a person's mind and entities who would separate a travelers' spirits from their body in order to take possession and clothe themselves in human flesh.

"Could you find them?" Elena asked.

"I don't know."

Elena's hand settled on the purse. She pushed it toward Aisling. "We could call this a third of your fee instead of half." She blinked away tears. "Please, I've got to know why they picked me. I have to know if I was just in the wrong place at the wrong time or if someone put Anthony up to it. He was arrogant and spoiled, but he had no reason to hate me or to strike out at Luther. I didn't see him or any of his followers at the club."

Aisling looked down at the brightly patterned purse. Temptation writhed with fear in her belly. The bills Father Ursu had given her represented more money than she'd ever possessed, and yet they weren't enough to buy fresh fruit or vegetables. The silver Elena was offering . . . it was a down payment on a dream Aisling had never dared to believe was possible for her or her family, a life without the fear of being collected by the authorities at will or evicted from land they didn't own.

She glanced at Aziel, but his eyes were hidden by the curl of his tail. He slept, or pretended to sleep, leaving the decision up to her.

Aisling pushed the pouch back to the center of the table. She couldn't agree, not now, when the hunger for security burned in her belly so hotly its presence nearly overrode her caution. "I need to think about what you ask."

Elena's lips tightened. Irritation flickered in her eyes, only to be followed by more tears. "I'm begging you. At least try. You saved my life last night. You're the only one who can help me."

"I can only promise to consider it."

Elena wiped the moisture from the corners of her eyes. She shoved one hand into the expensive jacket. She ducked her head as if struggling to regain her control, but Aisling was wary, suspicious of the easy tears after the flash of anger.

"Have you heard of Ghost?" Elena asked, taking her fisted hand from her pocket but not looking up.

"No."

"There's a club I go to sometimes, when Luther attends social functions with his wife. It's in the red zone." Elena glanced up then. "Do you know what that means?"

"No."

"The police don't patrol at all. They don't respond to calls there. You go into the area at your own risk, knowing it's dangerous. The clubs hire protection and serve justice in their own way. They lock their doors at dusk and don't open them until dawn. Some of the clubs are membership only.

"Some of them are open to anyone with the money to get in. Well, anyone human. No shapeshifters, vampires or other supernaturals.

"There are bouncers to make sure only the fully human are allowed inside. Most of the clubs don't look too closely when it comes to whether the humans have special abilities or practice magic. That's part of what makes the clubs fun."

She licked her lips. "What happens in any of the clubs during the night stays there. What happens outside the clubs isn't questioned either."

Aisling studied Elena's expensive jewelry and clothing. She looked beyond it, to the privilege and security it represented. Emotion roiled in her chest, anger and sadness, a railing against the injustice that someone who took survival for granted would seek her thrills in a place like the red zone, while others, like Geneva McConaughey, scraped and toiled to keep a roof over their head and food on the table as they raised children they hadn't given birth to.

The silence grew heavy around them. Aisling realized her own hands were clenched into fists. She forced her fingers open. She looked at the heavy coin purse on the coffee table and remembered Elena saying she'd been at a club before waking to find herself in the church.

Aisling made herself meet Elena's gaze and ask, "Is Ghost the place you were taken from?"

"No."

Elena edged her chair forward, crowding the coffee table so it moved to press against Aisling's legs. She opened her hand to reveal an etched container. It looked like a miniature snuffbox or a pillbox, something seen only in private collections and the history books Geneva collected when she could acquire them for almost nothing.

"Ghost is a . . . substance. An incredible, powerful substance." Elena rubbed her thumb over the top of the container. Her eyes sought Aisling's. Without saying anything else, she opened the box.

Fear rushed into Aisling with a force that left her heart pounding violently in her chest. Ghostland winds filled her thoughts with shrieks and wails and tortured summonses. She scrambled to her feet, intent on getting away from the sickly gray paste at the bottom of the container, but the table held her trapped.

Zurael hissed. His coils tightened on her arm as his head lifted from the back of her hand, his mouth open to expose deadly fangs.

Aisling twisted away, trying to escape the trap of furniture and spirit winds. Elena dug her fingers into the container then grabbed Aisling's bare arm.

There was no time for preparation, no time for Aisling to evoke the names of her guardians or set the necessary protections. Her spirit was ripped from her body and propelled into the ghostlands.

* * *

ZURAEL hissed for a second time when ice-cold wind buffeted him as if the spiritlands recognized what he was and tried to deny him entrance. The coils of his snake form tightened on Aisling's arm. Her whimpered protest sounded in his mind along with the racing beat of her heart. Her fear washed over his tongue to blend with his own.

His father's kingdom might be deep in the ghostlands, but it was a place apart from it. There were few exits, and those that did exist opened onto metaphysical pathways carved directly to the physical world now claimed by the alien god. Not even those who belonged to the House of the Raven entered this human-born land of cursed spirits.

Aisling's fingers pushed on one of his coils as if it was a bracelet she wanted to reposition. Confusion slid over Zurael in a hazy overlay that made no sense until images from other trips into the spiritlands slipped through his thoughts like the gray fog swirling around them. A spike of shock went straight to his core with the realization that he was a shadow in Aisling's mind and she was a shadow in his.

She pushed on his coils again, and he noticed she was completely naked, her golden hair unbound, and even in a snake's form he reacted to the sight of her. Heat swamped him, burned him almost to the point of pain.

She whimpered and shifted his coils again. Distress was written on her face.

With sudden clarity he realized he was hurting her. He was a creature of fire, and in this place the separation between form and essence was thin. If she stripped him from her arm and cast him into the mist, he would become *ifrit* as surely as those Djinn who'd killed the ones who bound them.

His coils tightened involuntarily. She whispered, "Stop. I can't think. I can't stay safe."

Zurael watched her face as he slowly loosened the coils. He felt her relief as the swirling gray mist caressed and cooled her skin.

The landscape cleared as her heart rate slowed and her distress faded. He looked around and was surprised by the barrenness, by the endless sea of empty gray.

He'd expected horrific sights and terrified beings. He'd imagined a bloody landscape filled with tortured screams.

As he thought it, the scene around them changed. A wall of gray parted to reveal the skeletal remains of burned-out buildings.

Men and women wearing tattered clothing sat in hollowed doorways, moaning, rocking, oblivious to anything around them. Machine guns rattled in the distance. Rats made no pretense of hiding as they feasted on human carcasses.

Elena stood in the middle of the street shrieking. She stopped when Aisling stepped through the opening and into the scene.

"This isn't what I want!" Elena screamed. Her terror became anger as she focused her attention on Aisling.

A man stepped out of an alley. His face was marked with a criminal's tattoos. His hands were bound behind his back. A metal cable twisted around his neck then trailed down his back. It slithered behind him as he walked toward Elena, though Zurael couldn't see its end.

"It's not what you want," the man said. "But perhaps it's what you deserve, sister dear. I see you are unfortunately . . . still alive."

Elena threw her hand up as if she could repel him with the gesture. She scuttled backward and sideways until she reached Aisling.

"No," Elena said, grabbing Aisling's arm just as she'd done in the living room with Ghost on her fingers. "Make this go away. This isn't what I want."

"What do you want?" Aisling asked.

Zurael saw the image form in Aisling's mind. He felt the spirit winds swirl and eddy as they gathered in order to do Aisling's bidding even before Elena said, "Sinead."

Time slowed. Aisling's heart lingered between beats.

The scene around them didn't fade, but a woman stepped through the grayness. Black leather molded to her body. Bloodred lips curled upward. Her laugh was a throaty invitation.

She slapped the riding crop she carried against her thigh. "So you found me at last."

Her attention shifted to Elena's brother. Her eyes widened momentarily. She laughed again as she reached up and fondled the tightly wound scarf around her neck. "It appears dear John and I met similar ends, though of course I went out thrashing in orgasm. I imagine he can't say the same."

Her hand left her neck. She offered it to Elena. "Come, my pet. Let's make your visit a good one."

Elena released Aisling's wrist and went to Sinead. The gray fog rose as soon as their hands touched. When they turned to leave, it engulfed them completely then spread to block out the gutted buildings and lost souls.

"Well, that's an interesting turn of events and a titillating secret I'm sure my sister prays won't get out," John said. "You'll come to regret saving her life. But who am I to complain?"

He shrugged and his hands were suddenly free. He stretched his arms and rotated his wrists and shoulders. "Your mistake is my gain."

He waved his hands in front of them and the mist at their feet thinned. Zurael felt Aisling shiver as gray faded to red clay, and the scattered bone-carved fetishes along with her discarded athame were revealed.

With a casual toss, Elena's brother threw the hawk figurine onto the ground. A hint of cruelty settled in his eyes. "Time to pay up."

Four

AISLING knelt on the ground. Zurael could feel the wild beating of her heart, but her hand was steady as she picked up the raven and stood it on the dirt. The spider came next, to the right and down, just as she'd positioned it earlier, east to the raven's north. South was marked by the serpent, west by the bear.

He rode the wave of her thoughts and knew whatever debt she owed would now be paid at a higher cost. And though he couldn't touch the names of the ones she offered her blood in payment to, he could sense she didn't fear the spirits represented by the fetishes.

Her heart thundered because she was afraid of what they might reveal to her. She feared what they might ask of her, what they might demand.

A tendril of guilt uncurled deep in Zurael's chest. He regretted his part in this. He'd acted without thought when he'd pinned her to the ground and kept her from making this offering of blood in the shaman's ceremony room.

Aisling leaned forward to pick up the hawk fetish. Unlike before, this time it didn't yield its position in the center of the other four.

Elena's brother clicked his tongue. Zurael's coils tightened involuntarily when she picked up the athame. He felt the streak of fiery pain shoot through her arm and forced himself to loosen his grip on her.

Aisling placed the tip of the blade to the right of the raven and drew an arc to the spider. She placed the tip of the blade to the right of the spider and drew an arc to the serpent, and then an arc from the serpent to the bear and back to the raven so they were all connected in a circle.

"Take my blood as you will," she whispered in a soft, melodic voice. "It is freely offered in payment for the aid you have given me."

A quick slash across her palm severed the lifeline in a symbolic gesture. Blood poured from it in an unnatural, steady river of red, despite the shallowness of the cut.

It splashed on the hawk, then spread outward, long fingers reaching for the other fetishes. But even when it reached them, the blood continued to flow from her palm, to deepen and pool until the hawk disappeared and nothing could be seen but a perfect circle of red and the four carved sentinels.

Elena's brother crouched down so his face was even with Aisling's. When his gaze traveled over her body and his hand went to his crotch, rage whipped through Zurael. With a hiss he lifted his head and opened his mouth, exposing the glistening, deadly fangs.

John laughed. He stroked his cock through the fabric of his jeans. "Your pet's jealous, beautiful. He might be long and thick, but I can please you better. What do you say, ang—" His words ended in a gurgle as the metal cable pulled taut, snapping his head back. A scream followed, a sound of such torment that Zurael's heart raced in sync with Aisling's.

The noise ended as quickly as it began. Elena's brother toppled forward with his knees underneath him and his forehead touching the red earth as though he were praying, begging for mercy. His panting sobs replaced the tortured agony of his scream.

He shuddered and cowered and finally calmed. In a subdued voice he said, "The one I serve sends you a glimpse of the future and a chance to change it. The choice is yours but the decision must be made before you leave here."

Dread vibrated through Aisling as she looked down at the pool of blood. The surface was slick and shiny, a screen for horrible images to play out on.

The breath caught in her throat as an orchard of trees rippled into existence. Her chest grew tight as the outline of a familiar house shimmered into place. The old barn and paddocks for the livestock followed. And despite the bloody medium the images were captured on, for one precious second the scene was beautiful.

Then came the bodies.

Spiderweb-thin lines provided just enough detail so Aisling recognized each one of her family members. They were scattered, as though they'd died where they'd fallen.

Pain lodged in her chest and throat. Tears fell from her eyes, dropping into the pool and sending waves across its surface until there was nothing but her own reflection.

"How can I stop this from happening?" she whispered, turning her head so she could look at Elena's brother.

As if her question released him from his supplicant's pose, he stood. "Find the ones responsible for creating Ghost, then kill them."

"Ghost is responsible for this?" She didn't doubt the vision, but she found it hard to understand how it could be possible. No one in her family would be tempted by a substance that cast them into the spiritlands without protection.

"And more," John said, waving his hand over the pool of blood.

Oakland's skyline came into view and with it additional carnage. Only in this scene the living danced with glee, their heads thrown back in howls of victory.

They feasted on the dead, but they weren't shapeshifters

scavenging or the creatures that emerged from hiding after The Last War and the plague. They were malevolent entities from the ghostlands who'd found a pathway back to the place they'd once called home.

Aisling shivered at the sight of their maniacal pleasure. It was her darkest fear that while she was in the ghostlands her physical body would be possessed and whatever tied her spirit to it severed.

She closed her eyes and sought a place of calmness. On the screen of her thoughts the sequence of events played out like a net she grew more and more entangled in—the guardsmen and Father Ursu arriving to take her from her home, the bishop and Father Ursu giving her no true choice but to enter the spiritlands in order to look for Elena, Elena's brother appearing, his help offered on the condition she remain in Oakland . . . Zurael.

She opened her eyes to glance at the serpent coiled around her arm. He burned with the fires of hell.

"I must personally kill the ones creating Ghost, or I may see them dead?"

John cocked his head. A heartbeat passed. "Either works, as long as the conduit is closed."

Aisling didn't know how the spiritlands were held open so the winds could flow over an earthly substance and create a doorway into the ghostlands. But she knew such a feat couldn't be accomplished unless powerful forces in the spirit world were involved.

"I will be protected?"

John's laugh was a sharp, angry bark. "What more do you need? You—" His head snapped back as the cable pulled tight.

Aisling braced herself for the sound of his screams, but this time they didn't come. The mist began to gather instead. It swirled around his feet and quickly swallowed his legs and hips, signaling that soon others would come to answer her questions, and their help would not be offered without a cost.

She looked down. The pool of blood held only her reflection. The raven, spider, serpent, and bear fetishes stood as sentinels. The beings they represented waited only for her decision before they would end the ceremony and accept her offering.

A heavy weight settled in Aisling's heart. She didn't know what stain would be left on her soul, but to save her family there was only one choice. "I will kill whoever is responsible for creating Ghost, or see them dead."

As soon as the words were spoken, the gray mist claimed Elena's brother. Then it rushed over Aisling with a force that drove her out of the ghostlands.

Zurael was aware of the ferret's presence immediately. Aziel was draped over Aisling's shoulder, close enough that he could launch himself and sink sharp deadly teeth into the snake's form.

Zurael hissed. He kept his fangs exposed as he slowly uncoiled himself from her arm and dropped to the dirt in the shaman's ceremony room.

Rage roared through him as he realized the true extent of the crime Elena committed when she forced Aisling—and him—into the spiritlands. The front door was unlocked. Their physical bodies left vulnerable.

With a thought, he changed from serpent to man. His attention shifted to Aisling.

Tenderness filled him as he crouched next to her. It flowed in unexpectedly and brought a protectiveness that went beyond keeping her safe while she served as bait.

He'd been a shadow in her mind. Now he knew she'd been ensnared in the same spider's web he'd been caught in.

Her eyes held the bruised look of one struggling with exhaustion. He found himself wanting to care for her and glanced at her hand, worried about the amount of blood she'd lost.

The slash across her palm was gone. For an instant he wondered if she'd paid with a part of her soul and the blood had been an illusion. But then she reached for the bone fetishes. They were bright red, as though they'd fed on what she offered.

The raven, spider, serpent and bear remained standing until she gathered them in her hand. The hawk lay shattered as if it had been sacrificed in order to give birth to a pentacle carved in onyx.

Uneasiness slid through Zurael when Aisling picked the talisman up and he saw the sigils carved into its black surface. They were familiar—making him think of the tomes meticulously cared for in the House of the Serpent—the volumes listing the enemies of the Djinn—the books containing the names of the angels.

Aisling ran her thumb over the pentacle. She compared the sigils etched into its smooth surface against the memory of those written on Elena. They weren't the same.

She startled when Zurael's hand gripped her wrist. Her pulse raced at the gentleness of his touch and the heat of his flesh. He was crouched next to her so it was impossible to miss the swelling of his cock in the molded leather of his pants.

An answering heat pooled in her woman's folds. Nervousness fluttered in her chest with the realization that her earlier fear had kept her from recognizing her body's attraction to him. She shivered as her eyes traveled up his torso to collide with Zurael's gaze.

Desire burned in the liquid gold of his eyes—there and then gone, as if he'd battled and managed to extinguish the flames fanned to life between them. "Do you recognize the sigils?" he asked.

"No."

"It's a protection charm?"

"I think so. I'd be of little use if I was thrust into the spiritlands every time I was in the presence of Ghost."

He nodded and released her hand. She pulled the soft leather pouch from underneath her shirt and placed the blood-fed fetishes and the pentacle in it before letting it fall back into place.

A low moan filtered in from the living room, reminding her of Elena and the silver coins. Nervousness fluttered in Aisling's belly along with deep anger. "I'll have to take her money. She'll never trust me with what she knows unless she thinks she's bought me with her silver. Other than Father Ursu and the bishop, I don't know anyone here."

Zurael cupped her cheek with his hand and sent her heart skittering in a dance of longing. His eyes met hers. "In the end you'll wish you'd never summoned me to save her life. She's already cost you much. Her selfishness could have cost your life today."

"But it gained me a chance to save my family."

Zurael stroked his thumb over her mouth. His cock pulsed when her breath caught in her throat and her eyelashes lowered in an unconscious invitation for his kiss. In the physical world her hair was braided, but the image of her in her astral state, naked with the blond locks flowing down her back, was burned into his mind.

He was a Serpent prince, a being who could take any form and no form. He could trace his line back to the first Djinn to be born from the fires of a molten Earth. She was all that he wasn't, yet he struggled to keep from answering her silent summons to touch his lips to hers and share his spirit with her.

She was forbidden fruit, a sweet temptation he was finding it harder and harder to resist. For all that his mind argued against knowing her in a carnal way, he couldn't stop himself from pressing his mouth to the corner of hers then kissing downward to the spot on her neck where her pulse pounded not with fear, but with desire.

Zurael luxuriated in the softness of her skin, in the heady scent of her arousal and the knowledge that he had the power to enthrall and enslave her. Her nearly silent whimpers made him want to stretch her out and cover her with his body.

He imagined himself thrusting into her. Plunging in and out until her low cries turned into pleasure-filled screams.

The groans from the next room grew louder. Their sexual nature became obvious.

Zurael smiled as Aisling's embarrassed blush burned his lips. The reminder they weren't alone gave him the strength to break the contact and rock back onto his heels.

Aisling rose to her feet and swayed under an assault of dizziness. Only Zurael standing and grabbing her arms kept her from toppling over.

"You've lost a lot of blood," he said, pulling her against him.

The sound of his steady heartbeat and the feel of his warmth chased the light-headedness away. She breathed in his exotic masculine scent and closed her eyes.

"Tea helps," she said, but she didn't have the energy to pull away from him and take the first step toward the kitchen.

For a long moment they stood together. Surprise made her eyes open when she realized Aziel was still perched on her shoulder. Confusion caused her to retreat from Zurael's light embrace.

In each of Aziel's lives he'd always been overly protective and aggressive toward any male who showed an interest in her. Yet now he allowed a demon prince to hold her.

A chill slid through Aisling as she wondered if Aziel was demon. She'd never seen his true form. She'd never been able to determine what type of entity he was. He'd rebuffed her efforts gently but firmly each and every time her curiosity led in that direction.

He was her companion long before he became her spirit guide. She'd loved him always. He wasn't a shapeshifter, but she'd never allowed herself to see his possession of his host forms as demonic.

People of faith painted all demons with a single brush. They saw them as malicious beings that served an evil master and sought the downfall of mankind. She had not found that to be the *only* truth. She had encountered such entities in the spiritlands, just as she'd encountered creatures that had once been gods but had later been named demons when one religion conquered another.

She had never looked for the gates of hell, but she didn't doubt such a place of punishment could be found in the ghostlands. When Zurael had called her a child of mud and promised retribution with his eyes, she'd thought he was a prince of hell. Now she wondered why it was *his* name Aziel had given her and what it meant that Aziel allowed Zurael to touch her.

"Why are you here?" she asked, lifting her chin as she met Zurael's gaze.

His hand went to her neck. His thumb brushed across her pulse. "Because you summoned me."

"Only the one time."

"Once is all it takes."

She shivered at the underlying menace in his voice, remembered too well his silky promise of retribution. She could still feel the phantom prick of his talons as he'd greeted her at the door earlier, but she refused to hide from the truth. "You came to kill me."

"Yes." His expression softened when she didn't pull away from him. He leaned in so his cheek touched hers. His breath was a warm breeze flowing over her ear. "Rest easy, child of mud. You're safe from me unless you summon me again."

She opened her mouth to say she wouldn't, then closed it again as the images she'd seen in the pool of her own blood rose from her conscience in warning. She would walk into the fires of hell if it meant saving her family.

Aisling stepped back and turned away. She was still weak and shaky, but somehow she made it to the living room door.

Her earlier blush returned with flaming heat. Elena was on the floor, her skirt up and her panties down to reveal the curls between her thighs. Her expensive blouse was parted, its buttons scattered in haste. Her bra was open so her fingers could pluck and pull at already bruised nipples.

Zurael cursed softly. He placed his hand on Aisling's arm and helped her to the kitchen.

Fine tremors ran through her hands as she filled the teakettle and set it on the stove then pulled chipped mugs from the cabinet along with a jar of honey. Frustrated tears wet the corners of her eyes when tea scattered on the counter as she attempted to fill the small metal tea balls with leaves. She hated the weakness that left her so shaky.

Aisling closed her eyes and tried to steady herself. She'd be fine as soon as she had something to drink.

Zurael left the kitchen. She heard him moving around, but she didn't open her eyes until he'd swung her up into his arms.

Her heart fluttered at the tenderness in his face. In two steps he was settling her onto one of the chairs he'd brought from the living room.

"I assume you'd rather have your tea in the kitchen," he said. "Under different circumstances the show your guest is putting on might be arousing, but at the moment I find nothing pleasant about her presence here."

Aisling nodded. She found it impossible to look away as Zurael took over the tea preparations. His movements were flowing, graceful. He was beautiful to look at.

Aziel rubbed his furry cheek against hers before sliding to her lap and hopping to the floor to disappear into the living room.

Zurael poured boiling water into the cups. His body hardened and burned with the feel of Aisling's eyes on him. Even without looking at her, he was intensely aware of her.

The tea steeped while he rummaged through the cabinet. He retrieved a can of peaches and placed it on the counter, then removed the tea ball and added honey before taking the mug to Aisling.

There were shadows under her eyes, a frailty to her features that made him want to gather her up in his arms and take care of her. He cupped his hands around hers to steady them as he helped her carry the mug to her lips.

His thoughts visited the House of the Spider and the tea he'd taken with Malahel and Iyar. He pictured Malahel's crystal altar and the stones he'd tossed, how Aisling's angelite had been touched by powerful forces as well as humans and angels. He'd assumed the dark stones represented beings in the spiritlands, but they could just as easily have represented powerful Djinn.

Ravens were spirit travelers like Aisling. They flew in the place where Djinn souls waited to be guided back and reborn, while Aisling walked the ghostlands created by human death and belief.

Spiders saw how the past, present and future weaved together. They worked the threads in subtle alterations that could change the entire design.

He wondered if Malahel and Iyar had known how quickly his mind would join his body in wanting her. If they'd sent him here for a reason beyond retrieving the ancient tablet.

Aisling sighed and lowered the mug to rest on her lap. His hands remained cupped around hers, trapping hers between the tea's heat and his own.

She closed her eyes and leaned her head back. "I'll be okay as soon as the tea and honey kick in."

Zurael left her long enough to open the can of peaches and put them in a bowl. He cursed himself for a fool as he knelt in front of her, picking up a peach slice with his fingers and holding it to her lips.

Her eyes opened to find his. A delicate blush of uncertainty washed over her cheeks as she accepted his offering.

His cock jerked in reaction to the touch of her tongue against his fingers. Lust burned through his veins.

She took a second slice, and a third. Her tongue lingered, gliding over his skin in pursuit of the peach juice. Her lips closed on his fingers briefly when he offered her a fourth piece.

He fought against the urge to pick her up and carry her from the room. It was easy to picture her naked, her lips on his cock, sucking it into the wet heat of her mouth.

Slice by slice he fed her the peaches. He watched her eyes grow dark with need and felt his own hunger grow as each piece left his fingers.

When the bowl was empty, he placed it on the floor then took the tea mug from her unresisting fingers and set it aside, too. Her eyes met his. Her lips parted in invitation.

With a low moan, he leaned in, desperate for the taste of her but still in control, still sane enough to keep from ravaging her mouth and sharing his spirit with her.

He pressed kisses along her jawbone before traveling to her ear. Panted when her fingers slipped through the opening of his parted vest and splayed across his bare chest.

She whimpered when he sucked on her lobe. She shuddered against him when his tongue traced the delicate shell of her ear before sliding into the sensitive canal.

"Zurael," she whispered, her voice stroking over him and making him hungry for the feel of skin against skin.

He jerked when her fingers found his tiny nipples. The muscles of his abdomen rippled as he fought the urge to take her hands in his and move them downward to his erection.

Elena's cries grew sharper in the next room. Her scream of orgasm cleared Zurael's mind with the suddenness of a dive into an icy stream.

He stepped back, breathing hard, unable to look away from Aisling's parted lips and soft, angelite-colored eyes.

The intensity of his need to protect her, to merge his body and soul with hers, was almost beyond bearing. He took another step backward, away from Aisling, though he feared no distance would be far enough to keep him from imagining them naked together and writhing in pleasure.

He glanced across the counter and saw Elena fumbling with her clothing. Her eyes were still closed, but her movements warned she'd returned from the ghostlands.

Zurael held the image of the serpent in his mind. He was glad to shift into its shape and escape the deadly temptation of Aisling.

Aisling picked up the discarded dishes, then rose to her feet. The light-headedness caused by loss of blood was gone, but in its place panicked confusion reigned.

She didn't recognize herself when Zurael touched her. She had no will to resist him, no desire other than to find pleasure in his arms.

Aisling shivered as she looked at the serpent coiled in her kitchen. His golden eyes followed her movements as she placed the dishes in the sink. His long, forked tongue flicked in and out.

She turned her head as images of him kissing her ear, assaulting it with a human tongue, sent a wave of longing straight to her swollen labia. Her panties were wet with arousal, and in the serpent's form he'd taste the scent of it.

Was she tempted by him because she was meant to be? Or because he was a demon of hell and demons were said to use temptation in order to lure humans to their doom?

Unconsciously her hand went to the place where her shirt hid the small pouch containing the fetishes and onyx pentacle. He'd come to kill her, but he'd said she was safe from him as long as she didn't summon him again.

He had no reason to seduce her. Her soul and her life were already in peril.

Zuracl's untouched mug sat on the counter. She fished the tea ball out and poured the tea into a pan. As it warmed on the stove she forced her thoughts away from the demon and onto the task ahead of her.

In the living room Elena rolled to her side. Her eyes fluttered open.

For a few seconds they remained unfocused. When they cleared, she sat up and casually closed her jacket, uncaring and unconcerned about what she'd done, what she'd risked for her pleasure.

Aisling banked her anger. She poured the tea. A lifetime of hiding her thoughts and emotions from anyone outside her family made it easy for her to take her seat on the couch as though the trip to the spiritlands had cost her nothing.

"This will help," Aisling said, offering the mug of tea after Elena reclaimed the chair she'd been sitting in earlier.

Elena took the mug. She trembled slightly as her attention shifted to the serpent gliding into the room, menace radiating along his patterned length.

This time Zurael didn't join Aisling on the sofa. He slid up the wooden leg of the coffee table and coiled himself on its surface within easy striking range of Elena.

Aisling used the fear she read in Elena's eyes to make a point. "It's dangerous to go into the spiritlands without proper protections."

Elena's gaze skittered up to meet hers, then immediately returned to the deadly snake. She licked her lips nervously but ignored the warning. "I was Ghosting. That's why I don't remember leaving the club or being at the black mass. I had to be sure you'd understand. I had to know if what I heard about you was true."

Aisling's heart jolted. It was her turn to feel a tremor of fear.

Like all the supernaturally touched children left abandoned on Geneva McConaughey's doorstep, Aisling never talked about her skill as a shamaness. She rarely used her talents openly. Until the guardsmen and Father Ursu arrived, she'd never gone into the spiritlands on behalf of someone she didn't trust or who hadn't been vouched for by someone she trusted.

"What have you heard?" Aisling asked, leaning forward, anxious, though some of her worry disappeared when Aziel emerged from the shaman's workroom and scampered over to settle on her lap.

"I overheard Father Ursu talking with Luther about you being able to guide a Ghost trip," Elena said.

Relief poured into Aisling. They may have mentioned her by name but they could have been talking about any shaman or shamaness. She had no formal training, no reason to think another gifted with shamanic ability couldn't do what she'd done.

A sudden chill swept in to chase the relief away. John's words tormented her from the spiritlands.

I see they've sent a sacrificial lamb. Or maybe that's Elena's role. Then again, maybe third time's the charm.

Aisling's stomach knotted as she looked around the worn, stark living room and thought of the abandoned fetishes and tools in the next room, of the man's clothing left hanging in the closet.

John's voice whispered through her mind. *They don't intend for you to leave. This is only the beginning act—if you survive it, of course.*

She shivered as she remembered the bishop saying she would have a choice between staying in Oakland or going home—only there never had been a choice. Powerful forces in the ghostlands had seen to that and bound her to look for whoever was creating Ghost. She wondered if those same forces had led Father Ursu to her and if the Church was also looking for the Ghost source.

Her attention returned to the serpent curled up on the coffee table. The presence of a demon prince suddenly seemed like a clear message, a warning against trusting Father Ursu or the bishop.

Aisling shifted her focus to Elena. She didn't know what Elena's role in this was. Maybe John was right and his sister was a sacrificial lamb—maybe they all were. At the moment it didn't matter. Elena was the starting point for finding the ones responsible for Ghost.

"I'll help you discover how you ended up at the black mass, but I won't hunt for Anthony Tiernan and his followers in the ghostlands, not unless there's no other choice."

"That's fine. You can search for answers at the club." Elena leaned forward eagerly but jerked back when she remembered the snake. "The man I bought Ghost from was new. He told me I'd have the best results if I found a private place where people couldn't interfere with my trip. He said it was a special batch, one guaranteed to take me where I wanted to go."

"Did it?"

"No, but it got me closer than I've ever been until today, with you."

Elena's eyes glittered with fevered intensity. "Find the man who sold me Ghost. Find out who he works for, but let me handle telling the authorities. You're new here. You don't know who can be trusted and who can't."

She leaned forward again, this time ignoring the serpent in order to whisper, "Don't tell anyone you can control the Ghost ride. It's not common knowledge, otherwise Father Ursu wouldn't have made Luther promise to keep their conversation confidential."

Horror shuddered through Aisling at the thought of being forced into the spiritlands again. Her hand twitched with the desire to hold the black onyx pentacle. "Tell me what I need to know about the club, and what you remember."

"The club is called Sinners. It's in the red zone. I've already told you about that. Do you have a map?"

"Yes."

"I'll show you where the red zone is and tell you how to get there by bus." Elena looked down at her watch. "You don't have much time. The buses will stop picking up passengers soon." She frowned as she took in Aisling's worn clothing. "You can get in wearing that, but if you look poor, you're asking for trouble. Do you have anything newer?"

There were only a few garments in the satchel Father Ursu had handed her in the car, but each item was nicer than anything she'd ever owned. It was silly to resist wearing the clothes she'd been given, but she clung to the familiarity of her own possessions because they connected her to a life that seemed to be slipping further and further away.

Aisling buried her fingers into Aziel's fur. She knew all too well what it meant to be poor and fair game. "I'll wear something else."

"Good." Elena's gaze lingered on the ferret then darted to the serpent. "Don't take your pets. The bouncer won't let you in with them, and if they're discovered inside, they'll be killed."

"Thank you for telling me," Aisling said and felt a small shimmer of gratitude toward Elena despite everything that had happened.

Elena placed her hand on the pouch of silver coins still lying on the coffee table. "This is between you and me. Luther believes I'm here to thank you for saving my life. I don't want anyone to know I've hired you. I don't want you contacting me. I'll return to check your progress when I can. Will you agree to those terms?"

"Yes."

Elena took her hand off the pouch. "Ghost sellers don't come to

Sinners every night. When they do, they arrive a few minutes before the club locks its doors. Until this time it's always been the same two people, a man with a cross branded on his cheek and a woman with a similar one branded on her shoulder. I think they'll talk to you when they find out what you are. It's possible the man who sold me the Ghost is competing against them. He didn't have a cross tattoo, but he was branded on the backs of his hands."

"What did the brands look like?"

Elena closed her eyes for a moment. When she opened them, she tilted her nearly empty mug and dipped a finger into the tea before tracing several wet symbols onto the coffee table.

"I think that's what they looked like but I'm not positive. Do they mean anything to you?"

"No."

Elena shrugged. "They're probably criminal brands then. I've heard there are places that don't bother with tattoos anymore because it's cheaper to use a brand and harder for a criminal to hide by paying someone to alter the design."

"I've heard the same thing. Besides the marks on his hands, what did he look like?"

"Short brown hair. A thin face. Pale. I wouldn't have noticed him at all if he hadn't been the last person to walk into the club before the doors were locked."

"Did he seek you out?"

"No, I was waiting with the others."

"People who wanted to buy Ghost?"

"Yes."

"How many others?"

"Six, I think. He took me aside after he'd sold to them. That's when he told me I'd have the best results if I found a private place where people couldn't interfere with my trip. I don't think he told the others that."

"Where did you go to use Ghost?"

"To one of the upstairs master bedrooms. The closet is long enough to lie down in and it has a door."

"Did he follow you?"

"I don't know."

"Did anyone see you go into the closet?"

"There was a threesome on the bed. There were people hanging around watching them. I didn't really notice who was there. What happens at the club stays at the club—that's one of the very few rules. The clubbers won't tell you anything, but the Ghost dealers, I think they'll be very interested in you."

Elena retrieved a thin billfold from another pocket and placed some money on the table. "This is enough to get you into Sinners a few times. It may take more than one visit before the Ghost sellers show up. There's food and drink for sale inside, but you're allowed to bring your own in." She cocked her head and studied Aisling in an assessing manner. "With your looks, you shouldn't have any trouble getting the men to buy you dinner and drinks. Rape's not allowed. Even drunk, the men who'll be in the club aren't stupid enough to try that, but just about anything else goes." She checked her watch. "You'll go to the club tonight?"

Nervousness tightened Aisling's chest. "Yes."

"Let me show you where it is on the map, then I need to leave. I've already been here a long time. I don't want to make Luther suspicious."

The map was still on the table pushed against the counter. It took Elena only a few minutes to show Aisling the bus route and the street Sinners was on.

As soon as she was gone, Zurael reclaimed his human shape. "I'll go with you."

"They won't let you in," she said and his husky laugh sent heated need spiraling through her.

Despite his intentions to keep his distance from her, Zurael couldn't stop himself from cupping her neck. The rapid beat of her pulse against his palm was echoed in the throbbing of his cock.

"Do you truly believe they can keep me out?"

The need to touch her was getting worse. The fascination she held for him was growing deeper.

A single hand's width wasn't enough contact. He leaned in and touched his cheek to hers as his arm went around her waist.

A groan escaped when he pulled her flush against him, and for a moment he couldn't speak. Sensation bombarded him. Lust burned through his veins like the molten rock the Djinn had risen from.

"Do you think I can't pass for human?" he whispered, kissing her ear, letting her feel the strength of his desire in the form of his erection.

Aisling wrapped her arms around his waist. She shouldn't feel such relief and comfort in being with him. It had to be wrong to lust for a demon. But she couldn't seem to stop herself from wanting him, from yielding a little bit more of herself each time he touched her. "We need to leave," she whispered, almost grateful to be going somewhere she wouldn't be alone with Zurael.

His hand left her neck and swept down her spine. She moaned softly as he cupped her hips and ground himself against her clit. He made her ache in a way she'd never ached before. He made her fantasize about things that shouldn't be allowed to happen.

She turned her head and kissed his neck. His hips jerked in response.

"Aisling," he said, and the sound of him saying her name made her labia swell and part in readiness for him.

Her hands moved up his sides and around to find his nipples. They were hard points against her palms. She rubbed over them and thrilled at the way he panted lightly and cupped her buttocks so he could pull her more tightly against his hardened penis.

"Tell me, Aisling. Can I can pass for human?" There was a dark amusement in his voice that made her shiver.

"Yes."

He laughed softly then set her aside. For an instant she felt bereft, rejected. But when her eyes met his, she encountered molten gold and a hunger to match her own. He lifted his hand but let it drop to his side before he touched her. This time it was Zurael who said, "We need to leave if we intend to take the bus."

Five

IT was a short ride. If they'd had more time before sunset, they could have walked it.

Aisling tugged at the unfamiliar clothing. She felt self-conscious in the expensive blouse and pants, like a field hand dressed up to impersonate a wealthy landowner.

Zurael took her hand in his. All along the street, chauffeured cars stopped to discharge their passengers before driving away.

Aisling's emotions ran the gamut from anger to sadness as she looked at the beautifully restored Victorians, housing clubs with names like Lust, Greed and Envy. She found it ironic that the powerful and privileged, the people who lived comfortably and without concern for what life was like for anyone outside their class, would gather here for their entertainment.

The Last War had been started by religious zealots, by people determined to cleanse mankind of sin. There were those who believed the plague finally ending the war was god-created and not war-born—apocalypse averted because mankind was forced to concentrate on survival instead of the afterlife.

Aisling knew only that the ghostlands were full of cast-aside gods, and human souls lingered or passed through at the will of something unknowable, that the spiritlands could be a place of heaven or hell.

She shivered and spared a glance at the demon by her side, became acutely conscious of the fiery heat of his palm against hers as they approached the club named for those who might one day find themselves in his domain.

Sinners was in the middle of the block. Despite its name, it was painted in cheerful yellow tones. Its windows were unmarred by bars, though Aisling didn't doubt some type of elaborate security was in place. Colorful curtains were pulled back. Well-dressed patrons lingered behind the glass and viewed the activity on the street.

Aisling rubbed her palm against her pants as they approached the bouncers on either side of the doorway. They were heavyset men with bulging muscles and hard, emotionless eyes.

"Hand," the one on the right said.

She offered her hand and felt nothing but callused skin against callused skin.

The bouncer's eyes narrowed slightly. He dropped her hand and turned his head toward his partner. "Gifted."

The second bouncer took her hand. "What are you?"

"A shamaness," Aisling said, feeling afraid and exhilarated at the same time at being able to acknowledge a gift she'd rarely admitted openly before.

"You can go in." The bouncer's attention returned to Zurael. Zurael's hand was already lifting. The contact was brief. "You're clear."

Aisling pulled out the bills Elena had given her and paid. The bouncer to the right opened the door.

A party was already in progress inside the house. People gathered in small groups. Most held crystal glasses full of colorful liquid.

More than one of the women paused in their conversation to give Zurael a hungry, inviting look while men stripped Aisling with their eyes.

Zurael took her hand again and led her to a bay window. Outside, the night was arriving rapidly.

Nervousness and curiosity warred inside Aisling. Everything around her was so different from anything she'd ever known.

Zurael pulled her back against his front, then settled his muscular arms around her waist. The image of the two of them captured in the window glass filled Aisling with a longing that went beyond the physical.

A man and woman joined them at the window, their predatory expression captured in the glass before they turned and in a perfectly choreographed move lifted their hands, hers toward Zurael's bare arm, his reaching for Aisling's.

"No," Zurael said with such deadly menace both hands dropped immediately.

"Not many people turn us down," the man said, leaning against the edge of the bay window, the woman next to him in matching red.

"You're new here," the woman said. "We can help you get into the swing of things. In fact, there's nobody better. Everybody follows our lead, especially when it comes to the voting."

The man met Aisling's eyes. "Come play with us. Alone, if your companion can't be persuaded. You'll enjoy it. I promise."

"No."

"Suit yourselves, though I think you'll find you've made a mistake in turning us down." He pushed off from the window bay, but not before Aisling saw the flash of anger at being rejected. The woman slipped her arm through his and they walked away.

Aisling's attention lingered on them. She wondered what the woman meant about the others following their lead when it came to the voting, but then her focus shifted to a man scurrying into the red zone from the direction of the bus stop just outside of it.

The people in the room migrated to the front windows. The conversation grew hushed, the atmosphere heavy with anticipatory excitement, like a collective beast getting ready to pounce.

Aisling's arms settled over Zurael's. Her fingers slipped through his.

The windows of the Victorians across the street were free of bars, too, and crowded with watchers. One by one the bouncers guarding the entrance to those clubs went inside before the hurrying man reached the sidewalks leading to their doors.

"He's not going to make it," someone whispered in the hushed silence of the room.

"He will," someone else said, a hint of regret in his voice. "Sinners is always the last to close."

As the man reached the bay window, excitement slid through Aisling. It wasn't the man who'd sold Ghost to Elena, but the cross on his cheek marked him as one of the regular dealers.

A deflated sigh went through the gathered crowd as the door to Sinners opened and the man darted inside. The bouncers followed.

There was the definitive sound of a lock clicking into place. A low-level hum signaled that some type of electrical current also served to keep the unwanted out.

Slowly the crowd dispersed. Elegantly dressed patrons re-formed into smaller groups. Some wandered up a beautiful wooden staircase. Others slipped into open rooms.

Aisling noticed that none of the interior rooms had doors, and understood the significance of Elena's comment. Why privacy was hard to find.

The man and woman in red lingered nearby. The Ghost dealer went through a doorway with a small flock of people behind him. Aisling forced herself to leave the comfort of Zurael's arms and walk across the room.

The dealer stood in an old-fashioned parlor. Furniture from the era, or copies of it, graced the room. There was a fireplace. The blackened and ash-coated tool set on the hearth indicated it wasn't just for show.

There was no attempt at concealment. Like disciples to a messiah, men and women gathered around the Ghost dealer. They offered silver, gold, jewelry. They received small metal boxes in return.

Aisling shivered at the sight of the containers. The one in Elena's possession had made her think of an antique pill- or snuffbox. Now she saw small metal coffins.

Three of the buyers hurried from the room. The remaining five settled on the chairs and couches. Aisling braced herself when their fingers reverently stroked the lids of the tiny boxes.

Zurael's heat warmed her back. She longed for the comfort and security his touch had come to represent, but she didn't blame him for standing apart until he knew she wouldn't be dragged into the ghostlands.

Aisling felt the spirit winds as soon as the first lid was opened. Her hand went to the hidden fetish pouch containing the pentacle.

The winds recognized her. They swirled around her but didn't pull at her spirit.

The Ghost users dug their fingers into the tainted substance. Some of them rubbed it on their bodies, while others licked and sucked it off their skin.

One by one they were taken.

Club patrons drifted into the room like theatergoers waiting for the show to begin. A few checked their watches. The Ghost seller moved to the fireplace and leaned against the mantel.

He surveyed the room, perhaps looking for other customers. Aisling tensed when his gaze settled on her. It was there for only an instant, then gone.

She'd expected to feel a jolt of recognition, to feel something of the ghostlands in him. Instead she felt nothing, as if he were only human, a man with no connection to the spirit world.

Aisling turned to look at Zurael. "I'm going over to him."

Zurael's eyes burned with an intensity that sent wild heat coursing through her. His hand curled around her forearm, possessive and protective, allowing for no argument. "I'll go with you."

She acquiesced. Until dawn arrived, they were all trapped in the house. There was little point in pretending she and Zurael weren't together.

The five men who were Ghosting started to moan. Like Elena they must have been seeking pleasure in the spiritlands. Zippers gave way. Hardened cocks emerged to be taken in hand. Hips rose as backs arched.

Aisling couldn't stop the blush from coloring her cheeks. She'd grown up on a farm and witnessed animals mating. She felt no shame in sexual desire or attending to those needs but she'd never imagined men and women, strangers, entertaining themselves like this.

She couldn't tell whether the Ghost dealer was monitoring those he'd sold to or whether he was merely watching them. His attention shifted to her as she drew near. "Last one," he said, pulling a container from his pocket.

Even as he said it, the spirit winds shifted and the rhythmic grunting of the men who were Ghosting was silenced. A coldness swept into the room along with a malevolent presence.

Aisling turned away from the dealer to look at the Ghosters. Their fingers were locked around their swollen organs, forgotten. They were all sitting, focused on her though they had the dead, empty eyes of zombies.

She heard a faint whispering, a command spoken on the spirit winds. Dull nothingness gave way to gleeful hatred in the men's expressions, and the Ghost dealer quickly left the hearth.

Instinctively Aisling grabbed the poker from the fireplace tool set. It wasn't as good as a hoe or pitchfork, but it would serve as a weapon.

"They mean to attack," she said.

Zurael was already positioning himself in front of her. The men didn't bother with their trousers before closing in.

Aisling stepped to the side even as the first one launched himself

toward where she'd been. A second man attacked as Zurael tossed
the first one across the room. The third and fourth were right behind him, and while Zurael dealt with them, the fifth leapt at
Aisling.

She swung the poker and hit his arm, but he kept coming, slam-
ming her against the wall. His fingers locked around her neck.

The thrust of the steel in her hand and her raised knee broke his
hold. But her freedom lasted for only a second before he was on her
again, his fingers a vise depriving her of air.

Aisling was vaguely aware of the room filling with shouts as the
bouncers rushed in. Zurael's arm went around her assailant's neck.
His hand grabbed her assailant's chin, and with a sickening crack he
snapped the man's neck before tossing him to the side.

For an instant Aisling flashed back to the black mass and the bodies he'd casually discarded. Her gaze met his, but unlike that night,
tonight Zurael's eyes promised protection instead of retribution.

"Put the poker down," a bouncer said. He was one of three closing in on them, leading with batons Aisling knew were capable of
delivering a shock large enough to render someone unconscious.

She dropped the fireplace tool at her feet. "We were only defending ourselves."

The bouncer shrugged but didn't turn away. He and his com-
panions stopped several feet back. They lowered their weapons to
their waists. Their bulk continued to trap Zurael and Aisling near
the fireplace.

Across the room additional bouncers hovered around the four
remaining attackers. Two of the Ghosters were once again lost in
pleasure. The other two were on their feet, dead-eyed, though Aisling
sensed a different spirit presence hidden in them, beings who'd
found a host and planned to remain in possession.

Slowly the room filled with the powerful and privileged. The air
grew heavy with anticipatory excitement just as it had right before
the club locked its doors. Conversation faded to hushed expectancy,
only to give way to a chant. "Vote! Vote! Vote!"

The word traveled through the club with pulsing intensity. It brought more elegantly dressed men and women crowding in.

When it reached a crescendo, the bouncer who'd pronounced Aisling gifted raised his baton. Silence descended.

The bouncer pointed toward one of the men who was Ghosting, his hips jerking as his hand worked his penis. "In or out?"

A feminine laugh answered. The woman dressed in red waved a hand and said, "His act has gotten old and boring. Out!"

Those around her took up the chant. They were only silenced when the bouncer lifted his baton.

The same routine followed for the second Ghosting man, and then for the two who stood like zombies. They were all voted out.

When the bouncer pointed his baton at Zurael, the woman in red licked her lips and undressed him with her eyes. "What do you say? Will you play nice if we vote you in?"

Aisling glanced up and shivered at the sight of Zurael's liquid gold eyes. They burned with a hatred so deep it was impossible to miss his intent to kill anyone who tried to force his or her will on him.

"I think not," the man in red said. "Out!"

The chant was taken up immediately. It rolled through the house and filled the air until it was silenced.

When the baton was pointed at Aisling, the man in red said, "Having second thoughts, beautiful?"

"But will she play or will she be as interesting as a stone?" his female companion asked.

A stranger stepped forward. He waved his hand in the direction of the four men who'd used Ghost. "You'll find it far more entertaining to vote her out with the others. She's a shamaness."

"An interesting piece of information, Peter," the man in red said.

The woman in red smiled, but the flash of her teeth made Aisling think of a vicious dog. The mood of the crowd became more predatory. She said "Out!" and the others joined in.

The bouncers grabbed the two Ghosting men by their arms.

People shifted, jostled, parted to form a pathway out of the room. With horrifying clarity Aisling understood what it meant to be voted in or out, as the bouncers dragged the men toward the front door.

Additional bouncers appeared carrying guns. "Out," one of them said, pointing toward the two spirit-possessed men. The entities from the ghostlands were only too happy to comply.

Pure terror at the prospect of being outside after dark held Aisling frozen in place for an instant. Then she gathered her courage and picked up the discarded poker. She wouldn't surrender this life without a fight.

Zurael leaned down. His soft chuckle melted some of the icy fear trapped in her chest. He brushed his lips against her cheek. "Tonight I am your weapon."

A bouncer pointed a gun at them. "You two, out."

No one tried to take the poker from Aisling as she walked from the parlor to the front door. Heavily padded bouncers wearing helmets had dragged the men still Ghosting out into the middle of the street and were hurrying back to the club, while other bouncers stood on the porch, rifles ready in case of attack.

Aisling's breath came in fast, shallow pants as she stepped through the door and onto the porch. Despite Zurael's confidence, his easy assurance he would serve as her weapon, her heart raced so fast she thought it might burst in her chest.

Her hand tightened on the fireplace poker. She forced the terror down. If she was going to survive, she couldn't afford to act in a blind panic.

People gathered at the windows in the other Victorian houses as well as Sinners. Low-wattage spotlights illuminated the street. The scene made Aisling think of ancient Roman coliseums and the men and women whose fight for their lives served as a spectator sport.

Her skin pricked. She felt the enjoyment of the strangers watching from the safety of the clubs. Beyond that, she sensed a feral hunger radiating from the dark alleyways between the Victorians.

As soon as the heavily padded bouncers stepped back into Sinners, the armed men retreated. The door closed. The lock clicked into place. The low hum warned of additional safeguards.

The street held the waiting silence of prey and predator examining their surroundings carefully before acting. One of the men in the middle of the street stirred and sat up. He looked around with the incomprehension of a sleeper waking in a strange place and wondering if he was still dreaming. When reality crashed down on him, he scrambled to his feet and took off running. The two spirit-possessed men followed him.

None of them got farther than a house-length away before the werewolves emerged from a night-shrouded alleyway.

Zurael fought the urge to take Aisling's hand and cripple her ability to protect herself. His mind sorted through possibilities even as he cursed the angels who patrolled this world. He could shift into nothingness, but he couldn't protect Aisling against this threat without a form. He could transport both of them to her house, but the rapid travel would alert the angels to his presence and lead them to him.

Savage snarling drew Zurael's attention to the man lying in the middle of the street, still lost to the spiritlands. Feral dogs prepared to claim the prize the werewolves ignored.

They circled and gathered around the body. They lunged in to bite. The boldest growled as they gripped arms and legs in their jaws and pulled in a bloody tug-of-war.

Zurael spared a glance at the windows crowed with spectators. The downed man held little interest for them. Most of the crowd watched as the werewolf pack toyed with the men who'd run, providing entertainment in exchange for the easy meal.

He could sense other predators waiting in the dark alleyways between the clubs. For the moment Aisling was safe on the porch, but she wouldn't remain that way for long.

The wolves couldn't kill him. Even the angels would probably try to capture him rather than destroy him if they came upon him. But Aisling . . .

Zurael looked at her and felt a fierce pride in her courage. Her face was strained. Her knuckles were white where they gripped the poker, but she wasn't cowering in fear, though he could smell it on her.

The werewolves tired of playing with their food. The night filled with the sound of screaming.

Zurael glanced up to witness the sick pleasure on the faces of the men and women safe inside the clubs, and decided on a course of action. He grabbed Aisling's hand and led her from the porch. When they reached the pitch-black alleyway, he pulled her into the concealing darkness and stopped. "Trust me," he said, taking the poker from her hand and tossing it aside.

He could feel werewolves closing in on them. "Climb on my back."

Aisling didn't hesitate. She wrapped her arms around Zurael's neck and her legs around his waist.

In the street behind her there was a sudden silence followed by the growling, snarling sounds of a feeding frenzy. In front of her she could hear the rustle of predators.

She gasped when Zurael's wings emerged and slid along her sides in a sensual caress. In her mind's eye she saw him as he'd been when she summoned him, black-taloned and black-winged, demonic.

From somewhere in the darkness a beast launched itself at them. The hot spray of blood struck Aisling's face and arms even as something gurgled and fell away.

She tightened her grip on Zurael. His wings were stretched out. She had only a second to wonder how he would defend an attack from behind, before she felt the swing of a powerful tail inches below her buttocks and heard the crack of bones being broken. Another attack followed, and this time the blood struck her back and soaked into her shirt. She closed her eyes and pressed her face to Zurael's neck.

Zurael felt no satisfaction in killing the werewolves. He was coated in their blood, but rather than draw more of them to him, it began to act as a repellent. They started howling, announcing the presence of a demon.

His lips curled in a fierce smile. Long ago, in an effort to make the Djinn bow down before the creatures of mud, the alien god created a single demon by cursing The Prince into a hideous image. In the millennia since then, the humans had followed the example of their god. They'd conjured up thousands of nightmare creatures, named them demon, and along with their wars and false prophets had given the Djinn a way to disappear from human memory.

Zurael clung to the darkness as he carried Aisling away from Sinners. Behind and in front of him natural and supernatural predators alike scurried out of his way.

As the adrenaline faded and he no longer feared an attack, he found it impossible to ignore the warm press of Aisling against his back. He was aroused, beyond aroused. Part of it was genetic instinct, the need to mate and ensure another generation after being in the presence of violence and death. The larger part of it was his fascination with her.

He stopped a block away from her house. The moon was higher, the darkness less complete. He assessed the area for danger and found none. With a thought the wings, talons, and barbed tail faded.

Aisling slid from his back without him saying anything. His body tightened in protest. He turned and took in the sight of her. She was pale, blood-covered, her eyes shadowed with emotions he couldn't read.

He took her hand and they hurried the remaining distance to her house. When they were safely inside, he followed her into the bathroom. Bloody clothes hit the floor an instant before she wrenched the shower curtain open.

In those first few minutes, as red water swirled around their feet before disappearing down the drain, Zurael wasn't sure she was aware of him. But when the water finally cleared, she looked up and met his eyes. Heated need flashed between them.

The reasons he'd stepped away from her earlier flickered through his mind briefly and then were gone. His breath caught in his throat when she lathered her hands and touched his chest.

His cock bobbed against his abdomen. Stretched upward as if it wanted to reach her fingers.

"You saved my life," she said, stroking across his nipples, then down his sides, driving the hunger higher with her caress.

He placed his hand on her neck and wanted to kill her assailant all over again for the bruises left on her throat. Her pulse thundered against his palm. Her eyes darkened with desire as he followed the delicate line of her neck to her shoulder. She licked her lips when his other hand settled on her hip, mimicking the slow slick glide of her fingers on his sides.

"We shouldn't," she whispered.

He knew she was right. He knew it didn't matter.

Her nipples were hard, tight points begging for his attention. She closed her eyes and arched her back when his fingers traced her collarbone, then slid down to circle a pale pink areola. He leaned in and captured its twin with his mouth.

Lust spiked through him as her belly rubbed against his cock. His hand moved from her hip to her lower back. Now that he was touching her he couldn't stop.

Her sweet moans turned the shower into a sultry paradise. Her aroused scent made his penis weep and throb.

Zurael wanted to bathe in her. To plunge into her wet, hot depths. He wanted to thrust in and out of her until she screamed his name and summoned the lava-hot release of his seed.

He burned for her with the primal fire of the Djinn. It snaked through his veins in a roar that couldn't be denied.

Zurael forced himself away from her breast and turned off the water. There would be other times for taking her in the shower. This first time he wanted her underneath him.

Aisling stepped from the shower stall. She toweled herself dry, though she could barely take her eyes off Zurael's glistening body.

He was hard muscle and easy strength, masculine promise and otherworldly sensuality. There were those who would burn her at the stake if they found out she'd lain with him. She didn't care.

She burned with the need to feel him against her, inside her. Longed to lose herself completely in the passion he promised.

Later she would remember what happened at Sinners. Later the guilt would assault her. For now she wanted her only reality to be what she shared with him.

She squeezed the water from her braid as best she could, then passed the towel to him. Watched as he rubbed it over his slick skin.

His cock pulsed when her gaze lingered on it. His testicles were smooth globes, like a stallion's.

Aisling shivered as she imagined him covering her like a stallion mounts a mare. She turned her head slightly, flushed and aroused, already wet and parted for him—a willing participant in a seduction that might leave her damned.

When his hand took hers, she entwined her fingers with his. Anticipation and need built with each step toward the bed.

He paused next to it and pulled her tight against him. She kissed his throat as her hands roamed over his back and buttocks.

When she would have lifted her face and sought his lips, he eased her backward, onto the blanket. "Zurael," she whispered, arching as his mouth found her breast again and he began suckling.

It felt as though his lips reached between her thighs and pulled wave after wave of pleasure from deep inside her womb. Her clit stood at attention. It throbbed to the rhythm of his mouth sucking her nipple.

His hands reached under her buttocks, urged her to spread her thighs so the slick folds of her labia and her erect clit were pressed against his heated belly. Aisling moaned. Her channel clenched and released. Her hands went to his hair.

She whimpered in frustration. His hair was wet and tightly braided, just as hers was.

He kissed lower. He teased her belly button with his tongue, stabbed in and out in the same way she wanted him to do to her mouth.

Lust made Zurael nearly mindless. The siren song of his name on Aisling's lips made him want to press his mouth to hers and share his soul. He was saved from temptation by the heady musk of her arousal, by the lure of her petal-soft lower lips and the feminine mystery of her cunt.

She was ready for him. Her folds were slick and swollen, open, like a night-blooming flower. He could no more turn away from the sweet nectar of her than he could turn away from water in the desert.

He pressed his mouth to her soft skin and reveled in the way she arched and cried his name. He swiped his tongue along her slit and found the taste of her more intoxicating than any wine.

Aisling was lost in sensation, in the hot press and retreat of his tongue. His name was a litany she repeated over and over again.

Her hands went to her breasts, cupping, rubbing, tweaking the hardened nipples as he laved and kissed her lower lips, as he thrust into her with his tongue. She cried out when his mouth found her clit and he began sucking. Her hips jerked to the rhythm he set.

She was helpless against him, helpless against what he made her feel. "Please," she said, panting, barely able to breathe under his onslaught.

He tightened his grip on her buttocks as if he were afraid she'd try to escape. His tongue joined his lips in tormenting her swollen clit. It swirled over the exposed head, stroked the sensitive underside until she was desperately fucking the tiny organ through his lips.

Aisling's hands left her breasts and grabbed the bedding as erotic sensation rolled through her. The sounds of his pleasure fed her own. The image of him between her thighs was burned forever in her memory.

His tongue was a flame licking over her, filling her, turning her blood into molten lava until finally her cunt clenched and spasmed in a release that left her crying, as if only tears could extinguish the fire inside her.

But even the wetness of her tears wasn't enough. She still ached. She still needed. She still wanted to feel his body against hers, in hers.

Zurael was desperate to couple with her, desperate beyond anything he'd known in centuries of existence. He wanted to lie on top of Aisling and press his mouth to hers. He wanted to share her taste in a deeply carnal kiss. He wanted to feel the slide of her tongue against his and swallow her whimpers as his cock pressed deep inside her channel.

Dangerous, she was so dangerous to him. If he wasn't careful, she'd possess his soul and command him, even without binding him with the incantation the god had given to his mud creatures.

He lifted his mouth from her lush, wet cunt but didn't give Aisling time to tempt him into crawling up her body.

Zurael positioned her on her hands and knees. He reveled in the way she went willingly, in the way she spread her thighs and pressed backward, enticing him to penetrate her.

Primitive pleasure surged through him at the sight of her readiness. His cock pulsed and leaked. His balls tightened in warning.

It was a torturous exercise in control to keep from impaling her with one hard thrust. He moaned as he pressed the tip of his penis against her heated opening. He panted and struggled to go slowly.

She was so tight, so hot. The walls of her sheath clung to him, measured him, fought him even as they called for him to go deeper.

"Aisling," he said, unable to stop himself from leaning over and kissing the delicate line of her spine.

She answered him by thrusting backward, by taking more of his cock and whispering his name. His hips bucked once, twice. It was enough to drive him all the way in, so close to her womb that his seed boiled with the need to escape and flow into her.

Zurael closed his eyes as her internal muscles rippled over his shaft in nearly unbearable ecstasy. His chest heaved with the effort it required to stay still. He wanted to linger in the first moment of being fully inside her. He wanted to capture it and hold on to it forever.

She was exquisite, innocent sensuality and a frailty that hid her strength. She was sweet temptation and deadly fascination.

Except for those moments in the ghostlands when he'd been a shadow in her mind, she was an enigma to him, an unexpected contradiction to long-held beliefs. He shouldn't want her but he did.

"Please," she said, moving, drowning his penis in slick arousal, searing him with a heat to rival the molten world that gave birth to the Djinn—flooding him with potent lust and an inescapable need to thrust.

Zurael's hand slid from her hip to the downy nest of pubic hair. His fingers found her clit.

Her hips jerked with the contact. Her cry matched his as her sheath tightened on him.

"Please," she said again, and this time he couldn't resist her plea. He couldn't fight the desire that ensnared them both.

He pulled his cock almost completely out of her slit and felt a savage pleasure when she cried at its loss, then welcomed it back with a shudder. In and out he thrust, slowly at first, then faster, harder. His reality became the hot, wet fist of her channel. His reason for existence narrowed to pleasing her, to making her scream as orgasm slammed through her, to filling her with his seed in an uncontrollable wash of lust.

When she cried out and her sheath tightened on him, Zurael followed her over the edge. He poured into her, died a little death because of her, and would willingly do it all over again.

Aisling felt sated, protected. Soft waves of pleasure rippled through her. Her cunt continued to spasm and grip Zurael's still-embedded cock as if it couldn't bear the emptiness that would come with releasing him.

Her heart warned against getting used to the feel of his strong arms around her and his warm chest at her back. He was temporary—in her life for reasons of his own or because he'd been maneuvered into guarding her. At the moment she was too grateful for his presence, too needy to question it.

The thoughts and memories she'd hoped to keep at bay crowded in. The guilt followed. "Those men died because I was there."

Zurael's arms tightened. He shifted position so his cheek touched hers. "They brought death on themselves."

Aisling shivered when his soft lips found the shell of her ear. His warm breath made her nipples bead. The arm resting under her bent and his palm covered her breast. She whimpered when his other hand stroked her belly before its fingers combed through her pubic down and found her clit.

"You were the only human in the club worth saving," he whispered.

His hips rocked in a gentle motion, timed to the subtle circle of his palm against her nipple, to the light press and rub of his fingers over her swollen clit, to the decadent hot swirl of his tongue in her ear.

Aisling closed her eyes. She let him chase away her guilt.

She met his thrusts and loved the feel of his hardness filling her, reaching deep inside her. He anchored her in a world where the only thing that mattered was the pleasure they shared, the panting murmured sounds as they climbed, the sharp cries as they found release.

Zurael kissed Aisling's shoulder as she drifted off to sleep. Tenderness filled him, a deep possessive satisfaction he'd never known before. It lasted until his cheek touched the leather string and his thoughts shifted to the pouch containing the bloodred fetishes and inscribed pentacle.

A cold knot formed in his chest and grew larger when Aisling's pet climbed onto the bed, its golden eyes boring into his. He worried over how he was going to keep her safe, not only from human and spirit enemies, but from the Djinn.

Six

AISLING woke to find Aziel curled up on her pillow. His eyes opened and held an intelligence far beyond what an ordinary ferret would possess.

He studied her as she studied him. What he read in her face, she could only guess. She thought she saw pleased satisfaction in his, but she couldn't be sure.

"I wish you would tell me what you know," she whispered, reaching over to stroke his fur, to scratch behind his ears, knowing even as she made the wish it was in vain. Whatever had brought Aziel into her life and kept him there, it remained a secret she couldn't unravel even in the ghostlands.

Behind her, Zurael's even breathing told her he still slept. His arm draped across her waist made her channel spasm and her cunt lips grow flushed and slick as memories crowded in.

She eased over to look at him. His was a beauty found only in the old mythology books, in the art books capturing the works of masters long dead, those whose paintings of angels and ancient gods once hung in fine museums to be viewed by rich and poor alike.

He was otherworldly. Temptation and damnation. A dangerous being tangled in the web of her life. One who might ultimately *take* her life.

She wanted to touch him, to trace the masculine lips, the firm chin and elegant nose. She wanted to lean in, press her mouth to his, her tongue to his, but didn't.

Continuing to lie with him might cost Aisling her soul as well as her heart. And though she couldn't find it in her to regret what had taken place between them the night before, it would be better not to repeat it.

As with Aziel, whatever had brought Zurael into her life remained a secret. But unlike Aziel, whose presence gave her strength, Zurael was a weakness she could ill afford.

Nothing good could come of loving him. She didn't know whether demons existed before mankind's evolution or were given life by human belief. But she did know there were dark, terrifying places in the spiritlands that claimed human souls, and she didn't doubt some of them were ruled by demons—a hell whether it was the one defined by the Church or not.

Reluctantly she eased from the bed and walked softly to the bathroom, needing space, distance, a chance to gain her balance. She wasn't used to days without the rhythm of chores, without the ebb and flow of voices as the younger children played and quarreled, made up and went about the work necessary to survive.

Her heartbeat stuttered in her chest as she unbraided her hair underneath the showerhead. The images captured in the pool of her blood played out in her mind and threatened her with despair. How was she going to prevent the slaughter of her family?

Aisling lifted her face and let the hot water cascade over her and wash her feelings of horror and fear away. She forced her thoughts to revisit Sinners, to consider a course of action that would lead her to whoever was responsible for Ghost.

I'll start by talking to the gifted around me, she thought as she lathered and rinsed her hair. The number of cars she'd seen in the short time before the sun set the previous day was an indication that those who were supernaturally touched might be set aside from the rest, but they weren't shunned by Oakland society. Only the wealthy and powerful would arrive in this part of town in automobiles.

Feeling refreshed, confident, she stepped from the shower and dried herself with a towel. Her nose wrinkled at the sight of her wet hair. A sigh marked her memory of the decadent luxury of using a hair dryer after showering at the church.

Movement drew her eye to the bathroom door. Her eyes met Zurael's in the bathroom mirror and her nipples tightened in response to his nearness, his nakedness.

"Allow me," he said, holding her gaze, stepping forward to take the brush from her unresisting hand.

He smelled of exotic spice, of desire borne on desert winds. A small moan escaped her when he gathered her hair and his scent settled around her in a sensuous fog.

The new day magnified, not lessened, Zurael's desire. It was a mistake to touch her like this, to slide his fingers through her hair as he untangled the wet, twisted locks and used the molten heat of a Djinn's birthright to speed the drying.

Hair was a Djinn's weakness. Outside the summoning and binding spells the alien god had given his mud creations, there were few ways to bend his kind to a will other than their own. But an incantation using hair was one of them. And just as he'd rarely touched his lips to another's in a sharing of spirit, he had rarely trusted another to undo his braid.

Dark amber turned to golden streaks of spun silk as he brushed Aisling's hair. His cock hardened further, its tip licking across his belly. A shudder went through him each time her waist-length locks touched his penis.

Her skin was soft, her body delicate, utterly feminine. Her scent, spring flowers and arousal.

With a low moan he touched his cheek to satin locks. Rubbed against the loose strands of her hair as he devoured her reflection in the mirror.

Lust rose like steam between them. The brush dropped to the floor.

Her nipples tightened, her eyes darkened. His hands settled on her breasts, cupped and weighed them before his palms settled over hardened tips.

Aisling's shiver had him pulling her back to his front so he could feel the length of her body against his. And still it wasn't enough.

The small triangle of dark, honey-gold down drew his hand to explore her slick, swollen folds and erect clit. Her mouth parted, her tongue darted out to leave her lips glistening.

"We shouldn't," she whispered, echoing his earlier thought.

"But we will," Zurael said, kissing her neck, her shoulder. His hands making her quiver with pleasure.

Worry flashed in her eyes. Reluctance built even as the sleek globes of her buttocks rubbed against his cock, enticed him to bend her over and thrust into the slick welcome of her sheath.

"You won't deny me," he said, caressing the naked tip and smooth underside of her clit with his fingers. "You won't deny yourself. Say my name, tell me you don't want to feel me inside you."

"Zurael," she whispered, closing her eyes and turning her face away from the mirror where the sight of her flushed, heated skin and ripe nipples attested to the truth of her desire. "What place do you call home? Who do you answer to?"

He guessed her questions were meant to shore up her resistance to him. To fight her desire for him.

"The names are not for humans to know or call upon. They are death."

His fingers tightened on her nipple. He refused to let her run away from what was between them.

"Does the daylight make you fear me? Do you remember what I looked like beneath the moon and regret letting me cover you, pierce you? Does my form change the nature of who I am? Does it define me?"

"No," she said, shivering as she opened her eyes.

"Then look at me, watch while I take you."

Aisling tried to resist his command. She willed herself to ignore the desperate craving of her body, to pull away, escape his voice, his heat, his arms and the need he generated in her. But she was helpless against him, just as helpless as she had been the night before.

With a moan, she obeyed. She turned her face and met his eyes in the mirror, didn't resist when he urged her to lean forward, to grasp the edge of the counter, to spread her thighs.

Her hips jerked. Lightning strikes of lust ripped through her as his cock bathed in her arousal, glided over her swollen folds and rigid clit. Kissed her belly in sweet torment and agonizing delay.

"Please," she whispered and tried to change the angle of her body so he would find her opening and press inside.

Zurael grabbed her hips. He kept her where he wanted her, though the image captured in the mirror revealed how much the effort cost him.

The muscles on his arms stood out as if he fought himself. His chest rose and fell in sharp, quick movements. But it was his face that sent erotic fear slithering downward to pool between her thighs and pulse into her woman's knob. He was beautifully savage. His eyes were molten gold, his expression dominant, possessive, his attention completely focused on her.

Aisling's breath caught in her throat. The batlike wings she'd seen twice before unfurled and opened on either side of them, and for an instant she was held on the edge, caught between the terror she'd experienced when she first saw him and the dark, dark desire he now generated in her. But then he moved, once again sliding his cock over her engorged clit and plump, wet folds—and she was lost.

"Please," she whispered, moving the little bit his hands on her hips would allow, trying to entice him into penetrating her.

Satisfaction softened the hard line of his mouth. Victory deepened the gold of his eyes.

The wings came forward, soft suede against her arms, forming a protective cocoon as he found her opening and thrust with a single, hard stroke. She cried out in relief, in need, obeyed his command to watch until ecstasy claimed her in a rush of lava-hot sensation and demon seed.

Aisling returned to the shower, this time with her hair braided and coiled to minimize the wetness, this time with Zurael accompanying her, bringing memories of the previous night, along with the urge to go to her knees and take him in her mouth.

She cleansed herself as quickly as possible and escaped, dressing hastily before retreating to the kitchen and busying herself preparing breakfast. If she'd been home, there would have been fresh eggs and fruit, sausage from a pig slaughtered the previous fall and milk brought in from the barn by whoever was assigned the task of letting the livestock out for the day.

Her heart lodged in her throat; homesickness blended with worry as her earlier panic threatened to reappear and trap her like delta quicksand. She forced the unwelcome emotions away, finding it easier when Aziel scampered in and climbed to his familiar place on her shoulder.

"Do you know him?" she asked, glancing in the direction of the bathroom and wondering again whether Aziel was demon also. "Is that why you offered me his name? Why his presence is allowed when you've bitten other men? Do you serve him?"

The ferret didn't answer, didn't acknowledge the question. His attention seemed fixed on the meager contents of the cabinet, and with a sigh, Aisling studied them, too.

She'd used coupons for flour and yeast when she'd gone to the grocery store, and the thought of making bread was tempting. But it'd only serve to delay the task of looking for whoever was responsible for Ghost.

As she pulled canned pears from the cabinet, panic flared with the memory of how Zurael had fed her peaches when she was left weakened by her blood sacrifice in the spiritlands. She had no will to resist him, no ability to. He'd proven as much to her with every sensual interaction, taken a bit of her soul each time he'd touched her.

She put the can on the counter, retrieved a small carton of eggs and the remainder of the chicken breasts. Her thoughts went to the pouch of silver she'd gotten from Elena, the handful of bills given to her by Father Ursu, the possessions left in the house by the dead shaman. She'd have to return to the grocery store, or trade with her neighbors for supplies.

Eventually Aziel would hunt and scavenge. But at the moment she hated the idea of letting him roam freely outside.

It was foolish to worry about him, to grieve for him when one day he didn't return, to imagine him dying and ache over the possibility that he suffered. But she'd never been able to stop herself from doing it, from fearing each of his deaths would be the final one, the one that took him permanently.

Zurael emerged from the bathroom wearing black pants and a black shirt. Her pulse quickened, and she hastily ducked her head to concentrate on fixing them something to eat.

He joined her in the kitchen, working by her side as if he'd always been there, his movements sure and smooth. "I thought I'd visit some of my neighbors," she said a short while later, after they'd eaten and taken care of the dishes.

Zurael cocked his head, his mouth curved upward in a smile that made her want to press her lips to his. "I believe one of your neighbors has come to you."

A knock on the door attested to the truth of his comment. Aisling rubbed suddenly damp palms against the comforting, worn fabric of the pants she'd been wearing when Father Ursu arrived at the farm. She hesitated, wondered if she should ask Zurael to hide his presence, then shrugged the question away, allowing the demon to make his own choice as she crossed to the front door.

Habit made her pause long enough to peek through the window before unlocking the door, opening the wooden one first and then the metal one. A flash of black at her ankles made her heart race in her chest. "Aziel!" But it was already too late; the ferret was out and disappearing around the corner of the house.

It would be pointless to shout or follow him, but the urge distracted her long enough that she flushed in embarrassment when she realized she'd ignored her visitor. "I'm sorry," she said, taking in the colorful long skirt and blouse, the black-and-gray-streaked hair and the wealth of hand-fashioned jewelry worn by her neighbor.

"So Henri is dead," the woman said. There wasn't even a hint of a question in her voice.

Aisling stepped back. "Would you like to come in?"

"I'm Raisa," the woman said, entering the house. Her attention moved past Aisling and sharpened with interest.

Aisling guessed Zurael had elected to remain in his human form. She turned slightly, indicating the shabby sofa and chairs. "Can I get you some hot tea? I'm Aisling." She didn't offer Zurael's name.

He stepped to her side. "The water is on in anticipation of tea." To Raisa he said, "Henri was the shaman who lived here previously?"

"Yes."

They crossed to the furniture, Raisa claiming a chair while Aisling sat on the couch. Zurael returned to the kitchen, though Aisling knew both she and her unexpected guest were aware of his presence.

"Do you know what happened to Henri?" Aisling asked.

"I saw his death and warned him against keeping his appointments. He ignored me." Raisa shrugged. "But what choice did he have? As you can see from his possessions, he wasn't a wealthy man, and the Church works with the politicians to keep those of us with special abilities contained in this area of town."

"You're a seer?" Aisling asked.

"I own a tearoom several blocks away. It's a popular meeting place, and considered neutral territory. I read the leaves for those who ask me."

Aisling's fingers worried with a mended tear at the knee of her pants. She considered whether Raisa could be trusted and how much she could ask without revealing her search for the maker of Ghost.

Zurael rejoined them, carrying two small mismatched cups on chipped saucers and setting them on the table. Aisling picked up the cup in front of her and noted the leaves it contained. Her eyes went to his face. Was it a challenge? Or was he merely curious about Raisa's abilities?

Aisling glanced at Raisa and found her watching them, taking in Zurael's physical closeness and her reactions to him.

"Do you know what happened to Henri?" Aisling asked, returning to the question Raisa had yet to answer.

Raisa lifted her cup to her lips and took a sip, delaying, perhaps also wondering what it was safe to reveal. "No," she finally said, lowering her cup and leaning forward as if sharing a confidence. "I suspect the Church had a hand in it. Henri was an unhappy man, given to bouts of melancholy as a result of his dealings with the spirit world. He often went to services, and occasionally the priest who brought you here visited him."

She took another sip of tea, perhaps waiting to see how Aisling would react. But Aisling said nothing. She'd felt the eyes of her neighbors watching her as she'd gotten out of the car with Father Ursu, had known it would lead to talk and speculation. She was new, unfamiliar to them. It would be the same for anyone taking up residence.

The silence dragged and hovered, wary but not uncomfortable. Raisa broke it by saying, "I've heard that the last anyone saw of Henri was when a car arrived at dusk and he came outside immediately, dressed as he usually dressed when he went to services or to confess the things weighing on his soul. He got into the car and his house has remained empty until now."

This time she set the teacup on its saucer and settled back in her chair. Despite her casual pose, Aisling was reminded of a bird of prey perched on a ledge, equally ready to remain or to leave for better hunting elsewhere.

It was her choice. Just as ultimately each decision was.

Aisling cupped her hands around the warm teacup and carefully chose her words. With no allies and little knowledge about Oakland, she had to take chances if she was to accomplish the task she'd accepted in the ghostlands. "Father Ursu took me from my home in the San Joaquin, just outside of Stockton. He brought me here as a favor to someone important to the Church. A woman went missing and her lover wanted her found, or wanted the closure of knowing she'd passed from this world. Father Ursu told me the police had discovered several bodies recently and there was reason to believe the victims were all murdered during the witching hour. They were afraid this woman was one of them, or would be."

Satisfaction danced in Raisa's eyes. "I thought as much. Did you find her?"

"Yes." Aisling resisted the impulse to look at Zurael or to tell Raisa how she'd found Elena.

Raisa leaned forward, the clacking of her necklaces a subtle drumroll. "Another shaman's house stands empty, in San Francisco. He was a man with more ambition than talent."

Aisling licked suddenly dry lips. "What happened to him?"

A shrug. "No one knows, which says much about the power behind his disappearance. He was not nearly the shaman Henri was, but still he had his uses to the vampires who control that city. Their minions have been looking for answers without finding any."

A shiver went through Aisling. She didn't want to think about what uses the undead might have for one who could visit the land of the spirits.

"Did your Father Ursu mention how many of the supernaturally touched are among those found murdered?" Raisa asked.

"No," Aisling said, unable to let the comment pass without adding, "He isn't my priest. I'm not a member of any church."

A slight nod, a sharpening of Raisa's gleaming, birdlike eyes, met her words. "There are whispers that some of the murdered were offered up as sacrifices. They were found with their hearts cut from their bodies or with sigils painted on them. But when their loved ones tried to reclaim their remains for burial, they were denied and given only ashes."

Raisa leaned closer. "I've heard rumors there was another disappearance last night, a governess serving a wealthy family. If it didn't impact their wealthy benefactors, the Church would turn a blind eye to what is happening. I think Henri was asked to seek out some of those sacrificed in an attempt to find out who killed them."

Aisling set the teacup down. She thought about the hours she'd slept, locked in a tiny bedchamber in the church, only to be awakened close to midnight and brought before the bishop and Father Ursu.

"What you say could be true," Aisling said, a knot forming in her belly. If a governess disappeared the night before, then there were more dark priests than the one Zurael had slaughtered. "How many gifted have been murdered?"

"I can't say for sure. Some go missing and are never found. Five have disappeared from families settled here for more than one generation. There have been others as well, recent arrivals, here and then suddenly gone—maybe by their own choice, maybe not."

Zurael said, "Who would know more about these disappearances?"

"Javier. The occult shop on Safira Street belongs to him. He has an ear in the human world as well as the supernatural one."

"Is there a newspaper here?" Aisling asked. "A library where I could look at past editions?"

A laugh of derision greeted her question. "There's a newspaper, but you won't find anything useful in it. Those who run this city ensure only the truth they peddle is printed."

"But there is a library?" Aisling pressed.

"Yes," Raisa said. "You've been to the church?"

Aisling nodded.

"Then you've been to the center of Oakland. The powerful govern from there. The library is several blocks away from the church. It's next to the building housing the police and the guardsmen."

Aisling wiped her palms against the knees of her worn pants. She hesitated to express an interest in Ghost, but if what Raisa said about the newspaper was true, then it seemed foolish to waste the opportunity to ask in the hope of finding answers at the library.

She startled when Zurael's hand covered hers, took it to his knee and held it there, this thumb lightly stroking across her knuckles like a tongue extending from the serpent tattooed on his skin. When she looked up, she found Raisa's gaze riveted to their joined hands.

"Have there been rumors of a drug called Ghost?" Aisling asked.

"Drugs aren't illegal here. Lawbreakers won't escape the tattoo or the death sentence for acts they commit while using them." Raisa shrugged. "The Church would ban them if they could. But even they don't have the power to do it. Too many of the founding families add to their wealth because of the drug trade. They won't allow the first ban because they know it'll only open the doorway to having others made illegal."

Aisling nodded. It was the same in Stockton. There were few resources, and even the most conservative didn't want to see them wasted on an effort to eradicate the substances humans used to escape the harshness of their reality.

It hadn't always been so. Geneva's history books were filled with stories of a prohibition on alcohol and, later, a war on drugs that left those in control of production and distribution wealthy and powerful beyond anything they could have accomplished otherwise.

"You've heard something about Ghost?" Aisling pushed, aware Raisa hadn't answered her question.

"Perhaps." Raisa touched her fingertips to the saucer holding Aisling's empty teacup. "May I?"

Misgiving coiled in Aisling's stomach. She wanted to say no, to turn away from the offered reading, the implied cost of having her question answered. But images of her family members scattered dead throughout the farmyard forced her to say, "Yes."

Raisa picked up the saucer and carried it to her knees, balanced it there as she stared at the pattern left by the tea leaves. Dark, bird-like eyes remained motionless, transfixed by whatever they saw.

Outside a cloud masked the sun and the light faded, casting the room in the same heavy gloom it had held when Aisling arrived with Father Ursu. Failure wafted through with the scent of Henri's soap, though his spirit wasn't present.

"Death drapes you like a billowing cloak," Raisa said. "It writhes at your feet and twines around you like a nest of serpents, so your touch becomes its harbinger."

A shudder went through Raisa, strong enough to make the tea-cup rattle against the saucer. She placed it back on the table and rose from her chair. "Speak to Javier about Ghost as well as those who are missing. If you will excuse me, I'll let myself out. I need to return to the tearoom."

Aisling stood and followed Raisa to the door, stepped outside in the hopes of finding Aziel waiting. She shrugged aside the reading as she watched her visitor hurry away. Given Zurael's presence, and hers in Henri's home, it was easy to see death in the tea leaves.

The sun left its hiding place behind the clouds when Aisling went back inside. Zurael was still on the couch. She bent to gather the dirty dishes. His hands circled her wrists, sending molten lava through her veins despite the deadly serpent tattooed on his arm in a wicked reminder of what he was.

His fingers tightened. Forced her to look up and meet his eyes.

Aisling shivered, grew short of breath at the carnal heat burning there. She remembered too well what it had been like to stand in the bathroom in front of the mirror, to obey his command and watch as he took her.

"We only have the daylight to find answers," she whispered, not wanting to compound her weakness by giving in to him again and losing the chance to visit the library and the occult shop.

Zurael read the resistance in her face, saw her fight the desire that sprang to life between them like a living flame. He knew he should fight it as well.

He'd meant to assure himself she was okay, unbothered by Raisa's reading. But as soon as he touched Aisling, he wanted nothing more than to pull her onto the couch, to strip her out of her clothing and cover her body with his.

He carried her hands to his chest and pushed them under his shirt. He held them against hardened male nipples, felt her touch all the way down to his cock.

A hiss escaped when she tried to pull away. A moan followed when her eyelashes lowered submissively and the tension left her so her palms softened and rubbed sensuously against him.

Lust roared through him, hot need. When she wet her lips, he was swamped with the impulse to toss the coffee table aside and put Aisling on her knees before him, to unbind her hair and guide her mouth to his throbbing cock.

She leaned closer, whispered his name on a breath that caressed his lips, jolted him into an awareness of the danger he was in. He stood abruptly and released her hands, stepped away from her before he yielded to the temptation of kissing her.

Confusion, embarrassment, hurt—Aisling's emotions danced across her face before her expression became guarded. She picked up the saucers and turned away from him, leaving him feeling regretful, confused.

He wondered again if Malahel and Iyar had known he'd be ensnared, entangled. He thought of his father positioned in front of the mural of Jetrel, talking of the past and the son who'd lost his life because of a human female.

Zurael's attention returned to Aisling. She stood at the sink, rinsing the dishes.

He willed his heart to harden, his mind to close to what her future held. Death.

Aisling dried her hands. She could feel Zurael's gaze blistering her, as if he held her responsible for the desire burning between them.

Nervously she touched her pocket, felt the folded dollar bills and the bus pass. Without looking at Zurael, she went to the front door and opened it, forced herself through it.

The demon could do what he wanted with the day. She'd known even as she clung to him in passion that it wasn't wise to forget what he was and what caring for him could cost her.

She had only herself. And Aziel. It was enough. It had to be.

Seven

THE street was quiet, though Aisling felt the eyes of her neighbors on her. It was unnerving to be in a place where her talent was named on the house, where the ability that led to suspicion and ostracism somewhere else was openly revealed.

A car turned onto the street and approached slowly. It glided across the open lane to stop along the curb just as she got to the sidewalk. Father Ursu emerged from the backseat. "I thought I'd check up on you and make sure you survived your first night on your own," he said, gaze flicking from Aisling to the house and back.

Aisling rubbed her palms over the fabric of her pants. A breeze swirled around her, hot like the desert and smelling of exotic spice, of Zurael.

"I'm fine," she said, wary, suspicious, wondering if he knew what had transpired at Sinners.

"Good. Have you met any of your neighbors yet?"

Was it a trap? Had Raisa's visit been prearranged?

Fear made Aisling's heart race faster. Worry, then embarrassment, sent heat to her face.

Geneva favored nonfiction books over fiction. But even in those there were stories of listening devices and hidden cameras used for spying in the days before finding food and safe shelter consumed rich and poor alike.

Thinking about it, Aisling felt sickened by her naïveté. She should have considered that the Church might be monitoring her activities, might know of Elena's visit and Zurael's presence.

"What happened to Henri?" she asked, trying to escape her embarrassment and worry.

Resignation and sadness showed on Father Ursu's face. "I've been his priest for years. His loss weighs heavily on me. He died in service to the Church. As I mentioned the other night, the police have discovered several bodies recently. There's reason to believe the victims were all murdered during the witching hour. Henri volunteered to go in search of answers but didn't return."

"Those found were sacrificed?"

"Yes." Father Ursu took her hands, and once again she felt the baby softness of his against the calluses that had marked hers from the time she was old enough to take on her first chore. "If the situation hadn't been dire . . . I'm sorry, child. But thanks to you, Elena has been returned to those who love her." Father Ursu smiled and glanced at the house. "And you've had a chance to spread your wings and escape the shadows. I understand the citizens of Stockton and the lands surrounding it don't welcome those with special abilities. Am I correct?"

"Yes," Aisling said, though she didn't let his show of friendship or change of topic derail her. She might not have had the courage to seek him out and question him, but he'd come to her, and after Raisa's visit, she wouldn't let him escape without providing answers. "What about the shaman in San Francisco?"

A shudder went through Father Ursu. "What of him?"

"I've heard he's missing."

"I'm not surprised. A man who serves the damned can't escape the righteous hand of God, not for long."

Aisling hadn't expected him to speak so candidly or vehemently, though she knew the position of the Church when it came to vampires and shapeshifters—to demons and those who cavorted with them. She stiffened and resisted the urge to look to the house. She pulled her hands from Father Ursu's grasp and jammed them into her pockets.

Father Ursu said, "Now that I've assured myself you're fine and settling in, I'll be on my way." He started to turn, stopped. "Forgive me, but I feel a measure of responsibility for you since I'm the one who brought you here. I can't leave without warning you to be careful, especially when it comes to men. You're a beautiful young woman alone for the first time and in an unfamiliar city. There are men here who'll prey on your vulnerability. It'd be wise to settle in first before becoming involved with someone. But if you find yourself falling under the spell of love, please feel free to come to me. The Church isn't without resources, especially when it comes to protecting those who've aided it." He smiled and patted her shoulder. "There, I've said my piece. Now I'll leave and let you get on with exploring your new city."

Aisling watched as he slid into the backseat of the waiting car. She expected Zurael to step out of the house as soon as the dark car rounded the corner and was out of sight. Instead it was Aziel who caught her attention, beckoned her forward with chatter before scampering away.

She followed him, careful to pay attention to her surroundings and not lose track of the way home, as he darted through alleyways and abandoned yards, always staying just in sight—until finally he disappeared into a lot overgrown with poisonous plants and needle-sharp bushes.

"Aziel," Aisling called, knowing it was pointless, but doing it anyway. They'd played this game many times and in all of his various forms.

There was no answering chatter, though the stillness of the yard told her she wasn't alone in it. In front of her a narrow path pushed through poison oak and thorns.

Partially concealed flat rocks on either side of the path drew her eye. When she moved closer, she saw the sigils etched on the slate-gray surfaces. They were common witch symbols, warning against trespass and theft.

"Aziel," Aisling called again. "Come out. I can't come in after you."

"You're the shamaness who lives in Henri's house now," a voice said, causing Aisling to startle and turn away from the path.

A heavily pregnant young girl stood at an opening in the thorn bushes that hadn't been there a moment earlier.

"Yes, I'm Aisling."

The girl nodded and clasped her hands over her swollen belly. Small white teeth worried her bottom lip. She was seventeen—maybe—pale-faced with shadowy, pain-filled eyes.

"I'm Tamara Wainwright. This is my family's garden. Is Aziel your pet? They say you have a ferret."

"Yes. Have you seen him?"

"No." Tamara's face tightened and she rubbed tiny circles on her abdomen. She glanced quickly in the direction of the nearest house before saying, "Would you like to look in the garden?"

Unless Aziel came to her, Aisling knew she wouldn't find him in the garden, but he'd led her here and so she said, "Yes."

Tamara stepped away from the opening and ushered Aisling onto the path before freeing a bush of long-needled thorns to fall across the entranceway. The abandoned lot was surprisingly deep, the tangle of thorns and poisonous plants thick until they abruptly gave way to order, to clusters of plants arranged to form a pentacle with an altar at its center.

"This is incredible," Aisling said, awed by the design and the fact that it survived the night's predators.

"My family was already settled in this area of town when law and order were restored and Oakland was reclaimed by the Church and the non-gifted humans. They say my ancestors sacrificed anyone who trespassed, and marked the edges of the lot with cursed blood." She shrugged. "I don't know if it's true or not. It was a long time ago. We don't practice black magic, despite what you might hear from others." Tamara's eyes hardened. "Or the Church."

Aisling sighed softly. Would she forever be linked to the Church and viewed with suspicion because of it?

"I know very little about Oakland or those who live in this section of it," Aisling admitted, hoping the truth would ease her way with her neighbors. "It wasn't my wish to be brought here from my family's farm outside of Stockton. But when the guardsmen arrived with Father Ursu . . . what choice was there?"

"The Church wanted something from you?"

Given what she'd already told Raisa, Aisling didn't see any reason to deny it. "Yes, an important man's lover was missing, and they wanted me to see if her spirit had passed into the ghostlands."

Tamara bit her lip and looked away quickly. "Were you able to find her?"

"Yes."

Tamara's attention returned to Aisling's face. Old eyes stared out of a pinched, young face. "But then they brought you here instead of taking you back home. They want something else from you. Others have gone missing. Henri couldn't find them. And then he was gone, too."

"Father Ursu stopped by this morning to check on me. I asked him about Henri. He told me Henri died in service to the Church. He admitted the police have found sacrificed remains, but he didn't tell me anything more." Aisling's hands curled into fists as she remembered the fear and embarrassment that had assailed her. "Do the police and the Church spy on those who live in this section?"

Tamara shrugged. "I'm sure they've got informants. But considering how many of the wealthy and powerful find their way here, what do they gain from knowing who visits which home or shop?

It's not illegal to visit and do business with us. It's not even considered a sin any longer—not if the Church wants to keep its influence in Oakland."

Aisling felt foolish for pushing, but she couldn't let the subject drop. "What about cameras and listening devices?"

Tamara's laugh was genuine. "Did you find them hidden in Henri's house? I'm surprised either the Church or the police would waste their time installing them. They don't work in this area. The signals are jammed by technology from The Last War." She flinched and rubbed circles lower on her swollen belly.

"When is the baby due?" Aisling asked, noting the small basket for collecting leaves and roots that had been left near one of the pentagram's points.

"In another week. It's a boy. He'll be born gifted. My great-grandmother's never wrong when she does her scrying using fire." Tamara glanced sideways at Aisling and worried her bottom lip. "Are there any plants you'd like from the garden?"

Aisling shook her head. There were only a few things she recognized, but nothing she wanted badly enough to incur a debt for. "I have everything I need. Thank you for offering."

Tamara pushed her dark hair behind her ears, making her look even younger. "Do you have a healing amulet? One that'll draw the poison from even the most venomous snakebites?"

Aisling startled, wondered briefly if Tamara somehow knew about Zurael and his serpent form, then dismissed the thought. Healing amulets were a common enough offering of witches, since few could afford to see a trained doctor.

She skimmed her fingertips over the bills folded in her pocket. It would be wise to have an amulet, but she couldn't afford one, not when her cabinets held little food and the silver coins were set aside for the dream of security for her family.

Tamara removed an amulet from around her neck. It was circular and multitextured, a hard disk made completely of intricately woven strands of dried plants. Aisling had never seen anything like it, though she recognized some of the sigils stained on it.

"My great-grandmother made this one. It's like the ones that saved my ancestors during the plague. None of them died, even when all of their neighbors and most of Oakland did. They steeped the amulet in tea as soon as the first symptom appeared, and kept doing it for three days to rid their bodies of disease. For things like poisonous snakebites or gangrene, the skin can be cut open and the amulet pressed against the wound so it'll draw out the toxin as it's absorbed by the blood."

"I don't have the money for such a powerful amulet," Aisling said.

Tamara hugged her extended belly. "I want to trade it for your services. My son's father is missing."

Sadness filled Aisling. "You think he's one of the sacrificed?"

Thin shoulders lifted in a shrug. "I don't know. When I'm able, I slip off to the library and check the newspapers for word of him. His family is influential. Even if I could approach them, what would I learn? He was a black sheep for his interest in sorcery. They've threatened to send him away plenty of times. If he told them about the baby . . ."

Her hands trembled as she stroked her stomach. "He wasn't happy about the baby. I knew he wouldn't be, so I didn't tell him until it became impossible to hide it. I didn't tell anyone—I was afraid of what my family would do. He used to meet me here or in an abandoned house we'd pretend was ours—where he was a great sorcerer and I was a powerful witch."

Tears trailed down her cheeks when she looked up to meet Aisling's eyes. "He was angry about the baby. For months and months he was angry. He didn't leave notes for me or answer the ones I left in our hiding places. Then a month ago I saw him and . . . We agreed to meet at the house." She wiped angrily at the tears. "I waited there so long it wasn't safe to come home until the next morning. He never came and I haven't seen him again. I just need to know if he's still alive. Will you help me?"

Aisling glanced at the offered amulet and was tempted. Surely Aziel had led her here for this purpose. Her family's survival depended on her being able to find whoever was selling Ghost. She couldn't afford to let injury or sickness stop her.

"You're offering the amulet in exchange only for learning if your child's father is dead?" Aisling asked, making sure Tamara didn't want or expect more.

Tamara wiped additional tears off her cheeks. "Yes."

"I'll look for your answers in the ghostlands."

A pale hand curled around Aisling's forearm. "Will you do it now? Here? The garden is warded and I don't want anyone knowing I've asked you to do this. I don't want my family to know I've given you his name." Her grip tightened. "You'll promise on your soul not to reveal it to anyone in *this* world."

"I promise."

"On your soul."

"On my soul."

"You'll do it now? Here?"

Aisling hesitated for only a moment before agreeing, then found a spot beyond the pentacle of the garden and sat cross-legged on the ground. She smoothed the surface of the dirt as Tamara filled her gathering basket with ash-rich soil and returned with it.

"I'll need the name," Aisling said, looking around quickly when a hot breeze tugged at her braid and filled her lungs with the exotic scent of spice underneath a desert sun. And though she didn't see Zurael, she imagined he was with her, then realized as she should have earlier, that a demon needed no form to be present in this world.

"Christopher. Christopher Alan Cooper," Tamara whispered, pulling an inexpensive ring from her pinky finger and offering it to Aisling. "He bought this for me. It's the only thing I have that was once in his possession."

Aisling took the ring and placed it on her own finger. Her heart raced as it always did when she was about to enter the spirit world.

Instinctively her hand curled around the hidden pouch containing her fetishes. She thought about calling on one of the fetish-linked spirits, but the price was always high, and after her last trip to the ghostlands, she was afraid of what they might demand.

Aisling took a deep a breath. She wished Aziel would appear and crawl into her lap. But nothing stirred other than the breeze-bent plants.

She used her fingertip to draw a circle around her in the dirt, adding the necessary symbols of protection. When the circle was closed, she dug her hands into the ashy soil, let it sift through her fingers like baker's flour as she got a feel for the weight and fineness of her drawing material. She pictured the sigil she would draw, one suited for the task, and a name she could call upon whose price for aid had never been more than she could pay.

When the soil was as familiar to her as what she used sitting on the floor of her family's barn, she slowly, painstakingly drew the sigil, one small handful of dirt at a time, the lines formed with the minute opening and closing of her fist.

By the time she was nearly done, her hand ached and a thin sheen of sweat covered her face. But looking down at her work, Aisling was satisfied. She felt calm as the last line fell into place and the gray swirling mass of the spirit winds rushed to meet and claim her.

"BACK so soon?" a familiar voice said when the gray settled to reveal Aisling's naked form and unbound hair. Dismay filled her as she turned to find Elena's brother instead of the spirit guide she'd expected. "You're disappointed," he said, licking his lips in a blatantly carnal gesture as his gaze traveled over her, settling on the triangle of dark gold curls between her thighs. "Well, I won't say I am." His eyes flicked briefly to the arm where Zurael had been coiled on her last visit. "And it's so much nicer without your pet. So much cozier." He offered his hand. "Walk with me? Let's get to know one another better."

Instinct made her hesitate to follow him. Caution kept her from taking his hand. Rarely did she touch a spirit in the ghostlands.

"Why have you come to greet me, *John Rousseau*?" she asked, stressing the name, guessing his surname was the same as Elena's.

John threw back his head and laughed. He reached back to tug at the long silver cable serving as leash and hangman's noose. It coiled around his hand. "Nice try, but that witch's trick won't work on me. As you can see, my soul is not my own, though at the moment my master's attention appears to be lax."

A sly expression moved through his eyes. "You asked who I served on your first visit. Would you like to see the place he calls home?" He leaned forward and whispered, "I'll let you in on a secret. He'd like for you to join him here. Your mother got away from him, or so they say. But that's a story for another day."

Cold chills and burning curiosity splintered through Aisling. She wasn't the only child to be abandoned on Geneva's doorstep with no history or clue to his or her parentage. She didn't feel alone or alienated or unloved because of it, though a small part of her had always longed for answers, wanted them desperately, especially when she realized she could travel to the spiritlands. But until now, those answers had seemed impossible to obtain.

Temptation eroded her sense of purpose. It pushed back the urgency of her tasks in both the ghostlands and in Oakland.

John gave a sigh. He made a show of rolling his shoulder, and as he did so the grayness on that side gave way under a subtle breeze.

A row of Victorian houses with Sinners at their center became a backdrop for a group of hollow-eyed men. They stood, their attention focused on her. Their faces undamaged though their bodies were ripped open, the organs hanging and bones broken, the carnage mixed with bloody, torn clothing.

Bile rose in Aisling's throat. Guilt lodged in her heart at the sight of the men who'd been Ghosting, whose deaths had come because of her presence at the club.

John shuddered dramatically. "Your work? I'm sure they had it coming to them, but what a way to go." He stroked the cable around his neck. "It makes my own demise seem humane."

Once again he offered his hand. "Shall we appease your curiosity about the being who would claim you as his own?"

Wicked amusement made John's eyes gleam. His words of her being claimed by a being in this realm brought thoughts of Zurael and made Aisling hesitate just long enough for Tamara's ring to draw her attention, to make her question John's purpose and remember he'd yet to demonstrate he'd come as a result of the sigil she'd drawn before entering the ghostlands.

"Why have you come to greet me, John Rousseau?" she asked, repeating the sentence she'd met him with.

"How boring. I'd hoped we could spend some time together." He cupped the front of his pants. "Not that I'd risk eternal torment and damnation by actually fucking you. But even a dead man can fantasize." His eyes traveled over her again. "Oh yes, a man can certainly fantasize, which I intend to do. Until we meet again," he said, his voice lost in a swirl of gray as he was reclaimed by the ghostlands.

Aisling rubbed her arms, conscious of the stares of the men who remained against a Sinners backdrop. She closed her eyes, willed the scene away and felt the spirit winds caress her naked flesh.

Relief filled her when she opened her eyes and found unending grayness. She rubbed her palms against her thighs, more conscious of her lack of clothing in the spiritlands than she'd been for a long time, and unnerved by it.

A small man dressed in a brown suit stepped into view. His expression remained somber, his demeanor respectful. His gaze remained fixed on her face as he approached.

He was a figure out of one of Geneva's history books, a man wearing a bowler hat—a derby from the 18 and 1900s—a time well before The Last War. His manner suggested a man with a task to perform. And though she'd never seen him before, Aisling wasn't surprised when he doffed his hat to reveal the sigil she'd used in asking for aid.

"I am Marcus. How may I serve you?"

Aisling removed the ring from her finger and offered it to him. "The man who gave this to his lover was named Christopher Alan Cooper by his parents. I want to know if his spirit passed through this land or can be found lingering here."

Marcus took the ring. His hands were as delicate as a woman's and it fit easily on the same small finger Aisling had worn it on.

He closed his eyes and Aisling wondered if perhaps a part of him searched the ghostlands, or if he simply spoke with the being whose sigil she'd drawn. When he opened his eyes, he said, "For the answer to your question, you'll owe a shaman's task, one not meant to be either difficult or dangerous."

"I accept."

Marcus rotated his wrist. Inside the derby hat a new sigil replaced the one he'd first revealed. "The bearer of this mark will call upon you for your service."

Aisling memorized the symbol, then nodded. He placed the hat on his head. "Follow me."

As always, time and distance were immeasurable, meaningless. Phantom hands, tendrils of hot and cold, glanced over her bare flesh as they walked. Nothingness gave way to building-lined streets, to a bridge separating two cities and a distant skyline that was now home.

"This is San Francisco," Aisling said.

"An illusion of it, yes."

She looked around, absorbed everything she could, so if she ever found herself in the city across the bay, she'd know something of it. They continued walking along streets lined with shops. It took Aisling a block to notice how thoroughly those offering ordinary services and products were integrated with those operated by humans with supernatural gifts.

A small Italian bakery stood next to a palm reader. An apothecary shared a painted mural front with a witch's candle and herb shop.

"Do the people mingle freely as well?" Aisling asked her guide as they passed a grocery store. Its front was a large window of glass, an open invitation for burglary and theft.

"For the most part." Marcus stopped in front of an occult shop. It was the last one on the block and close enough to the bay that Aisling could hear the phantom lap of water against the docks and shore.

He pointed out a symbol etched in the glass next to the door. A serpent held an apple in its mouth. From a point behind its head to just before the tip of its tail, the three segments of its S-shaped body were impaled by an arrow. "This is the mark of the ruling vampire family here."

Aisling noticed that the other shops also bore the symbol. "They own these businesses?"

Marcus shrugged. "In some cases, perhaps. In most, those who do own them have paid for protection with money or services rendered. San Francisco is a deadly place to cause offense in, as the man you've asked about discovered."

The door opened easily enough to reveal a pale corpse lying amid chaos. The twin puncture marks of a vampire's fangs in his throat revealed the cause of his death. The transparent nature of the form told Aisling it wasn't Christopher Alan Cooper's spirit but an illusion provided for her benefit.

"He died here?"

"Yes."

She studied the scene more closely and realized the illusionary doorway Marcus had opened led to an interior room in the shop, an office instead of a place where merchandise was displayed.

A flat stone with unfamiliar text engraved on it was close to Christopher's hand. But it might easily have ended up on the floor during his struggle with the vampire who'd discovered him trespassing.

Or maybe Tamara's lover hadn't come as a thief at all. Maybe there'd been a disagreement or he'd failed to live up to a bargain he'd made.

"What did he do to offend?" Aisling asked. "What brought about his death?"

Marcus removed the ring from his finger. In the dim light of the shop it was dull and cheap. "For a shaman's service yet to be performed you've been given fair value and then some. Would you add to your debt for additional answers?"

"No," Aisling said, taking the ring and letting the spirit winds cast her from the ghostlands.

TAMARA'S face was tight with fear and her arms wrapped protectively around her swollen belly. Her gaze darted nervously to a point behind Aisling, and Aisling knew what she would find there.

Heat, the exotic scent of Zurael. Aisling turned her head and saw him crouched behind her. He was a portrait of deadly power, his attention focused solely on her, his eyes promising retribution for some sin he'd judged her guilty of.

With the swipe of her hand, Aisling erased the circle with its protections and the sigil she'd used to summon a spirit guide. Against her palm the ring felt cold.

She opened her fist and offered it to Tamara. "I'm sorry," Aisling said, her tone imparting the news.

Tears welled up, emphasizing the bruised look in Tamara's eyes. "You're sure?"

"Yes."

"Do you know how?" Tamara whispered. "Where?"

"San Francisco."

Tamara's face grew paler. "Vampires?"

When Aisling nodded, Tamara drew a deep, shuddering breath but held her tears inside. She took the offered ring and exchanged it for the promised amulet before rising unsteadily to her feet. "I'll let you out of the garden now, before someone in my family comes to check up on me."

Aisling looked at the sky and frowned with dismay at how much of the day she'd lost in the ghostlands, where an hour could pass in a minute, or a minute could be stretched to a painful eternity. Zurael shackled her upper arm with his hand, burned her with heat similar to what she'd experienced when he'd accompanied her in serpent form to the spiritlands.

A small hiss escaped when she tried to pull out of his grasp as they walked. In front of her, Tamara shivered and hastened her steps.

They exited in the same place they'd entered. But when Aisling turned, wanting to offer a word of comfort for Tamara's loss, she was met by a wall of thorns and poison oak.

"You risked yourself unnecessarily," Zurael said. There was purring menace in his voice as he pulled her against him and cupped her face with his free hand, forced her to meet the molten gold of his gaze.

Aisling wet her lips, nervous, unexpectedly excited at the same time when she felt his cock respond, pulse against her belly as his face tightened with lust. She shivered at the need he could generate in her with a look, a touch, tried to remember why she should fight it.

"I did what I had to do," she whispered. "For my family. The amulet was worth the risk. It was worth an even greater risk than the one I took."

She wasn't like him. She wasn't even sure how to kill a demon, or if they could be killed.

"I did what I had to do," she repeated, lifting her chin, speaking the truth she was coming to dread. "You won't always be here to protect me from harm."

A dark thought passed through his eyes, there and gone, instantly replaced by fierce possessiveness, but not before Aisling's heart spiked with fear. His grip on her tightened, and the heat between them built as though it would reduce their clothes to ash so flesh could touch, meld, turn two beings into one living flame.

"For the moment, I am here. There's no escape from this spider's web for either of us," Zurael said as thick waves of lust pounded through him, urged him to press his lips to hers, to thrust his tongue into the wet, heated depths of her mouth in preparation for stripping them of their clothing and taking her.

She made him forget his obligations, his home. She tangled him deeper in strands of desire and passion, until the thought of being separated from her became a painful agony. Only the programming of a lifetime, the horror of being discovered in the spiritlands and made *ifrit*, had kept him from joining her in the circle, coiling around her arm in serpent form and going with her as he had before.

Her nipples were hard points against his chest. He could feel the tiny tremors running through her, the electric combination of fear mixed with arousal.

Intoxicating. Mesmerizing.

He tried to remember a female of his own race who'd affected him as Aisling did, but couldn't. Instead images from the tapestries on the walls in the House of the Spider flickered through his thoughts, carnal scenes of humans, Djinn and angels.

His cock ached and he found himself leaning forward, lost in blue eyes, drawn by wet, parted lips. Their breaths mingled. Honey gold and desert spice filled his lungs, drove the air out in sharp pants.

Her whimper was music to his ears. Her lowered eyelashes a submission he feasted on.

She was so fragile, so delicate, so utterly desirable he forgot how dangerous she was to him. Their lips were nearly touching when some tiny part of his brain overrode the needs of the flesh, reminded him that to kiss her was to deepen his physical enslavement as thoroughly as if an incantation had been used to secure him to a hollow vessel.

A shudder ripped through him as he forced himself away from

GHOSTLAND 125

her, turned aside so she couldn't see what it cost him, how he still struggled with the need to finish what he'd begun. And though separating was his doing, his choice, the desire to prove to her she wanted him flared hot and white in his chest when she immediately put more distance between them, as if it were she who wanted to escape the entanglement of their souls and not him.

"How much of what I've learned from Father Ursu and Tamara did you hear?" Aisling asked, somehow managing thought with a mind hazy with desire, a body tormented by lust-abraded nerves crying for intimate contact.

"All of it," Zurael said, acknowledging his ability to follow her unseen.

Aisling slipped the amulet necklace over her head and tucked it underneath her shirt. She glanced at the sky again. "When I left the house, I intended to go to the occult shop Raisa mentioned. There's still time to get there and return home before it's dusk."

"A good plan," he said and started walking.

Aisling didn't immediately hurry to catch up with him. He confused her, one minute darkly possessive, lust blazing in his eyes, the next pushing her away, his features remote, tight, as though he were angry at her for his lust.

Desire pooled in her belly. Her cunt lips were swollen, parted, open for him, despite her knowing it would be wiser to keep her distance. Tears threatened to escape, and she told herself their appearance was because of the need pulsing through her with no hope of being satisfied, and not because his actions hurt her.

Her hand shook slightly as she curled it around the hidden pouch containing her most powerful fetishes and drew comfort from the tiny carved figures. Zurael's footsteps slowed subtly to allow her to catch up, to walk at his side. Resolve stiffened her spine, and when she reached him she repeated the question he had yet to fully answer. "Why do you stay here if you no longer intend to kill me for summoning you?"

He stopped and turned, cupped her face again. She shivered

when she felt sharp, deadly talons brush lightly over the skin of her neck. "Because I am hunting and my prey will be drawn to you."

"I'm bait?" Aisling whispered, feeling the sting of tears return with the thunder of her heart.

Amber gold darkened with unfathomable emotion. Zurael leaned in. He touched his cheek to hers as his free hand went to her side and pulled her against him so she felt the rigid length of his erection.

"At your summons I killed those who intended to make a human sacrifice. By my own choice I will kill any others who follow that same path. Your search for whoever is responsible for Ghost, and mine for the guiding hand behind the dark masses, are tangled strands in the same spider's web. There is no escape for either of us."

His tongue caressed her earlobe and sent a jolt of icy-hot desire straight to her clit, caused her to grind against his hardened cock. She felt his shudder of pleasure. When he released her and stepped away, she read his intention to have her again when they returned to the house. Her body rejoiced even as her heart and mind argued against it.

Eight

AISLING was worried by the time they arrived at the occult shop. It'd taken far longer than she'd anticipated and would take them even longer to return home.

The shadows were deep in places and the area felt deserted. The abandoned buildings and rubble remains of war-torn streets were already being reclaimed by wild creatures as well as supernatural ones.

Eyes glowed from dark hollows and disappeared in a blink. The wind brought whispered voices, but whether they belonged to her imagination or some fey beings, she didn't know and wouldn't risk discovering.

There were other buildings, their doors shut and barred, their interiors darkened. The occult shop stood alone, apart, an inscribed circle painted in red on the concrete sidewalk surrounding it.

The sigils were traditional, simple, so common Aisling thought perhaps they were done for show, for those humans without inherent magic, rather than with the true intention of keeping spectral beings out.

"Can you cross the circle?" she asked.

Her question was greeted with an amused chuckle. "Yes," Zurael said, proving it by stepping forward and pushing the door open, holding it for her to pass through.

A woman looked up just as a crystal embedded in the forehead of a primitive statuette behind the counter flared red and stayed that way for a long moment before going dark. "Cool," she said, tugging at a ring pierced through her eyebrow, then rubbing her palm over a shaved, almond-colored head. "That's never happened before. I'll have to tell Javier."

"He's not here?" Zurael asked.

"No," she answered, sparing him a quick glance before asking Aisling, "So what are you? You're not a witch or a sorceress. We get plenty of them in here and the crystal's never reacted."

"A shamaness."

Aisling didn't know what to think of the woman's claim that the crystal had reacted to her presence. She moved closer, studied the crude figurine. It reminded her of the artifacts she'd seen in Geneva's books on ancient history, of something unearthed long ago and created millennia before then, in what was once called the Holy Lands, though in the end those same lands became the birthplace of The Last War.

"You're the one who has Henri's house now?" the woman said, drawing Aisling's attention away from the primitive statuette.

"Yes."

"I'm Aubrey, Javier's assistant and apprentice. Shop's open for a few minutes more. Since you're new to Oakland, here are the rules. Cash only. If you want to trade services, you have to wait until Javier's around to negotiate. Candles and supplies are for sale. The books aren't unless there's already a duplicate made up."

She lifted a hand holding a pen. "If you want a book you can pay to have us copy the entire thing; sometimes we do it by hand, other times we do it on a copy machine. You can also buy copies of a page or more. Price varies depending on the book. You take your chances if you try to memorize the information and leave with it. If we catch you copying it yourself, you get a warning the first time; after that you're banned."

The pen tilted to point out a collection of books in a glass case at the end of the counter. "Those come out one at a time and have to be looked at right there. They're spelled and you don't want to know what'll happen if you try to leave with one of them." Aubrey glanced down at the counter, to a page she was copying by hand. "I need to get a little more of this done, otherwise I'd give you a tour of the books. Ask if you have questions."

Aisling nodded and began exploring. Zurael did the same.

The shop was larger than it had looked from the front, but laid out in a way so whoever was tending it could keep an eye on any visitor. Candles, pentagram jewelry, fetishes, herbs, wands, caldrons and athames—all were available and with plenty to choose from. But it was the sheer number of books on magic and witchcraft that left Aisling both awed and wary.

An entire wall contained a library of handwritten spell journals, individual Book of Shadows that no living witch would have willingly parted with, much less shared for a price or allowed to be copied by someone she didn't know or trust. Most were old, probably salvaged from homes where entire families had been lost to plague and war.

Aisling turned away from them, saddened by the loss they represented. She joined Zurael at the glassed bookcase and immediately understood the stiffness of his posture, the menace she read in him when their eyes met. Among the texts there were books filled with demon names and rituals for summoning and commanding them, as well as books on Satanism and performing black magic.

A chill slid up Aisling's spine at the sight of them. "How can you offer these?" she asked, her voice holding the horror and disbelief she felt.

Aubrey looked up from her work. Pierced eyebrows drew together in puzzlement. "Haven't you ever been in an occult store before?"

Aisling shook her head. If one existed in the San Joaquin, it was a well-kept secret, even from Geneva, whose sheltering of those with otherworldly gifts was known, though never flaunted.

Aubrey spared a glance at the glassed bookcase. "Javier's collection is amazing, but it's nothing compared to the store in San Francisco." She shrugged. "Selling information isn't illegal. Nine times out of ten it either doesn't work for the untrained or it ends up getting them killed. And if it does work, and they get caught doing something they shouldn't with it, then they're punished. Believe me, the Church sees to that."

Aisling couldn't let the subject drop. "People have disappeared. There have been human sacrifices."

Aubrey's hand tightened on her pen. "The police have already been here, several times, asking who looked at the books. We cooperate with them. There's no guarantee of privacy. Anyone who shops here knows that." She put her pen down, glanced at the growing dusk and slid off the stool. "I need to close the shop now."

Zurael said, "Will Javier be here tomorrow?"

"Maybe. He comes and goes."

Aisling worried about asking further questions and revealing where her true interest in visiting the shop lay, but she couldn't waste the opportunity. "Do you know anything about men and women who have crosses branded into their skin?"

Aubrey shook her head. "Sounds like they're religious zealots, maybe members of one of the cults that live outside the city. There's a place called The Mission at the other end of Oakland, just before The Barrens. Ask there. We don't get many true believers here."

"Have you heard of a substance called Ghost?" Aisling asked.

"No. Is it something we should carry here?"

Dread at the possibility made a knot form in Aisling's stomach. "No, you shouldn't offer it for sale. Anyone who uses it invites death."

"You'd be surprised how many customers, especially untalented humans, are turned on by the prospect of dangerous magic." Aubrey came out from behind the counter and Aisling stopped her with a touch to her wrist.

"What about these symbols?" Aisling used her finger to draw imaginary lines on the countertop.

Aubrey picked up a pen and pulled a sheet from the pad of paper. "Use this."

Javier's assistant stiffened when Aisling re-created the branded patterns Elena had traced in tea on the coffee table after the trip to the ghostlands.

"They're punishment brands for someone caught using magic that's against the law," Aubrey said, immediately shifting away from Aisling. "Now I really need to close up and leave."

"Do you know of anyone who wears these brands?" Aisling asked, but Aubrey was shaking her head no and opening the front door for them to leave before the words were completely out.

"SHE lied about knowing of someone with the brands," Zurael said after they'd put some distance between themselves and the shop.

"I thought so, too. But we know more than we did." Aisling slid her hands into the roomy pockets of her work pants to keep from curling one of them around Zurael's arm as they walked. It worried her that in such a short time his heat and scent had come to represent security. "Tomorrow we can visit The Mission and ask about the man and woman bearing the cross brands. It doesn't seem likely that religious zealots would frequent places like Sinners or sell something like Ghost."

Zurael's hand stroked down her spine and made her shudder with pleasure. "Humans have a long history of seeking enlightenment through mind-altering substances. But I agree, the man we witnessed selling Ghost at Sinners didn't appear to be doing so with the intention of converting followers or leading them to salvation."

Even though she didn't believe in the Church's vision of heaven and hell, Aisling worried for her soul. She knew too well how choices made in life followed a person in death.

"Is there such a thing as salvation?" she asked, curious what a being who most likely called one of the dark places in the spiritlands his home would say.

Zurael laughed and stopped walking. She stopped with him and both of them turned.

He cupped her face and brushed his thumb across her lips. In the fading light the liquid gold of his eyes held both amusement and desire. "I'm not the one to ask about salvation for the children of mud. Until I met you, I would have seen them all destroyed in the fiery burn of justice and retribution."

"And now?"

Zurael leaned in, unable to stop himself from pressing a kiss to her forehead. "And now there is at least one I would argue should be spared."

He closed his eyes and inhaled her scent. It filled his lungs and dissolved into his bloodstream, surged downward until desire pulsed through his cock in time with his heartbeat and the whispered sound of her name across his soul.

His fingers traced the delicate bones of her spine, slid over the gentle curve of her buttocks. Had the first son of The Prince felt this way about the human female he'd become obsessed with?

Zurael rubbed his cheek against Aisling's silky hair as his father's imagined voice issued a warning through time, drew his thoughts to the moment they stood together in the Hall of History, before the mural of Jetrel. *She became his weakness, the bait used to trap him.* And overlaid on the Prince's words were those Malahel had spoken of Aisling. *It's good you already intend to kill her. She is dangerous to us and will be made even more so if she learns what's written on the tablet.*

Fierce protectiveness surged through Zurael when Aisling's arms wound around his waist and she pressed more tightly to him. He would argue she be spared.

She'd admitted she didn't know how to bind him and wouldn't have summoned him if the need weren't urgent. He'd been a shadow in her mind when they were together in the ghostlands. He could attest to the truth of her innocence when it came to the Djinn. He would offer his belief that powerful forces were at work and had ensnared her in a trap the Djinn benefited from.

His palm glided upward. The heat intensified between them. Worry for her made him ask, "How were you able to draw the brands Elena showed you?" They'd been inked in tea on the coffee table and gone within seconds, so quick they'd left little impression on him.

"I have a memory for things like that. Sometimes it feels as though I've seen them before, even though I know I haven't."

"Like an ancestral memory. You know nothing of your parents?"

"No." Aisling's lips brushed his earlobe and sent lust boiling through him so he ached.

His hands curled into fists at her back with the material from her shirt gathered in them. Her soft moan was echoed by his as the contours of her breasts and the hard points of her nipples became more pronounced.

It would be so easy to urge her into the shadows, to press her against the wall of an abandoned building and take her there. Or to command her to grip a windowsill as he'd commanded her to grip the counter in front of the mirror so he could mount her as he'd done then.

A shudder went through Zurael. Arousal leaked to coat his cock head in molten desire.

"We need to keep walking. It'll be dark soon," she said, her breath hot on his skin. It drew his thoughts to her lips. It renewed his fantasies of placing her on her knees before him so he could know the feel of her mouth and tongue on his cock.

He opened his hands, freed her shirt in favor of sliding over delicate, feminine curves to cup her hips. "Do you think I fear the dark or the creatures that roam in the nighttime, Aisling?"

"No." She pressed a kiss to his collarbone. "But I do. And it would be better if my neighbors didn't see me out in it and wonder why I'm not a prisoner to it as they are."

Reluctantly Zurael set her aside. Misgiving, guilt, worry forced the lust to recede into the background. At Sinners he'd accepted Aisling's need to approach the Ghost dealer. The task of finding its source was hers, set before her by the spirits protecting her in a land the Djinn feared. But in the occult shop he'd struggled against letting her question Aubrey and draw further attention and danger to herself.

It was only a matter of time before Aisling's questions would ripple outward and turn the hunted into hunters. If they viewed him as no more than her lover, her companion and bodyguard, then they would underestimate how lethal he was. They wouldn't know until the moment of their own deaths that there had never been a possibility of defeating him or harming her. But looking at her standing before him, fragile and soft, intoxicatingly feminine, he felt a soul-deep fear for her.

Zurael knelt on the ground. He swiped his hand across the loose earth, smoothed it into a dark tablet. A few sure strokes and he'd drawn a symbol representing the name of a lesser angel killed by the Djinn in some ancient battle. It was one he remembered from his childhood and the endless hours he'd spent studying the tomes kept by the House of the Serpent.

He let the symbol remain for a heartbeat then cleared it with the sweep of his hand. "Can you draw it?"

She laughed softly and his chest tightened. The ease in which she knelt and recaptured the name in quick lines across the dirt, the talent she took pride in and performed with confidence, was the very thing that would make her death necessary if she were to see the text written on the tablet he'd been sent to retrieve.

"Close your eyes," he said, an ache forming in his chest when Aisling complied with a smile, trusted him so easily when he might bring only death to her.

This time he wrote several sentences using script and symbols many of the Djinn no longer studied or remembered. It was an account from a history text, a record of angel sightings in long-dead and forgotten cities.

"You can look now," he said, watching her closely, giving her only enough time to scan each line once before he cleared it away. "Can you copy it?"

Her eyes met his. Pleasure had given way to somber expression, to private, guarded thoughts he longed to coax from her as much as he feared what they might reveal.

She leaned forward. Her hand moved with the same sure confidence she exhibited when re-creating only a solitary symbol. There was only a brief hesitation on the name of an angel whose purpose the Djinn had never been able to determine, before she moved on to complete the task, her perfect accuracy deepening his fear for her.

He had to ensure she never saw the tablet he sought. Even the pleading of a Serpent prince wouldn't spare her from a Djinn assassin if she did.

Zurael erased her work and stood. He offered his hand because he couldn't stop himself from wanting the feel of her skin against his. A shudder went through him when she placed her hand in his in a simple display of trust. Pain over possibly betraying her lanced his heart even as his cock responded by growing harder and fuller.

They resumed walking. Silence reigned between them, though around them the increasing dusk brought the sounds of insects and frogs, of swaying weeds and the rub of leaf against leaf—the thinly veiled hush before the predators stirred and woke, arrived to claim the night.

"In Stockton the Church or a religious council is always involved when magic practitioners are on trial," Aisling said as they drew close to her home. "It happens rarely, since few admit openly to being gifted, but if the brands Elena saw are punishment brands as Aubrey said, then Father Ursu might be able to identify the man who sold Ghost if he was judged here. If nothing else, he'd know what offenses they represent."

Zurael's hand tightened on hers in protest. He didn't trust the Church not to set Aisling to a task in the spiritlands if she went to them. Father Ursu may have claimed Henri's death weighed heavily on him, but that hadn't stopped him from going with armed men to take Aisling from her home and family.

"It would be dangerous for me to be with you if you go to see him," Zurael said.

In a non-corporeal form, as he'd been when he followed her from the house, he was nearly impossible to kill or detect. But he was also at his weakest, when a spell trap set for any number of other beings would also ensnare him. He would expect such traps at the church, just as he'd expect one of those rare humans who could read heavily masked auras to be present. They'd think him demon instead of Djinn, but the damage would be done and the risk for Aisling increased unnecessarily.

"You asked Raisa about the library. Let's look for information there first. If you ask Father Ursu about the brands or the man who wears them, he'll wonder what your interest is, perhaps have the authorities intervene and collect the man for questioning."

"You're right," Aisling said, and he could hear the worry in her voice. "We might never get a chance to talk to him if the police or Church get to him first."

They rounded the corner and her house came into sight. He felt her tension build with each step. Several times she called for the ferret, Aziel, but there was no flash of black or chirped greeting.

Zurael pulled her keys from his pocket as they neared the front door. He laughed at her consternation when she realized she'd been in such a hurry to escape his presence earlier that she'd left without them.

She took them from him, glanced around again, though the yard was overgrown and held a number of places for her pet to hide. "Maybe he'll show up once I start cooking dinner," she said, worrying her bottom lip. "I can leave a window open for a little while longer."

Zurael's thoughts went to the few things she had in her cabinets.

In the Kingdom of the Djinn, few knew hunger. Even the *sila*, those of lesser birth who had no ability to change shape or become non-corporeal, didn't lack for food or shelter unless they were cast out into the elements by their houses or clans and not accepted into another.

His life had been one of luxury, of fine food and respectful servants, of incredible freedom borne along with the heavy weight of responsibility that came with being The Prince's son. Until he'd been summoned, he'd never known true fear, had never experienced so deeply the emotions that buffeted him when he was in Aisling's presence.

"Let me provide tonight's meal," he said, and as soon as the words were out, he saw the opportunity they provided for him to return to the occult shop.

"Full darkness will be here in— "

He stopped her by the touch of a fingertip to her lips and felt his heart fill with tender warmth when a fleeting look of worry moved through her eyes before she gave a slight nod, accepting he would be safe out in the night, where she wouldn't be.

"I'll travel fast and be back soon," he said, finding himself suddenly reluctant to leave her.

She nodded and turned back toward the barred, metal door, slid the key into the lock and opened it enough to unlock the wooden door behind it.

He couldn't resist the temptation to touch her one last time, to trace her spine and feel her shiver as desire flared inside her as surely as it did inside him. When he returned he'd have her again. He'd know the silky heat of her wet core, the ecstasy of being buried so deep inside her their heartbeats blended and pulsed in sync with one another.

"I'll have to close the windows before you get back," Aisling said, letting the exterior barred door close as she gave Zurael the house keys.

Somehow he managed to part from Aisling, to seek the shadows and will his physical shape to fade. He became a swirling, eddying wind that twisted, picking up random twigs and leaves as he retraced their steps to the occult shop. He knew even as he did it there might be no chance to examine the primitive statue and perhaps destroy it.

Javier's assistant had assumed the crystal in the figurine's forehead reacted to Aisling because she was first through the door. But he'd seen images of similar statuettes in the history books of the Djinn, and all of them were dangerous tools in the hands of someone capable of summoning and binding those who could shed their physical form.

What had taken quite a bit of time to do as a man took only a few minutes without the hindrance of flesh. With a thought, unseeable particles condensed, re-formed and clothed him in the manner he'd chosen when he left the Kingdom of the Djinn.

From deep in the shadows another presence emerged. The aura was heavily masked but recognizable to Zurael. He turned and said, "What brings you here, Irial?"

"My father sent me," Irial said, stepping closer, the green of his eyes a sharp contrast to the stylized raven marking his cheek.

Where Iyar en Batrael was the pitch-black of night, the eldest prince of the House of the Raven was the golden-brown of the forest floor in evening light. Teeth flashed white, but the amusement didn't quite reach the green of his eyes as he said, "I think my father worries the little shamaness will distract you from your task and perhaps be your downfall. From what I've witnessed, even from a safe distance, he has cause for concern. Beyond that, I'm simply a messenger boy, sent to gather what you've learned so he can feed the information to Malahel en Raum in silken threads for whatever web the two of them are weaving."

There was no reason for Zurael to withhold most of what he'd learned, though he carefully parsed through it, avoided mentioning Aisling's ability to quickly memorize script and symbols. And underlying his recounting was a subtle message: He didn't view her as an enemy of the Djinn. He would see her spared.

Irial's face was grim by the time Zurael stopped speaking. He glanced at the occult shop. "I can feel the traps from here. They're powerful. I'm not sure it would be safe for you to enter the shop again, even in a corporeal form."

Frustration spiraled through Zurael, but he wasn't foolish enough to ignore Irial's assessment. Irial was gifted with the ability to recognize the presence of entrapment spells before they could be triggered.

"We can get closer," Irial said, "I want to see the figurine."

AISLING remained on the door stoop long moments after Zurael disappeared. She'd been so anxious to return to the house, to escape the impending darkness. But now the thought of going inside alone held no appeal.

"Aziel," she called, knowing it was useless but unable to stop herself from doing it.

Goose bumps rose on her arms as she left the stoop. She was determined not to give in to the fear and uneasiness that being completely by herself engendered.

Resolutely she forced herself to go around the corner of the house, as Aziel had done when he'd escaped earlier in the day. But there was no sign of him in the tangled weeds and rubble.

She frowned as she imagined the work it would require to reclaim the yard. Perhaps Henri's size had kept him from tackling the physical work necessary to garden, or perhaps, as the gloom of his house indicated and both Raisa and Father Ursu had alluded to, he suffered from depression and had no energy for managing a yard.

"Aziel," she called again before returning to the stoop and glancing to the spot where Zurael had disappeared into the shadows. Need for him coiled in her belly and snaked up her spine to her breasts. Each time she resolved to keep her distance emotionally, to deny the desire for him, her resistance melted against the lust that flared between them.

Aisling shivered. Her nipples tightened and her clit stiffened against panties wet with arousal as she remembered the light scrape of his talons against her neck after they'd left Tamara, the heated promise in his eyes and hard intent of his body after they'd left the occult shop.

Another shiver passed through her, this time with thoughts of the script and symbols he'd drawn in the dirt. So many of them were vaguely familiar—perhaps ancestral memories as he'd claimed. But if they were . . .

A cold knot formed in Aisling's stomach and banked the fires of need. If they were the memories of her ancestors, did that make her part-demon? What other symbols and script would Zurael know so readily and use to test her with?

She wiped suddenly damp palms against her pants. Her heart beat so loudly it drowned out the call of insects in the deepening menace of dusk.

Shall we appease your curiosity about the being who would claim you as his own?

You asked who I served on your first visit. Would you like to see the place he calls home?

I'll let you in on a secret. He'd like for you to join him here. Your mother got away from him, or so they say. But that's a story for another day.

I'd hoped we could spend some time together. Not that I'd risk eternal torment and damnation by actually fucking you. But even a dead man can fantasize.

The taunts Elena's brother had spoken in the spiritlands whispered through her mind, haunted her with a different meaning than the one she'd attributed to them before. She'd thought John spoke of lust, but what if he spoke of her father?

Aisling curled her hand around the hidden pouch containing her fetishes, pictured again the mix of script and sigils Zurael had drawn in the dirt, the one among them she knew by heart. It was a name Aziel had given her long ago, her most powerful protector though he'd refused to answer her questions or speak of the being the sigil represented.

He'd cautioned her against using the name unless she feared for her soul. He'd warned the cost of summoning her ally and drawing him to her was beyond any she could imagine paying.

Aisling shook off her thoughts and went inside. She moved from window to window, noting as she secured them that the bars she'd set ensuring they couldn't be raised higher from the outside remained in place.

The shaman's workroom drew her. The sight of the stones and unfinished forms waiting on the workbench, the fetishes guarding the room, didn't offer her respite from the unanswered questions and haunting fears circling inside her, not only about her unknown parents and her own identity, but about Zurael and Aziel. If they were both demon, then were they her father's enemies or his allies?

She glanced at the bed of dirt in the center of the room but knew she didn't have the courage to seek John out in the ghostlands and ask him to show her the place his master called home. And beyond that, she feared what the knowledge would cost her, what it would mean to her.

With a sigh Aisling forced the swirling chaos of her thoughts to still. She picked up the box of matches on Henri's workbench and lit several lamps rather than use electricity. Then she turned her attention to examining the large fetishes Henri had positioned around the room to guard him when he journeyed in astral form.

She lifted an owl carved from a heavy greenish-brown stone she didn't recognize. Henri's work was less detailed than her own, lacking the tiny lines that made some of her larger pieces seem real, as though they could actually house the spirits of the animals they represented.

For an instant she flashed back to the primitive figurine at the occult shop. She hoped the library would have history books covering ancient times so she'd get a chance to learn more about the statuette, but she didn't count on it. During the years of plague and lawlessness so many books had been destroyed—burned to provide heat and light, and in some cases because those who came across them found the ideas and thoughts they contained offensive. Any truly valuable books surviving had long since disappeared into private collections

In Stockton there was only a small library because the city government saw no reason to spend money on books when the rich and powerful had their own and the poor who struggled in the city or on the land had little time to read or even to learn how. And even if they had, most were wary, worried their choice of reading material would be noted and judged by the Church and those they supported to power. Aisling wondered if it would be different in Oakland, or if word of her visit to the library with Zurael would find its way to Father Ursu as it seemed the trip to Sinners had.

A presence in the doorway made her glance up. Adrenaline poured into her bloodstream at the sight of the stranger standing there, blocking her escape. Her hand instinctively tightened on the owl fetish.

He was only slightly bigger than she, small against other men, which had perhaps led to the violence he'd been found guilty of. The tattoos of a lawbreaker marked his face, one on each cheek, both proclaiming the nature of his crimes—a serious assault against a lover and another against a family member. A third conviction and he might well be executed, but Aisling doubted he'd ever be found if he escaped from her house.

Zurael. She cried his name, but she wouldn't wait for him to rush to her rescue.

The man stepped into the room. His eyes traveled over her and made her skin crawl.

A length of cord unwound when he opened a hand. He grabbed its end and pulled the cord tight, snapping it with a violence meant to add to her terror.

She didn't dare look away from him, though she frantically sifted through her memories of what was on the workbench behind her. There were mallets and chisels, but none of them would give her the reach or the weight of the fetish in her hand.

"Who sent you?" Aisling asked, managing to push the words out, sure his presence in her home wasn't accidental.

"You'll know when you're dead," he said, snapping the cord again before slowly wrapping it around his hand, covering his knuckles with it and kissing them like a prizefighter might do his bare flesh.

He grinned and licked his lips when Aisling grasped the owl with both hands. "I like it better when it's not easy."

Every muscle in Aisling's body tensed as he took a step toward her. Her breath moved in and out of her lungs in fast pants.

There was no point in screaming. Even if her neighbors heard her, they wouldn't brave the night to come to her aid.

Death. Delay. They were the only two options.

Aisling didn't let the open doorway tempt her into making a wild dash into another room. But she cursed her ignorance and her ready acceptance of Zurael's protection for not having paid enough attention to the details that could make a difference between life and death. She had no idea if there were locks on the internal doors, if they were strong enough to last until Zurael's return.

At home she knew every hiding place, every defensible space, each room that offered a safe refuge and a chance for survival from not only supernaturals should they attack, but from bands of outcast, lawless humans. Living in the country—on land with an abundance of food, water and shelter—was dangerous, though other than those times when the landowners came with their militiamen, or the police came on some pretext, she'd never felt threatened.

She kept her attention on her assailant's eyes—counted on his intentions arriving there first and giving her enough warning. How many times had the eldest of Geneva's fostered children drilled and driven that point home to the youngest as they were growing up? How many bruises had blossomed on her skin in the course of learning how to defend herself?

There was only a second to act and she did it—swung the large fetish like a club without stopping to question or second-guess her instinct.

Her attacker howled with pain as the carved stone struck his forearm. Fury contorted his face, chased away the sick amusement she'd seen when he taunted and toyed with her.

Pain screamed through Aisling as he landed a blow to her chest. Agony spread in her stomach when the steel toe of his boot struck her, driving her backward against the workbench.

Rational thought left her and she fought, swinging the fetish as primal sounds and whimpers blended, escaped along with the sound of her breathing.

The will to kill, the necessity of it, rode her. It fed on terror-fueled surges of adrenaline and gave her strength without hesitation.

She managed to drive him back a step, and rather than cower she advanced, swung again, and the sickening crack of a broken bone sent savage satisfaction through her.

He lunged and she sidestepped, used the fetish like a baseball bat and sent him into the edge of the workbench. He struck headfirst and fell to the floor. Didn't rise.

Aisling tightened her grip on the fetish. Her stomach roiled with the choices in front of her: kill him as he lay unmoving or get close enough to tie his wrists and ankles.

Small tremors warned of larger ones to come. It took her a few seconds to realize the whimpering sounds of an injured animal were hers.

She dared to glance away from her assailant long enough to scan the workbench. There were some strands of wire within arm's reach. She picked them up, and the tremors grew stronger at the thought of putting the fetish down so she could secure her attacker.

Aisling watched him carefully as she slowly knelt. She willed herself to strike first, to club him if he moved at all.

She couldn't kill him in cold blood. But she wouldn't let him subdue her.

He remained completely still, so still she paused to see if his chest rose and fell. When she couldn't be sure, she dropped the wire in order to check his pulse.

A wrenching shudder gripped him just as she placed her fingers on his throat. His eyes opened, revealing shock and horror in the instant before his spirit entered the ghostlands, leaving a hollow body staring at the ceiling.

Relief came and Aisling sat on the floor. Tears emerged to run freely down her cheeks in a release of fear at first, and then in acknowledgment of the agony radiating from her stomach and chest where her assailant had struck her.

For long moments she gave in to emotion and pain, buried her face against her knees and hugged them to her, until the need for answers pressed her into action.

Unlike the men who'd been Ghosting at Sinners, she felt no guilt over this man's death. He'd meant to kill her.

The tattoos on his face told of his crimes—assault against a family member and against a lover, both offenses inflicting damage severe enough for him to be charged. She guessed his victims had been women, glanced to the cord still wrapped around his knuckles and doubted he'd been warned of Zurael's presence.

Had her attacker slipped into the house when she'd gone around back to call for Aziel? Or had he entered earlier in the day to lie in wait?

Aisling forced her arms away from her knees and knelt next to him. She braced herself to touch him, to search his pockets for answers. She tried to close her mind, but it was impossible to hide from her gift. The absence of a soul made the body nothing more than an already-decaying husk of flesh.

There was folded paper money in his front pocket. She set it aside, wondered if it was what he'd been paid to kill her.

Her pulse leapt when she found keys in a second pocket. She wouldn't be sure until she tested them, but they looked like duplicates of the ones she'd given Zurael so he could get back into the house when he returned with dinner.

Physical pain screamed through Aisling when she rolled her assailant over. It continued to pass in waves that made her want to curl into a ball.

There were no answers to be found in the back pockets, and she knew she didn't have the strength necessary to undress him in case there were hidden pockets sewn into his clothing or identifying marks on him. She wondered if they'd find a cross branded into his flesh but knew looking for it would have to wait until Zurael returned.

Aisling rose to her feet, swayed and nearly collapsed. Her hand curled around the healing amulet she'd gotten in payment from Tamara. If it was as powerful as the witch claimed . . . If she could just make it to the kitchen and boil some water . . .

But what if there's a next time? She'd only just started looking for whoever was creating Ghost.

The tears she'd fought successfully returned with indecision. She had no way of knowing how much of the amulet's healing properties would be leached away if she steeped it in tea, even for only a few minutes, and used it now.

Aisling closed her eyes. She forced herself to combat the waves of pain and nausea with steady breathing and sheer determination. If she wasn't better in a little while, she promised herself, she'd use the amulet. And the promise helped.

Breath by breath her strength returned. She took a step, then another. Found the second easier than the first.

Her destination was the couch, where she could curl up and wait for Zurael. But as she passed the bed of dirt in the center of the room, she remembered asking, *Who sent you?* and heard her assailant reply, *You'll know when you're dead.*

Aisling shivered as, unbidden and unwanted, an idea came to her. If she followed him into the ghostlands, she might gain the answer to her question. If she got to him before his soul was claimed, he might gladly exchange the name he held for what protection she could offer—even if it was only temporary.

Nervousness made the nausea intensify. She worried that she might have internal injuries making her bleed into her stomach. Shortness of breath and the rapid beating of her heart made the pain in her chest seem sharper, more piercing. But the idea of following her attacker was unshakable.

Slowly she sat on the red dirt. As she enclosed herself in a protective circle, she thought of the names she could call upon for help, and discarded them in favor of a more powerful spirit guide. The price she paid would be higher, but she'd never traveled to the spiritlands when she was in pain or weak. She didn't know whether her astral form would be more vulnerable because of her physical injuries. When the circle was closed, she pulled the pouch containing the fetishes from underneath her shirt and spilled them across her palm just long enough to select a falcon, its wings and legs outstretched.

Aisling placed the falcon upright on the dirt and retrieved the small ceremonial athame from its hidden sheath sewn into the back of her pants. With a quick slicing motion she made a shallow cut across her lifeline.

Her blood welled, beaded. When there was enough of it pooled in her palm, she cleared her mind of everything but a single word, a single name. She held her hand over the falcon so her blood fed it, and called the one she needed as the spirit winds swept in, cold and fierce, to claim her.

Nine

ZURAEL wasn't surprised to look through the window of the occult shop and see a bare spot on the shelf where the figurine had been. "It's gone," he said, wondering if the shop assistant removed it or if the unknown Javier returned and did so after learning the crystal had flared to life.

Next to him Irial shrugged and said, "Which only increases my interest in it. Given the protections around the shop, I suspect it's still inside, hidden away. Perhaps you can convince the shamaness to steal into the shop and retrieve it for you."

"No. She's too important to risk."

"For the moment."

Zurael stiffened but held his words. He sensed Irial was baiting him, poking at him with a verbal stick as the truly foolish might do to a snake with a wooden one. But he didn't make the mistake of labeling the eldest Raven prince a fool.

In the darkness between them, Irial's teeth flashed white. "I'll return to my father's house and leave you to return to the child of mud. The shamaness is beautiful, Zurael, but she's dangerous. I only had to look once to know she affects you physically. Don't let her be your downfall. Stop coupling with her before you're lost to the Kingdom of the Djinn."

Irial's form gave way to a swirling breeze. An instant later Zurael's did the same, and he gained some relief from a cock hardened by the mention of coupling.

He felt the urgent need to return to Aisling, but he pressed forward in the opposite direction, toward the wealthiest area of town so he could provide the promised meal. With no flesh to slow him down, he moved quickly, though not as quickly as if he had simply moved through time and space between two places, leaving and arriving within a fraction of a second, regardless of the distance between the two points.

All Djinn had the ability to travel in such a manner. But doing so anywhere other than their kingdom prison resulted in the equivalent of a sonic boom on the metaphysical plane and left a trail for angels to follow.

He took form again a safe distance beyond where streetlights blazed defiantly against the darkness in an expensive, wasteful use of resources. The rich and powerful flirted with danger here. They walked the street, moved from bars to restaurants to chauffeured limousines, flaunting their wealth and their ability to pay armed bodyguards to insulate them from attack, to die in their place if necessary.

In his search for Aisling, he'd come here first, expecting to find her among the privileged. Now he could never picture her here. She belonged with—

Zurael cut the thought off, but unbidden came the image of her lying naked among pillows on his bed as a desert breeze made the thin curtains enclosing it flutter and part to reveal her waiting for him. Even if he wished it, she couldn't enter his father's kingdom.

But that didn't stop liquid hunger from spreading to his cock and testicles so he fought the urge to take himself in hand, to lose himself in the fantasy of coupling with her on silken sheets.

Aisling. She'd made him come to crave her body, the feel of her skin against his and the tight fist of her sheath around his cock. He should burn with the need to destroy her for how thoroughly she'd ensnared him. Instead he felt only the burning desire to get back to her and take her repeatedly, to hear her whimpered cries of pleasure and submission.

A shudder went through him as he once again imagined Aisling on her knees before him, her eyes dark with need, her lips slightly parted, glistening and ready to take him into her mouth. His cock urged him to hurry and his mind echoed the thought, forced him from the night and into the bright lights.

He realized his mistake immediately. The absence of bodyguards drew unwanted attention and aroused suspicion. Guns slid from openly worn holsters. Knives glinted underneath street and restaurant lights.

Zurael continued toward the closest restaurant—one offering Italian food—as if unaware of the alarm his presence caused. There were wards in place; sigils painted on the building warned of their existence. He doubted he'd be allowed inside and was relieved when a pale, frightened waiter was forced through heavy front doors to stand shaking between two armed guards.

The human offered a menu, his eyes never lifting to meet Zurael's, for fear of being mesmerized. Vampire. It made Zurael chuckle when he realized that's what they thought he was, and the reason they refrained from attacking. Even the wealthiest and most powerful of the children of mud would be cautious about raising a hand against a vampire who approached them without threat in such a public setting.

A quick glance at the menu and Zurael made his choice. He pulled a small gemstone from his pocket and handed it to the waiter to pay for the meal.

The red stone was a bauble of little value to the Djinn, but the waiter's eyes widened and he hurried back inside with it. The restaurant owner himself brought out the food when it was ready. He rushed to assure Zurael that no offense was meant and babbled about his inability to change the wards preventing vampires from entering the building.

Zurael took the meal and retreated to the shadows. Once again he let his form fade into a swirling mass of unseen particles.

He was anxious to return to Aisling, and it showed in the force of the breeze he traveled in. By human standards it didn't take long. By his own it seemed to take forever.

Fear gripped him when he re-formed in darkness and found Aisling's pet scratching frantically at the metal door. The scrape of Aziel's claws was a scream in the stillness of the night.

THE cold, gray fog of the ghostlands settled at Aisling's feet. It twined around her ankles in greeting like Aziel had once done as a cat.

From the white-gray nothingness, a welcome figure emerged, a beautiful woman wearing a silken, flowing robe made of woven feathers. "The soul you seek has already been claimed. He resides now in a place you can't visit, or I for that matter."

Aisling thought of the blood-fed fetish and wondered if the payment already made would gain an answer to another question. She couldn't quiet the doubts and fears that had plagued her earlier, or dismiss her curiosity. "Does my father reside here? Is he demon?"

The spirit guide lifted her arm and the material gave the illusion of a wing unfolding. She offered a hand and Aisling took it without hesitation.

Warmth flowed into Aisling, as if in this land of gray, the sun still found its way in. With a gentle tug, she was pulled forward. The woman leaned in, pressed a kiss to her forehead. "You will know in time. For now I give you something of greater value. Return to your body and find it healed."

Aisling returned as her front door crashed open. Before she could react, Aziel was there, followed immediately by Zurael.

She hurriedly slipped the bloodred falcon into her fetish pouch. Zurael's eyes flashed with fury and the same promise of retribution she'd seen when she returned from the ghostlands in the witch's garden.

"You followed him into the spiritlands," he hissed, sparing a quick glance at her assailant's body.

Aisling's chin lifted though a shiver of erotic fear slid down her spine to stroke between her thighs in response to his expression. Phantom talons scraped across her neck as real ones had done earlier in the day. And in that instant the healing she'd been given by her spirit guide was far more important than answers about her father.

With a confidence that was part bravado, Aisling erased the protective circle. Aziel jumped onto the front of her shirt and scrambled to her shoulder as masculine fingers wrapped around her arms and pulled her to her feet.

Molten eyes narrowed, bored into hers. "Are you hurt?"

"Not now."

"What happened?" Zurael asked, barely able to contain the guilt-laden fury he felt for not having anticipated their enemies would strike so quickly.

Aisling told him, though he'd guessed much of the story when he saw the dropped owl fetish, the folded bills and the house keys on the floor near the body.

He stripped her assailant with barely contained violence. Other than the tattoos of a lawbreaker, there were no clues to his identity.

Aisling discovered a concealed knife and garrote in the man's clothing, nothing more. Her hands trembled slightly as she set them aside. "There's no way of knowing who sent him."

Zurael stood and pulled her to him so he could bury his face in the silk of her hair. "No one is beyond suspicion." His lips brushed the delicate shell of her ear. "I'll dispose of him. Our dinner is next to the front door."

"I can't—"

"You will. By your own hand or mine. You will eat."

He released her and knelt next to the corpse, lifted it in his arms and stood. "Open the window, then close it behind me. Lock the front door. I've still got your keys."

Zurael didn't wait for her to respond. He let his physical form dissolve, and when she opened the window he joined the night long enough to take her assailant's remains to a deserted area.

This time when he returned to the house, he found the living room glowing with candlelight and Aisling waiting for him. She'd set the table and transferred the food into serving dishes. He laughed when he found the ferret on a chair busily eating from a saucer of food in front of him.

"Aziel couldn't wait," Aisling said, her soft voice winding its way through Zurael's chest and downward to curl around his cock. In a heartbeat the hunger for food was replaced by a different hunger.

He didn't yield to the temptation to carry her from the room, but he couldn't stop himself from going to her. Her assailant's possessions were on the counter separating the kitchen from the living room. "The keys fit your locks?"

"Yes."

He leaned in and pressed a kiss to her forehead.

"Do you know who my father is?"

The question surprised him, made him curious. "No. Why do you ask?"

"I think . . . I thought he might be demon because of something Elena's brother said in the spiritlands."

"John is not someone to be trusted." And because Zurael wanted to give her something more, he said, "If it eases your mind, I know your pet is something other than what he appears, but I don't know what."

"Neither do I," she admitted. "The names you wrote in the dirt—"

"Are the names of my enemies," he said, unable to keep centuries of rage out of his voice.

Wariness flickered in her eyes. She stepped away from him, but he caught her arm before she could retreat further. A small tremor passed through her, and he again fought the urge to carry her to the bedroom, to whisper that she had nothing to fear from him as he coupled with her.

"The food will be cold if we don't eat it soon." He brushed his knuckles across her lips, then stepped away before the temptation she presented became too great.

She settled onto a chair across from him and he hated the distance. But she ate, and as she did, the candlelight caressed her features, made the angelite blue of her eyes become violet and the gold of her hair darken to rich honey.

Zurael found it impossible to take his eyes off her. He ached to free the coil of her braid and unbind her hair, to comb his fingers through it in a rare intimacy.

Desire filled the space between them. It grew and pulsed in the air as wax-fed flames undulated in a sensuous dance of heat and light. His breath escaped in a rush when she lowered her eyelashes to shield her expression in an effort to hide from the lust.

The fantasies that had tortured him throughout the day rushed in along with new ones. Protective, possessive urges filled and overwhelmed him. She was delicate vulnerability hiding strength of character, a female created for a man's pleasure, for *his* pleasure.

Zurael waited until they'd finished eating. As she cleared the table, he went into the bathroom and turned the faucets on so water began filling the large, claw-foot bathtub. From a shirt pocket he pulled several of the substance-filled beads the Djinn used for bathing and during sensual play. He set them at the edge of the tub and didn't allow himself to wonder why he'd brought them with him when he left his father's kingdom, professing a desire only to kill the one who'd summoned him.

Aisling stood in front of the sink, preparing to wash dishes. Zurael stopped in the doorway as he had on the first day, only instead of watching her with suspicion and fighting the desire raging through him, he said, "Disrobe, Aisling."

Color rose to her cheeks, and a tremor in her hands served as acknowledgment she'd heard him. He read her intent to deny him in the curl of her body before she whispered, "We shouldn't."

The truth only inflamed him further, filled his head with the roar of lust and his cock with aching need. He pushed away from the doorway and went to her, trapped her between the sink and his hard body.

"I could take you here, now, as I did earlier today in front of the mirror. Do you remember how you begged me to fill you, Aisling? How you cried out in release when I did?"

"Yes," she said, shivering against him, exhaling on a shaky sigh when his hands traveled up her sides and around to take possession of her breasts.

Zurael pulled her back more tightly to his front. He needed to feel her against him, wanted to feel the instant she softened and surrendered, gave herself over to him completely. He traced the shell of her ear with his tongue. "Obey me tonight, Aisling."

Aisling closed her eyes against the desire pulsing through her, burning her from the inside out and making her cunt lips slicken and part. He was dangerous to her, more so now that she knew the depth of his rage toward her most powerful protector, the one whose sigil he'd drawn in the dirt. Yet still she was a moth to his flame, helpless against the needs of her body and the security she found in his arms.

She felt bereft, lost, when his hands dropped away from her breasts and his heat left her back. Lust swirled in her belly when he once again said, "Disrobe, Aisling."

She didn't understand herself when she was with him. Didn't understand the dark cravings, the need to submit that blossomed inside her. He was beyond anything she'd thought to experience with a lover, anything she'd done previously, though the farm's remote location and Aziel's presence as guide and guardian hadn't allowed for much beyond fumbling, hurried experiments with passion.

The need to obey and please him turned her nipples into hard knots and her clit into a stiffened, erect knob. Her fingers trembled as they worked to unbutton her shirt, slowing the process of disrobing as he'd ordered, but intensifying the desire burning between them.

Zurael's sharp inhale as her shirt fell away made her heart flutter with satisfaction. His command to turn around made her cunt clench.

Aisling turned to face him. She looked at him from beneath lowered eyelashes and wanted to go to her knees like a supplicant in front of an ancient deity. In the candles' glow he was a being made of golden light, a predator with no equal. He was raw power and invincible strength, masculine perfection almost too painful to behold.

"The rest of it, Aisling," he said with a purring, sensual menace that made her shake with need.

His gaze scorched her when the cloth binding her breasts joined her shirt on the floor. She trembled at the hungry look in his eyes but knew instinctively that while he might demand her obedience, he was just as much a slave to desire as she was.

Embarrassed, vulnerable heat added color to her cheeks as she removed her short boots and socks then slid her pants and underwear to her ankles before stepping out of them. He'd seen her naked before, already knew her body intimately, and yet it was different stripping at his command. It was both arousing and erotically frightening to stand in front of him while his eyes traveled over her bare flesh as if she belonged completely to him and was his to do with as he pleased.

He stepped in to her, hard heated flesh and leather, desert wind and exotic spice. His hands went to the coil of her braid and unwound it, freed the locks so they fell in honeyed waves to her buttocks as they did each time she entered the spiritlands.

He cupped her breasts, rubbed his thumbs over nipples that ached for his touch, his mouth. Golden eyes darkened and became molten.

"Do not touch me," he ordered, his harsh voice revealing what the command cost him as his hands trailed down her sides and he knelt in front of her.

She widened her stance without being told, though her hands curled into fists in an effort to keep from freeing his braid, from tangling her fingers in his hair and pulling him to her parted slit and wet channel.

Her clit hardened further, so the soft, delicate hood no longer concealed the tiny, sensitive head. "Please," she whispered.

He cupped her buttocks and kept her from pressing against him in sultry invitation. He leaned forward, slid his tongue through her wet folds and over her hardened knob, sent nearly unbearable ecstasy through her, before abruptly standing and lifting her with casual strength then carrying her into the bathroom.

Zurael placed her in the nearly filled tub. He turned off the faucets before stripping out of his clothing, his eyes never leaving her.

He was heavily aroused, his cock hard and thick. The testicles hanging beneath it made Aisling think of a stallion, a bull. He was elemental man and primordial force.

Despite his command that she not touch him, it seemed the most natural thing in the world to rise to her knees when he stepped into the tub, to grasp his hips and press her mouth to his hardened flesh. Satisfaction roared through her when he groaned her name and tangled his fingers in her hair, held her against his rigid cock.

He shuddered as she measured his length in kisses, in the wet trail of her tongue. He panted when she nuzzled the heavy sacs containing his seed, heated them with her breath.

"Take me in your mouth, Aisling," he said, buttocks flexing, hands clenching and unclenching in her hair.

She ignored his command, and the shift in dynamics was intoxicating, thrilling, too heady to resist. She'd never felt so feminine, so powerful.

One hand left his hip to cup his testicles, to weigh them. He was silky smooth, hot in the palm of her hand. She traced the ridges and veins on his shaft with her tongue, sucked on them until his fingers tightened painfully on her hair and his breath came in ragged pants.

"Obey me, Aisling. Now."

His voice promised retribution, punishment, complete domination if she didn't yield. And her cunt clenched, her body hungered for it. She was beyond reason, beyond denial.

She curled a hand around his cock, defied him by pressing her mouth against the velvety soft tip of him, parting her lips only enough for a shallow kiss, for the dart of her tongue to explore the tiny slit.

When he thrust, she tightened her grip on him, warned with the press of teeth, the increase of pressure around his testicles, that she wouldn't be rushed.

Zurael raked his fingers through her hair. He rubbed golden strands of it against his belly and thighs as he fought to regain control of himself and the situation.

Lust, desire, brutal need whipped through him in a heated maelstrom. He would punish her later, make her scream and beg for release.

She would learn the cost of disobedience. She would experience true submission.

He leaned over, scraped his nails against her back, her buttocks. Felt her jerk when he traced the tight pucker of her back entrance. He would have her there, too. He would have her in every way a man could claim a woman.

"Take me in your mouth," he said, straightening, finding her breasts, her nipples, his fingers ruthless, making her whimper, shudder, surrender.

He nearly came when she sucked his cock head into the wet heat of her mouth and assaulted it with her sinful tongue. His hips jerked, thrust. But the tight fist of her hand kept him from forging deeper, from knowing the ecstasy of fucking all the way in and out of her mouth.

Zurael panted, groaned, fought against the restraint she imposed on him. He rubbed and tormented her breasts and nipples, whispered what he intended to do to her later. He dared her to continue defying him, but she didn't yield. She drew it out until their skin was slick with sweat and the sounds of pleasure echoed continuously against the bathroom walls.

"Aisling." Command had gone to plea, to naked supplication. And finally she relented.

He threw his head back and closed his eyes. His hips jerked, pistoned, the frantic thrust and retreat beyond his control as she took him deeper, let him take her as he'd fantasized.

The pleasure was nearly unbearable, and yet he fought against release, tried to draw it out. He forced his eyes open, wanted to memorize the sight of her kneeling before him, his cock sliding between her lips, her eyelashes lowered in submission, in the pleasure she found in the primitive, carnal act they shared.

She made his heart and soul sing, made him feel masculine, powerful, complete. "Aisling," he whispered, wanting her more than he'd ever wanted anything in his centuries of existence, knowing all he'd ever have were what precious memories he made with her.

Eyelashes lifted to reveal eyes filled with unfathomable emotion, and he lost what little control remained. He thrust, panted, shuddered in ecstasy as he came—and nearly cried when the heated release only left him craving her more intensely.

Zurael sank into the water and pulled Aisling against his chest. His mouth pressed against her ear, his tongue traced the delicate shell then fucked into the sensitive canal as his fingers found her clit.

"Please," she said, clinging to him, rubbing her mound against his hand, wanting release from the tight coil of need.

He should draw it out, reduce her to helplessness as she'd reduced him, but the danger was too great. A tilt of her head and their lips would be close, nearly touching, and the temptation to do the forbidden too great to resist.

He found her plump folds and shoved his fingers into her slit. Retreated. Repeated it over and over again, his palm striking the naked head of her clit until the water was sloshing violently and she was keening, slumping, limp with the pleasure he'd given her.

Zurael turned her in his arms, kissed her neck, her shoulders. He murmured words of satisfaction as he stroked her breasts, her belly, cuddled her until both of them recovered from the first rush of passion. Then he picked up a translucent bead of soap and crushed it between his fingers, worked the lather in his hands before applying it to her silky skin.

The way she melted against him, went boneless as he bathed her, was deeply satisfying. He lingered, saved her hair for last. And the intimacy of washing it, combing through it with his fingers, was nearly his undoing, even though he knew it didn't mean the same thing to humans as it did to the Djinn.

After the soap had dissolved as if it were never present, Aisling turned and rose to her knees. "My turn."

Zurael's cock hardened at the sight of her breasts, the nipples begging for his touch. Memories of the pleasure she'd given him, when he stepped into the tub and she knelt before him, left him struggling against the urge to stand.

She reached behind him and slowly freed his braid. Waves of incredible sensation rippled through him as she combed through his hair with her fingers.

When she started to pick up a light blue bead, he nudged her hand to a translucent one. She crushed it between her fingers and he gave himself over to her care, moaned as she stroked his chest and teased the small nipples before grasping his cock.

Zurael allowed her to bathe him as thoroughly as he'd bathed her. He willingly turned his back to her and tilted his head so she could wash his hair, touch him in ways he'd never allowed a female to.

It gentled him for a while, chased away thoughts of dominance, of punishing her for her earlier disobedience—even as it filled him with the need to possess her completely, in every way. His cock throbbed, leaked, was more than ready to provide the lubricant necessary to work its way into the virgin orifice he'd traced earlier.

Zurael turned and captured her hands in one of his, saw need in her eyes, a vulnerable tenderness that made his heart and soul weep. "Aisling," he whispered, pulling her to him, enjoying the press of her breasts against his chest, the way she trembled in reaction to the desire between them.

He held her, ran his hands over her as he kissed her neck, her shoulders, her ears. He built the fire between them until she was clinging to him, then turned her, put her on her knees and urged her to lean over, to grasp the edge of the tub.

She spread her thighs willingly, and the sight of her parted folds nearly distracted him from his purpose. Thoughts of pushing through wet lower lips, of being gripped by the tight muscles of her sheath, made him take himself in hand to stop from moving closer and impaling her with his cock.

He tightened his fingers, let a hint of pain clear the lust so he could concentrate on preparing the way to even greater pleasure. She pressed backward when he palmed her buttock, but when he grazed the rosette of her back entrance she tried to escape his touch, whispered, "*no*," as she'd done other times, the word lacking resolve.

"Yes," he said, moving closer, sliding his penis between her thighs, coating it with the arousal he found there as he rubbed over her swollen labia and clit.

She whimpered in response, tried to cant her hips so he'd find her hot opening. His hands on her buttocks kept her from doing it; his thumbs exploring the crevice between the silky cheeks reinforced his intention to take her there.

When she was shivering with need, he reached for the light blue bead he'd kept her from selecting earlier. It crushed easily between his fingers. The lubricating oil warmed immediately, tingled briefly as it penetrated skin in search of nerve endings.

Aisling jerked when he applied it to the tight pucker of her anus. She tensed, but within seconds she was panting lightly, responding to his commands as he stretched and prepared her, tempted her with the press of his cock head against her opening.

Lust flooded Aisling. Colors exploded on the insides of her eyelids.

Her cunt clenched and her skin slickened with sweat as she pressed backward, and took him into her forbidden entrance as slowly as she'd taken him into her mouth.

His tortured breathing echoed her own. His words of praise and husky pleas filled her with the desire to please him.

She moaned when he was all the way in, felt as though every nerve ending called his name, demanded she move, pull away from him—but not so far he would escape.

Pain and pleasure blended into indescribable ecstasy as she yielded to dark cravings. And he rewarded her with guttural cries and the hot wash of seed, with shuddering release.

They bathed again, sharing the soap generated by the last of the beads. And as he'd done once before, he used demon heat to speed the drying process as he brushed her hair and then his own before they left the bathroom.

Aisling pulled the sheet back, prepared to slide beneath it. He stilled her with a hand to her wrist, a carnal reminder. "You disobeyed me earlier. I told you not to touch me."

Dark lust and erotic fear chased away the deep contentedness, the desire to cuddle and sleep.

She licked her lips. It was a provocative reminder of just how she'd disobeyed him, by taking him in her mouth. It was a subtle challenge for him to deliver the punishment he'd promised.

Molten eyes darkened, narrowed. Before she could do more than gasp, razor-sharp talons slashed the sheet she was holding, left only a long strip of fabric between fingers that shook slightly.

He released her wrist and took the cloth from her hand. "Get on the bed, Aisling."

The command in his voice, the knowledge of what he intended, made her shiver and ache, gave birth to a hidden fantasy as she did as he ordered. His face tightened as he read her desire, scented the arousal rushing to coat her inner thighs, her flushed folds.

Aisling was acutely aware of the cool sheet against her heated skin as he bound her wrists and secured them to the bedpost. It was a symbolic admission of how helpless she was against him. A gesture forcing her to admit how much she liked having him above her, straddling her so his rigid cock and heavy testicles rubbed against her abdomen as he looked down at her with possessiveness in his eyes.

"Zurael," she whispered, unable to think past his name, past the masculine satisfaction edged with desire she saw in his face.

She cried out when he lowered his head and took a nipple between his lips, tortured her as she'd tortured him—with teasing swirls and licks, light touches when she craved the fierce suction of his mouth.

He tormented her until she writhed and thrashed and pleaded. And then he kissed downward, pinned her splayed thighs to the bed with ruthless hands, pleasured her with his mouth and tongue— taking her to the edge of release over and over again—but didn't let her come until he thrust his cock into her channel and made her scream.

Ten

AISLING woke to incredible warmth and feelings of profound security. The first was reality, the second illusion, though she didn't try to banish it. Instead she allowed herself to savor the heat of Zurael's skin as he held her in his arms, his hand cupping her breast, his chest against her back. She allowed herself to linger in a fantasy where she was safe, loved. Complete in a way she hadn't known she could be until he was in her life.

An ache formed in her chest. Her heart and mind warned her of the foolishness of weaving images of the future with him in it. And yet her labia grew slick and parted as memories of the night rushed in—the carnal pleasure he'd shown her and the things she'd allowed him to do to her.

A shiver went through her. She snuggled more deeply into Zurael's sleeping embrace, welcomed the feel of the erection pressed against her buttocks. She understood dominance and submission, accepted it as the natural order of things when it came to the domesticated animals she'd grown up tending or the wild ones she'd observed. But when it came to humans, gifted and normal alike, she'd always equated it with weak and strong, with loss of power and the helplessness of being at another's mercy.

Zurael had shown her differently. But in the process he'd peeled away some of her protective armor, made her crave something she might not ever find with another man—with a human.

Her world had always been insular, limited but made safer by those limits. There'd been Aziel, her family, the people Geneva trusted. There'd been long days of physical work. Evenings spent reading or exploring the spiritlands with Aziel.

Sometimes there were dreams of having a home, a husband, children, of living in a place where she wasn't feared, hated, looked at with suspicion and hostility. But more often there were nightmares of militiamen driving them from the farm. And underneath dreams and nightmares alike was a simple reality she greeted each morning: She had little control over her future, so she needed to make the most of each day.

Masculine lips against her shoulder pulled Aisling from her musings. She moaned when Zurael's hand left her breast and slid downward over her abdomen, before slipping between thighs she parted willingly for him.

"You're remembering the night," he said, his voice husky with satisfaction as his fingers bathed in her arousal, then went to her stiffened clit.

"Yes," she whispered, need for him rising to a flash point with his touch, his attention.

Words Zurael had never spoken to any female fought to escape as Aisling pressed against him in subtle offering and sweet submission. He wanted to demand that she acknowledge his dominance, wanted to hear her say she belonged to him in all ways and always would.

The very strength of his desire to possess her so thoroughly revealed how dangerous she was to him, had his heart and his mind urging him to erect an emotional barrier.

There was no future with her. He couldn't remain in her world. She couldn't enter his.

Fear sliced through him like an angel's icy sword. He had yet to ensure she would be safe from the Djinn.

"Aisling," he said, desperate to keep her safe. Unable to fight the feelings she engendered in him, the need that was more than physical, though he knew only the physical could be satisfied.

She edged upward, whispered his name as her hot, wet cunt lips kissed the tip of his penis. He shuddered and let her engulf him in the fiery heat of her tight channel, gave up the uncertainty of the future in favor of the ecstasy to be found in the present.

AFTERWARD they showered and dressed. Aisling went to the kitchen, and Zurael found himself once again lounging in the doorway, watching her as she prepared their breakfast.

Her movements were smooth, assured, pleasing in a way that surprised him. Until Aisling, he'd never given much thought to the effort behind the meals served him. They were prepared by servants, served by servants, the remains taken away by servants, all at his command.

Even by the standards of the poorest Djinn, the meals Aisling made were meager, and yet . . . His chest filled with emotions he didn't want to identify as he watched her combine the leftovers of the previous night with what she had available. He knew he'd prefer a meal made by her hands to the most extravagant feast presented to him by servants.

Aziel joined them for the meal. He chirped and chattered in between bites, then stood on his hind legs and stared into Aisling's face when the plate she'd placed on the chair seat was clean.

Her laughter made Zurael smile. The simple joy she took in teasing the ferret about becoming fat and lazy as she slid the last bite of food from her plate to his, made Zurael want to take her into his arms and press his lips to hers in a joining of souls.

"Do you know what he says?" Zurael asked, his curiosity about Aisling's pet renewed.

She hesitated slightly. "Only in the spiritlands. And only if he chooses it."

"He was there the night you summoned me."

"Yes. Sometimes he goes with me." She stood and gathered their dishes, her unbound hair becoming a curtain hiding her face from him.

He let the conversation drop, not wanting to admit to her that he no longer felt even an ember of the fury and rage he'd experienced when she'd whispered his name on the spirit winds and commanded his presence. Not wanting to admit he trusted her as no Djinn should ever trust a human.

Zurael followed her into the kitchen and stopped behind her as she washed the plates and silverware. Her body vibrated subtly against his, telling him without words how much she craved the physical contact.

She moaned when he cupped her breasts, whispered his name as he stroked and pet her, nuzzled the silky fineness of her hair and luxuriated in the feel of it against his chest.

He wanted to undo his pants and let the golden beauty of her hair cascade over his cock. He wanted to once again see it spread across the bed, interwoven with the raven black of his.

"We need to go to The Mission and the library," she said when the last dish was drying in the rack next to the sink. But she didn't move from his arms.

His cock pulsed in protest. His hands lingered at her waist. Images of pushing her pants down and bending her over the counter, as he thrust through gold satin and found heated ecstasy, invaded his thoughts—warred with images of urging her to her knees, of thrusting into her mouth as her hair wound around his legs and pooled at his feet like sunshine.

"I know," he said, forcing himself to step away from her.

A final shiver slid through Aisling. Somehow she managed to leave the kitchen instead of begging Zurael to touch her again.

Her vulva was swollen, the folds slick, but she knew the day needed to be faced and the task of finding the ones responsible for Ghost and the human sacrifices resumed. She went into the bedroom and gathered all of Henri's clothes. She returned to the kitchen only long enough to stuff them into a burlap bag, then went to the workroom and did the same with the clothes Zurael had stripped from her attacker.

"You're taking them to The Mission?" Zurael guessed from the doorway.

"Yes." At home nothing was wasted. Cloth was salvaged and reused until it eventually disintegrated.

He took the sack from her as she passed him, and the gesture made heat flare in her heart. Aziel waited at the front door. At her nod he climbed up to drape across her shoulders.

A quick touch to her front pockets confirmed that the bus pass and folded money were there. The sudden dampness of her palms revealed her nervousness about leaving the house after coming back to it and being attacked.

Zurael's hand cupped her cheek and forced her gaze to his. Heat flared again in her chest, not the hot burn of lust but something deeper, something that would leave a gaping, charred opening when he was gone from her life.

His thumb brushed across her mouth. "Trust me to protect you."

"I do."

It was several blocks to the bus stop. As they walked, Aisling could feel the eyes of her neighbors. Watching. Speculating. She wondered what Raisa had told them, if any of them had witnessed her assailant letting himself into the house, if they'd also taken note he never left it.

The bus was old, a belching shell of salvaged metal and parts. The woman driver squinted when she noticed Aziel. "Keep him under control or I'll put you off," she said as Aisling ran the card

Father Ursu had given her through the slot twice, worried as she did so that he'd get a record of it and know she didn't travel alone.

They walked past cages full of squawking chickens to claim vacant seats at the back of the bus. A dog barked from the arms of an elderly woman. A young boy turned, talked excitedly to his mother and pointed to Aziel while the other passengers averted their eyes.

It was a long trip to The Mission, not because of the distance but because of the number of stops the bus made. They traveled past the church, past the library, skirted the edges of places where the wealthy lived, before entering a section where the poorest of the poor lived.

The bus stopped. Its driver announced they were at the route's end point.

Only Aisling and Zurael remained. As soon as they were clear of the doors, the bus drove away.

Few signposts stood. Aisling was thankful The Mission's location appeared on the map Father Ursu had given her. Without a word, Zurael passed her the sack of clothing so both of his hands would be free. They began walking toward the bay, then along its edges.

Houses huddled together in clusters, like tiny outposts of civilization reclaimed from the horror of the past. Rubble, burned-out buildings and cars, blackened remains, all crawling with heavy vines, separated one group of salvaged buildings from the next.

In theory, any abandoned property was up for grabs, belonged to whoever was willing to restore and defend it. Aisling doubted the reality here differed from the one in Stockton. There would always be the rich preying on the poor, the strong bullying the weak, demanding payment or tribute.

Closer to the center of town, the reclaimed trucking depots and docks along the bay were guarded by men carrying machine guns, just as the waiting warehouses and the incoming boats were guarded, escorts standing ready to protect the cargo. At the outskirts of town, residents took their chances against human and supernatural predators alike.

Aisling knew they were nearing The Mission when she saw the children along the banks, manning a long row of crude fishing poles. They wore rags, but they laughed and teased, played tag and threw a ball, stopped occasionally to check the lines or pull a struggling fish from the water.

A wave of homesickness washed through her at the sight of them. The work of survival was different on the farm. But the joy of having food and shelter, family though few were related by blood, erased the sting of having been abandoned and chased the dark shadows of fear away.

Determination and resolve returned to her in a rush. Regardless of what it cost her, she wouldn't allow the future she'd seen in the spiritlands. She wouldn't allow her family to be slaughtered.

The laughter of the children slowly subsided as she and Zurael drew near. Some of them gathered in small groups to watch the two of them pass, while others turned their backs. Their expressions ran the gamut—fear, suspicion, weary indifference. Hope. Several started forward, only to be caught and pulled back by those near them.

Next to her Zurael stiffened, as if unused to the attention of so many children, but Aisling didn't have time to question him. Her attention was drawn to The Mission's front door.

A woman was hurrying away, leaving a toddler behind. The child screamed and cried, tried to follow, but its tiny wrist was tethered to an iron railing by a strip of cloth.

Pain radiated through Aisling's heart. A knot formed in her throat as she rushed forward. The front door opened just as she knelt in front of the devastated child.

Aisling spared a glance, saw an older woman and a teenage girl, but concentrated her efforts on freeing the child from its tether. When it was done the teenage girl took up the abandoned toddler and disappeared inside.

The older woman said, "That child won't be free to adopt for a month, maybe longer. I like to give the parents a chance to change their minds." Her attention was on the spot where the mother had disappeared from sight. She turned her head and looked at Aisling, then Zurael. "There are plenty of other children here in need of homes. You'll need references, and there are fees to be paid. The ones to the government aren't negotiable, but the ones to help keep The Mission going are. Proof of marriage is optional. Proof of residency isn't."

"We aren't here to adopt," Aisling said, remembering the burlap sack she'd dropped in her haste to free the screaming toddler. She picked it up and offered it the woman. "I thought you could find a use for the material."

The woman took the bag, opened it and nodded. "Come inside then. I've got enough time to give you a quick tour. I'm Davida."

"I'm Aisling."

Davida's glance sharpened when Aisling didn't offer Zurael's name and he didn't introduce himself. But a slight shrug indicated it wasn't important to her.

"The Mission got its name before The Last War," Davida said. "It was a homeless shelter originally, then later a drug rehabilitation center. During the war it was a church. At the start of the plague it was a place to bring the dying. Now it's a place for the children. The guardsmen and police come this far, but they don't go farther—into The Barrens—unless they're hunting. Sometimes children find their way here from The Barrens. Sometimes parents bring them. But just as many come from the other direction, from people barely surviving on the work they can find in Oakland."

Inside the building it was hushed but not quiet. Girls of all ages worked at household chores, talking quietly among themselves.

"We try to teach them what life skills we can," Davida said, entering a room where girls and boys alike were sewing clothing and patchwork blankets. She opened the burlap sack and dumped its contents onto a table.

Aisling said, "Keep the bag if you've got a use for it," and it joined the pile.

The next room was the nursery. They stopped beside a table

where a teenage girl was in the process of changing the diaper of a newborn. "He was left at dusk last night," Davida said.

Aisling's throat tightened painfully with thoughts of her abandonment on Geneva's doorstep. It'd been at the edge of dark, just before the final check on the livestock and barring of the doors.

There'd been others abandoned, before and after her, but none had been left in the moments before the predators claimed the night. Later, when Aisling's supernatural gifts began to emerge, Geneva said she was relieved. Given the time of Aisling's arrival on her doorstep, she'd feared Aisling would turn out to be a shapeshifter and put them all in mortal danger.

Aisling reached out and took the infant's tiny hand in hers. So small. So helpless. "Will you find a home for him?"

"I don't know. There are too many children. It's a struggle to feed and clothe them. And ultimately, despite what moral training we provide, far too many of them return to the streets when they get older. They disappear into The Barrens and join gangs of lawbreakers, only to end up hunted by the guardsmen.

"If only there were fewer children. I try to make sure the ones who are adopted, all of them, but the small ones in particular, go where they'll be treated well and cared for. But it's hard. There are days . . ."

Davida sounded tired, defeated. She shrugged and turned away. "At least I don't have to deal with the ones who aren't normal. The police come for those."

A chill of horror spiked through Aisling. "What do you mean?"

"Some of the children come to us damaged beyond our ability to cope with them. Brain damaged, physically damaged. Some are already more like wild animals than humans."

"Gifted?" Aisling asked, forcing the word out as she remembered how difficult some of those taken in by Geneva had been at first.

"Is that what you call it?" Davida's voice held a certain chill. "No, that's one good thing I'll say for those who've been cursed, they take care of their own."

"What do the police do with the children you send them?" Zurael asked, speaking for the first time.

Davida spared him a glance. "I don't ask."

The toddler abandoned minutes before their arrival was still screaming as they entered the next room. From the clothing, Aisling thought the child was most likely a little girl. She'd been set on the floor among wooden blocks and other children, but it was no consolation. A teenage boy and girl monitored the children while cleaning household items that looked as though they'd been salvaged from a long-abandoned home.

An open doorway led to a small fenced yard. Colorful balls littered the lawn in front of a large sandbox where several young children played.

Aziel stirred from his position on Aisling's shoulder. His head lifted, and some of the children in the room squealed with the realization he was a live animal.

Soft chirps and the direction of his gaze told Aisling he'd found something of interest in the small yard. When he would have slid from her shoulder, Davida's frown warned it wasn't acceptable.

Aisling saw the instant Davida stiffened and could guess at the direction of her thoughts—that she was in the presence of one of the cursed and Aziel was a witch's animal familiar.

"What section of Oakland do you live in?" Davida asked, confirming Aisling's suspicions.

She tried to deflect Davida by saying, "I'm new to Oakland. Until a few days ago, when Father Ursu came to get me, I lived with my family in Stockton. Does the Church offer assistance?"

"Occasionally."

Aisling breathed a sigh of relief when another woman stopped in the doorway and summoned Davida for a discussion.

Aziel dug his claws into her shirt, reminding her of his interest in something outside. A quick glance at Davida and Aisling went into the play yard.

The ferret wasted no time. He jumped from her shoulder and raced to the sandbox.

Aisling followed, and as soon as she saw the crude sigils a tiny blond girl was drawing in the sand, she knew immediately what Aziel had wanted her to see. He didn't resist when she scooped him up and placed him on her shoulder.

The sight of the symbols brought a lump to Aisling's throat. She pictured her youngest sister. She'd been about the same age as the child now studying Aziel intently when she'd begun scribbling similar sigils. Three years later, when she turned seven, it had become apparent she had a witch's innate talent.

Aisling knelt and casually smoothed the sand to erase the symbols. The braver children began petting Aziel, while the more timid hung back.

If only she could get the little girl to Geneva. But even as she thought it and pictured the pouch of silver coins she'd gotten from Elena, Aisling knew it was impossible.

Travel was expensive and dangerous. There were men and women who'd think nothing of taking her money then claiming afterward that the child had been accidentally killed en route.

Aisling's heart ached at the thought of leaving the little girl, of not being able to do anything immediately, or make any promises. But given Davida's coolness toward the gifted, she didn't dare say anything about the child. And even if she could produce the necessary paperwork, Aisling knew she was in no position to adopt the little girl. Her own future was uncertain, threatened, and though she refused to dwell on it and live in terror, she'd known when she agreed to the task in the spiritlands that it might lead to her death.

Still, hope settled in Aisling's heart. If what Davida said was true, and the gifted took care of their own, then she would find a home for the child if she had to visit every house in the area set aside for those with otherworldly talents.

"What are your names?" Aisling asked, careful not to show a

particular interest in any of the children though she tried to memorize every distinguishing feature of the undiscovered witch.

Zurael crouched next to her, studying the children intently as one by one they gave their names. The little girl was Anya.

Curiosity made Aisling turn to him and say, "You seem fascinated by them."

His eyes met hers and her breath caught at the burning fury in them. His arm made a sweeping gesture encompassing the children not only in the sandbox but in the building and manning the fishing poles along the water. "In the place I call home, the birth of a single child is call for a kingdom's celebration. And here—it is wasted on those created of mud. Like the earth they walk on and the air they breathe, they aren't worthy of what they've gained."

Davida appeared in the doorway before Aisling could think of anything to say. Rather than linger with the children and risk revealing her interest in Anya, Aisling rose to her feet.

"Sorry for the interruption," Davida said. "Let me finish showing you around."

Workrooms followed. Then crowded dormitory rooms and a kitchen connected to a dining area.

As they walked back to the front door, Aisling said, "In Stockton, lawbreakers are tattooed, but since coming to Oakland I've seen both a man and a woman branded with the sign of the cross. What are they guilty of?"

Davida laughed. "Only of being devout in their faith. They belong to the Fellowship of the Sign. Its members have carved out a community in The Barrens, or beyond. Several I thought lost eventually found their way to God when they were taken in by the Fellowship. They come back to help occasionally. And when the number of adults in the community expands, they offer a home for some of the children."

"You've visited their community?" Aisling asked.

"No. I've had to act on faith that I'm doing what's right for the children."

They reached the front door and were ushered out.

The worst of Zurael's rage faded as they distanced themselves from The Mission. It cooled with the need to remain vigilant.

"You did well in drawing her out," he said as they passed the clusters of houses separated by remnants of destruction and nature's reclaiming of the land.

Aisling glanced up at him, her eyes troubled. "I didn't ask about Ghost or whether people have gone missing in this area, too."

"I doubt Davida would have anything to offer about either. It's better you left those questions unasked and didn't alert her to your true interest in the Fellowship of the Sign."

"How are we going to find their community or get there without trusting Father Ursu or Elena?"

Zurael chuckled. His hand curled around her arm and he stopped walking, turning her to him as he did. "Do you think the wings I've worn in your presence are useless except for show and defense? Do you think I'm limited to only the forms you've seen so far? If necessary we'll search The Barrens and beyond."

"You can fly?" she asked, making him groan when her hand settled on his chest.

"Of course, but first we'll try to get a better idea of where to look for the Fellowship's compound. And tonight, I will do a preliminary search of The Barrens."

Zurael covered her hand with his and tormented himself by guiding it beneath his shirt to a male nipple hardened by the desire that needed only a touch, a look from her to flare to life. He closed his eyes when she rubbed her palm over puckered, sensitive flesh. He knew he had no one to blame but himself for the throbbing ache in his cock and the fiery need coursing through his bloodstream.

"Aisling." It was warning and plea, curse and benediction.

A soft feminine mouth pressed to his, shocking him, tempting him nearly beyond reason. He jerked away, stepped back. Only the deeply ingrained training that came with being his father's son, a prince in the House of the Serpent, kept him from responding to her overture, from parting his lips, taking what she offered and returning it, sharing breath and spirit with her.

She pulled away from him and resumed walking, but not before he saw the hurt in her eyes, the tremble of pain that spiked through her the same way it did him when he witnessed it. He wanted to grab her arm and haul her back into his, to finish what she'd unknowingly started, or if not, then to explain how dangerously he already cared for her.

Zurael remembered too well standing in the Hall of History, then taking tea in the House of the Spider, unable to hide the lust she'd inspired in him from those he was with. Fear permeated every cell when he thought about an assassin from the House of the Scorpion being sent for Aisling after the tablet was reclaimed. He could keep her safe from the Djinn if Malahel and Iyar stood with him, if The Prince agreed. But if they knew how thoroughly she'd ensnared him . . .

Zurael allowed her to put physical and emotional distance between them. It wouldn't last. Just as he'd catch up to her once they reached the bus stop, the wall of hurt separating them would fall under the onslaught of passion as soon as they touched again.

Aisling pulled the silence around her like a protective blanket. She willed herself to concentrate on the scenery she passed as she walked to the bus stop, on the tasks in front of her as she got onto the bus, anything but Zurael.

How often had she told herself to deny the desire? To fight the attraction? It was a mistake to accept more than his protection and aid, to continue allowing him access to her body.

For comfort she plucked Aziel from her shoulder and cuddled him against her chest. "As soon as we get back to the house, I'll see what I can do about finding a place for Anya," she said, rubbing her cheek against his soft fur before restoring him to his usual spot.

She sighed in relief when the bus stopped in front of the library and she escaped the close confinement. Zurael followed her into the building, seemed content to let her take the lead. But then this was her world, not his.

Some of the tension eased from Aisling as she looked around. Surprise made her gape when she saw the row of computers against one wall, each one claimed by a citizen sitting on a stool.

The entire space labeled "library" was hardly bigger than the shaman's house she now called home. It held few books; those she could easily see were set aside in an area enclosed by short walls so children could be contained and kept away from the racks of magazines and newspapers.

Aisling browsed the magazines on her way to the newspapers. Most were about cooking or construction, salvage and reclamation of the land, crafts and gardening, practical topics, though a few dealt with beauty and fashion, sports and the pleasures only the rich could afford.

The newspapers were all local. Oakland. San Francisco. San Jose. There were editions going back several weeks. She spared a glance at Zurael. "Can you read them?"

His expression became one of dark amusement. "Of course." And despite the fact that he was the one who'd shunned her touch and sent pain crashing through her, he leaned forward and lightly scraped his fingernails against her neck in a subtle reminder of his talons. "I don't spend all of my time lost in fantasies of retribution."

She looked away from him. Knew he wouldn't miss the tight points of her nipples against her shirt. But she refused to let him see desire in her eyes. "We should start with the Oakland papers. I'll take today's."

Aisling didn't wait for him to answer. She rummaged through the papers on a table and quickly found what she was looking for, then retreated to a chair away from the other patrons.

Within minutes she felt chilled to the core at what she'd discovered. A touch to Zurael's thigh and he leaned over to read the article about a body found in an area plagued with violence.

Final Judgment For Another Sinner! the story caption proclaimed above a picture of a partially savaged man lying among rubble. A smaller insert showed the brands on his hands.

The damage done to him by nighttime predators was severe enough to make cause of death unclear, but then that wasn't of interest and the reporter made no apologies. It was the brands that fascinated, that provided shock value and titillation for the reader.

Aisling shivered as she looked at the insert of the hands and overlaid them with the symbols Elena had traced on the coffee table in tea, the ones she'd drawn for Aubrey the previous night at the occult shop. They were the same. And the punishment brands burned into his flesh were for a crime she was equally guilty of, for summoning a demon, for lying with one.

Zurael's lips against her ear distracted her from the downward spiral of her thoughts. "I will kill anyone who threatens you," he said, the heat of his breath no match against the deep chill inside her, his promise feeding her fear of punishment, not reducing it.

Aziel made his presence known. He slid from her shoulder far enough for his front feet to find the pouch hidden underneath her shirt. His weight pressed the fetishes against her chest in a reminder she had powerful allies.

Aisling closed her eyes. She forced the fear away. If she was going to save her family, she couldn't worry about her own fate.

"What's been done can't be undone," she murmured, stroking Aziel's soft fur then repositioning him on her shoulder before resuming her search through the newspapers.

It was Zurael who found the next item of interest. Aisling immediately recognized the man pictured, just as she remembered his words at Sinners. *You'll find it far more entertaining to vote her out with the others. She's a shamaness.*

Her stomach knotted when she learned Peter Germaine was a man of power—a deputy police chief, the brother of the mayor— and no friend to any human who'd been graced with otherworldly abilities.

"Interesting," Zurael said. "Did he want you dead because he knew you located his brother's lover? Or did he influence the others because he hates and fears those with gifts he doesn't have? Perhaps my curiosity will get the better of me and I'll hesitate long enough to ask him before I mete out the punishment he deserves."

There was no heat in Zurael's voice, no passion. He might have been talking about plans to weed a garden or clean livestock stalls.

Aisling opened her mouth to protest his casualness, to argue against what he planned, but the words remained trapped in her throat. The images Elena's brother had conjured in the spiritlands drifted into her thoughts on icy winds—the hollow-eyed Ghosters standing in front of Sinners, their attention focused on her, their faces undamaged though their bodies were ripped, torn so organs hung and wet bones gleamed.

Your work? I'm sure they had it coming to them, but what a way to go, John had mocked. And she couldn't bring herself to tell Zurael she didn't want him to kill the man who'd so casually suggested she be put out into the predator-filled night.

She shivered. The icy winds settled around her heart like heavy weights as she worried about the corruption of her soul, the ease in which she accepted the slaughter of a human unable to protect himself against a being like Zurael.

Did it prove she was half demon? Her father's daughter? Or did it only mean that in summoning Zurael, in coupling with him, in coming to—care for him—that the humanity to be measured and judged when she entered the spiritlands the final time was leaching away?

Aisling ducked her head and resumed looking through the paper on her lap. She filled her mind with information as she scanned articles about her new city.

Geneva and the farm seemed a lifetime away. A world away. And by the time she came across a picture of the man and woman in red, Aisling wondered if she could truly return to a place where her gift had to be hidden.

Like Peter Germaine, Felipe Glass, the man in red, was involved in law enforcement. He was in charge of the guardsmen, powerful in his own right but also wealthy. Aisling wouldn't have been surprised to learn the woman in red was a mistress, but found she was Felipe's wife, Ilka, the daughter of a founding family.

It helped having names for those faces at Sinners. Aisling doubted they had anything to do with Ghost or the black masses, but she felt better knowing who they were, even if it only confirmed a belief she'd held all her life: The police and the guardsmen couldn't be trusted.

She passed the newspaper to Zurael without comment and continued through those remaining. There was no mention of Ghost, no mention of the Fellowship of the Sign in any of them.

"You're tired and hungry," Zurael said when they'd reached the end of the stack. His voice was as caressing as the knuckles he stroked across her cheek. "Let's get something to eat."

There were restaurants and food stalls across the street. Aisling touched her pocket and felt the folded money there. The craving for fresh fruit, for bread and cheese, rose and made her mouth water. She fought it, told herself not to waste the money, but an internal voice overrode her long-ingrained frugality. It reminded her that some of the bills in her pocket had probably been paid to her assailant to bring about death, whispered that she should use it to sustain life.

They were nearing the door when one of the patrons left his spot in front of a computer. Aisling slowed. She looked longingly at the machines capable of housing huge libraries of information, and which had once been so commonplace even children owned and used them.

"Do you know how to use one?" she asked Zurael.

"No. There is no power to run technology such as this in the place I call home."

Aisling rubbed her palms against her pants and approached the available machine. In the days before The Last War there'd been satellites and land networks allowing for instant communication using computers. Children no longer used books in school, and rarely used pencil and paper, just as the majority of people paid for everything through accounts accessed by magnetic cards like the one she'd used on the bus, instead of using cash.

Relying on technology to such an extent was a foreign notion, intimidating. Yet the possibility of having so much knowledge readily available was exhilarating.

The young librarian who'd been stationed behind the counter stopped next to them. "Do you need some help? Please say you do. I've got hours left on my shift and am going a little crazy just sitting around reading magazines."

"I've never used a computer before," Aisling admitted.

"It's easy. You'll be a pro in minutes. Take a seat. I'm Cassandra, by the way."

"I'm Aisling."

She sat and felt even more intimidated in such close proximity to the screen and keyboard.

"Don't panic!" Cassandra said with a laugh. "Don't freeze up. Believe me, this is simple. Child's play. They say before The Last War toddlers used to learn their alphabet and numbers by playing computer games. Believe me, you'll wonder why you haven't been a regular library visitor. This is your first time here, right?"

"Yes."

"I thought so. It won't be your last. You probably noticed how often there's a waiting line for the computers. Hopefully we'll be getting more of them soon."

Cassandra leaned over and touched the sole icon on the screen. "Okay. Here's the big picture. We're on a limited local area network. What that means is enough cable has been salvaged so computers like these, and the ones owned privately, are connected to huge computers where information is stored. What's stored in the mega computers is stuff like news, books that have been input, you name it. Content depends on who owns the huge computers, so take what you read with a grain of salt. Are you new to town, or just to the library?"

"I've only been here a few days," Aisling said.

"Do you like it?"

Aisling's earlier thoughts returned, along with the unsettling realization that she could no longer see herself content with the life she'd lived in the San Joaquin. True, there was violence and prejudice here, the powerful preying on the weak, but there was also freedom and the opportunity to openly use her gift to help others.

"Life here is different from anything I've ever know. But yes, I think I could come to like it very much."

"Where are you staying?"

Aisling hesitated only a second. "In the area reserved for those with special talents."

"Cool! Let me guess . . ." Cassandra tilted her head. "Witch, warlock and ferret familiar?"

Aisling laughed, though a blush rose in her face. "Shamaness. Friend. And pet."

"Even cooler." Cassandra turned to the computer in front of them. "Okay, back to work. The easiest way to find what you're looking for is to type in a word or a couple of words and do a search. Now, hand on the mouse, and I'll walk you through it."

Aisling put her hand on the "mouse" and was absolutely amazed at the world that opened up by her doing so. True to Cassandra's words, within minutes she wondered why she'd ever felt overwhelmed by such simple technology.

"I think you're good to go now," Cassandra said, stepping back and beaming with satisfaction. "I'll leave you to it. Shout out if you hit a snag."

"I will," Aisling said, waiting just long enough for Cassandra to move away before typing in *Fellowship of the Sign*.

Only a few references, *links* Cassandra had called them, came up. When Aisling followed them, they didn't provide any more information than what she'd already learned from Davida at The Mission.

She typed in *Ghost* and was immediately overwhelmed with possibilities, all of them connected to sightings of spirits or old-fashioned horror stories. And even after she'd added and subtracted words as

Cassandra had demonstrated, there were no references to the substance called Ghost.

Aisling closed the browser and stood. Despite not finding anything about Ghost or the Fellowship of the Sign, she felt exhilarated, empowered in a way she couldn't completely put into words.

Zurael's chuckle and the warmth she saw his eyes only increased
her sense of accomplishment. "I'm impressed," he said, and the liquid heat in his voice found its way to her breasts and cunt.

She glanced away quickly. "Ready to eat?"

"Yes."

They went across the street, to a food stall serving soup and salad.
Aisling's euphoria over mastering the computer lasted until she saw
Cassandra leave the library and enter the building next to it. Fear and
worry edged in, with the memory of Raisa saying the library was
next door to the building housing the police and guardsmen.

A deep sadness invaded Aisling's soul at being presented with
evidence of how dangerous it was to trust, at having been so foolish
as to set aside a lifetime of caution. She'd been as easy to question
as a child, had casually revealed enough information to lead the authorities to her, and had never wondered whether the computer would
save the contents of her search after she'd closed the browser.

"Your world is far more treacherous than mine," Zurael said,
pulling her back against his front, surrounding her with his heat, his
strength. He gave her the security she craved but made her consider
again the ease with which her humanity was leaching away—as time
and time again she found what she needed in a demon's arms.

Eleven

AISLING studied the witches' home from the safety of the cracked and broken sidewalk. Elaborate sigils were carved into the door and the window frames as well as the posts marking the front corners of the yard.

A short wrought-iron fence stood guard against the fey in a not so subtle warning. And though Aisling wasn't magic sensitive, as some of the gifted were, she could feel the ley line humming through the souls of her feet, rising from the depths like a great whale close to breaching the surface of the ocean.

Tamara might have claimed her family didn't practice black magic, but Aisling knew the Wainwrights were more than witches whose craft was tied to the elements and their goddess. At least some of them would be sorceresses, able to pull on the rich power pulsing through the ley line their house sat on.

Instinctively her fingers curled around the fetish pouch beneath her shirt. She glanced at Zurael and thought about returning from her trip into the spiritlands to find Tamara's face tight with fear and her arms wrapped protectively around her swollen belly. At the time she'd attributed Tamara's reaction to Zurael's unexpected arrival and the menace radiating from him; now she wondered if Tamara had guessed what he was.

"I don't think it's safe for you to come with me," Aisling said. "I haven't got an affinity for spell magic, but I can feel a ley line close to the surface here. It's strong enough to power any number of entrapment or revelation spells."

Aziel nuzzled the side of her face in approval, then surprised her by jumping from her shoulder to Zurael's, the unusual behavior making her wonder again about Aziel's true purpose in giving her Zurael's name.

"I can feel the line as well," Zurael said, accepting the ferret's presence without comment. "You won't linger?"

"As soon as I tell them about the child at The Mission and either get their promise to retrieve Anya or the name of someone else to talk to about her, I'll leave."

"Your pet and I will wait out here then."

Aisling pushed through the wrought-iron gate and walked to the front door. The decision to come here for help was an easy one to make. The only other gifted person she'd met since moving into the shaman's house was Raisa. And given Father Ursu's arrival minutes after Raisa's departure and then the attacker who'd been waiting later, Aisling wasn't prepared to trust the tearoom owner.

A thick brass gargoyle with a ring held in its mouth served as a door knocker. An older version of Tamara responded to Aisling's use of it. She studied Aisling for only a second before looking past her and smiling slightly. "You must be Aisling. I'm Annalise, Tamara's mother. She's unavailable at the moment. Can I help you?"

"I hope so. I'm here about a child who needs a home."

Dark eyebrows rose, the smile widened. Ice slid down Aisling's spine with the impression that she'd been expected.

Annalise stepped out of the doorway and confirmed Aisling's suspicion by saying, "Come in. Levanna is waiting in the parlor."

The inside of the house reminded Aisling of the luxury she'd found at the church, though the prewar artwork gracing the walls or residing on polished wooden furniture would have been viewed as sinful and destroyed if it had come into the hands of the religious. Naked men and woman danced and worshipped. They coupled in rites of fertility, their faces and bodies full of emotion and life.

"Ah, the shamaness is here," Levanna said from the couch, her voice strong despite the frailty of a body shrunken and bent by age.

She wore a long black dress and was kept warm by a fringed shawl draped over boney shoulders. Her hair was silver, her eyes made sightless by cataracts, though Aisling imagined the Wainwright matriarch hadn't needed them to see for a long time.

Annalise sat on the couch next to Levanna while Aisling claimed a chair across from them. "Tell us about the child," Annalise said, and Aisling did, tracing on the coffee table the symbols she'd seen Anya draw in the sand and feeling relief when Annalise nodded, recognizing their importance.

"It's good you came to us about her," Levanna said. Her hand went to the spot where the ends of the black shawl overlapped, her fingers caressing the amulets and charms she wore. "It's too late to retrieve Anya today, but first thing tomorrow we'll send someone in good standing with the authorities to get her. We can ensure she has a good home, if not with us then with others who will attend to her training and care."

Cataract-blinded eyes met Aisling's as Levanna's hand fell away from her shawl to reveal a pendant. The gold sun caught and held Aisling's attention. Tendrils of awe and dread slid through her like whispers too faint to hear, knowledge just out of reach.

Annalise freed her from the amulet's fascination by saying, "Tamara told us about her visit with you and why the Church brought you to Oakland. She confessed what she asked of you. I'm not surprised the father of her child met the end he did. He was like a lot of the rich younger sons who've taken to dabbling in magic and lost their lives because of it. You've heard a male sex witch has disappeared?"

"No. Raisa came by my house yesterday and introduced herself. She didn't tell me about the sex witch, but she told me a governess went missing."

"We heard about that as well. The governess wasn't one of us, though we're making inquiries," Annalise said. "We don't know the details of the witch's disappearance yet. His family hasn't come to us or asked for aid, but others have told us he went missing, along with the son of his wealthy patroness."

Levanna leaned forward abruptly and the golden sun swung toward Aisling, making her breath catch involuntarily though there was no logical reason for her to react to the pendant.

"In my dreams I saw a dark priest and his followers slaughtered by a powerful demon," Levanna said. "If you're not careful, you'll meet the same end as Henri and the vampire's shaman. There are beings of absolute evil trying to break into this world and reclaim it. But despite our efforts and allies we haven't been able to find the human servants who call those beings master."

Aisling's breath froze in her lungs. After trusting Cassandra so readily at the library, she didn't dare risk making the same mistake by acknowledging what happened the night she'd gone into the ghostlands to find Elena. "Do you know what happened to the vampire's shaman?" she asked instead.

"He was not a powerful shaman, yet his screams lingered and echoed in a nightmare shared by many of us with talents that brush against the spiritlands," Levanna said, subtly acknowledging she was more than a witch who practiced nature-based magic. She settled against the back of the couch once again and tilted her head slightly toward Annalise. "Only my granddaughter saw anything of his passing."

"He was strapped to a bed in a cold basement room of the church," Annalise said. "Bishop Routledge was there, as was Father Ursu. There was only a sliver of awareness between his waking and finding himself there, and when they anointed him with Ghost and told him to seek its source. That's all I saw before the screaming began."

Zurael's words whispered in Aisling's thoughts. *No one is beyond suspicion.*

They were followed by John's taunt in the ghostlands. *I see they've sent a sacrificial lamb. Or maybe that's Elena's role. Then again, maybe third time's the charm.*

Elena's visit and the pouch full of coins took on a new meaning, making Aisling wonder if the Church had played a role in her abduction, if the man branded for summoning and lying with a demon had repented his sins and sought penance from the Church, only to be disposed of when it was done.

Aisling didn't think it was likely that there were two men wearing the same brands. She didn't think it was a coincidence he'd been killed.

She shuddered, glad she hadn't gone to Father Ursu with questions about the Ghost seller. "Do the vampires know what happened to their shaman?"

Levanna said, "Those in power know. But they bide their time and pretend ignorance. If the Church has suspicions about who is behind the creation of Ghost, then it's someone they're afraid to act openly against.

"The vampires are content for the moment to let the Church's game play out. If the barrier between our world and the spirit world breaks down because of Ghost, then the humans without gifts will once again fear those of us who have them. Their fear will lead to blame and to violence, both of which will soon spill over to the vampires as the Church and its allies are given an excuse to claim the wealth accumulated in San Francisco."

Aisling nodded in understanding. Stockton and the surrounding areas had come under Church and non-gifted human control because of violence waged as a result of fear and blame. It'd happened long before she was born, when a wave of disease killed children by the dozens.

Weres and vampires were hunted and slaughtered, blamed for carrying the sickness. Some of the gifted were killed as well, accused of creating the illness through magic or for harboring the supernaturals responsible for it.

Levanna's hand lifted to the sun pendant and drew Aisling's eye. "You should return home in case the family of the young sex witch comes to you on his behalf. Travel carefully. We will send word tomorrow when the child has been retrieved from The Mission."

Aisling took her cue and left.

"You had a successful visit?" Zurael asked as Aziel launched himself from his shoulder to hers.

"Yes."

Aisling told him what had transpired with the Wainwright witches as they walked toward her house. When they rounded the corner, they saw Raisa waiting there with a young woman.

"I don't like this," Zurael said. "We don't know where Raisa's loyalties lie. If this is about the missing sex witch, it could be a trap set for you in the spiritlands."

Aisling shivered as Levanna's warnings slid down her spine like ice. "I'll be careful."

"You'll turn them away without offering your services."

She stopped and he turned to face her. Strength of purpose gave Aisling the courage to stand up to him. "I'll listen to what they say and make my own decision."

"More is at stake here than some stranger's life," he said, fury in his eyes.

Feminine intuition guided her actions, steered her away from anger and hurt. She placed her palms on his chest and felt the wild, fast beat of his heart. He was worried for her, afraid. "I know what's at stake. But I'm not without protectors in the spiritlands. Trust me."

The anger fled from his expression. His hands framed her face. "I already trust you far more than is wise or safe for either of us."

She wanted to lean into him, to wrap her arms around his waist and press against his hardened body. She wanted . . . impossible things, even if there'd been time to pursue them.

"They're watching," she whispered. "They're waiting."

Zurael released her and they continued to the house.

"This is a neighbor, Nicholette," Raisa said in greeting. "Her brother is missing."

Dark smudges underneath light brown eyes gave Nicholette a bruised, fragile appearance but didn't diminish her beauty. Her hand trembled slightly when she took Aisling's. "We're new here and I can't offer much in the way of payment, but I'll give you whatever I can if you'll . . ." Her lips trembled. "Please, can you find Nicholas?"

"Your brother is the missing sex witch?" Aisling asked.

"Yes. He's also my twin." Delicate fingers tangled and twisted in strands of wavy brown hair.

Aziel's sharp claws slid through the fabric of Aisling's shirt. She said, "Let's go inside and you can tell me what you know."

When they were seated, Nicholette said, "My brother was with a client last night. It was an overnight visit, not the first with this woman, though all the others were . . . spontaneous . . . or at least he didn't go to her home intending to stay."

"But last night he intended to stay," Aisling said.

"Yes. He'd scheduled the visit." Nicholette glanced down, smoothed her hands over the bold flowers captured in the material of her dress. "Some clients are easier to . . . serve than others. He expected to return shortly after dawn. He scheduled another appointment at noon."

So he'd have an excuse to leave.

The words hovered unspoken in the air. Aisling's stomach tensed at the thought of intimacy, of engaging in the sexual act with someone she didn't care for.

There were places where all sex witches were labeled prostitutes. Just as there were practitioners who were non-gifted humans making a living selling sex. But true sex magic was powerful, and those born with the ability to wield it were as talented as any healer, as holy as any priest or priestess called to serve a fertility deity.

"Nicholas didn't return from his overnight visit," Aisling said.

"No." Haunted eyes met hers. "I thought he'd been delayed. His client . . . She's very demanding and not used to being denied. We have no telephone. Noon came and went. With each hour I felt more anxious. Finally, I went to his client's house. Things were in an uproar there. One of the family cars was found abandoned shortly before noon. There was blood on the seat." Huge tears welled up and spilled down Nicholette's cheeks. "She has a son, older than Nicholas and me. This morning her son offered to drive Nicholas home in exchange for using the car. They left just after dawn."

Aziel slid from Aisling's shoulder and shocked her by scrambling across the coffee table to settle on Nicholette's lap. Nicholette gave a watery smile, busied trembling hands by stroking his fur.

"What area of town?" Aisling asked, hating that she felt a touch of jealousy at Aziel's defection, hating the hint of insecurity that made her glance at Zurael to see if he, too, wanted to go to Nicholette and offer comfort.

"The car was found on Rhine Street," Nicholette said.

Petty emotion gave way to icy chill. It couldn't be a coincidence. Nicholas was taken to serve as bait in a different kind of trap, a direct challenge from someone who knew about the death of the dark priest and his acolytes on that same street.

"Can you find him?" Nicholette asked. She touched a delicate hand to her chest. "He's alive. I think I'd know if he weren't. But the disappearances . . . the deaths . . . Raisa said you found a wealthy man's mistress who was also taken. Will you help me?"

Nicholette's gaze slid to Zurael then back to Aisling. "My brother and I can pay you in a trade of services, or with fresh food. We've got a few chickens and a small garden."

Heat moved through Aisling's cheeks in acknowledgment of the
first offer, though she couldn't imagine any other lover than Zurael—or the need for one. A touch of homesickness spun through
her with thoughts of garden-fresh produce.

It was Aziel who decided her. Their eyes met and his communi-
cated a message as clearly as if they were in the spiritlands. He
wanted her to accept the task of looking for Nicholette's brother.

"I'll help you," Aisling said and felt Zurael stiffen next to her.
His displeasure was like a living flame reaching out to surround her
and steal the air from her lungs.

Aziel slid from Nicholette's lap and onto the floor. Aisling watched
as the ferret jumped onto a chair, then the eating table, raced across
the counter with seeming abandon and sent the saltshaker bouncing
to the floor and spilling white crystals as it rolled.

It was a message. Aisling couldn't be sure of its meaning. She
wouldn't know if she fully understood it until she was in the
spiritlands—and even then, confirmation would come only if she was
proven right or Aziel joined her and elected to communicate mind
to mind.

The magic in the living world wasn't readily accessible to her,
not in the way it was to witches or sorcerers or those with healing
gifts. She'd rarely been able to leave the ghostlands in an astral
state as she'd done the night she'd located Elena. But thinking back
on it now, comparing what she'd done that night to other times
when she'd been drawn back to the living world while traveling
outside her body, Aisling couldn't repress a shudder. In every in-
stance, a magic practitioner was involved, either performing a ritual or shoring up a curse—their acts thinning the barrier between
the world of the living and the dead. If Nicholas was still alive, she
would find him only if he was in the hands of a dark priest as Elena
had been.

Aisling's hand went to the hidden fetish pouch. Misgiving filled
her, worry that it was a trap.

Aziel returned to Nicholette and climbed onto her shoulder. He nuzzled her hair, her ear, and she laughed softly. "Is he always so affectionate?"

A tiny ache speared through Aisling's heart. On rare occasions Aziel had stoically allowed himself to be handled by some of the children in Geneva's home, but he'd never been demonstrative with anyone other than her.

"I don't know much about a shaman's craft," Nicholette said. "Will you look for Nicholas now?"

Aisling hesitated before answering, not wanting to reveal the limits of her gift. She could find Nicholas now if he were already dead, or she could find him alive but only if he were in the hands of someone using him to work magic, as she suspected. It wouldn't be a comfort to Nicholette to learn either.

"I'll have to wait until after dark."

Nicholette's face lost the color it'd gained because of Aziel's antics. Fear and worry returned with a tremor. "If you find him, there'll be no way for me to get to him. Maybe for his client's missing son, the police or guardsmen would go out in the night, but . . ." She glanced at the window, to the approaching dusk. "There's no time to get to his client's house."

Caution and compassion fought inside Aisling and struck a balance. She leaned forward, touched her hand to the back of Nicholette's. "I'll do what I can to find Nicholas and help him. Go home or stay with friends tonight, be with someone."

Aisling could read Nicholette's desire to remain. But she couldn't offer that comfort, and Nicholette didn't press, perhaps believing a shaman's magic required privacy similar to a sex witch's.

"Can I return at first light?" Nicholette asked, her hand trembling under Aisling's.

"Yes. Do you have something that belongs to Nicholas? Or something he's given you?"

Nicholette pulled her hand out from underneath Aisling's and unclasped a necklace. An entwined couple hung at the end of a thin chain, their sexual joining captured in jasper. "Nicholas wears an identical amulet. Our mother had them made for us. They were crafted from the same piece of stone since he and I are twins. I think this will be better than anything else I can give you."

Aisling took the necklace. And minutes later, her guests departed, hurrying to stay ahead of the darkness.

ZURAEL didn't like the jealousy burning in his veins. It was unfamiliar, uncomfortable, unwelcome. He'd known almost from the first that Aziel was more than he appeared, but witnessing the silent communication between Aisling and the ferret, how easily she let herself be guided by a creature whose true nature she didn't understand, had left him edgy, unsettled—feeling challenged—as if his possession of her was an illusion. He wanted to argue against Aisling searching for Nicholas—not because he hadn't been touched by Nicholette's distress, but because he knew it was a trap of some kind, and he couldn't protect Aisling in the spiritlands.

He studied the ferret sitting at Aisling's feet in the kitchen and waiting for her to finish preparing the meal. In his mind's eye he was once again in the House of the Spider, sitting before Malahel's altar and seeing the stones he'd cast.

Had one of them represented Aziel? Or did Aziel serve a greater power?

Zurael's attention shifted to Aisling. The fire burning through him intensified, jealousy yielding to something more primal and threatening to burn out of control.

Images of tethering her to the bed, of having her helpless, her world reduced to him and the pleasure he gave her, tempted him to abandon the course of action he'd set for himself. He closed the distance between them without intending to, pressed his hardened cock to the curve of her buttocks, only to be assaulted by different images, recaptured moments of taking her anally.

"You're trusting him with your life," Zurael said, his mouth finding the satin skin of her neck as his hands stroked up her sides then around to claim her breasts.

"I always have," Aisling said, but the huskiness of her voice and the way she softened against him kept the words from inflaming him further.

Zurael closed his eyes and fought the need pulsing through him. They didn't have time, not if he intended to make the most of the night by searching The Barrens, as he'd told her he intended to do after they'd left The Mission. Still, he hesitated over leaving her body unprotected while her spirit traveled in astral form.

He'd seen the protective sigils carved into the wood around her windows and doors, but they hadn't kept him out, wouldn't have protected her from death the first time he entered her home if killing her had remained his purpose. Few of the Djinn dabbled in spell craft, fewer still—if any—understood or used most of the magic wielded by human sorcerers and witches.

"I can search tomorrow night," he said.

"You might have to do that as well. Finding the Fellowship's compound is important. I'll be okay by myself tonight."

It was a show of weakness, an admission of the power she held over him, but Zurael couldn't force himself away from Aisling. He stroked her, placed kisses along her neck, held her against him while she prepared their meal, and only reluctantly released her so they could eat.

When the meal was done, he gathered her in his arms again, hungered and burned with the need to carry her into the bedroom and couple with her. "Promise me you'll be careful."

"I will be. Promise me the same."

Zurael laughed. "There's little I fear in this place." And for an instant he was trapped in the warmth of her concern, caught in angelite eyes and unfamiliar tenderness. But too soon it faded, replaced by a remembrance of rage and true terror, scenes of the dark priest and his acolytes. "Do not summon me."

"I won't," she whispered, shivering at the promise of death in his eyes, but he didn't offer comfort. If she summoned him while he was in her world, the angels would hear it and come.

Zurael stepped away from her. With a thought, he let flesh and blood, muscle and bone give up their shape, become the potential for a swirling wind before gathering, re-forming into an owl.

At Aisling's gasp of surprise and pleasure, Zurael spread his wings so she could further admire him. He allowed her touch and wasn't any more immune to her as an owl than he'd been in the serpent's form.

An owl-voiced protest escaped when she stopped stroking him. He watched with approval as she wrapped a burlap sack around her arm before offering him a place to perch.

Sharp talons dug into the material, touched her skin. He used his wings for balance so he wouldn't pierce her flesh as she lifted and carried him to the back door, offered him the night.

Zurael hesitated for an instant, torn between the urge to remain with her and the need to take flight. Finally, reluctantly, he launched himself from her arm and headed toward The Barrens.

What had taken a good part of their morning now took only a short time. He soon flew over The Mission, its doors locked and most of its windows dark.

There was no sign of human life close to the city, but the streets weren't empty. A flash of gray marked the presence of a lone were-wolf. Larger packs of feral dogs ran boldly through abandoned streets. Somewhere in the distance, a cougar—Were or pure animal—screamed.

Beneath the owl's wings, bats swooped on insects. Cats hunted for rats in blackened, fallen buildings while others yowled from the hoods of rusted cars, announcing their desire to mate.

The farther into The Barrens he traveled, the more nature dominated. Trees grew among rubble. Vines crawled over objects and sites no longer identifiable.

He looked for light, for fire. Listened for the sound of voices. He abandoned his task only when he required food in order to sustain flight. And in those moments he savored the hunt, the kill, relived the primitive beginnings of the Djinn when this land belonged only to them and they hunted it just as he was hunting it, in whatever form would bring success.

Thick forests of pine, juniper and oak rose and went on for miles. He banked and circled, knew the night wasn't long enough to search where leaves and darkness created an impenetrable shroud of secrecy.

The passing of time was marked by the way the light changed as stars were added to the sky and the moon traveled across it, by in the rising crescendo of insect song, the howling of wolves and yipping of coyotes.

He flew and perched. Waited and observed. Took flight again and again, until the sound of engines and gunfire exploded into the night, abruptly silencing all other noise and filling the air with the promise of unnatural violence.

The jeeps arrived moments later, four of them racing down parallel streets. Spotlights struck the sides of long-deserted buildings and patches of vegetation. Any movement caused a barrage of bullets, followed by whoops and hollers.

A feral dog lost its nerve and darted from underneath a burned-out car. Its body danced over cracked sidewalk long after it was dead.

"One confirmed kill! You got that?" a man yelled and radios crackled to life, each of them repeating, "One confirmed kill. Got it."

Hatred and fury roared through Zurael. He only barely suppressed the impulse to become a thing of human nightmare, a demon swooping from the sky to deliver terror-filled death to the guardsmen in the jeeps.

AISLING knelt in the shaman's workroom, laughing at Aziel's antics, enjoying the moment even as the time to enter the ghostlands approached. The ferret sat on top of a mound of salt, gleefully digging into the white granules and tossing them onto the floor underneath the table.

She'd assumed the heavy sack contained cheap stones used for making inexpensive amulets or fetishes. But when she entered the workroom, Aziel's chatter insisted she open the bag.

Have I been doing it wrong all along? she wondered, thinking on how Father Ursu had given her the bowl of salt the night she searched for Elena, and how Aziel had tossed those grains to the floor, too, subtly telling her she was to form a protective circle using them.

Aisling rose long enough to find a container, a can that had once contained peaches. She dumped the collection of polished stones it held on to the workbench, couldn't stop herself from remembering how she'd returned from her unwilling Ghost trip into the spirit-lands to find herself in this room, and how Zurael helped her to the kitchen, fed her peaches by hand. It was the beginning of her downfall, her seduction.

Aziel chattered urgently. He tossed more salt onto the floor, his movements shifting from playfulness to the beginnings of agitation, hinting that his uncharacteristic show of affection toward Nicholette was more than a means of communicating to Aisling that she should agree to search for Nicholas.

She knelt and filled the can full of salt then took her place on the dirt in the middle of the room. The ferret scrambled onto her lap. But when she would have traced protective sigils in the dirt as she cast a circle in salt, Aziel went completely still—his signal for her to stop and think, to consider past lessons—and she understood she needed to duplicate what she'd done the night she searched for Elena.

Do not summon me.

Zurael's earlier warning, the promise of death she'd read in his eyes, made her heart race just as surely as did the knowledge that she'd encounter another dark priest tonight. Only a lifetime of trusting Aziel gave her the courage to allow the spirit winds to rush through her, to pull her into the world of the dead.

When the ghost winds settled, Aisling welcomed the gray nothingness around her, the calm stillness requiring no action, no decision, no payment. It could last seconds, minutes, hours if she let it, and a part of her *wanted* to let it go on, but instead she lifted her hand and touched the necklace she'd gotten from Nicholette, let her fingers caress the entwined lovers carved from jasper.

Gray swirled and parted, allowing a familiar figure to step through, though it wasn't the one Aisling expected. Sinead's husky laugh filled the space around them, became the purr of a predator. "You'd prefer John?" she asked, touching the scarf tied around her neck, stroking the instrument of her death as she lightly tapped the crop she carried against her leg. "Oh, he's dabbled in the sex trade, if you can call taking money so guardsmen can have a little sport on their days off being part of the pleasure business."

Sinead glided forward, leather and perfume, crackling dominance. "Umm, a natural submissive," she said, circling Aisling, crowding her, making Aisling self-conscious of her nakedness in the ghostlands. "You'd be a fun one to train, but I don't think that's why you're here. Am I right?"

Aisling took the necklace off and held it between them. "I'm searching for a missing sex witch," she said, and the spirit winds rose, shimmered over the jasper and made it appear as though the man and woman writhed, their bodies glistening with sweat as they fucked.

Sinead licked her lips. "What a temptation. Who is she?"

"The witch I'm looking for is named Nicholas. This is his sister's necklace."

"A pity." Sinead tapped the crop against the leather of her pants. "A pity it's the brother and not the sister. But better for you." She closed her hand around the lovers trapped in jasper. Her eyes lost focus until a sly smile formed. "Oh my, this is a delicious turn of events. Karmic fate for those who have the luxury of believing in such things. I can take you to him. If we hurry you might even arrive before he's welcomed to this world." Sinead released the necklace and again licked her lips, made a show of caressing Aisling with her eyes. "It will, of course, cost you, and even here my time is valuable."

Aisling steeled herself against reacting to the blatant display. It was part of the bargaining process, something she'd learned early on. And because she knew that only those who lived fully in this realm could conceal themselves in clothing, she didn't wish to look down and find herself wearing it.

Sinead circled. Tapped the crop lightly on her leg. "I could do so much with you if you put yourself in my hands for training. Men and women alike would line up, all vying for the privilege of hearing you call them Master." She stopped at Aisling's side, her breath a cold whisper across bare flesh. "Or have you already been claimed? Shown the pleasures of being submissive?"

Zurael's image came to mind before Aisling could prevent it. Her body responded instantly, tightening her nipples and sending heat coiling through her belly.

Sinead moved around to stand in front of Aisling. She shifted her attention to Aziel, for the first time acknowledging she could see him. "Too bad you're already claimed, but not by this one I don't think."

Aisling slipped Nicholette's necklace over her head. She wondered if Sinead recognized what Aziel would be if he took his true form.

Sinead's eyes lingered on the jasper amulet before moving to the pouch containing the fetishes, then abruptly lifting to Aisling's face. She tapped the crop lightly against the palm of her hand, the sound rhythmic, like a clock ticking away the final moments of Nicholas's life.

"Very well, my price. I will lead you to the sex witch Nicholas. In exchange you will bring Elena to me after she meets her death."

Aziel's sharp claws dug into Aisling's bare shoulder, urging her to hurry while also warning her to be cautious. She shivered, recognizing both trap and the high cost of the favor.

"You will take me to Nicholas as quickly as possible, before he can be killed?"

Sinead closed her hand around the end of the crop, slid it back and forth through the fist of her fingers, mimicking the sex act. "Yes, I'll concede that point."

Her smile was sharp, her eyes hard. "I won't yield on the other demand, so don't waste your time—or what little of the witch's that remains—in trying to put limitations and restrictions on the task I want you to perform. In my own fashion I love Elena, as one does a well-trained and obedient pet. Bring her to me in death and I will take you to the witch in time for you to call on another to save his life."

Promise me you'll be careful.

I will be.

But the thundering race of Aisling's heart made a lie of her words. What Sinead asked was outwardly simple, but could ultimately cost Aisling more than she could afford to pay. There was no way of knowing, in this moment, who might claim Elena's soul at death, where Elena's spirit might go when she entered the ghostlands.

Aisling shivered. In her mind's eye she saw Nicholette's fear for her brother, and she ached for her. But to risk so much for a stranger . . . She wavered, torn, also seeing the images of her family's future captured on a slate of blood. Only slowly did she become aware of the tension vibrating through Aziel as he waited for her to decide.

You're trusting him with your life.

I always have.

"I'll pay your price," Aisling said.

"Come then."

They walked through gray nothingness and swirling ghost winds until Sinead stopped. No blood seeped into the spiritlands the way it had the night Elena lay on the altar to serve a dark mass.

"Here we are. With time to spare. As promised."

Aisling nodded, accepting the incurred debt before closing her eyes and willing herself to sink through the barrier separating spirit world from living one.

The scene that greeted her differed from what she'd expected, but was equally horrifying. Black candles lit a room laid out in preparation for an unholy ceremony. Nicholas lay gagged, struggling and fighting against tethers, cuts marring the perfection of his body—small knife wounds made to draw blood for the now-familiar sigils painted on his skin.

Two robed figures were in the room. As they approached the altar, one of them parted his robe to reveal a stiffened cock. He slid his hand up and down his shaft. "We've got time. Plenty of ceremonies start this way. Besides, aren't you curious about why your mother is so hot for him?"

"I'd rather piss on him than fuck him."

"Suit yourself. But not until after I'm finished with my fun."

Reflexively Aisling touched the entwined couple of Nicholette's necklace. A matching one seemed to writhe where it lay on Nicholas's heaving, fear-slick chest.

Aisling curled her fingers around the fetish pouch, pressed the jasper pendant to soft leather. *Aziel?*

He shifted on her shoulder, studied the scene intently. *This isn't the trap I expected, the one I wanted you to see and understand. There's no spell here to capture anyone you might summon. I will give you a name. But you will have no control over the one you call.*

The black-robed figure climbed onto the altar and knelt between Nicholas's legs. His hands reached underneath splayed thighs, wrenched Nicholas upward and Aisling shuddered in revulsion of the rape about to take place.

There was a fleeting thought to ask what it would cost her, but she didn't give it voice. *What is the name?*

Irial, Raven prince, son of Iyar en Batrael.

Not even a heartbeat passed between the end of Aziel's silent communication and Aisling's spoken summons. This time she felt no shock of terror when the demon arrived, black-winged and black-taloned, furious death given physical form.

The robed figures died in a spray of blood, their heads nearly severed from their bodies. When the demon's attention turned to Nicholas, his fury like waves of lava—uncaring who was destroyed in the flow of molten hate and deadly retribution—fear engulfed Aisling.

It tried to freeze her in place like a rabbit in the shadow of a hawk, but she managed to say, "No! Please don't!" and the sound of her voice turned Irial away from the altar.

Everything she'd seen in Zurael's face the night she summoned him, she saw again in Irial's. The demon rushed toward her, as if only just then understanding she was the one who'd called his name on the spirit winds.

The protective circle flared to life when he got to her, flashed in his green eyes like small flames burning with the absolute promise of death. But then his head turned slightly, and he stilled completely at the sight of Aziel.

Furious rage and unrelenting hatred gave way to subtle surprise and a glimpse of understanding. The threat of violence disappeared like a doused fire.

Aisling became aware of Irial's masculine perfection, how similar he was to Zurael. And as if thinking it forged a link between them, Irial met her eyes again. Only this time a stylized raven graced his cheek the same way a serpent coiled around Zurael's forearm.

"Do you trust that one with your life, little shamaness?" Irial asked, tilting his head toward Nicholas, who lay shivering on the altar, streaked with gore, his ankles and wrists raw and bleeding from his struggles.

The ease with which Irial identified her, the casualness of his address, made Aisling's heart race. But she didn't hesitate in saying, "Yes. His sister asked for my help. I trust him." She glanced at the bodies on the floor then back at Irial. "Will you free him?"

"I will free him."

"Thank you."

Irial's eyes darkened, and for the first time they swept downward, over her nakedness. "I understand better your allure," he said before turning his back and walking to the altar.

Unbidden, the spirit winds swept in, but rather than restore her to her physical body, they carried her back to the ghostlands, to another room and another circle, to a place that once made her think of ancient Greek temples but now made her think of desert lands and a time before humans existed.

Arched doorways formed the walls on all four sides. Gauzy, pastel-colored curtains held the gray of the ghostlands out. Sigils created with priceless gems sparkled in the stone floor. Some glowed so brightly they would imprint on her retinas if she looked at them too long.

Aisling sighed in relief. In the spiritlands all things came at a cost. There'd been no time to contemplate the price of saving Nicholas, no time even to ask what would be required of her. Now she knew she was to pay Aziel for Irial's name.

It was a heavy price, but one she had always paid willingly. The other spirits who guided her took her blood or a promise of service. Aziel took a part of her soul, what the ancient Egyptians had once labeled *ka*, the life force.

Aziel slid from her shoulder and settled on one of the jeweled symbols as he'd done any number of times before, as he'd done in each of the forms he'd taken as her companion.

He recognized you, she said, thinking of the instant when Irial saw Aziel, wanting answers, as she always had, but wanting them more desperately now.

Perhaps.

You're demon. She made it a statement. Hesitated slightly then added, *As is my father.*

Aziel's amusement reached her, a sharing of emotion rather than thought, the bond between them stronger in this place. *What's in a name, when it's given by another and not claimed by the one it's given to?*

The question made Aisling blush and look away. Memories of a similar question crowded in, where she stood naked in front of the bathroom mirror with Zurael.

Do you remember what I looked like beneath the moon and regret letting me cover you, pierce you? Does my form change the nature of who I am? Does it define me?

No.

Then look at me, watch while I take you.

Without conscious thought, Aisling's fingers curled around the entwined lovers of Nicholette's necklace, and in the cool of the spiritlands the jasper was warm against her palm. A fleeting, hazy image appeared, an impression of Nicholette writhing on silken cushions in this circle, the curtains in the archways billowing as a man lay on top of her, thrusting into her—and Aisling knew Aziel's interest hadn't been feigned.

She let go of the necklace, didn't want him to feel the childish, selfish insecurity that attacked her and held the larger fear of losing him at bay. But in this place, it was impossible, the bond between them too strong, too deeply ingrained. He'd been with her from her earliest memory. He was father and brother, spirit guide and best friend.

It's not time for me to leave you yet, he said, and his love surrounded her like a blanket, warmed her so deeply that there was no room for fear or worry about the future.

She let her mind drift, only barely noticing the sigils, flaring and subsiding in random order, as if an unseen hand played notes she couldn't hear. Tiredness came first, with the faint outline of her clothing as her life, her *ka*, drained away. Exhaustion came next and she wrapped her arms around bent knees, could almost feel the fabric of the pants she wore in the living world. Lethargy followed and she rolled to her side in a fetal ball, closed her eyes because she didn't want to see how close to physical death Aziel would take her.

Twelve

ZURAEL rose onto an elbow and gently brushed the hair away from Aisling's face. She slept deeply, with the insensibility of the dead. And though her bare skin was warm against his, he shivered as he remembered returning close to dawn to find her curled in a ball on the red dirt in the shaman's workroom, unresponsive to his touch and voice, her skin chilled and pale.

"Aisling," he whispered, leaning down to trail kisses over her soft skin, to touch his lips to hers and tempt fate by doing it. How had she come to matter so much to him? When had the thought of her death become unbearable?

He curled his arm around her waist and pulled her more tightly against him, pinned her unresisting thighs to the sheet. He was hard, as he always seemed to be when he was with her. But it wasn't the ache in his cock that guided his actions or urged him to cover her completely. It was the desire to possess her, to protect her.

She stirred as if responding to his closeness, his need to know she was whole, undamaged, safely returned from the spiritlands. Some of the worry loosened in his chest, burst in a wave of heat that had him touching his mouth to hers again, almost daring her to wake, to defy the future by taking his breath and spirit as easily as she'd summoned him from his father's kingdom.

Movement ended the moment. Zurael turned his head and saw the ferret.

Aziel was in the doorway, bold now where he hadn't been willing to show himself earlier in the face of Zurael's anger at finding Aisling still as death on the floor.

A knock on the door came and Aziel turned, retreated to the living room. Reluctantly Zurael left the soft heat of Aisling's flesh, slid from the bed and pulled on a pair of pants. More of his tension left when her eyebrows drew together and her mouth formed a frown over his absence.

He forced himself from the room to answer the front door. It was Nicholette.

Her gaze went behind him, searching for Aisling, then down to the ferret, who wound himself around her ankles like a cat before disappearing back into the house. When Zurael didn't call for Aisling, she said, "I brought fresh bread and vegetables from our garden. It's not enough, not nearly enough for what Aisling did. But it's all we can spare. We're leaving Oakland."

Nicholette's knuckles were white where her hands gripped the coarse burlap. She offered the sack to him and he took it.

"Please tell her we'll never willingly talk about what happened. Tell her no one knows Nicholas is safe. His client will never accept that her precious son brought about his own death. If she learns that Nicholas is alive, she'll blame him and find a way to have him arrested."

Fear settled like ice in Zurael's chest. Dread tempted him to ask how Nicholas came to be alive and free while his client's son was dead. Caution kept his lips sealed. If Aisling had summoned another Djinn . . .

Aziel returned, carrying Nicholette's necklace in his mouth. Her worry faded. Laughter and warmth shone in her eyes, highlighting her exquisite beauty and delicate features. She was breathtaking, though Zurael didn't desire her physically.

Nicholette knelt and took the necklace from Aziel. She stroked his head and back for long moments before slipping the chain over her neck and standing.

"I need to leave now."

"I'll pass on your messages."

Nicholette spared one last look at Aziel, then turned and hurried away. Zurael watched her for a few minutes, felt the eyes of unseen neighbors noting his presence, but even that couldn't pull him from the icy foreboding of his own thoughts.

He returned to the bedroom, intent on rousing Aisling, demanding answers. But the sight of her sprawled in the center of the bed, the covers kicked away to reveal splayed thighs and pink-capped breasts distracted him. Lust flared, as fast and dangerous as a flash fire.

Zurael crossed the room and stripped out of his pants without being aware of doing it. His cock was a hard ridge along his abdomen, his testicles a heavy, full weight.

He wouldn't yield, he told himself as he knelt on the bed next to her. But then her eyelashes fluttered, parted, and he was captured in blue shaded to violet, in a whirlpool of desire he had no resistance to.

"Zurael," she whispered, and he answered her call, responded to the subtle arch of her back by leaning over her.

With a moan, he latched on to a nipple, sucked and bit as she twisted and writhed, moved so his chest hovered above her face. She captured the loose strands of his hair and pulled him downward until she could press her mouth to his flesh.

Razor-sharp desire spiked through him when she bit down on his nipple. His hips jerked with each touch of her tongue, each suck, and he would have surrendered his seed if she hadn't taken his cock in hand, cupped his testicles and prevented release with the tight band of her fingers.

"Aisling," he panted, and did the unthinkable. He yielded his power to her. Submitted by repositioning them so he lay on his back and she knelt, her knees on the mattress near his head, her sinful mouth kissing downward toward his throbbing penis.

He palmed her breasts. Tortured her nipples and kissed the silky skin of her belly, bathed in the scent of her arousal when he was presented with her heated lower lips.

A shudder went through him as her mouth captured his cock head. He wouldn't beg, he told himself, *she* would be the one to plead.

His hands abandoned her breasts in order to cup her buttocks. He pressed his lips to slick, swollen folds. Probed her wet core with his tongue.

She bucked, whimpered. Took his penis between her lips and sent raw pleasure through his shaft—and he knew the depth of the lie he'd told himself.

Her name became a plea in his thoughts as liquid hunger consumed him. His hips jerked, lifted off the mattress in urgent rhythm.

His cock fought to surge deeper, but her hands prevented it. Had she asked, he would have done anything she wanted if she'd just take him further into her mouth, if she'd just bring him to completion.

A soul-swallowing lust held him in its grip. He was consumed by a carnal claiming he would never have allowed himself with another Djinn.

Aisling's fragile, delicate beauty was a trap he couldn't escape. The more he thought to possess her, the more possessed he became.

His tongue stabbed through wet folds, licked over the tiny head of her clit. "Aisling," he whispered and nearly cried when finally she gave him what he craved beyond anything else.

She took him deeper. Stroked him with her tongue. She sucked on him until his mind was white heat and screams of unbearable pleasure as orgasm claimed him.

He felt boneless beneath her. Echoes of his release trembled through him, but he had the presence of mind and discipline to return what she'd given him, to send her over the edge with his tongue.

THEY showered and dressed. Zurael waited until Aisling was in the kitchen, pulling loaves of bread and freshly harvested vegetables from the burlap sack he'd left on the counter, before he trapped her between his arms.

Somehow he resisted the urge to press against her, to get lost in the sultry heat and sweet allure of her. "Nicholette was here. She and her brother are leaving Oakland without telling anyone he's alive. They want you to know they'll never willingly reveal what you did." His voice became barely more than a growl. "What name did you call last night, Aisling? Who did you summon?"

"Irial."

Zurael went rigid with shock. Fear for her froze the air in his lungs. It made his heart stutter and miss a beat.

Aisling turned and placed her hands on his chest. Calm blue eyes met the molten, raging gold of his. "He would have killed me if he could. He intended to. But when he saw Aziel on my shoulder, his anger disappeared completely. He asked me if I trusted Nicholas with my life since he'd witnessed everything. When I said I did, Irial agreed to free Nicholas. What happened after that, I don't know. I couldn't stay any longer."

Zurael pulled Aisling into his arms and rubbed his cheek against the silk of her hair. Hope rose where fear had been. If the House of the Raven stood with him about sparing Aisling's life . . .

He shivered when she pressed kisses to his chest. His cock hardened, and he felt her smile against his skin, answered it with one of his own.

A knock on the door kept him from urging her to her knees or taking her against the counter. He stepped back, but followed her into the living room.

Raisa stood on the stoop. Bird-sharp eyes shone as they took in

Zurael's bare chest and Aisling's heightened color. "I hope I'm not interrupting. I saw Javier this morning. He mentioned you'd stopped by the occult shop looking for him. I took the liberty of telling him about our visit the other day. I told him I'd suggested you go there with your questions. He's willing to meet you for lunch at my tearoom. As I mentioned during our earlier visit, my shop has always been a safe place, a neutral zone for those touched by the supernatural. There's no way to reach Javier now, but he said he'll stop by in an hour, just in case you can make it."

Aisling said, "I don't know if I can."

"I'm sure Javier will understand if you can't on such short notice." She glanced at Zurael, then back at Aisling. "Nicholette didn't answer her door this morning. Did something happen—"

"There's still hope," Aisling interrupted. "Or at least there was . . ." Her voice trailed off, giving the impression of worry. "If you'll excuse me, there are some things I need to do before I'll know whether I can meet Javier for lunch."

"Of course."

"You handled that well," Zurael said moments later, when they were in the kitchen again. "Curious she should arrive this morning with an invitation and a question. What happened last night?"

Aisling told him, though not what transpired with Sinead before or Aziel afterward, and not how she'd come by Irial's name. When she was finished, she said, "I think I should meet Javier for lunch."

Zurael pulled her into his arms. "*We'll* meet Javier for lunch."

She placed her hand over his heart and felt its steady, reassuring beat. "Do you think it's safe for you to go with me? The books in his shop—"

"Probably have very few incantations in them that would be dangerous to me even if done correctly and by a powerful sorcerer."

The beat of Zurael's heart remained steady, sure, until she stroked the tiny male nipple. Then it jumped and raced, sent a surge of pleasure through her.

"We don't have time," he whispered, his breath warm against

her ear, his lips capturing the lobe, sucking, sending a hot stab of lust to her clit.

"I know." But she didn't pull away from him.

He slid his hands under her shirt, caressed her back with heated palms and gathered her closer so her mound was pressed against the rigid line of his erection. "This is dangerous, more dangerous than you can imagine," he said, rocking into her, panting softly as she did the same, riding the thin edge of control until the lust burning between them calmed enough for them to separate.

Aziel emerged from the workroom and scurried through the door. Aisling picked him up, started to tell him he had to remain here, then thought better of it when she remembered the lesson he'd intended for her when they found Nicholas.

This isn't the trap I expected, the one I wanted you to see and understand. There's no spell here to capture anyone you might summon.

He'd always been more sensitive to spell magic than she, though they'd rarely encountered it when they lived with Geneva. She settled him on her shoulder. "If it's a trap, I think Aziel will warn us."

.

FROM behind curtained windows and screened doorways, Aisling felt her neighbors watching them as they walked past. Chauffeured cars dropped off wealthy clients, the drivers leaving or remaining at the curb.

She tensed when a jeep came into view. It was several blocks away, but the camouflage green and brown marked it as belonging to guardsmen. Instinct, a lifetime of habit, made her turn into the nearest alleyway.

Zurael's fingers curled around her wrist, halted her when she would have hurried forward. "No," he said, pulling her behind a wall of shrubbery and using his arm to trap her back to his front.

The jeep's engine was distinctive. It drew near, slowed as it passed the alleyway, but didn't stop. "Wait for me here," Zurael said before the warmth of flesh became a swirling, heated breeze.

Leaves kicked up, allowing Aisling to follow his progress until he was beyond the row of shrubs. She gasped when he returned without warning, greeted her with the touch of his lips against her neck. "They showed no particular interest in your house."

"When Father Ursu brought me here, he told me the police and guardsmen don't patrol this area."

"Perhaps they're looking for Nicholette or her brother. Or they might be here on personal business."

Rather than retrace their steps to the main road, they continued down the alley and exited onto others just like it, until they emerged onto the street that would take them to Raisa's Tearoom. As they passed the Wainwright house, the front door opened.

"Hold on," Tamara called. "We were just about to send someone with a message for you."

One hand supported Tamara's extended belly while the other grasped the railing as she descended the porch steps. Happiness rose inside Aisling. "You've got Anya?"

Tamara was shaking her head as she reached them. "No. There's an approval process, which mainly requires paying fees to the government and the Church. By the time it was done and the couple we sent got to the The Mission, the child was gone."

Aisling could barely breathe. "Gone?"

"Yes. The matron wouldn't provide any information about who took Anya or where she was taken, until the couple we sent reminded her it was a matter of public record and told her they intended to pursue it. Then she admitted to sending the child into The Barrens along with some of her playmates—to some religious community she claims exists there."

"The Fellowship of the Sign," Aisling said.

Tamara's face tightened. "That's the name our friends heard. The matron had no right to send any child into The Barrens without government approval—which I doubt she has. It's beyond the reclaimed area of Oakland. It's still considered lawless."

Aisling felt heartsick. She worried for Anya more than the other children.

She'd been so sure Davida hadn't noticed Aziel going to the sandbox, calling attention to the symbols Anya had drawn. Perhaps it was a coincidence . . . or more likely, given Davida's dislike of the gifted, she hadn't known Aisling was interested in a particular child. Instead she'd sent Anya and her playmates away thinking she was saving them all.

"Levanna wanted me to tell you we won't give up. We're trying to find out more about the Fellowship of the Sign and how we can find them in The Barrens."

"You'll tell me as soon as you know?"

"Yes." Tamara grimaced as her unborn child kicked. "I need to get back inside."

Aisling waited until they were a distance away from the house before stopping and turning to Zurael. "They'll be on foot. Walking with children and having to remain on guard will slow them down. Even if they left early this morning, you could catch up to them. And if their compound is in the forest past The Barrens, you'd be able to follow them home."

"I can't be in two places at once."

She smiled at the fierceness she heard in his voice. "I trust Raisa enough to believe I'll be safe at her tearoom."

Zurael cupped her face in his hands. His eyes glittered with harsh regret. "And when you return home, Aisling? I've already failed to protect you once."

"It wasn't your fault." She saw he was going to argue, and prevented it by putting her hands on his chest, stroking over the firm muscles and hard nipples. "This is our best chance of finding where Ghost comes from. The longer it takes and the more people we ask questions of—the closer we get—the more dangerous it's going to become."

Aisling felt his tension against her palms, his resistance. She felt him struggle against the truth of her logic and finally yield to it.

"Promise me you'll send Aziel into the house to make sure it's empty before you go inside."

"I promise."

His hands tightened on her face. His eyes bored into hers. "Be safe," Zurael said before releasing her and walking away.

Aisling glanced at the sun's position in the sky and hurried toward the tearoom. She stopped at the shop's perimeter when Aziel's claws dug into her shoulder. There were round tables set outside, enclosed by a short wrought-iron fence that looked as if it might once have encircled a prewar garden. Umbrella poles rose from the table centers and a light breeze made the material flutter softly.

Sigils were carved into the gate and the redbrick pathway leading to the front door. Aisling took them in with a glance, recognized them all as standard wards against the use of magic on the premises. Still, she paused, waited for some sign from Aziel because she knew that despite the sigils she could see and read, there might be others she wasn't aware of that could offset them and allow for subtle manipulations.

"Aisling?" a man's voice called.

She turned her head. "Javier?"

He was so average-looking that a blink made it hard to remember what he looked like—or so she thought until Aziel drew blood with his claws. Then she realized Javier wasn't just the owner of an occult bookstore but a sorcerer in his own right—one strong enough to create a glamour spell to mask his appearance or to dim it so he became forgettable.

Aisling turned her head, just enough to brush her cheek against Aziel's in acknowledgment of his warning. The ferret turned his attention to the tea shop and chirped softly, lifted and lowered his head as if saying yes, then slipped from her shoulder and scampered away before Javier reached them.

"I hope I didn't scare your pet," Javier said, offering his hand to Aisling.

A small tremor of nervousness went through her before she could stop it. The fetishes gave her some measure of protection, but caution had ruled her for so long she still hesitated before touching her hand to his.

Javier's smile reached his eyes. It was charming, persuasive, memorable, as if some of the concealing glamour had faded, thought Aisling, though more likely it had changed for another purpose.

He carried her hand to his mouth and pressed a kiss against the back of it. "My assistant didn't do you justice when she described you after your visit to the shop. You're beautiful. Enslaving, even."

Aisling stiffened at his choice of words and the sly gleam that had entered his eyes. She pulled her hand from his and glanced at the tearoom.

"Shall we?" Javier asked.

Aisling preceded him through the open wrought-iron gate. "I'd like to sit out here," she said, feeling safer in the open.

"A good choice." He pulled a chair out for her when they reached a table. She slid into it and scanned the area beyond the fence, but didn't see Aziel.

Raisa emerged from the shop with menus. Simple pictures accompanied the descriptions of food choices, a selection of sandwiches and fruits and cheeses suitable to accompany tea. The teas were listed also, but Raisa recited them rather than ask if Aisling could read. When she'd finished speaking, Javier said, "My treat, of course."

Aisling fought the urge to touch the folded dollar bills in her pocket. "No. I'll pay for my own."

"An independent woman. I like that," Javier said. "But then I suspect there's nothing about you I wouldn't find delightful."

His flirting made her uncomfortable. The isolation of the farm outside Stockton hadn't prepared her for dealing with it, and Zurael's presence in her life made it more unwelcome than it would have been anyway. She needed only Aziel's reaction to Javier, and her own leeriness about sorcerers and the spell magic they played with, to leave her uninterested in Javier—other than for what information she could gain from him.

They ordered and Raisa went inside the shop. She returned long enough to bring them their tea service before retreating again. Aisling struggled to find the best way to pose her questions.

Javier leaned forward to ask his own. "Aubrey said you mentioned Ghost. You've encountered it?"

"Yes," Aisling said, knowing she'd have to give up some information if she hoped to gain any.

His lips curved in a conspiratorial smile. "I'll admit to trying it. *Once.* I'll also admit to being extremely grateful I survived the experience. But I'm sure you understand Ghost better than I and have greater reason to fear it."

Aisling parsed through his words, considered the possible meanings. His tone was conversational but his eyes were intent.

"Do you know where it comes from?" she finally asked.

"No, and I suspect it would be very dangerous to get too close to its source, either in this realm or another. The power necessary to create a substance like Ghost, one that allows untalented humans such easy and ready access to the supernatural realms . . ." He gave a dramatic shudder. "I can only imagine what kind of entities are behind its creation."

His words rang with truth, enough of it that Aisling felt some of the tension leave her. Raisa appeared with their food and left again.

Aisling studied Javier while they ate. She couldn't be sure, but she believed whatever disguising glamour he'd been cloaked in had disappeared as they passed through the wards guarding Raisa's establishment. She thought she was seeing him as he truly was— physically at least. He was attractive, deeply tanned as Zurael was. But where Zurael was a muscled predator with a long mane of hair, Javier was lean, his scalp shaved and free of stubble.

"I find you very attractive," Javier murmured, as if reading her thoughts about his appearance. "I think you'd find we have a great deal in common if you'd spend some time with me. And I'm very interested in your work."

She looked down, not wanting to encourage him.

"You asked about Ghost," Javier said, filling the silence. "I'm curious, understandable given the wide range of books I've acquired over the years. Under the right circumstances, could you summon a lingering spirit and require it to possess the physical shell left empty by someone foolish enough to Ghost?"

Images of both Elena and Nicholas—the sigils painted on them—rose like an icy tidal wave. And this time some of the ancestral memories were freed from Aisling's subconscious.

Her skin crawled as she realized the nature of what the dark priests, or perhaps more accurately, the dark sorcerers, were trying to accomplish. They weren't making an offering to a Satan-like god. They weren't making a human sacrifice to feed a spell or gain power. They'd been trying to trap a demon in human flesh, where its strength might be limited though its knowledge would be vast. No wonder Zurael hunted the one guiding them in their pursuits.

Javier's hand captured hers, forcing her eyes to his. "I've shocked you with my question. And now you're wondering if I have something to do with the sudden rise in sacrificial victims. A reasonable question, one the police ask me almost every time they find a body these days."

He grimaced and leaned forward, offering a confidence. "What they seem to forget, though I'm sure they're aware of it—or at least those in power are—is that I spent a great deal of my childhood in the tender care of the Church. The Church itself helped arrange for me to open my store. What better way to monitor how far the non-gifted humans are straying than to know what sinful reading material interests them?"

Javier brushed his fingers over Aisling's knuckles. But where Zurael's touch sent liquid hunger through her, Javier's deepened the chill spreading with every heartbeat.

If he'd thought to deflect her suspicion, he hadn't. He'd solidified it instead.

She'd wondered if the Church played a role in Elena's abduction when she found the connection between it and the branded man who'd sold Ghost to Elena and taken her from Sinners. And now Aisling had another link, this one between the Church and a man whose store was visited by humans without supernatural abilities. Men like Anthony Tiernan, the dark priest Zurael killed. Men like the son of Nicholas's wealthy client, the pretend sorcerer Irial killed.

Aisling escaped Javier's grip when Raisa returned to take away their empty plates and offer dessert. "None for me," she said through frozen lips, fumbling as she pulled the folded money from her pocket and counted out what she thought she owed.

It was an effort for Aisling to control her desire to escape Javier's presence and hurry home. She scanned the area past the wrought-iron boundary of the tearoom for Aziel, for Zurael—and found neither.

Javier followed Aisling's lead and paid for his lunch, too. Raisa lingered as if hoping for an invitation to sit or read the tea leaves. When one didn't come, she walked away slowly.

"I didn't mean to frighten you with my confession, Aisling," Javier said, "but apparently I have and I'm sorry for that." A small smile curved his lips. "I shared a little known fact, my connection to the Church, with you, because I hoped to put you at ease, to show you we share a certain *dangerous* predicament in that we share an undesirable connection with the Church, one we have to handle with great care given their financial and political resources."

Aisling forced calm into her limbs. She forced herself to meet his gaze. His nearly black irises made her think of the soul-stealing entities that could be found in the spiritlands. And in a moment of clarity she realized *this* was the true trap, the one she'd expected to be waiting for her when she went searching for Nicholas.

"I don't trust the Church," she admitted, willing to draw Javier out, to delay the moment when she had to leave the tearoom, because now the walk home seemed far more treacherous.

"You're smart not to trust them," Javier said, relaxing, seeming to accept that he'd managed to reduce her fear. "They have their own agendas, one of which is to find Ghost, I think. I can't imagine they're thrilled with the prospect of having its use spread through the wealthy classes. No telling what voices those in power might start hearing, and what Church whispers might no longer be heard because of them."

Aisling nodded, encouraging him to continue. She believed Annalise Wainwright's vision was true and the Church had sent the vampire's shaman to his death trying to find Ghost. She suspected Henri had lost his life for the same reason.

Javier's reasoning was in keeping with what she knew of those whose lives had moved beyond the daily struggle for survival—but she would find it equally believable that he was behind the creation of Ghost.

He leaned forward and said, "I'm afraid I can't stay much longer. It's a hazard that comes with owning the shop. Not all the guardsmen serve only the city or the Church. Some of them are in the pocket of wealthy and powerful families who've recently lost loved ones in magic ceremonies gone wrong. They're looking for someone to blame and I make a wonderful target.

"I wasn't lying earlier when I said I find you attractive, Aisling. I think we could be very good together." Javier reached out to stroke her cheek, but even for answers she couldn't bear his caress.

She jerked back. His eyes flashed, narrowed, then slowly filled with speculation. His voice lowered to a whisper. "Does the demon who accompanied you to my shop serve you so willingly, *kill* for you so willingly, because you've enslaved him with sex, perhaps even love, Aisling? It's a dangerous game to play with a demon. I wonder if you're equally ensnared."

Aisling did her best to hide the alarm she felt. She refused to acknowledge his reference to Zurael.

Javier smiled and leaned back in his chair. "Gaining access to your special gifts interests me far more than access to your body. I'm content to share nothing more than a working relationship with you."

His absolute confidence unnerved her. Every instinct shouted that she was in the presence of the man who'd orchestrated the dark ceremonies—the man Zurael hunted.

Aisling doubted Javier would admit his guilt, but she pushed anyway. "I won't work with you. Those who practice black magic and attempt to gain power by human sacrifice are damned to dark, horror-filled places in the spiritlands."

Javier's eyebrows lifted. "Are you saying you fear for your soul? I rather imagine there's a place in hell for you already, at the side of your demon lover."

He opened his jacket. From a deep inside pocket he retrieved the figurine that had been behind the counter of his shop. His thumb stroked the red crystal set in its forehead. "My assistant mistakenly thought this reacted to your presence. I didn't disabuse her of the notion. It's an old artifact, predating much of civilization.

"Before The Last War it spent centuries in the hands of various private collectors, all of whom gained possession of it through illegal means. I believe it was originally relegated to a storage room in a museum after being found by archaeologists, though it disappeared shortly thereafter and was sold on the black market.

"If there are a handful of these statuettes still in existence, I'd be shocked. I'd be equally shocked if even a handful of people would recognize it and understand its true purpose.

"You've no doubt guessed, but I'll tell you anyway. Humans—gifted and non-gifted alike—have always called upon otherworldly beings. Angels, gods, demons, devils—name them what you will, through ritual sacrifice, ceremony or rite, prayer and incantation, we've tried to enlist their aid, *compel* their aid."

Javier's eyes glittered. His thumb again stroked the darkened gem in the figurine's forehead. "This particular statuette was used by priests. It served to warn them whenever malevolent spirits were present, beings the Church would label demons. Imagine my surprise when despite the wards protecting my shop *against* such entities, it flared when you entered the shop accompanied by one of them walking around in daylight in human form."

He placed the figurine on the table between them. "Do you know what happens to those found guilty of consorting with demons? They're branded, and regardless of gender they become fair game, though women suffer far more than men do. After all, if someone is willing to lie with a demon, then how can they protest sex with a human, willing or not?"

His smile became predatory. "I think you understand now why I'm so confident we *will* be working together. The Church won't protect you. You're every bit as disposable to them as Henri was. In fact, you're something of a liability to them. Here's another little known fact. As I mentioned when we sat down for lunch, I spent a great deal of my childhood in the *tender* care of the Church, much of it with Father Ursu, who *saw* the dark nature of my soul—read my aura and the strength of my inherent gifts—then tried to scrub it clean."

Aisling's stomach knotted. She remembered Father Ursu closing his eyes in the hallway of the farmhouse as if he looked elsewhere to ensure she was the one he should take to Oakland. She thought about his interest in Aziel and wondered if he'd seen a demon's aura.

If her suspicions were right about the Church being behind Elena's abduction, and if the vampires were right about the Church being afraid to openly go after whoever was responsible for Ghost—had they used her, knowing, hoping, she'd summon a demon if she found Elena in time to keep her from being sacrificed? Was it a test to see if she could be used to do something they couldn't? And if she succeeded, would she be branded, put to death for consorting with demons, for carrying a demon taint?

Javier stood abruptly, jerking Aisling from her private horror. He captured her face between his hands before she could evade him. "I need to be on my way now, but I'll be in touch soon. Give what I've said some thought, Aisling. I'm sure you'll see the benefits of us joining forces. Imagine what could be gained if even a handful of the wealthy and powerful lost their souls to Ghost—or permanently for that matter—while their bodies housed entities you and I could command."

His hands dropped away from her face. He picked up the figurine. "Just a friendly warning, if you truly care for your demon lover, don't send him after me. I'm well protected."

Javier turned and left the patio area. When he stepped beyond the wrought-iron fence marking the tearoom boundaries, he glanced down at the figurine as if checking it for the presence of a demon, then hurried away.

Aisling shuddered. Icy fear coursed through her, propelled by the fast beat of her heart.

"Did you have a nice visit?" Raisa asked, startling her.

"Yes," Aisling said, and somehow she managed to sound calm underneath the birdlike-scrutiny of Raisa's dark eyes.

Aisling stood. "The lunch was wonderful, as was the tea. Thank you."

Raisa nodded but didn't reach for the dishes on the tables. The silence hung between them, demanding to be filled with confidences, but Aisling wasn't tempted. She said good-bye and left.

Nervousness trailed her as she hurried toward home. Despite having seen the guardsmen earlier, Aisling worried about what might be waiting for her in the alleyways more than she worried about being out in the open.

Her thoughts raced. Lunch with Javier played itself over and over again in her mind.

There was no sign of Aziel. She couldn't help but think he'd somehow sensed the figurine in Javier's possession. He'd known the crystal would flare in his presence and confirm her suspicions about his demon origins.

Worry for Zurael knotted Aisling's stomach. She couldn't hide from him what she'd learned. And when she told him, he would hunt Javier.

She turned the corner and stopped at the sight of a car parked in front of her house. It was black, its windows tinted. From a distance she couldn't determine if it belonged to the Church or if it was the one Elena had arrived in.

Indecision held her motionless. The lack of safe places to go kept her from simply turning and running.

The driver's door opened. A man emerged from the car as though he stepped out of the pages of one of Geneva's history books. He wore a brown suit with a matching derby hat—just as Marcus had in the spiritlands when she'd gone looking for Tamara's lover.

Aisling knew in a heartbeat he'd come to collect the ghostland debt. And strangely enough, the thought of it calmed her.

The man took his hat off and nodded respectfully when she reached him. "I'm Marcus, sent to fetch you, miss."

He caught her surprise and smiled as he placed the hat back on his head. "The Master calls us all Marcus, after a favored servant when he was a boy. Says it's easier all the way around. Any other name and we've outlived our usefulness to him and know it."

Marcus patted his vest pocket and pulled out a folded piece of paper. "You'll want to see this before getting into the car with a stranger."

Aisling took the paper from him and opened it. She found what she'd expected, a single sigil, the same one the Marcus she'd encountered in the ghostlands had shown her inside his bowler hat.

"Do we need to leave now?" she asked. There was no sign of Aziel, and Zurael wasn't back from his search of The Barrens.

Marcus tugged on a gold watch fob. An old timepiece dropped to his hand. He looked down at it. "We've got a few minutes—just—before we have to be on our way. Don't worry about meals. Cook will serve you. But I'm afraid I won't be able to drive you home until after sunrise tomorrow."

Aisling glanced at her front door, remembered her promise to

send Aziel in before going in herself. "I'll need clothes. And to leave
a note. Would you mind going inside with me?"

Marcus pocketed the watch. All affability left his face. "There's
been trouble?"

"Yes."

"Then I must insist on going in first to make sure it's safe. The
Master would be displeased if something happened to you. Not that
I would countenance it either, miss."

He reached under the car seat. Aisling half-expected him to pull
out a Prohibition-era tommy gun. Instead he retrieved a wooden
truncheon.

Marcus slipped the rope loop at one end over his wrist, then
tapped the palm of his hand with the billy club before nodding, apparently finding the weapon satisfactory. He followed her to the
front door and waited while she unlocked the doors, but then insisted she remain on the stoop while he went inside.

A few minutes later he emerged and held the door open for her.
A tug to the watch fob brought the timepiece out of his pocket
again. "I'm afraid we're going to be cutting it close if we don't leave
quickly."

Aisling hurried to her bedroom to gather a change of clothes
and something to sleep in. Marcus cleared his throat. "The Master
won't expect you to be dressed on par with a coming-out party. He
understands you've only recently arrived in Oakland. But you might
want to pack your best for the appointment tonight."

"Thank you, Marcus."

"My pleasure, miss."

Aisling packed her clothes, then went to the kitchen to search the
drawers for the tablet of paper she thought she'd seen there. It was
underneath frayed dish towels and yellowed from age.

A pencil was there, too, its tip broken. She used a knife to sharp-
en it.

There was so much to tell Zuarel, none of which she wanted to leave in writing. She hesitated, pencil point on the paper, and asked, "Where are we going?"

Marcus shook his head. "I'm not at liberty to say. You're leaving a note for someone you care about?"

"Yes."

"Then assure them your physical safety is guaranteed. As my counterpart said when he struck this deal with you, tonight's work involves a shaman's task not meant to be difficult or dangerous. You understand we can't offer assurance when it comes to the use of your gift. But to the best of our ability we'll see no harm comes to you."

Aisling nodded her understanding and acceptance. She had to settle for telling Zurael she was paying a debt incurred and would see him in the morning.

Only when they got to the Bay Bridge and San Francisco loomed ahead of them did her nervousness return like a gust of icy wind. Suddenly references to the Master took on chilly meaning, as did the clothing Marcus wore—clothes centuries upon centuries out of style.

He slowed to a stop at the guard booth.

"Authorization!" the guard barked.

"Certainly."

Marcus pulled a piece of paper from his pocket and handed it to the guard, but not before Aisling saw the green of printed money held firmly to the back of the paper.

The guard slid the bills into his sleeve as he held the paper underneath a scanner. When the scanner beeped, he returned the paper to Marcus.

"Everything is in order. By law I must remind you that under the terms of the compact between Oakland and San Francisco, the bridge closes from dusk until dawn."

As soon as they pulled away from the booth, Aisling said, "Marcus, do you serve a vampire?"

Thirteen

"YES, miss, I serve a vampire. But unless you do something exceedingly foolish, which I can't imagine you doing even on such short acquaintance, your physical safety is guaranteed."

Aisling rubbed icy palms against her pants. A hundred questions crowded her thoughts, raced through her mind with the pounding of her heart.

In astral form she'd felt the presence of a vampire a couple of times, but she'd never seen one, never spoken to one, either in a corporeal form or a non-corporeal one. What she knew of them was gained from gossip and books, from exaggerated tales and the faded memories of the elderly people who visited with Geneva.

"How long have you served him?" Aisling asked.

Marcus glanced at her as they reached the mid-span of the bridge. "Several hundred years."

Aisling gaped. She studied his face, thinking maybe he had a subtle sense of humor.

He caught her looking at him and asked, "Where did you live before Oakland?"

"On a farm outside of Stockton."

"Ah, that explains it then. There are very few vampires in that area. It's human-dominated, nontalented and heavily influenced by organized religion as I recall. I'll hazard a guess and say you've never spent any time in the company of vampires."

"I've never met one," she admitted.

"Well then, if you don't mind my offering a little advice, just treat the vampires you'll meet tonight the way you'd treat any other client. Vampires understand business transactions, and for humans, it's safer not to mix business affairs with social ones. Once that line is crossed, expectations change and things become a bit trickier to navigate.

"They don't tend to like idle conversation and they won't appreciate any questions not pertaining to the task you're to do for them. I can't speak for vampires elsewhere, but the ones who claim San Francisco adhere to strict codes of privacy and silence. I'll mention to the Master where you've come from. He'll pass the word on discreetly, though it's probably unnecessary. They won't expect you to understand even the rudimentary rules of their society."

"Thank you, Marcus."

He reached over and gave her hand a pat. "You'll do just fine, miss."

"Aisling."

He chuckled. "The Master would have my heart if I was so informal with you while I'm serving as guard and chauffer."

"Marcus, have you really served him for several centuries?"

"Yes indeed."

"You're not a vampire."

"No. I'm not sure I'd want to take that step even if the Master thought I'd earned the privilege of being offered a place in his family beyond servant." He glanced at Aisling. "I'll not say too much about it, but given your line of work, I think you can understand how tricky it is for a soul not to get caught up in moving on to what comes after dying. Sometimes the body restarts but it's just a husk that has to be destroyed before something else takes up residence in it. Other times there's no flicker of life after the heart stops the first time. The blood is just not strong enough to get it going again.

"So many don't make it through the change. But I imagine that's the way it's supposed to be. The world would be overrun with vampires if every person lived through it. And some family lines have a better rebirth rate than others."

Aisling looked out the window as the city approached. She could guess the nature of the service she would be required to perform but she didn't want to examine it too closely. "Did you know the San Francisco shaman?"

Marcus snorted. "A piece of work that one was. More ego than talent, but some ability is better than none. That's what kept him alive, though as far as I know none of the most powerful families used him. Didn't want him capitalizing on their name, I suspect.

"I don't know the ins and outs of it and I'm not asking you to elaborate, but even vampire servants talk. They whisper the Church brought you here and you survived whatever task they set you to—where their own shaman didn't. You'll do just fine with the vampires. Give them honest work and they won't hold the outcome against you if it doesn't turn out the way they hoped. Like I said earlier, they understand business."

"You gave the guard money so you could bring me to San Francisco without anyone knowing it," Aisling guessed.

Marcus chuckled. "Exactly right. The Master could easily have arranged authorization for you to cross the bridge, but he prefers to keep his affairs private."

The car left the bridge and entered the city. The silence settled around them like a comfortable blanket as Aisling took in her surroundings. Unlike Oakland, here she saw no burned-out buildings or charred vehicle remains. There were large gaps where buildings had once stood, but they were free of rubble. Residences and shops stood side by side on some streets but were completely separated on others.

Marcus slowed and turned. "This is Telegraph Hill. The Master's ancestors settled here in the eighteen hundreds, back when they were all fully human. They've kept a presence here ever since."

At the bottom of the hill the houses were small and packed together. As they climbed, there were fewer houses. And those were hidden behind stone walls or dense, high hedges.

Near the crest of the hill Marcus turned into a driveway. The heavy gates swung open to reveal a huge house. As he drove around to the back, he said, "The Master's old-fashioned. Servants and tradesmen have their own entrance. It's the same way with the powerful families, only they've got an entrance set aside for petitioners, too."

Marcus braked to a stop. "Now, you stay put. It's only fitting I open the door for you given your special talent."

Aisling caught herself smiling. Even after her experience in the library—trusting Cassandra only to realize later the librarian was probably spying for the police or guardsmen—when it came to Marcus, suspicion couldn't gain any purchase. She liked and trusted him, which made entering a vampire's lair an adventure rather than a nightmare.

The furnishings were old-fashioned, the halls dim. Heavy drapes covered the windows in the rooms they passed.

The hallway ended in a T. Marcus pointed to the left, where a doorway stood open at the end. "When you get hungry, that's the kitchen. Cook knows to expect you. There's an eating nook there or you can do like most of us do and eat at the counter if it suits you."

They turned to the right, then right again at the next hallway. Halfway down he paused in front of a door and opened it. "These are your quarters."

Marcus stepped aside, allowing Aisling to go in first. He followed and indicated a pull cord. "If you need something, tug on this and a maid will come."

Aisling barely heard him. Her attention was riveted to the television set. "Does it work?"

"Yes indeed. We get local stations as well as the national news feeds. Cook will make you up a tray if you decide you want to stay in your room and watch television."

"I may just do that," Aisling said, barely able to contain her excitement. She turned to Marcus and touched his arm. "Thank you for making this easy for me."

Marcus doffed his hat. His face reddened with a blush. "My pleasure, miss. I'll be back to fetch you when the Master's ready to see you. It looks like you'll be content to stay put. It'd be best if you didn't go exploring."

"I won't go any farther than the kitchen."

"Good. I'll leave you then."

Time passed in a whirl of changing scenes as Aisling watched TV. She hadn't realized how starved she was for information until it was there for her to consume. At home the radio was often on as they went about their chores. And from time to time, Geneva traded for television parts and got the set in the living room running, but even so, the choice of programs seemed as limited as the life span of the TV.

Dinnertime came and went without her noticing, until a knock on the door revealed a portly woman in a cook's apron carrying a tray of food. "Marcus said I should bring this to you. The Master's awake. He's got to take his sustenance yet." Cook's eyes strayed to the bed. "And sometimes that leads to a bit of a delay if you get my meaning. But you best be eating dinner and getting ready to be summoned. Marcus will be around when the Master wants to see you."

Aisling thanked the cook and took the tray of food. After she ate, she put on the same long, modestly designed black dress she'd been given to wear the night Father Ursu brought her to Oakland.

It didn't look the same on her. When she'd worn it before, she'd felt lonely, diminished, helpless and frightened. But tonight, its stark simplicity seemed to emphasize her blond hair and the blue of her eyes.

"Ready, miss?" Marcus asked from the doorway, making her blush at having been so absorbed in studying her image that she hadn't heard him enter.

The furnishings grew more elegant as they moved from the servants' area to the one that housed the Master and his family. Aisling would have loved to ask Marcus questions, but she took her cue from him and remained silent.

Finally he stopped and ushered her into a sitting room done in dark red velvet. It graced the walls, the sofa and chairs, hung in front of the windows in heavy folds.

"Well, come closer, girl," a cranky voice said, drawing her eye to a wrinkled old man sitting in deep shadow in an overstuffed chair. He motioned with his hand. "Come on, girl. I'm not going to bite you, not on first acquaintance anyway."

Aisling obeyed. Her heart pounded, more from uncertainty than fear. The vampire in front of her wasn't anything like she'd imagined.

He thumped his walking stick on the hardwood floor, and she grew apprehensive that he could read her mind when he said, "You think every vampire gets turned in the prime of life?"

"I believe you're the first she's ever met, sir," Marcus said from the doorway. "Until recently she's lived in the Stockton area."

"Primitive, backwater place." The Master rose from his chair with the aid of his stick. "They still unenlightened there, girl?"

"They fear supernaturals and don't welcome humans with otherworldly gifts."

The Master snorted. "Place has been an armpit for centuries." His gaze traveled over her, taking in the dress before lifting to spear Aisling with shrewd eyes. "You'll do nicely, I think." He switched his attention to Marcus.

Marcus said, "The car is ready, sir."

"Good, good." The Master thumped his walking stick against the floor twice to punctuate his words. "Let's get going then. Can't keep Draven waiting."

The old man moved like a young man despite his frail appearance. He strode down the hall—the walking stick an accessory and not a necessity—and forced Aisling to hurry in order to catch up with him.

A dozen questions came to mind, piling one on top of the other until she shook her head to still them before climbing into the back of a long, sleek, gray limousine and taking a seat across from the Master. Curiosity kept her fear at bay as Marcus drove them to an estate surrounded by walls. But it returned with a rush when she saw the emblem carved on the heavy metal gates. A serpent held an apple in its mouth. From a point behind its head to just before the tip of its tail, the three segments of its S-shaped body were impaled by an arrow.

"You recognize the symbol?" the Master asked.

"It belongs to the ruling vampire family in San Francisco."

"Quite so." His eyes caught and held hers. He leaned forward abruptly and warned, "The Tassone aren't a family to cross. Remember that."

She nodded because it seemed to be expected of her. Then the car was stopping and Marcus was there, opening the door.

From the darkness two men appeared out of nowhere, their arrival so stealthy Aisling knew they were both vampires. Without a word they escorted Aisling and the Master into the house, one guard in front and one behind.

Incredible wealth met Aisling wherever she looked. Artwork graced the walls. Figurines adorned the polished wood surfaces of antique furniture, while larger statues, many of then on pedestals, served as focal points. But it was the library they passed that made her breath catch and her steps slow for an instant.

"Draven will see you now," the vampire leading them said, stopping at an open doorway.

The vampire seated behind the desk was everything Aisling imagined one would look like, and it was clear why once they'd been confused with incubi and succubi. He made her think of sex as his blue eyes mesmerized and held her in place until turning to the Master.

"You both may have a seat," Draven said, indicating two chairs placed in front of his desk.

"Thank you for seeing me on such short notice, Draven." The Master's voice was deferential.

"You're here with a petition." The statement didn't hold even the slightest hint of interest.

The Master nodded. "Several of my business investments have paid off. I want to bring in more workers."

"How many more?"

"One hundred head."

"Permanent?"

"Yes."

"Single or with families?"

"There's usually less trouble if they have families to worry about."

"Your one hundred could easily swell to several hundred." Draven steepled his fingers. "Which means you need housing for them."

"Yes. I'd like to put them on Tempe, Kenin and Grandin, and offer them protection as part of their incentive package."

"I can see your problem. All three of those streets border your territory and are controlled by the Tucci family. They'd consider your actions one step away from annexation of their property."

"That's why I've come to you with my petition."

Draven's gaze moved to Aisling and pinned her to the chair. "You must believe you've got something I'd consider very valuable. I'm skeptical. I don't lack for female companionship, and I have little need to enter into potential alliances as a means of satisfying physical desire."

"The girl's a shamaness. She owes me a shaman's task."

Something flickered in Draven's eyes. "You're Aisling, the shamaness Bishop Routledge ordered brought to Oakland."

She shivered under the intensity of Draven's stare and the knowledge that he knew who she was. "Yes." It came out little more than a whisper.

He continued to study her for long moments as her heart pounded furiously in her ears regardless of how hard she tried to quiet it. Finally he turned his attention back to Marcus's master. "You offer me a fool's bargain."

"Not at all. It's me who stands to lose something of value and gain nothing in return. If she's successful in whatever task you set her to, then I would expect to gain housing and protection rights on Tempe, Kenin and Grandin for my one hundred head plus any dependants they choose to bring with them. If she fails, I'm out what she owes me."

"Leave her. Have your man come for her before dawn. You'll have your answer then."

The Master stood and left the room. Aisling wet her lips. Marcus's conversation as they'd entered the city earlier kept her quiet in Draven's presence.

Without a word he rose from his chair and came around the desk like a lithe, predatory cat. He wore black trousers, and combined with the white shirt and the long hair pulled back and secured by a jeweled clasp, his appearance made her think of a sea pirate.

She stiffened when he cupped her chin. Shock bolted through her when he said, "Tell me your mother's name."

The thunder of her heart became a buzz of anticipation. The skills she used in the spiritlands slid into place. An answer given freely was lost forever. "Do I remind you of someone?" she countered.

Draven's sensuous lips hinted at a smile. "Yes, you do, though I've only seen her a few times over the years. She doesn't call this city home. You could be her twin . . . or her daughter. Give me a name and I'll tell you if it's familiar."

"I don't know one. I was left on a doorstep as a newborn."

"Ah, it happens often, though not here in San Francisco."

"This woman I remind you of, was she a shamaness?"

Draven rubbed his thumb over her cheek before he released her chin to lean against the edge of his desk. "I've heard rumors to that effect. If they're to be believed, she was very gifted, perhaps too gifted. She chose a vampire's long life over remaining human and one day returning permanently to the realm of souls."

For a moment old hurts threatened to overwhelm Aisling. She'd been abandoned at the edge of dark, when the predators began stirring, when the sunlight had faded enough—she imagined now—for a vampire to rise and move unseen to the doorstep, knowing there were humans in the barn who'd soon be rushing for the safety of the house.

Your mother got away from him, or so they say. But that's a story for another day.

John's taunt in the ghostlands coiled around Aisling with the chill of the spirit winds to remind her of what she suspected her father was—demon. Had her mother discovered it too late? Been so horrified by what she'd done that she preferred to risk everything? In all the times Aisling had traveled to the ghostlands, she'd never encountered a vampire's soul.

"How did you come to be in Thaddeus's debt?" Draven asked, drawing Aisling's thoughts back to the present.

She smiled at learning the Master's name. "I needed information in the spiritlands and traded to get it."

"You've been formally trained?"

"No."

"But your gift must be strong or you wouldn't have survived your night in the church. Other shamans have died there."

Aisling shivered at the deadly coldness of his voice as well as the reminder. Since he hadn't posed it as a question, she didn't offer an answer.

"Do you know what task I would set you to?" he asked after a long interlude of silence.

"I . . . I can guess." Her breathing grew shallow with the thought of witnessing the death of a human and the birth of a vampire, of being a part of it.

Draven straightened away from the desk abruptly, making her jerk in reaction. "Come with me."

He didn't look back to ensure she obeyed. But then he didn't need to. Vampires were said to have incredible hearing and a keen sense of smell. He probably heard the way her heart raced, probably smelled her fear.

Draven led her upstairs, where even greater wealth was on display. Toward the end of the hallway, he stopped and rapped on a door before opening it and going inside.

"Nice of you to wait for me to say come in, Draven," a male voice chided as Aisling followed Draven into the room.

"This is the shamaness from Oakland," Draven said, ignoring the rebuke.

A bare-chested blond turned in his chair. His eyebrows went up in surprise when he saw Aisling. "She looks like—"

"I thought so, too. She owes Thaddeus a shaman's service."

The blond went completely still. "And he's offered it to you?"

"In exchange for an intercession with the Tucci family. One that's easy enough to accommodate."

"Tonight?"

"She's here for the night. I'm sure Thaddeus aimed high but will settle for low. I imagine he's off arranging another deal in case this one doesn't materialize."

The blond's attention returned to Aisling. Sea-green eyes and flowing hair gave him the appearance of a buccaneer, too. And even though he wasn't vampire—yet—Aisling knew few women would be able to resist him.

Silence settled like a heavy taffy being pulled between the three of them. She resisted the urge to rub her palms against her dress, fought to keep the nervousness from escalating into unstoppable tremors.

Finally the blond said, "Well, I guess tonight is as good a night to die as any." He glanced around the room before locking his eyes to Draven's. "Here suits me."

Aisling was acutely aware of unspoken words between the two men, though she had no idea what they were. After a long pause, Draven said, "Here it'll be. I'll leave you two alone for a few minutes while I arrange for a guard and escort."

He closed the door behind him. The blond stood and met Aisling in the middle of the room. He took her hand in his. "Under the circumstances, I'd say we should introduce ourselves. I'm Ryker."

"Aisling."

"Tell me you've done this kind of thing before, Aisling."

"No."

"Oh well, I've always enjoyed firsts." His eyes danced and his smile was infectious.

"The woman I resemble—"

"Can't be named in your presence at this time or Draven would have done it. He's a law unto himself, in case you haven't guessed; otherwise you wouldn't know of her existence at all. Are you familiar with the term *omerta*? The old Mafia families used it."

"It was a code of silence, wasn't it?"

"And loyalty. You'd do well to remember that vampires are extremely fond of the concept of *omerta*." Sea-green eyes grew serious. "Whatever happens here tonight, Aisling, don't speak of it."

Worry and sadness knotted her stomach as she looked up into Ryker's handsome face and imagined it drained of color, still and lifeless in death. "Why do you want this?"

"My reasons are my own."

"But the risk—"

"Is acceptable to me."

The smile returned to his eyes. "The thought of me being a vampire doesn't terrify you at all. It's the thought of my human death that has your heart racing and your eyes clouding with concern. Am I right?"

"Yes," she whispered.

"I want this, Aisling. I don't have any doubt Draven's blood is strong enough to kick-start my heart, but if it were as simple as that then there'd be a lot more vampires." Ryker's knuckles brushed her cheek. "Even on such short notice and having only just met you, my gut tells me I'm lucky Thaddeus wanted something from Draven."

Ryker's hand fell away. He stepped back as Draven entered the room. The vampire's gaze flicked to Aisling then back to Ryker. A dark eyebrow lifted. "Ready to start?"

"Ready," Ryker said. His eyes found Aisling's and filled with mischief. "I've always imagined I'd end up dying in bed, though not necessarily my own. Can you do whatever you need to do there?"

Heat rushed to her face. She laughed despite the cold, heavy fear that rushed to settle in her chest.

"Yes," Aisling said, following him to a bed large enough to hold three or four people, then coloring further when Draven removed his shirt and joined them on the mattress.

With a casualness that spoke volumes, Draven opened a nightstand drawer and removed a knife. "Insurance," he said, slicing his wrist deeply enough to draw blood.

"You *do* care." Ryker mocked her, leaning down to press his lips to Draven's wrist.

The men didn't touch otherwise, and Draven's expression gave no clue to his thoughts. But Aisling found the sight of them together arousing. She found the act itself erotic, deeply intimate.

Courtesy demanded she turn her head, but she couldn't look away, couldn't keep her gaze from dropping to the fronts of their pants as the men sat next to each other, cross-legged, one knee nearly touching. She closed her eyes then, tried to close her ears to the soft sound of Ryker drawing Draven's blood into his body. She concentrated

instead on what would come next. On what would be required of
her next.

Her hand crept up to the pouch containing her fetishes. She
quieted her mind and let memory guide her.

There'd been a child once, when she was a child herself. He'd
fallen into a canal before he knew how to swim. His uncle pulled
him out and forced the water from his lungs. He pressed on the
boy's chest until his heart beat on its own, but the boy didn't regain
consciousness.

They came to Geneva because a doctor was too expensive and
they feared the worst. Geneva took Aisling with her.

Aziel wore the body of a cat in those days. He'd guided her
through the gray mists of the spiritlands to a hill overlooking a
playground. The boy was there, giggling wildly as his father pushed
him on the swing while his mother pulled food from a wicker picnic
basket and placed it on a blanket spread out on the grass.

You can call the boy to you, there's still time, Aziel told her, words in
her mind rather than a voice. *They can't keep him from answering if
you do.* But Aisling shook her head. She'd been young enough then
to fantasize about being reunited with her mother and father, as if
she'd somehow been lost instead of abandoned.

He's happy to be with his parents.
Is that what you want to tell his uncle and aunt?
Yes.

And that's what she'd done, only realizing later—after the happy
images from the ghostland were replaced by the stricken, haunted
expressions of the boy's aunt and uncle—that by her choice she'd
left them to finish what the water had been kept from doing.

The mattress shifted beneath Aisling. She opened her eyes to
find Ryker lying down. Draven knelt beside him, the knife still in
his hand. Both of them were looking at her, waiting for her.

There'd be no circle, not with a death required. She crawled to
Ryker's opposite side and took his hand in hers, wove her fingers
through his.

"When Ryker returns, he'll be in the grip of bloodlust," Draven said, radiating complete confidence, as if there were no doubt about the outcome. "Leave the room immediately. There's an escort waiting outside the door to take you to your quarters. Remain there until Thaddeus's servant arrives before dawn to take you home. You're ready?"

The tightness in Aisling's throat made speech impossible. She barely had time to nod before there was a flash of silver and a sharp cry of pain as Draven drove the knife through Ryker's chest and pierced his heart.

She was jerked into the spiritlands with the same abruptness as when Elena forced the Ghost trip on her. Only the gray fog immediately parted to reveal a dock, a sailboat swarming with partially dressed men and women.

"Ryker!" they yelled, in unison and apart. "You're here! Come on!"

Ryker's laugh poured over Aisling, carefree and happy. He seemed unaware of their interlocked hands as he hurried toward the boat, dragging her with him.

For an instant she wavered, let him draw closer to his friends. He was almost to the dock before a sense of urgency made her dig her heels in and say his name.

Ryker faltered. She called him again and he started to turn away from his friends.

A woman on the boat shed her wrap to reveal tanned skin and a model's body. An equally gorgeous man moved to her side and slid his arm around her bare waist. "Come on, Ryker! Don't tell me you've forgotten what it's like. Sail with us."

This time Ryker's laugh was masculine and appreciative. "How can I say no?"

He jerked Aisling forward with renewed determination to reach the boat. "What about Draven?" Aisling said, desperate to get his attention as they reached the wood of the dock. "Draven's waiting for you. He's expecting you to come back to him."

Ryker faltered again. He turned toward her. His eyebrows drew together in puzzlement. The voices from the boat grew more demanding.

Aisling wished the fog of the ghostlands would block the sailboat and silence the voices—and as if hearing her call, the spirit winds came in a breeze that sent Ryker's hair and her own dancing until a shroud of gray was wrapped around them.

The confusion slowly faded from Ryker's eyes. As it did, Aisling said, "You wanted me to take you back to Draven."

Ryker's hand went to his chest, where the knife's blade had left only a small deadly wound. He glanced down and took in his nakedness, then hers. The infectious smile returned. "Another first. Draven will be sorry he wasn't included. He has a decided preference for blondes. Shall we return?"

"Yes," Aisling said, and the ghostland cocoon expelled them.

Aisling scrambled from the bed and ran to the bedroom door. Behind her came the sound of thrashing, curses.

She opened the door and was immediately grabbed and pulled through it by one of the vampires stationed in the hallway. Even if she'd been tempted, there was no chance to look back.

The door shut. A second vampire moved to stand guard.

"This way," the one who'd pulled her from the room said.

Aisling followed him to a suite like something out of a magazine depicting the lives of the rich. A large-screen television took up a great part of one wall, in an area with a couch and chairs. In the next room a huge canopied bed was placed in the center, amid plants and flowers of all descriptions.

Beyond the bedroom was a bathroom with a sunken tub. She touched the sparkling faucets and couldn't resist the idea of submerging herself in heated, bubble bath–infused waters.

Aisling stripped as the tub filled. When her fingers brushed over the fetish pouch, her thoughts went to the woman who might have given birth to her before becoming a vampire. She opened the pouch and removed a single fetish—the one representing her most powerful protector, the being she was beginning to think was demon—her father.

Unlike the others, most of which were made of bone, the one she examined was clear crystal, with no shape other than the one she'd found it in on the day Aziel led her to it. The being it represented was the only entity she could call upon who wasn't bound by the spiritlands—though Aziel had warned her more than once that the cost of saying the name and summoning her guardian was beyond any she could imagine paying.

Ice slid through Aisling's veins. Was he so frightening? Was the place he called home so terrifying that becoming vampire was preferable? Or was the woman Draven and Ryker spoke of an unknown sister, a cousin or aunt?

Aisling returned the crystal to the pouch and got into the tub. She let the heated water and luxurious bubbles turn her mind away from answers she might never have, questions that might cost too much to ask.

Zurael's image rose in her thoughts. With it came memories of what they'd done together when they shared a bath.

Aisling closed her eyes and glided bubble-slick hands over her breasts. Her nipples firmed as she imagined that her palms and fingers were Zurael's, stroking, admiring, bringing pleasure.

Desire made her cunt clench in reaction. In her mind's eye she saw the two of them standing in front of the bathroom mirror, saw his wings unfold behind them as he pierced her with his cock.

Demon. And she was helpless against the need he inspired in her.

She abandoned a breast, smoothed downward to swollen cunt lips and an erect clit. Hidden by bubbles, her toes curled as sweet sensation spiked through her when she rubbed the tiny bared head, slipped her fingers into her slit.

A moan escaped as she forged in and out of her channel, slowly at first, savoring the fantasy that it was Zurael's tongue, Zurael's penis. Then faster, even though she knew the ecstasy would never rival what his touch did to her.

IT was nearing dawn when Zurael finally tired of pacing the confines of Aisling's house. Hours had passed since he got back from The Barrens. It felt like a lifetime.

He'd thought spending the darkness in the owl's form, searching as he'd done before, would ease his worries for Aisling and make her absence more palatable. It did neither.

Once again he picked up the note she'd written, examined it for clues as to who'd come to claim the debt she owed. It didn't escape him that only her physical safety was guaranteed.

A shudder passed through him when he considered what might happen to her in the spiritlands. When she got back—

His cock answered for him with a sharp pulse.

Zurael shed his clothing and escaped to the shower. He couldn't afford to lose control when she returned.

Water cascaded over heated flesh. A moan escaped when he took himself in hand.

When he'd returned the first time to find the note, he'd known only misery waited for him between the sheets of Aisling's bed without her there. And so he'd flown. He'd hunted through the night and tried desperately to avoid the truth of his misery.

Aisling. Her name echoed each time his fisted hand moved up and down on his shaft. Images of her filtered through his mind as fire built in his testicles.

His thighs bunched. His buttocks flexed.

He fucked through the tight fist of his hand. Slowly at first, then faster. Until, with a shout of her name, release came in hot jets of semen—but brought only a moment of peace.

Zurael dressed. He rubbed his chest as he paced, felt the hollow place that widened each time he thought of the future.

The dawn came. Faded to morning.

A scratching at Aisling's front door had him flinging it open. Dismay filled him when he saw Aziel, but it passed when the sound of a car drew Zurael's attention away from the ferret.

The two of them remained motionless in the doorway. They watched as a black car rolled to a stop in front of the house.

Aisling emerged. She stopped to say something to the driver, then turned and hurried up the walkway.

Her smile pierced Zurael's heart. The sight of her rushing toward him filled him with emotion he wasn't brave enough to name.

He welcomed her into his arms, buried his face in the gold of her hair and held her to him until she laughed and pushed at his chest. "Aziel expects a greeting, too."

Reluctantly Zurael released her. A spike of anger stabbed him when she cuddled the ferret in her arms, rained kisses on Aziel's head.

"Why didn't he accompany you?" Zurael's voice held the bite of his anger.

Aisling stepped farther into the house. He followed, closing the doors behind him, then listening as she told him about the meeting with Javier.

It was as Malahel en Raum and Iyar en Batrael had thought it would be. The one behind the sacrifices, the one believed to possess the tablet, wanted Aisling.

"I will deal with him," Zurael said, determined to protect her, even as the worry for him that he read on her face nearly undid him.

"I'll help you. I'll be your bait," Aisling murmured against Zurael's chest, but before he could reply, a knock sounded at the door.

He didn't recognize the woman, though the likeness to the witch Tamara suggested it was her mother. Aisling greeted the woman by the name Annalise and invited her in.

"I only have a few minutes," Annalise said, sparing him a glance before focusing on Aisling. "Levanna dreamed last night. In her dream you passed The Mission and followed the early Church's symbol of a fish into The Barrens. It led you to the child. She's beyond our reach, but not yours. Will you go for her?"

Aisling didn't hesitate. "Yes."

Annalise pulled a braided band of leather from her pocket. Aisling tensed at the sight of the sun hanging from it. "Levanna sends this for protection. Do you accept it?"

This time there was a tiny hesitation before Aisling answered, "Yes."

Instead of handing Aisling the charm, the witch tied the leather around her wrist. The sun amulet swung from a thinner strap connected to the larger one, so it lay against Aisling's palm.

"You've got powerful, dangerous enemies who can travel between worlds freely," Annalise said when she'd finished the task. "Touch this to their skin and will them away from you; it will force them from this world and back to their own."

Zurael gripped Aisling's wrist as soon as Annalise left. He studied the charm.

A memory stirred, an image from one of the books in the library of his father's house, but it remained elusive. Finally he lifted his eyes and met Aisling's. He saw her determination—not only to go for the child, but to find the Ghost source.

"Gather food and we'll leave now," he said, willing to put off his hunt for Javier in order to keep her safe.

Fourteen

ZURAEL worried it was a trap. Twice police cars had pulled along-side the bus. Once a guardsman's jeep had slowed at an intersection and waved the bus onward when it would have yielded the right of way.

Aisling's fear washed over him each time the authorities were present, fear so deeply ingrained in her she couldn't prevent her rapid breathing or the tiny tremors that shook her. And yet she didn't turn back from the task.

He took her hand as they walked, felt the tension in her slide away. Her courage amazed him. Her trust destroyed him. He couldn't allow anything to happen to her.

They passed the houses huddled together in worn-down poverty and gritty survival, the vine-controlled wastelands, the burned out, rusted shells of other structures, until eventually they came to the place where ragged orphan children fished on the banks. The Mission followed—a last vestige of civilization before The Barrens.

Zurael thought he caught a glimpse of Davida in an upstairs window. His suspicion that it was a trap set for Aisling grew.

Hidden eyes followed them. He felt the gazes—curious, apathetic, hostile, suspicious. Predatory.

His hand fell away from Aisling's. He studied their surroundings, looking for danger. Prepared to kill anyone or anything that dared attack.

Having explored The Barrens on wings, Zurael chafed at the pace they were forced into because of the necessity of having to look for the fish symbol. He hated that Aisling was so vulnerable, so very human in a place filled with danger.

She slowed at the first blackened shell beyond The Mission. It stood at an intersection, though nothing remained on three of the corners and the road had long ago cracked and become pocked with holes.

A school of crudely drawn fish was ankle-high on the strongest of the walls still standing. Each swam in the same direction, face pointing forward, through the intersection.

"We're going to find them," Aisling said, excitement and anticipation making the blue of her eyes rival the sky.

Without conscious thought, Zurael leaned forward. He was a short breath away before he realized the danger, how close he was to touching his lips to her.

He stood abruptly and turned away. But not before his heart wrenched at the sight of Aisling's uncertainty.

They continued on in silence, their progress slow. The continued sensation of being watched, considered prey, kept him at her side instead of scouting ahead.

They stopped long enough to eat lunch. Then later, dinner.

The daylight grew into evening light, but neither suggested they turn back toward Oakland. It became harder to locate the symbols of early faith.

Several times they hid as jeeps driven by guardsmen patrolled.

A helicopter in the distance, its arrival too sudden and unexpected, caught them out in the open, though it didn't veer toward them.

Crickets and cicadas came to life. The rumble of car engines purred in the dusk all around them, alternating between growing louder and fading.

Zurael considered shifting to the demon's form and flying with Aisling to safety but thought of the game he'd witnessed the guardsmen playing each time he'd been in The Barrens. The risk was too great. He couldn't protect her from bullets, or a fatal fall, if he became formless.

"We need to find shelter," he said, studying what remained from the time when one city merged into another and another until little was left besides concrete and steel and teeming masses of humans penned in a place that would ultimately make their slaughter easy.

Nature was in the process of reclaiming much of the area they were in. The vines once developed by scientists to leach industrial poison from the soil now covered the horror left by man's temporary rule of Earth.

Aisling pointed at what might have once been a secure storage shed. "How about there?"

Zurael studied it for a moment. He compared it to the larger structures around them, most with gaping holes, to the cars buried beneath shrouds of thick stems and shiny leaves. He nodded. The walls of the storage building were concrete, the roof solid metal. They'd be trapped, but the narrow doorway allowed for a defensible space.

The wind brought the sound of hounds baying. Next to him Aisling shivered and rubbed her arms. He ushered her into the building and indicated a corner for her to settle into just as the sound of a helicopter reached him.

It was a risk, but this time he deemed it necessary. He crossed to her and knelt in front of her, noting how fragile she was, sitting on the floor with her knees to her chest and her arms wrapped around her legs. The desire to protect her filled him with the primitive, explosive heat of molten rock.

"I won't be far," he said, unable to stop himself from stroking her cheek, from brushing his thumb over her lips and losing himself in angelite eyes.

Pride spiked through him when she pulled a long kitchen knife from the burlap sack holding what remained of their food. She laid it on the ground next to her. "I'll be okay."

Zurael shed his physical form and moved away from her, motes of dust and dirt, lightly tossed leaves and insect carcasses the only things marking his exit.

The drone of engines assailed him, vibrated through him. Wildlife scattered and darted into hiding places ahead of the rumble announcing the approach of man.

A small swarm of the finger-length fey who feasted on blood raced after a fleeing deer, hoping for a meal before deep nightfall forced them to their nest.

Their wings glittered with the colors of sunset. Their upper bodies and faces were vaguely human though their minds were those of a savage hive insect.

Zurael moved away from Aisling's shelter cautiously, gauging the distance to ensure he could get back to her if danger threatened. The baying of the hounds grew closer, coming from the same direction as the sound of the helicopter's rotors. He couldn't see the helicopter until he reached the end of his self-defined tether to Aisling. Then uneasiness filled him at the spotlight illuminating the ground beneath it.

He'd witnessed the guardsmen carousing in The Barrens, casually slaughtering anything that crossed their path, but tonight was different. They were hunting something specific, and coming toward where Aisling hid.

He shifted his attention to the closest buildings. Reevaluated them. The storage shed was a defensible position against wild animals, humans and supernatural beings, but it wasn't safe against armed men.

Zurael returned to Aisling. "Let's find another place."

She rose to her feet without argument. At the doorway he lifted her in his arms.

With a thought, the wings unfurled, unhindered by the Djinn-created fabric of his shirt and jacket. In two steps he was airborne, her weight negligible, her soft, joyous laugh sending heat cascading into his heart as he flew the short distance necessary to reach a hole in the third floor of a building that looked relatively stable.

"That was wonderful!" she said, eyes sparkling, voice breathless and cheeks flushed, for an instant unafraid of anything.

He wished he could keep her that way. But all too soon the blood-hounds arrived, baying, noses to the ground. They went directly to the place Aisling had been, then circled in confusion at the lost track as guardsmen arrived in jeeps.

Fury filled Zurael. The witches would pay for their part in sending Aisling into a trap. "Stay here," he said before once again becoming a swirl of air.

In the desert a single Djinn could become a sandstorm deadly enough to bury large caravans of men and machines in a matter of moments. He had less to work with in The Barrens, but Zurael was determined to disrupt the hunt for Aisling.

Leaves and sticks, rocks and small scraps of metal—all gathered in the violent energy of his unformed mass. Men cursed and dogs yelped when he bore down on them, blinding them temporarily, making them bleed when debris struck them. Some ducked into the shelter he and Aisling had abandoned, while others raced toward the building where she was now hidden.

Rage gave the winds more force, but the vines reclaiming the land covered the loose material that would make him deadlier. As the first of the guardsmen neared the building Aisling was in, Zurael shot upward, using all the gathered energy to reach the helicopter.

It rocked, tilted, might have escaped his assault, but the open door where a man with a machine gun sat allowed the gathered debris to distract the pilot in a critical instant. The humans screamed as the helicopter spun out of control before striking the ground.

Zurael returned to Aisling. Beneath them, men rushed to the downed helicopter. Radios squealed. Panicked, angry voices reported the crash and were told additional guardsmen were being dispatched. Already there were too many of them, spread too far apart and too heavily armed, too nervous, for Zurael to attack with Aisling close by—and even if he could buy her time to escape, there were other predators to worry about.

Machine-gun fire exploded, vented in fury or fear at some movement in the shadows. Next to him, Zurael could feel Aisling shiver, could hear the shortness of her breath as she remained completely motionless, not giving in to the primitive instinct to run.

Guardsmen pulled the bodies of the pilot and his passenger from the twisted metal. "There's nothing we can do for them," an authoritative voice said. "Newman, get the heat sensor out. Alvarez, get the dogs. Refresh their memories with the scent article. Let's finish this. These men died because of magic. Anything that moves and isn't one of us, shoot to kill."

Two men peeled away from the crash site. One headed toward a jeep, the other to where the bloodhounds milled around the concrete-block storage building.

Zurael turned to Aisling. What he intended was dangerous, but there was no other way.

He gathered her in his arms and lifted her. "Put your legs around my waist," he whispered.

Returning to Aisling's home wasn't an option. Not tonight and not with her.

In his mind's eye he saw The Barrens as he'd seen it as an owl, considered the abandoned buildings where he'd perched and watched the activity beneath him. He chose one to shelter in, but fixed the roof of another in his mind to transport to—a place he hoped to launch from before the first of the angels arrived, summoned by the sound of him breaching the metaphysical plane.

With a thought, the batlike wings appeared again; only this time he allowed the full demon form to manifest. His fingernails elongated into sharp talons; a deadly barbed tail completed the look. Zurael smiled at the irony of appearing in the image once forced onto The Prince by the alien god—of possibly using it to defeat an angel.

A burst of machine-gun fire, and the seemingly instantaneous impact of bullets against the building, served as a trigger for their departure. He curled an arm around Aisling in a protective gesture, then willed himself to the rooftop fixed in his thoughts.

As he'd feared, no sooner did his feet touch the flat surface of the roof than the night sky opened in a blaze of light. White wings stretched in what the humans saw as a glorious display.

Zurael set Aisling aside then moved to stand between her and the angel, but not before he heard her gasp of awe and saw it in her eyes. A deadly blade formed in the angel's hand. It glowed like the sun, but despite what the humans believed, it wasn't a weapon of fiery glory. It was a creation forged in the coldest, deepest realms of space, because only such a thing could prevail against the fire of the Djinn.

Satisfaction moved through Zurael when the angel made small slicing motions with the blade, indicating his intention to fight. An older angel, one from a higher order, would use his voice as a weapon. But by his actions, the angel in front of Zurael had revealed his status, his inexperience when it came to the Djinn.

Zurael moved forward and to the side, wanting to draw the angel away from Aisling before the fight began.

The angel's eyes flicked briefly to Aisling. He spat the word "Abomination," then lunged toward Zurael, blade in front of him as though he were fencing.

Zurael easily eluded the thrust. A laugh escaped. He slashed, sending severed wing feathers fluttering to the rooftop.

The angel swung then, eyes glowing, the arc of his swing carrying the blade to where several steps and a lunge were all it would take to reach Aisling.

Zurael launched himself upward and the angel followed, knowing he had the advantage with the extension of the sword.

Pride might keep the angel from summoning others to assist with the kill. But it was no guarantee others wouldn't soon arrive, alerted by the sound of Zurael's passing through the barrier, drawn by the trail his energy signature left when he transported between Earthly locations.

He dropped to a far corner of the roof, and waited until the angel was nearly on him to turn into a swirling mass of particles. The ice chill of the blade barely missed him before Zurael reclaimed the demon's shape. Struck and drew blood this time.

A scream erupted from the angel, the enraged sound of a bird of prey instead of a man. He lunged forward, swinging the sword with savage ferocity as his blood left a trail across the roof.

Zurael retreated, driven backward by the near mindlessness of the assault. Out of the corner of his eye he saw Aisling trying to stay far away from the fighting. But her movement drew the angel's attention. The sudden gleam in the angel's eyes was the only warning he gave before halting his wild swings and launching himself toward her.

Too late Zurael realized it was a trap. With the swiftness of a falcon the angel turned, slashed, opened a deep wound across Zurael's chest.

Cold seeped into Zurael, so pervasive it froze the breath in his chest and filled his mind with the sound of his own scream of agony. Only his training saved him from a death blow. Instinctively he twisted away, used the barbed tip and whiplike strike of the demon tail as a weapon.

The angel screamed. The blinding glow of the blade disappeared as his concentration faltered and his sword arm slickened with blood.

Zurael tried to move in for the kill. But the cold was spreading, making his reactions slow as it seeped deeper into his being in an effort to reach and extinguish the Djinn fire at his core.

Aisling.

The heat she generated in him, the protectiveness he felt for her helped him fight the angel's icy poison.

His flesh mended, chased out a chill that should have required a visit to the House of the Cardinal in order to heal so quickly. But just as he was mending, so too was the angel.

Zurael lunged forward, talons drawing blood, turning white feathers crimson.

The angel jumped back, knocking Aisling to the ground. Deadly swords appeared and elongated in both of his hands. "Abomination!" he said, slashing downward at Aisling.

"No!" It was wrenched from Zurael, torn from the depths of his soul in the same instant Aisling's stark face and terrified eyes were seared into his mind.

He flung himself forward and was greeted by a blinding flash, a boom so loud it shook the building and rolled across The Barrens like a shock wave from the human's destructive bombs.

For a second he was frozen in place, held in a doorway of ice and infinite darkness. And then he returned to find Aisling rubbing her hands over his chest, calling the Djinn fire at his core with her worried touch and angelite blue eyes.

"Are you okay?" she said, her voice quivering, not hiding her fear for him.

He grabbed her wrist, suddenly aware of the sun-shaped charm trapped between her palm and his flesh. The memory that had eluded him earlier returned with clarity.

In his mind he located the book kept with so many others in the House of the Serpent library. Turned its pages and saw the powerful token. "You touched the angel."

Aisling shivered. "I sent him home, wherever that is."

Zurael read her face, saw her thoughts as clearly as if they were his own. She was a child of the ghostlands, but she was still human. She still had a human's instinctive, genetically programmed reaction to the alien god's warriors—to cower and worship, to prostrate herself in their glorious beauty and accept their judgment.

Fierce emotion gripped him, mixed with pulsing pride. She'd been found in the presence of what she thought was a demon and named an abomination, yet she'd had the strength of will, the presence of mind, to use the charm the witch had given her and cast the angel from the human world. She was as worthy as any Djinn.

Clouds covered the moon, offering some protection. He peeled his bloody shirt off. And because it wasn't of the human world, he was able to will it to ash so it wouldn't be used to track him.

Zurael scooped Aisling up in his arms. In three steps they were airborne, flying rapidly to a place where he hoped they'd be safe from both guardsmen and angels.

His emotions churned. A lifetime of belief and teaching was lost to their chaos, in the lava-hot flow of desire coursing through his bloodstream.

Zurael was barely aware of landing on the fifth-story ledge of what might once have been an apartment balcony. He had no conscious thought of entering the darkened space other than a predator's quick, instinctive searching for the presence of others.

He was feverish, burning from the inside out. He became more so when Aisling whimpered, so attuned to him that she kicked off her shoes so he could strip her from the waist down before pressing her back to a smooth wall.

Her arms went around his neck, her legs around his waist, trapping the hard length of his cloth-covered erection against her fevered, wet folds. "Aisling," he whispered, glad the clouds no longer obliterated the moonlight so he could see the exquisite beauty of her face.

She was delicate and desirable. Had enslaved him from the first moment she whispered his name on the spirit winds—only now he acknowledged it willingly.

"Aisling," he whispered again, touching his lips to hers, parting them with his tongue and taking her breath, her spirit, her moan of pleasure—and returning the same.

He'd worried over it, feared it. But as he felt their souls touch, dancing and merging like twin flames, euphoria filled him.

Despair to match the height of his joy would follow if he was separated from her for any length of time. But he couldn't care in that moment when they were one being.

In heated darkness their tongues rubbed and twined, teased and tormented. It was beyond anything he'd ever experienced. It became something he'd forever crave.

Each of her whimpers lodged itself in his heart, filled him with a satisfaction like no other. He smoothed his hands over her back, felt a renewed surge of primal satisfaction that she accepted him regardless of what form he took.

With a thought, the wings and demon-tail disappeared. His hands left her long enough to free his erection from his pants so he could grasp her hips and lift her until his cock head was positioned at her opening.

They both shuddered with ecstasy when he slid into her hot core. He groaned when she freed his hair, tangled her fingers in it and held him tightly to her as her tongue twisted and mated with his.

Sensation bombarded him. Savage emotion ruled him. An uncontrollable hunger swept through him with the devastating force of molten lava.

Aisling belonged to him. No one—not angel or human, supernatural being or Djinn—would deny his claim or take her from him. No one—not even The Prince would keep them apart.

He freed her hair and reveled in the silky feel of it. He gave her his breath when her lungs screamed for air.

His cock mimicked the thrust of his tongue, plunged deep and hard, with dominating force. And she responded with moans of pleasure. She welcomed his aggression by softening against him, becoming more submissive; she acknowledged by her actions that she belonged to him completely and without question.

Her tight channel clenched and unclenched on his cock, sent waves of raw, nearly painful pleasure up his spine and into his heart. *His!* She was his. The sureness of it was reinforced each time his penis surged in and out of her.

He wanted to linger, to savor the intimacy of their first kiss, the sharing of breath marking the first true joining of their souls. But the night was still young, too full of predators to be guarded against. And the hunger raged too fiercely. It commanded the jerk of his hips, the tightness of his testicles, the undeniable need to imprint himself so thoroughly on her that every cell would hold his name, answer to his call.

He changed the angle of their bodies, felt her quiver each time he struck her clit. Primal satisfaction filled him when she fought to get closer, to take him deeper, to feel the hot splash of his seed.

Each thrust was a claiming, a declaration of intent. They would be together.

Aisling's cry of release spilled into him where their lips touched. And like Djinn fire, her ecstasy burned through him, triggered his own, so wave after wave of semen jetted through his cock.

Long minutes later he pulled from her sheath and reluctantly stood her on her feet. Heartbreakingly beautiful eyes met his as she touched her kiss-swollen lips and asked, "Why?"

He knew she was asking why he'd repeatedly refused the intimacy of kissing until now, but he had no answer for her, nothing he could reveal until after they'd found whoever was creating Ghost, until after he'd dealt with Javier and returned to the Kingdom of the Djinn with the tablet, until after he'd fought for and won a future with her.

"Let's find a more defensible room," he said, touching her lips lightly with his before taking her hand and leading her deeper into the building, to a windowless area with only a solitary door to guard.

Aisling dressed then settled into a corner, knees hugged to her

chest. For a while she was content to puzzle on the question of Zurael, the change that had taken place between them. So many other
times he'd turned away from her when she'd thought to touch her
mouth to his.

She wet her lips, relived the fire of his kiss, those moments when
the only breath he'd allowed her was his own, as if her very life belonged to him. Her nipples and clit pulsed with renewed need,
ached for his mouth and hands.

He stiffened in the doorway. His nostrils flared as if he could
scent her arousal. Tiny nipples grew tight and the serpent he wore
on his forearms rippled.

Their eyes met and held.

Feminine satisfaction curled in her belly and breasts. The fast,
rough coupling had left him craving more. It was there in his taut
muscles, the tightness of his features, the cock once again pressed
huge and hard against the front of his pants.

She wanted to stand and go to him, to lose herself in the pleasure, the safety and peace she found in his arms. She wanted to keep
the angel's judgment—the word *abomination*—from her mind and
avoid the truth of her own demon origins, the worry about her soul
that she'd never struggled with until Zurael and then the angel
appeared.

But a cougar's nearby cry urged caution. The sounds of rustling,
of movement in other parts of the building, kept her in place. The
drone of a helicopter in another part of The Barrens reminded her
of the danger if they had to give up this hiding place.

She pulled her attention away from Zurael. The sun-shaped
amulet pressed against her palm. She'd thought at first it was meant
to protect her against Zurael, then later, when it became obvious
the guardsmen were hunting her, she'd wondered if Tamara's family
had sent her into a trap. Now she didn't believe either was true.

Aisling flexed her wrist, exposed the golden charm. "Would this
work on you?"

"No. It's meant for the *heavenly* host."

She trembled at the fury and hatred in his voice. But she didn't back away from her train of thought. "Levanna knew I might need this. The Wainwright matriarch wouldn't have given me such a powerful charm if she didn't want me to find the Fellowship of the Sign and return with Anya. I think she guessed what you are and knew I'd be safe in The Barrens from anything but an angel."

Zurael nodded. "I thought it was a trap also. Now I think otherwise. The guardsmen wouldn't need the hounds, not if they knew the trail we were following."

An icy chill swept into Aisling's chest. It settled around her heart like a frigid fist as she remembered the guardsmen calling for a scent article.

Fear for Aziel froze the breath in her throat. In her mind's eye she saw the guardsmen storming into her house so they could get something of hers to present to the bloodhounds, their heavy boots and guns deadly to the ferret trapped inside with them.

She shivered and once again hugged her knees to her chest. She told herself Aziel was clever. He'd find a hiding place.

For long moments the worry and fear crowded in. They only lessened when she accepted that she couldn't change what had happened, acknowledged that it wouldn't have been better to bring Aziel into The Barrens.

If he was a lesser demon, as she suspected, then he would have become a target for the angel's attack. And unlike Zurael, he wouldn't have been able to defend himself. Aziel was trapped in whatever body he wore.

Aisling turned to the question of the guardsmen and who might have sent them. She and Zurael had witnessed Cassandra going into the building housing the police station and guardsmen shortly after they'd left the library after searching the Internet for information about Ghost and the Fellowship of the Sign.

Twice police cars had pulled alongside the bus, and once she'd seen a guardsman's jeep. If they'd been after her, watching her, determined to prevent her from entering The Barrens, then wouldn't they have stopped her sooner? And if they were selling protection, or involved in distributing Ghost—then wouldn't they know where to find the Fellowship's compound?

Aisling's eyebrows drew together. She felt like one of the farm dogs chasing shadows and rustling leaves—until she thought about Father Ursu and Bishop Routledge. The magnetic strip on the back of the transit bus pass would reveal she'd gone to the stop closest to The Barrens for a second time, traveled again with a second person, only this time hadn't returned home.

She'd slept at the church. Her scent would be on the towel she'd used after her shower, on the sheets and pillow. Annalise Wainwright's vision had confirmed Father Ursu and Bishop Routledge's desire to find the Ghost source.

"The Church might have sent the guardsmen, hoping we'd lead them to whoever is responsible for Ghost," Aisling said, tensing with her next thought. What if the guardsmen had been ordered to bring her back alive? What if it was the helicopter's crash that changed the nature of their hunt?

A knot formed in her stomach with the added deaths laid at her feet, the ever darkening stain on her soul. She closed her eyes and pressed her forehead against her knees.

Almost instantly Zurael was there, his fingers tracing the vertebrae of her spine, already knowing her so well he could guess at her thoughts. His breath was hot against her ear, his lips soft. "The hunted always have a right to defend themselves."

A soft whimper escaped when his tongue caressed her earlobe. A second followed when it circled the shell of her ear then slipped inside.

His hand pushed between her chest and knees, possessively stroked her breasts, her nipples, forced her to open from her defensive posture. "You need to sleep," he whispered, palm gliding downward. "We lost ground coming here to escape the guardsmen and reduce the risk of encountering another angel. We'll have to make it up on foot tomorrow."

Her cunt lips grew flushed and slick, parted with the same ease as her thighs when Zurael's hand slipped beneath the waistband of her work pants and her panties. On a moan, she tilted her head backward, welcomed the way he covered her mouth with his and demanded entry with the dominant thrust of his tongue.

The fingers tracing her spine went to her hair, speared through it, making it impossible to escape even if she'd wanted to. His palm burned where it cupped her mound possessively. His fingers slid inside her, and she lifted her hips so he could thrust deeper.

Zurael's groan fed her desire, her confidence. She wasn't alone when it came to the shattering intensity of the hunger that flared to life when they touched.

His grip on her hair tightened. His tongue probed, thrust in the same rhythm as his fingers forged in and out of her channel and his palm glided over her hardened clit.

When she would have sought breath, he allowed her to take only his. When she would have let ecstasy consume her, he forced her to wait.

He was relentless, unyielding. He demanded everything from her.

And she yielded.

He became her world. The only reality until sweet oblivion claimed her at his command.

Fifteen

THE smell of meat cooking on an open fire made Aisling's stomach clench painfully. It came on a pine-scented breeze along with the sound of music intermixed with human voices.

She touched the knife strapped to her thigh with strips of burlap. The food she'd packed for their trip into The Barrens had been eaten hours, and miles upon miles, earlier, before the first rays of light streaked across the sky.

They'd made up much of the distance they'd lost, by risking the darkness. The sun was rising when they left the ruin of civilization and slipped into thick forest.

At random intervals they continued to find the ancient believer's symbol carved into a tree or scratched on a cluster of rocks. Narrow deer trails led them deeper into a place where only a little bit of sunlight filtered in, where Nature had reclaimed what had once been ravaged by man. Twice they'd startled foxes from hiding, once they'd found the prints of a large cat—a cougar maybe, or jaguar. Aisling couldn't tell whether they were pure animals or Were animals.

Zurael stopped her with a hand to her elbow, urged her from the trail and behind a tree so wide she couldn't have gotten her arms around it if she'd tried. "Stay here," he whispered, becoming part of the breeze before she could speak.

Aisling slipped the long-bladed kitchen knife from its crude sheath of burlap and waited. Her stomach growled. Her mouth watered as the smell of baking bread joined the cooking meat. Calls of "Amen!" accompanied stomping and clapping, a tambourine and cymbals—the sounds of worship arriving with the tantalizing smell of food.

The hard knot of hunger in Aisling's stomach became an icy dread. Hot acid rose in her throat.

The promise she'd made in the ghostlands weighed heavily on her: to find whoever was creating Ghost and kill them—or see them dead.

What if it wasn't a single person but an entire congregation? What if every member of the Fellowship of the Sign could be judged guilty, save the children?

She shuddered. Understood as she hadn't before, that when Aziel offered Zurael's name, he'd given her the weapon to use for this task.

The soft swirl of leaves at her feet warned her of Zurael's return. She didn't flinch when he solidified next to her, his fingers locked around her wrist to keep her from accidentally using the knife on him. "They worship without having guards posted," he said. "It's safe to get closer."

Aisling sheathed the knife. The voices and music got louder as they moved forward. Her curiosity and trepidation mounted with each step, until once again Zurael pulled her from the path, this time guiding her deeper into the forest until they reached a high spot where the undergrowth provided cover and yet allowed them to look down and witness the gathered church members.

The service was being held in a small clearing. Aisling scanned the gathering for Anya, her tension mounting until she realized she didn't see any children younger than six or seven.

She looked at the men's faces and felt relief when she didn't find the face of the Ghost seller who'd been at Sinners the night she and Zurael went there.

Wooden picnic tables were set up in rows on the opposite side of the clearing. In front of them were several fire circles, each with a spit being turned by a teenage girl dressed in dark, somber clothing, her attention split between the meat she was tending and the preacher who stood behind a wide stone altar.

Two small boys managed fires on either side of the altar, prodding them, raking coal or wood into piles to keep them burning red. And on the altar itself, Aisling counted fifteen rectangular boxes, set haphazardly, as if they'd been placed there in offering.

She wondered what they held, until the rattling began. It came fast and furious. Soft, like the rustle of leaves. The bursts of sound long and short, each different, all distinctive. Especially to one who'd grown up on a farm in the country. Rattlesnakes.

The preacher walked around to stand in front of the altar. His voice carried, deep and rich and persuasive. "Brothers and sisters. You're here because God led you here. You're here, part of this community or getting ready to join it, at his will. You already know his words, the words Mark tells us about in chapter sixteen, starting with verse fifteen, but I'm going to tell you again!"

A chorus of "Amen!" met his words

He lifted his arms and pointed toward Oakland. "And He said, 'Go into the world and preach the Gospel to every creature. Those who believe and are baptized will be saved. Those that don't believe will be damned. And *these signs will follow* them that believe.

" 'In My name they will cast out devils.

" 'They will speak with new tongues.

" 'They will take up serpents—' "

The preacher opened the closest box and reached in without looking. He pulled out a heavy-bodied rattlesnake.

" 'And if they drink any deadly thing, it will not hurt them.

" 'They will lay hands on the sick, and they will recover.' "

The preacher reached into a second box, pulled out another rattlesnake, this one green and gray, long and thin.

He raised his arms, holding both of the snakes so the rattles ended up next to his face like beaded hair. "And they went forth and preached everywhere, the Lord working with them and confirming the Word with signs following. Amen!"

"Amen!" the congregation shouted, and a woman started playing a drum, its beat commanding, pulsing through air and earth alike, demanding movement.

Men and women danced, some in place, some toward the altar and the fires the two small boys were tending next to it. An older man reached the preacher and was handed a snake. He draped it around his neck, then opened a box and pulled out another one, holding it to his chest before offering it to a girl who looked sixteen.

The smell of burning flesh reached Aisling. She looked in horror at a teen standing next to a fire, his face a mask of spiritual ecstasy as he held a branding iron against his chest. When he lifted it, he wore the sign of the cross.

Others, some with brands, some without, joined him. And as Aisling's attention shifted between the two fires, the small boys reheated the irons then offered them to any who came. And lost in faith, or held by it, no one screamed as their flesh burned.

When she finally turned away from the sight, Aisling saw all the boxes open. Men and women both, old and young alike, passed snakes around, handled them. And the rattle of the snakes blended in perfect harmony with the throb of the drum.

A woman in the congregation stood and began prophesying. An older man fell to the ground, writhed, then began speaking in tongues.

Aisling shivered, unable to turn away from the scene. It was equally fascinating and repelling, horrifying and amazing. And for the first time she fully understood how mighty civilizations and the world as it once was had come to be destroyed because of religion.

Slowly the energy and ecstasy of the worship service faded,

controlled by the slowing, softening beat of the drum. The snakes were returned to their boxes, and the peopled gathered close, surrounded the preacher for a final prayer, one said in low, murmured tones that didn't reach beyond the circle of church members.

When it ended, the women and girls went directly to the picnic tables—all except for the drummer. She moved to the preacher's side.

Wicker picnic baskets were pulled from underneath the tables. Plates and silverware, tablecloths and finally dishes of food were laid out.

Movement at the end of the clearing drew Aisling's eye. Zurael murmured, "There's the child."

The little girl was subdued where the children not being carried by young teens were already tumbling toward the adults and the food like eager puppies. And as if the children's appearance was the sign to begin the meal, the men still at the altar picked up the snake boxes and went to the picnic tables.

The boxes were set on the ground, on benches, on the tables, as if they were hymn books set aside after the worship service. The rattle of the snakes slowly faded, giving way to the sound of conversation and laughter as people took their seats and began to eat.

Aisling's stomach clenched painfully. Her mouth watered.

She turned to look at Zurael, her eyes catching on the serpent tattoo coiling around his forearm before lifting to meet his eyes. Hunger or insightful observation, the words came from nowhere. "If I go alone, with you in a snake's form, they might welcome us with less suspicion and talk more freely in front of us."

Denial flashed in Zurael's eyes. His features tightened.

Aisling touched her fingertips to his lips with a confidence that once would have been foreign to her. "Don't say no. This is the best way. Let them think I'm one of them, someone whose faith is marked by a sign they believe in."

His hand lifted to become a fiery shackle around her wrist. A violent storm raged in his eyes, only yielding to the calm of deadly promise. He pulled her fingers from where they touched his mouth. "We'll approach the gathering as you suggest. My ability to protect you is limited by the serpent's form. Be warned, Aisling. Anyone who threatens you will be dead before they strike the ground. I won't risk your being harmed."

The fingers around her wrist tightened, then disappeared as he pulled away and became the serpent he'd been the day Elena visited, the day he and Aisling were taken unwilling into the spiritlands by a Ghost touch. She picked him up and draped him over her neck as she'd seen the worshippers do, as she'd once done with Aziel when he wore the body of a king snake.

Worry for Aziel distracted her. She stumbled, sending a covey of quail flying from cover with the noise she made.

Aisling forced herself to concentrate on the moment, on the task at hand. It was easy enough to rejoin the trail. Far harder to leave the shelter and protection of the forest.

Her heart raced in her chest. She knew that in the serpent's form, Zurael would taste her fear.

Whether it was the eruption of the quail or simply a testament to how alert they were to their surroundings, despite the ease in which they were gathered around the picnic tables, all eyes seemed to be on her the moment she stepped into the clearing.

The preacher rose from the table, as did the woman drummer. Both came forward to greet her with smooth confidence, the force of their personalities reaching her before they did.

"Welcome. I'm Brother Edom and this is my wife, Sister Elisheba."

The preacher's voice was the warmth of home, the promise of family and safety. His eyes were a father's, a brother's, seeing past the sin to the good that lay beneath and offering forgiveness, understanding.

"Come, join us for the meal," his wife said in lyrical tones, her eyes soft, offering a mother's love, a sister's friendship. "What should we call you?"

Their charisma was nearly overwhelming. It pressed against Aisling's psyche as if seeking hollow places to fill and gain anchorage in.

Her fingers curled unconsciously around the hidden fetish pouch. And with a suddenness that left her swaying slightly, she was free of Edom and Elisheba's subtle influence.

Aisling looked down at the ground, hoping they saw success in her unsteadiness, instead of failure. "Call me Aisling," she said in a whisper.

"You look tired and hungry, worn from your trials," Elisheba said. "Let us wash your feet and welcome you properly."

"No," Aisling said, deciding it was best not to let them pull her too deeply into their world. "I can't stay."

She dared to lift her face and meet their eyes again. In them she saw pity and regret, gentle understanding and infinite patience. But unlike before, she didn't feel buffeted by emotions.

"We understand," Edom said. "For some it takes time to believe and accept that God offers a taste of paradise on Earth for those who do His work. Come share a meal and fellowship with us."

Aisling followed them to the picnic tables and was introduced. A place to the left of Elisheba was rapidly cleared for her, though when the others retook their seats, they noted Zurael's presence and didn't sit within striking distance.

A plate loaded with sliced pork was set near Aisling. Her stomach growled so loudly that heat flashed to her cheeks. But the people around her laughed with good humor and pushed other food in her direction.

She ate, though after the first few bites Zurael's weight draped over her neck grew heavier and her conscience made the food lose some of its taste. She hated the thought of him being hungry in the midst of such a feast, but consoled herself with the knowledge he could hunt later or find the Fellowship kitchen and slip into it unseen.

When the meal was finished, young girls collected the plates while older ones served dessert. Boys of all ages stood, drifting closer to the table where she sat, apparently drawn by Zurael.

"He looks poisonous," one of them said, his gaze riveted on Zurael.

"I think he might be," Aisling said and there were appreciative murmurs from the boys when Zurael opened his mouth to reveal deadly fangs. "He was at the edge of the clearing. I picked him up after witnessing the worship service."

Several of the boys nodded.

Edom said, "The Spirit came on you, Aisling. It pulled you through a doorway and into fellowship—not just for your sake, but for ours!"

"Amen!" the people within hearing range said.

"It sent you as testament to The Word," Edom said.

"Tell us more," came the refrain.

"God is a living god," Edom said. "He's a spirit. He doesn't have a body. Except us. We're his body."

"Amen!"

"We're his hands and his mouth. We're his way into this world!"

"Amen!"

"Amen!" Edom said, leaving a pulsing, energy-filled silence that Aisling filled by asking, "Is that why you make and sell Ghost? So people will be open to The Spirit?"

She thought they'd be defensive, frightened that she knew about Ghost. But her question was greeted by smiles of understanding and nods of encouragement, by murmurs of "Welcome, Sister."

Their reaction confused her. It made the knot in her stomach grow heavy and cold. Her conscience shuddered and her soul recoiled at the thought of overseeing the slaughter of people who seemed strangely innocent, unaware of the devastation that would one day be unleashed because of their beliefs.

Edom leaned forward, eyes shining with the fervor of his faith. "Today isn't the first time The Spirit has come on you, is it? It came knocking when you were in one of those places of sin in the city—places with names advertising their wickedness.

"Lust! Greed! Envy! Those are just a few of the clubs people flock to, trying to fill an emptiness that can only be filled by Him!

"Don't worry, Sister, we're all sinners. We've all got things in our pasts, deeds and thoughts we're ashamed of.

"You're not the first person to seek pleasure using the stuff people have taken to calling Ghost. You're not the only one to end up confronting the ugliness, the evil that's slipped into your life while you weren't watching. You're not the first person to make a pilgrimage from the city looking for redemption, answering the call.

"Well, you've found Him and you've found us. Amen!"

"Amen!" came the refrain, thundering through Aisling like a death knell.

"So you make Ghost?" she asked again, needing to be sure but dreading hearing them admit it.

Edom's frown told her the question was unexpected, unwelcome after the passion of his words.

Elisheba covered his hand with hers and gave Aisling a small, knowing smile. "I've heard some become addicted to Ghost because it leads to unparalleled physical ecstasy. But once you've known true spiritual rapture, Aisling, you won't crave Ghost anymore.

"None of the Fellowship members use drugs. They're high on God and the life he's brought them to. We don't make drugs here. We take a small amount of money in exchange for distributing Ghost. And we sell it only in the red zone, where those who buy it might find salvation instead of damnation."

"Do you really see it as only a drug?" Aisling asked, her voice edged with both horror and disbelief.

Faces closed. Friendliness disappeared. Eyes darted back and forth between her and the preacher and his wife.

A toddler wobbled over and stood between him and Elisheba. "Up, Mommy!" the little girl said, and some of the smiles around the table reappeared briefly.

Edom measured his congregation. His expression grew somber and pensive, the charisma folding in on him, making him seem thoughtful, a man not afraid of searching for and confronting the truth.

"What do you mean?" he asked and Aisling wondered if some of the Fellowship members were opposed to selling Ghost, if maybe they weren't only sheep after all.

She gathered her thoughts. Chose the words and arguments that would ultimately lead them to tell her who they distributed Ghost for.

"You spoke about The Spirit coming on a person, knocking and opening a doorway to redemption and salvation."

Aisling paused and from somewhere behind her the space was filled by a soft "Amen."

"Well, Ghost can serve that purpose. I'm taking it on *your* faith. It can bring the light."

Brother Edom nodded. "Amen. It can bring the light."

"But I know for certain it can bring the darkness. It can open the door and let evil in. I've seen it myself."

"Tell us about it!"

Aisling held back a smile. She felt a rhythm settling in, understood the addictive power of the word.

"What Brother Edom said was right. I was in a place of sin. A place that boasted of it in the name it goes by."

"We've been there, Sister."

"Brother Edom was wrong when he said I was using Ghost. I wasn't. But there were men who were.

"Men who bought it from one of you. Who rubbed it on themselves and ate it. Who found the pleasure Sister Elisheba spoke of and became an obscene show for others in that place."

"Tell us more!"

"I was there when an evil presence swept into the room like an icy wind. I witnessed as it called others to join it and they moved on the men, slid into them like a hand goes into a glove."

"What happened then?" came a chorus of voices.

"Evil recognized evil!" a strident male voice answered, and Aisling turned her head to see the Ghost seller who'd been present that night approaching the tables, his finger pointing accusingly at her.

He was dirty, his clothing torn and his eyes burning with zeal. The shoulder-length brown hair was tangled and matted, wild— and for an instant his image was overlaid onto one she'd seen in an art book—of the Christians' savior raging as he cast moneylenders from the temple.

"Evil recognized evil," the man repeated. "They attacked her and were thrown out of the club. The men were torn apart and eaten by wolves and dogs while the shamaness and her lover ran and the sinners inside cheered for the beasts. And now evil has come into our home, like some of us said it would when we argued against taking money for distributing Ghost.

"You were wrong, Edom, to deal with the wicked, to send us out to their places of evil. And now we'll all pay for it unless He sees that we can abide by his word and are worthy of protecting."

The man opened two of the boxes and, without looking, reached in and pulled out snakes. They rattled furiously, struggled and writhed in his grasp, mouths open.

"You shall not allow among you anyone who is an enchanter, or a witch, or a consulter with familiar spirits, or a necromancer. You shall not allow them to live!" he screamed, hurling the snakes at Aisling and reaching for more of them.

People surged upward from their benches. They scrambled to get away from the snakes that coiled and struck and slid across the wooden table.

A child screamed repeatedly, shrill and terrified.

Zurael lunged. He deflected a snake before it could reach Aisling, then raced forward.

A man yelled as a snake swung around and bit his cheek while he tried to subdue the Ghost seller.

Zurael struck and retreated. Returned to coil at Aisling's feet, mouth open, his upper body raised and swaying.

The Ghost seller fell, dead before he reached the ground—just as Zurael had promised would happen to anyone who threatened her.

The air vibrated with the rattle of snakes, then was pierced by the screams of a child abruptly silenced.

Men closed in on the freed snakes, recaptured the ones that held their ground, hunted the ones that slipped into the forest.

Only slowly did chaos give way to calm.

Aisling heard the sobs then, the pleading, impassioned prayers. She turned to find Elisheba and Edom kneeling on the ground next to the chubby toddler.

The child was unconscious, shivering. Puncture marks marred her throat and arms where she'd been bitten.

They'd used a knife from the table to slice open her skin. Now they feverishly tried to draw the venom out with their mouths. But the toddler's condition was testament to how quickly it had already spread.

Aisling took off the necklace with the witch's healing amulet on it and knelt next to Elisheba. "Will you accept my help?"

Edom looked up and spat blood. His eyes bored into hers, not with the charismatic charm that seemed to offer forgiveness and understanding, but with a diviner's intensity, as if he was looking for the black stain of evil on her soul.

He glanced at his child. For a horrifying second Aisling thought they'd deny her help.

Elisheba reached across the tiny body and placed her hand on his arm. "Edom, please," she said and he nodded.

Aisling hoped the amulet was as powerful as Tamara claimed. She pressed it to the wound on the girl's neck.

The effect was immediate. The little girl stopped shivering. Her eyelashes fluttered, fast at first, then slower, as if she were being drawn back to awareness at the same rate the venom was being absorbed by the amulet.

Underneath Aisling's fingers, the woven strands of the amulet softened and took on the texture of wet yarn before hardening again, turning from pale gray to black, and finally crumbling from the outer edges inward.

The angry streaks on the child's arms and neck, left by the spreading venom, receded. Disappeared.

A whimper heralded the little girl's return to consciousness. Elisheba stroked the damp, silver-blond curls and whispered prayers of thanks. She cried in joyous relief when her daughter's eyes opened and chubby arms reached upward.

All that remained of the amulet was a large coin-sized circle. It had stopped changing against Aisling's fingers so she lifted it away from the child's skin.

Edom said, "Will you give what aid you can to Brother Samuel?"

"Yes," Aisling said, looking for the man who'd been bitten on the cheek as he tried to subdue the Ghost seller.

Brother Samuel was lying on a picnic table, moaning in pain. His face was already grotesquely distorted by the swelling, his chest rising and falling rapidly.

Aisling wasn't sure there was enough of the amulet left to save him. But she hurried to him.

Someone had cut across the puncture wounds left by the fangs, but little blood seeped from the opening. "Hold him down," Aisling said.

Guided by instinct, by her experiences with the fetishes she carried and the entities they represented, she pulled her athame from its sheath at her back and cut across the man's cheek, deepening the wound already there until it bled freely.

He screamed and thrashed. Lifted from the table.

Out of the corner of her eye, Aisling saw Zurael prepare to strike.

"No!" she said and quickly pressed the amulet to the man's skin.

He shuddered. Continued to struggle until what remained of the amulet grew soggy, then hardened and finally fell away.

"I'll be okay now," the man croaked, rolling to his side and vomiting when the others released him. His skin was clammy, but the swelling was gone from his face.

On another table lay the body of the Ghost seller. Guilt hovered over Aisling for bringing death with her. But she didn't allow it to settle on her. In her mind's eye she saw the vision of the future captured in a pool of her own blood in the spiritlands—the gleeful images of a world where malevolent spirits easily found pathways back to the place they once called home.

Aisling glanced around her and was met by somber expressions. She turned to find Edom and Elisheba standing, the little girl in her mother's arms.

Tension mounted in the silence. And into that silence came the slightest rustle of leaves as a breeze rose from her feet, swirled around her, lifting her hair and making her think Zurael had shed the snake's skin and now waited to take on a far more deadly form than the serpent's.

"If you were guilty of creating Ghost, more of you would be dead, perhaps most of you," she said, deciding to tell them the truth. "I came here looking for the person responsible for it."

Edom met her eyes for a long moment. A slight tremor went through him before he seemed to gather his natural charisma. He glanced around, pausing on some of the older members of his church, and said, "God is a living god. He's a spirit. He doesn't have a body, except us."

"Amen."

"Usually when He comes on us we're in a prayerful state. He tells us to take up the serpent, to put *His* mark on our flesh. But not always."

"Amen."

"There was a time *He* moved on me and I saw an angel."

"Tell us more."

"You want to hear it was a beautiful sight."

"Yes, Brother."

"You want to hear I was filled with *His* glorious love."

"Yes, Brother."

"Well, I'm not going to tell you either of those things. I'm going to tell you it was a terrible sight. It filled me with fear, the same fear I have now, standing in the presence of this stranger—this stranger who appeared with signs following!

"But I'm thankful for the fear! I'm thankful for the chance to make things right before it's too late."

Edom pointed at the corpse laid out on the picnic table. "Brothers and sisters, we've been fooling ourselves about Ghost. It cost us a good man."

"He was a good man," came the reply.

"Brother Scott saw the message *He* delivered in that place of sin but didn't know how to interpret it correctly. We've been telling ourselves it was all right because we weren't breaking any laws, because what little money we took for it went to do *His* work. But no more!"

"Amen."

"We won't be part of the devil's plan."

"You got that right, Brother."

"Amen," Edom said, releasing the hold he had on his congregation and turning to Aisling, motioning her forward. "Only a few of us know where the drug comes from. It's best if we keep it that way."

The gathered church members dispersed, respecting the need for privacy. Women and girls started clearing the picnic tables. Men and boys clustered around the corpse, discussing burial details.

"She doesn't think we know who she is," Elisheba said when Aisling stood next to the preacher and his wife. "Edom and I are the only two people who've seen her face. If she guesses that we recognized her, the guardsmen will be given an excuse to kill us and none will question it or be the wiser."

"Who is she?" Aisling asked.

"Ilka Glass," Edom said, naming the predatory woman in red who'd so easily swayed the crowd at Sinners so they voted the Ghosting men out to their deaths. "She's the wife of the man who's in charge of the guardsmen."

"And powerful in her own right," Elisheba added. "She's the daughter of one of the First Families to reclaim Oakland. Her husband has never come with her, but he must know or be a part of what she's doing. There are more guardsmen hunting The Barrens on the days she gives us Ghost and collects what we took from those who bought the previous batch."

A man's voice interrupted. "Brother Edom, what should we do about this? It's still full."

Aisling shivered at the sight of the small, coffinlike container the Ghost seller offered her at Sinners in the seconds before a coldness swept into the room along with a malevolent presence.

Last one.

"Bring it here," Edom said, and as if picking up on Aisling's thoughts, he added, "We don't have any more Ghost. Brother Scott took all that was left of what we got last month to the city. We won't accept any more of it if it's offered to us after the next full moon."

"That's when you get it?" Aisling asked, knowing the full moon was a week away and not surprised a substance like Ghost would most likely be created at a time when power for many supernatural beings peaked and the barrier between this world and the spirit one thinned.

"We get it the day after the full moon," Elisheba said.

The man who'd discovered the container walked as if he was carrying a bomb that might detonate in his hand, or an item that might cause the heavens to open and a bolt of lightning to strike him. When he reached them, Edom took it from him and shoved it into Aisling's hands. She fought the impulse to hurl it aside and wipe damp palms on her pants.

Her heart raced. She braced herself, almost expecting the spirit winds to claim her despite the onyx pentacle hidden in her fetish pouch and the thin slice of metal keeping the powerful substance contained.

Nothing happened.

Her heart rate slowed. The breath she was holding eased out.

Aisling slipped the container into her jacket pocket. Women and young teens were picking up baskets and gathering the smaller children, intending to return to the Fellowship compound hidden from view.

"Ghost wasn't the only reason I came here," Aisling said, finally locating Anya standing apart, her features wearing the shell-shocked expression Aisling had seen often enough on the faces of those left on Geneva's doorstep. "I came for one of the children brought here from The Mission."

"Recently?" Elisheba asked.

"Yesterday. She has a home elsewhere."

"Ah, those children haven't been taken in by families yet," Elisheba said, relief in her voice. "Edom?"

He nodded. "Take the child with you. If you've been to The Mission, then you know there are many others we could raise in our community."

Aisling glanced at the sky. The return trip would be faster since they wouldn't need to search for the symbols leading to the Fellowship. If they hurried, they should make it back to the outskirts of Oakland in time to catch the bus and get Anya to the Wainwright house before dark.

"We'll leave now," she said, surreptitiously looking for Zurael but not seeing the serpent.

"May The Spirit stay on you," Edom said.

"Amen," Elisheba murmured.

Aisling went to Anya. The little girl took her offered hand, and surprised her by saying, "I dreamed you came for me."

A wave of homesickness assailed Aisling as she thought about her sisters and brothers, especially the young, gifted ones. "I'm taking you to a family where you'll belong."

Anya nodded solemnly.

A church member gave Aisling a basket packed with food as they passed. "For your journey. May The Spirit stay on you while you're in the land of sin."

"Thank you."

At the edge of the forest Aisling felt the hot breath of a swirling breeze pass by her. From the dark shelter of pine and oak, Zurael emerged to block the path.

Anya's hand tightened slightly on Aisling's. In the same solemn voice with which she'd greeted Aisling, she said, "You're magic. Like the ferret."

Zurael chuckled and the gentle expression on his face as he looked at the child sent warmth cascading down to Aisling's toes. She handed him the food.

He leaned in, whispered a kiss across her lips. "Thank you. We'll have to hurry if we hope to make it."

They traded off, each of them carrying Anya, alternating between walking and running. They raced the sun, dodging the guardsmen and lawless humans patrolling The Barrens in the daylight.

It was a relief to get to The Mission. To hurry past it and climb onto an empty bus.

Tamara and her mother were both on the Wainwright porch when Aisling, carrying an exhausted and sleeping Anya, turned the corner with Zurael. The child didn't wake when she was transferred to Annalise's waiting arms.

Aisling's fingers went to the sun-shaped pendant at her wrist. Annalise shook her head and whispered, "Levanna wants you to keep it."

The dusk approached too rapidly for them to linger. But Aisling wanted to. Her heart felt strangely heavy, her arms empty now that Annalise had Anya.

"Visit the child when you can," Annalise said with an understanding smile.

"I will."

Aisling left the porch and joined Zurael where he waited beyond the warded boundaries of the witches' property. Her thoughts shifted from Anya to Aziel and her pace quickened.

Destruction and devastation greeted her when she opened the door. The old, tattered furniture was turned over, tossed against the wall and left broken. Cabinet doors hung open in the kitchen. But it was the silence, the emptiness, the fear of finding Aziel dead that numbed her to the core.

She didn't protest when Zurael urged her forward and to the side, closing the door behind them so a guardsman driving by wouldn't know they were back. "Let me check the other rooms," he said, voice soft, his knuckles brushing her cheek, his eyes burning with fierce tenderness.

Aisling nodded and leaned against the wall for support. Guilt swamped her.

How easily she'd convinced herself it was Father Ursu who had sent the guardsmen after her, using bedclothes or a discarded towel from her night in the church as a scent article. How easily she'd pushed aside her worry for Aziel, told herself he was safe in the house. If only . . .

"Aziel's not here," Zurael said, and she sagged, torn between relief and dread.

Sixteen

RAGE coursed through Zurael over the violation of Aisling's home and the pain radiating from her with the loss of her pet. He felt savage, barely in control—with no outlet for his fury other than passion.

He took her in his arms and crushed his mouth to hers, promised her with the force of his kiss that he'd see her pet returned and her suffering avenged. She softened immediately. Clung to him for strength and comfort, and in doing so, gentled him.

As they'd traveled through The Barrens, they'd decided on a plan of action, reasoned that the best place to hunt the ones responsible for Ghost was Sinners, where there would be no repercussions from either the humans present or the law.

"If the man in charge of the guardsmen and his wife know anything about this, we'll learn it tonight," Zurael said, parting from the kiss just long enough to say the words before recapturing her lips.

He rubbed his tongue against hers. Didn't know how he'd ever resisted the lure of her mouth, the soul-shattering intimacy of sharing a kiss.

A desperation settled over him. If they were successful tonight in destroying those responsible for Ghost, then he would have to turn his attention to his own task and she would become bait in a trap for Javier.

He could see no other way. But the thought of her being in danger—

It couldn't be helped. Until he'd returned to his father's kingdom with the tablet in his possession, their future together was uncertain and her life would be at risk from the Djinn.

With a groan he picked Aisling up and carried her to the bathroom. He set her on her feet next to the shower stall.

"We need to hurry if we're going to get to Sinners," he said, stripping before reaching in to turn on the water.

Her clothes fell away quickly and he shivered in ecstasy at the feel of her skin against his. They stepped underneath the water, already lost in the steamy cocoon of passion.

Zurael lifted her, impaled her. His tongue thrust against hers with the same urgency as his cock plunged into her slit.

He promised himself that one day he would lay her on a bed covered with silken pillows and sheets. He would spend hours pleasuring her with his mouth and hands—and being pleasured in return. But here, now, with the night swiftly approaching, he coupled with her furiously. He swallowed her cry of release and came in a shuddering, hot eruption when her channel tightened like an erotic fist around his penis.

They hurried through the remainder of their shower, then dressed and ate. A knock sounded as they were ready to leave.

Aisling went to the window and peeked out, felt her breath freeze in her lungs at the sight of a priest's black robes.

"It's Father Ursu," she said, keeping her voice low enough so it wouldn't be heard through the door.

A warm swirl of air greeted her announcement. She turned to find the room empty.

She didn't think it was a coincidence that Father Ursu had arrived so soon after she'd used the bus pass, though unlike before, she'd slipped it through the magnetic card reader only once, then used folding money to pay Anya and Zurael's fare—hoping the Church wouldn't take the time to question the bus driver and discover she hadn't been traveling alone. She opened the door but blocked it with her body so Father Ursu couldn't enter and delay them from getting to Sinners.

Worry creased his forehead. His eyes were kindly until he glanced behind her, to the devastation of the living room.

Surprise registered in his face. And though she would never trust him, she didn't think it feigned.

"What happened here?" he asked. "Who did this?"

"I don't know who's responsible. It was like this when I returned home."

His attention shifted to the right. "At least your pet wasn't harmed."

For an instant the sight of the black ferret left Aisling giddy with happiness. But when he didn't chirp a greeting or move from his position next to the workroom doorway, she knew it was Zurael and not Aziel.

She fought the worry that threatened to crush her with thoughts of Aziel, realized Zurael's appearance was meant to get a reaction from Father Ursu, to gauge whether or not he might know where Aziel was.

Aisling considered what she'd seen in Father Ursu's face and heard in his words. Once again she thought they were unfeigned.

She realized he must have questioned the driver who took them to the edge of Oakland the day before. Otherwise he wouldn't have known Aziel wasn't with them.

Uneasiness knotted her stomach when she looked at Father Ursu and caught him with his eyes closed, his eyebrows drawn together, his attention still on Zurael.

Javier's words rang in her mind. *I spent a great deal of my childhood in the tender care of the Church, much of it with Father Ursu, who saw the dark nature of my soul—read my aura and the strength of my inherent gifts.*

Father Ursu opened his eyes and caught her looking at him. "Aisling," he said, and the weight he gave her name invited confession—as if he'd read Zurael's aura and knew she consorted with a demon. "May I come in?"

"I'm just on my way out."

"This close to dusk? Do you think that's wise?"

She thought it better to deflect him if she could. "I'm not going far. Just to a friend's house."

A disappointed expression settled on his features. "I suspect the *friend* you intend to visit is the very one I'd hoped to speak with you about. As you know, Henri's death weighs heavily on me. I was his priest, and more often than not, the only friend he felt he could talk openly to. I feel a great deal of responsibility toward you as well. You're a beautiful young woman out on your own for the first time and alone in a strange place. Just because I wear the robes of the Church doesn't mean I don't understand loneliness or the temptations of the flesh."

Aisling couldn't prevent the heat from rising in her cheeks. She glanced beyond him at the growing dusk, wanted to bolt from his presence and his false attempts to befriend her.

Father Ursu's face softened, invited confidence. "Last night it was brought to my attention that you'd gotten off the bus near The Mission and hadn't caught it for a return trip. I suspected, given your history, you might have decided to help Davida with the orphans. But I was still concerned enough to contact her. She told me you'd been there in the company of a man previously, and she'd seen you entering The Barrens with that same man earlier in the day."

Aisling's heart raced along with her thoughts. Questions formed but she didn't speak, because asking them would also reveal what she knew, what she guessed.

When she didn't say anything, Father Ursu's sigh filled the space between them. He made a point of looking at the devastation behind her in the living room. "Aisling, have you considered that what happened here is a result of your involvement with your *friend*? No decent man would take a young woman into The Barrens."

She kept her silence, and his expression became grave. She willed him to say more, to answer the questions she didn't dare ask.

He said, "A couple of guardsmen lost their lives in The Barrens last night because after speaking to Davida, I grew very concerned for your welfare and initiated a search."

Aisling sagged with a lessening of the guilt over leaving Aziel behind. She'd been right in thinking the Church was behind the search, had probably offered the linens she'd used as scent articles.

Her reaction seemed to satisfy Father Ursu. She wondered if he'd suspected her of having something to do with the deaths. She thought maybe the purpose of his visit had been accomplished, but then he said, "I'm afraid the Church incurred quite a bit of expense on your behalf, Aisling."

An icy finger traced her spine. This was the very thing she'd worried about from the first and sought to avoid—being entrapped by debt.

She met his gaze boldly, refusing to become a victim. "It was your choice to initiate a search."

A part of her expected him to point to Zurael, to hint she could find herself accused of consorting with a demon. Instead he nodded his head in agreement. "You're correct. The Church can't expect you to reimburse it for the expense of the search. However, quite some time ago Henri tithed this house to the Church. While he lived in it, there was no reason to expect rent from the property. But with his death, and the cost incurred because of the search, those in charge of the Church's finances have successfully argued this property should be offered to someone able to pay rent. At Bishop Routledge's insistence, they're willing to give you a week before vacating or signing a rental agreement."

Aisling could guess at their plan. If they believed Ghost was made during the full moon, then that would be the time to use her as their weapon against its maker.

She didn't ask what the rent would be. She knew it would be set impossibly high—so that with the threat of eviction looming over her, she'd think it a godsend when they offered to let her perform a task in exchange for being able to remain in the house.

It would explain why Father Ursu didn't hint about her alliance with a demon, about the taint he might well see on her. To accuse her might make her flee, or it could bring suspicion on the Church if during a trial they were found to have used her services while suspecting she might summon a demon in the course of doing the task they asked of her.

But even guessing at their plan, even knowing if she was successful tonight, there would be no need to search for the ones responsible for Ghost, fear threatened to crowd in. She would have to seek shelter elsewhere. She wouldn't willingly enter into a contract with the Church and give them leverage over her.

Aisling kept her worry for the future hidden and held at bay, reminded herself that whoever had destroyed her furnishings hadn't found and taken the purse of silver coins.

It would buy her time. The sun pendant at her wrist made her hope the Wainwrights would serve as important allies if the Church threatened her with accusations of practicing black magic.

She glanced again at the darkening sky and said, "I need to leave now."

Father Ursu frowned, perhaps expecting her to cry in fear over the threat of being put out on the street, to beg him to intercede on her behalf. But the darkness held danger for him, too, and he contented himself with saying, "I'll check in on you in a few days."

* * *

THE same two bouncers guarded the front door of Sinners. They showed no surprise when Aisling and Zurael approached. But then Aisling suspected they were used to seeing people narrowly escape death, only to return on another night to court it.

She shivered, preferring the dark and the predators that lurked outside to the ones who glided through the hallways of the restored Victorian. She was acutely aware of the casket-shaped Ghost container in her pocket, of the strangers who even now gathered at the windows of the clubs lining the street in anticipation of a night of excess and violence.

The bouncer to the left took the offered money. The one to the right opened the door.

Aisling wiped damp palms against her pants and tried to slow the wild throb of her heart. It would be over soon, she told herself. She—they—could get through what came next. And then her family would be safe.

She willed herself to slide her hand into her jacket pocket and touch the small metal box. It was the only way. The best way. The surest way to get Ilka and Felipe Glass to answer the questions put to them.

Aisling's stomach knotted as she imagined dipping her fingers into the gray substance and then touching them, using Ghost to cast them into the spiritlands in the same way Elena had done to Zurael and her.

Her skin grew clammy thinking about committing such an act. But by her agreement in the spiritlands, she had to kill them or see them dead if they were guilty of creating Ghost.

The thought of Zurael going to their home in order to force them to come to her scared her. He'd be vulnerable there. The rich and powerful could afford wards and traps, and if they were truly guilty of making Ghost, then they'd have allies in the spiritlands, entities that might be capable of killing Zurael. She couldn't bear the thought, couldn't imagine living with the guilt if he died because of her.

This was the only way. The best way. But a chill swept through her. Could she really do it? She'd been so sure, so confident when they were miles and hours away from confronting Ilka and her husband.

In The Barrens she'd revisited those moments in the spiritlands with Ryker. She'd drawn upon the memory of the spirit winds coming to wrap them in an impenetrable cocoon after she'd wished the fog of the ghostlands would block out the sight and sound of his friends calling him. But as they were about to step into Sinners, old doubts assailed her.

She had no formal training. What if she was wrong? Not just about her ability to summon the winds, but about being able to control the Ghost trip as Elena had claimed to overhear Father Ursu saying.

There'd be no circle of protection. Nothing to keep malevolent beings from finding her except her faith in those she would call before entering the spiritlands.

Zurael's fingers circled her arm possessively as they stepped through Sinners' doorway. She glanced up at his face and took comfort in the fierceness of his expression.

Ilka and Felipe wore red again, only tonight it was the color of old blood. Aisling could feel the attention of those gathered on the first floor shift away from the street outside and sharpen with predatory interest on her and Zurael.

Titters of anticipation formed an undertone to clinking glass and murmured conversation. A few spared glances at Ilka and Felipe.

As they'd done on their previous visit, Aisling and Zurael moved to the bay window. She settled against him, her back to his chest.

His arms went around her. His lips trailed tender kisses along her neck.

The sight of them captured so intimately in the glass mesmerized Aisling. It blocked out the noise, the presence of others.

Something had changed between them in The Barrens, after the fight with the angel. But she was too much of a coward to speak to him about the future. She was too afraid of learning she'd followed in her mother's footsteps and, in taking a demon for a lover, had been granted a place in hell.

A shudder went through her before she could stop it. Zurael's arms tightened. "We can abandon this plan and make another," he whispered, misinterpreting the source of her anxiety.

"No," she managed, seeing Ilka's and Felipe's approaching images in the glass.

"You're back," Ilka purred, eyes bright, gleaming, as if the danger of confronting someone she'd led the vote against, someone who'd survived what waited in the darkness, excited her sexually.

She leaned forward, offering a glimpse of cleavage, a hint of a nipple. Her fingernails were long, painted red to match her outfit and lipstick. They hovered in the air then slowly descended toward Zurael's arm.

Against Aisling's back he vibrated with suppressed fury, making her think of the steady, unmistakable sound of a rattlesnake before striking. But Zurael allowed Ilka's hand to settle on him as they'd agreed upon in The Barrens, and Aisling hated the sight of another woman touching him.

"So this time you're interested in playing," Felipe said, following his wife's lead, leaning forward, stripping Aisling with his eyes.

It was all she could do to tolerate his nearness. Every cell screamed in protest when he ran his fingers down the line of buttons on her shirt.

Bile rose in her throat. She couldn't speak, couldn't utter the words necessary.

"You might say we couldn't stay away," Zurael said, his voice low, dangerous, his hand moving lower on Aisling's belly, his touch possessive, blatantly sexual. "But we don't intend to be entertainment tonight."

Ilka's laugh was a husky trill of victory. "Everyone's entertainment here. See and be seen, though I guess you weren't here long enough last time to understand the fun of Sinners."

Her hand slid upward. Her fingers curled around Zurael's biceps as Felipe's returned to the top buttons of Aisling's shirt and freed them, exposing the upper slopes of her breasts.

"Not here," Zurael growled, grabbing Felipe's wrist with snake-like quickness.

"Somewhere private," Aisling said, finally managing to break through the paralysis of her revulsion.

"Hmmm," Ilka said, shifting her attention to Aisling for the first time and leaning forward so their lips nearly touched. "Privacy is possible, for some. Have you ever been with a woman?"

"No." It was barely a whisper.

"Then I'll tell you a little secret. It drives men crazy. Turns them into stallions." She ran her tongue along the seam of Aisling's mouth as her hand cupped Aisling's breast. "But you already know what it's like to be mounted by a stallion, don't you?"

"Yes," Aisling said, fighting to accept Ilka's touch, blanking her mind to it.

"Not here," Zurael said, seeming to prove Ilka's claim by knocking her hand away, then possessively capturing Aisling's nipple with his fingers, tormenting it until a small moan of pleasure escaped despite their audience.

Ilka licked her lips. "Ummm, delicious. We're going to enjoy playing together."

"I think privacy is in order," Felipe said. "At least to begin with. Some treasures aren't meant to be shared—at first."

They pushed away from the bay window with perfectly synchronized grace. Felipe offered his arm and Ilka took it. Neither looked back as they walked away, their footsteps unhurried, the crowd parting in front of them as if they were royalty.

Zurael's lips found Aisling's ear. "Do it quickly. I can't tolerate them touching you."

Speculative, appraising glances followed them as they trailed Felipe and Ilka up the stairs and down a hallway that had no doors, until they turned a corner.

Felipe stopped in front of the only room possessing a door and produced a key. An anticipatory smile formed on Ilka's dark red lips. Her eyes traveled to the front of Zurael's pants. "It's little more than a closet. But I think it'll be perfect for getting better acquainted."

The door swung open. Aisling trembled and felt Zurael's fingernails sharpen and curl in a hint of the deadly talons they could become. He leaned in, brushed a kiss across her cheek and ear, whispered, "Release me from my agreement, Aisling. Let me do what needs to be done."

"No," she said, and they entered the room.

It was small, confining. A bed and two chairs took up much of the floor space.

One of the walls resembled a tack room. It was lined with ropes and leather straps, riding crops and other things Aisling couldn't identify. Restraints were bolted to a second wall and on the bed frame as well.

Aisling's thoughts flashed to when Zurael had tethered her wrists to the bed, to the pleasure she'd found. She met his eyes, saw the hot desire in them, the promise.

Heat gave way to icy chill when Ilka and Felipe stepped into the room and locked the door behind them. Dark red fingernails settled over Zurael's heart. "You I think we need to chain to the wall."

"No, please. I want him on the bed with us," Aisling whispered, letting them hear her fear, using it to her advantage as she endured Felipe unbuttoning the front of her shirt.

Ilka's attention shifted. Her eyes traveled over the length of Aisling's bared skin. She licked her lips and reached for a wooden rod studded with metal, pulled it from its place on the wall. "Only if he behaves. Only if you both behave."

Felipe's hands went to Aisling's shoulders. He started to slide the jacket off so the shirt could follow.

Her heart tripled its beat. Her breath grew short.

"I'll do it," she said, turning her back to them in a seemingly shy gesture.

"Delicious," Ilka purred.

Aisling's hands shook as she slipped the small, coffinlike tin from her pocket and tucked it in to her breast band. She shrugged out of her jacket and shirt, baring her upper body except for the fetish pouch and the wide strip of cloth she used to bind her breasts.

"How quaint and old-fashioned," Ilka said. "What a lovely blindfold that'll make. Or maybe we'll use it as a gag."

Aisling carefully unwound the breast band, making sure the Ghost container remained pressed to her skin until the last moment, when both ends of the binding cloth touched her knees. Fear knotted her stomach, but it didn't stop her from opening the tin and dipping the first two fingers of both hands into the gray substance, then silently calling the names of the entities who'd witnessed when this task was set before her in the spiritlands.

She let the container and cloth fall to the floor as she turned. She took advantage of Ilka's and Felipe's attention being drawn to her exposed flesh, paused only long enough to ensure that Zurael was free of their touch before stepping in to them and grabbing their wrists.

Understanding flashed in their eyes in the instant the wild rush of the spirit winds jerked their souls from their bodies and hurled them into a swirling, dense fog. Aisling knew her guardians had come to her aid when the gray mist held Ilka and Felipe in unseen restraints.

Fury and murderous rage gave way to cunning speculation and they stopped struggling. "Aren't you the clever one," Ilka said. "It's rare someone bests us, but apparently we're your prisoners, for the moment. What do you want? Revenge? No I think you're far too intelligent to waste such a luscious opportunity on something like that. We can offer so much more."

"I want to know if you're responsible for creating Ghost."

Ilka laughed, and her laugh held the supreme confidence of someone who'd always had the security of power and the protection of wealth, who'd believed since birth that the city was her playground and she could do anything she wanted in it.

Felipe chuckled. "I told my dear wife it was a mistake to vote you out of Sinners. Ilka found it hard to believe we'd been so easily manipulated into doing something not in our best interests. It looks like I've been proven right."

"What can I say? I got caught up in the moment, as one does at Sinners. Afterwards I regretted it of course, but there was nothing I could do."

"True, but I think we can strike a bargain with the shamaness. She's got a family of sorts, sharecroppers on a farm outside of Stockton I believe my captain said in his report. I suspect she'd like to know they're not only safe but have the security that comes with owning their own land. Between the guardsmen I control and the real estate your family owns, we can come to a satisfactory arrangement."

"You're getting ahead of yourself, Felipe. It's possible this is her way of getting rid of the competition and taking over the trade in Ghost herself."

"True. But somehow I don't think she intends to eliminate us. I have to go with the situation as I see it." Felipe made a point of examining Aisling's nakedness then his own and his wife's. "I believe play *is* on the agenda for the night, once we can reach an agreement. And I will point out, even before Aisling's trip to the library, I did tell you it was a mistake to use those snake-handling religious fanatics to distribute Ghost. It was only a matter of time before someone made the connection and found their way to the Fellowship."

Felipe smiled but there was only calculation in his eyes. "For the record, Aisling, I had nothing to do with the bloodhounds being sent after you last night. It was a routine search, even if Father Ursu initiated it. I wasn't in the office and it didn't need my approval."

Their complete lack of conscience sickened Aisling. Their lack of fear worried her.

She could feel the spirit winds thickening, buffeting against her as if being pushed back by something fighting to get through the gray barrier forming a protective cocoon around them.

"Where's Aziel?" Aisling asked.

"Aziel?" Felipe's puzzlement seemed genuine.

"My pet. The ferret I brought with me to Oakland."

"I don't know."

Pain slid through her heart like a knife's blade. But she believed him. He had little reason to lie and had already demonstrated a complete confidence that he would bargain his way out of a situation that would have left most cringing in terror.

"Are you responsible for creating Ghost?"

Ilka's smile was sly. "We've got a silent partner. But you must have already guessed that. Otherwise you wouldn't have dared use Ghost on us. If we give you his name, will you kill him?" She laughed. "Not that I blame you. Not that Felipe and I would object. We could sell so much more than our partner produces. And you'll find it's easier to gather the necessary ingredients with guardsmen helping—especially when some of the ingredients need to be brought in alive. Even in Oakland, where there are plenty of poor and destitute, it's not all *that* easy to make someone disappear."

Aisling's stomach lurched and roiled. "Who's your partner?"

"Can't you guess?" Ilka said. A silky taunt.

And playing back the things they'd said, what had happened the first time she and Zurael visited Sinners, what they'd learned since then, Aisling could.

It was a mistake to vote you out of Sinners. Ilka found it hard to believe we'd been so easily manipulated into doing something not in our best interests.

You'll find it far more entertaining to vote her out with the others. She's a shamaness.

An interesting piece of information, Peter.

"Peter Germaine," Aisling said, naming the mayor's brother, the deputy police chief who was no friend to any human with supernatural gifts.

Almost as soon as she'd spoken, Aisling thought she must be wrong because he'd have to be gifted to make Ghost. But before the doubt could settle in, Ilka's expression offered confirmation, and Felipe echoed it by asking, "Now what?"

The gray wall of fog parted and Elena's brother stepped through to stand next to Aisling. "Felipe! Ilka! You can't imagine how glad I am you're finally here. I should have guessed you had something to do with Ghost."

John rubbed his fingers over the cable around his neck as if stroking a dog's collar. He leaned in so his face was inches away from Felipe's, but the other man didn't blink, didn't seem to see Elena's brother.

"Still under Ilka's thumb?" John asked. "Still letting her call the shots? I'm curious. Did she order my death? Or did you resent losing business to me? A pathetic reason either way. I hardly made any profit supplying entertainment for your guardsmen, not by the time I shaved my rates to undercut yours. But then dear Ilka never did like me, did she? And if I remember correctly, she absolutely loathed my sister—not that I blame her there. I wish dear Elena could join us, it's the only thing that would make this show better, but I'm still going to enjoy it immensely."

He turned to Aisling. "Did you fantasize about me the way I did about you?"

"Why are you here?"

"To set the stage, my beautiful ang—" The steel cord pulled taut, his back arched, and the tattoos of a lawbreaker stood out in stark relief on his face.

John went down to his knees. The metal leash grew slack.

A hint of madness glittered in his eyes. He whispered, "I keep forgetting that where you're concerned I have to be very, very careful not to offend."

He reached for Aisling, as if he'd use her to pull himself to his feet. She stepped back, felt the rub of coarse fur against her bare skin and knew the entity represented by the bear fetish stood behind her.

John scrambled to his feet and began walking a circle. The thick strand of cable he'd hung from at his death trailed behind him. And as he paced out the design, the ghost fog thinned to reveal men, women and children by the dozens—all of them staring at Felipe and Ilka with feverish intensity—prevented from moving closer by the boundaries of the circle.

Aisling recognized four of the dead immediately. Their faces were undamaged though their bodies were ripped open. Organs hung by strands of muscle and sinew. Intestines looped to the ground through bloody, tattered clothing. They were the Ghosting men who'd died the night she and Zurael first went to Sinners.

Beside and beyond them were others who'd shared the same fate, men and women sent to their deaths when Felipe and Ilka led the vote. And intermixed with those were victims who'd been executed with shots to the head, who wore ropes or twisted wire around their necks. But they weren't the most horrible of the dead.

Hollow-eyed children and young women stood with gaping chest cavities, their hearts extracted. And seeing them, Aisling knew this was what Ilka had meant when she said, *Some of the ingredients need to be brought in alive.*

She'd wondered how the spiritlands could be held open so the winds would flow over an earthly substance and create a doorway into the ghostlands. She'd known such a feat couldn't be accomplished unless powerful forces in the spirit world were involved.

Those beings would demand death. They would devour innocence and enjoy the screams of terror that came with it. They would find it amusing to use the hearts of the sacrificed as bait for souls yet claimed.

"Do you judge your prisoners responsible for the creation of Ghost?" a deep, masculine voice asked, and Aisling turned to face the entity whose name she'd called upon for protection.

She didn't know whether it was his true form or the one he offered because her mind could accept it. But he was as she'd expected to find him—appearing like a shaman of old, a human form draped in the pelt of a bear.

His face was hidden from her though his eyes shone through the snarling headdress. His human arms disappeared into folds of fur, his hands and fingers becoming bear claws.

"They aren't solely responsible," Aisling said, "but they are guilty."

"Then you must kill them or see them dead."

A shudder went through Aisling. She'd been witness to so many deaths. The Ghosting men. Those Zurael and Irial struck down. The assailant she'd killed in her home. What were two more? Especially these? And yet she knew these two would leave her changed forever. That by killing them here, in the spiritlands—on a circular stage created by a soul she'd come to believe was in her father's possession—she was being drawn deeper into a world belonging to Zurael's enemy.

She looked past the circle at the silent, waiting dead. They would kill for her. She had only to break the circle John created with the cable linking him to his master, and they would rush in.

But the risk was great. She might be killed. If not by them, then by what would follow.

She felt the phantom weight of the athame she wore in a sheath at the middle of her back, but when she glanced down, the naked view of her skin was unbroken except for the fetish pouch around her neck.

The old shaman's arm lifted, drawing her attention back to the savage headdress, the yellowed bear teeth and impenetrable eyes, the wrists disappearing into fur and claws.

Without warning he struck. Raked the sharp claws down her face.

Pain drove her to her knees, an agony that left her gasping, sobbing, unable even to scream as a thousand shards of ice sliced through her eyes, leaving her terrified that when she opened them she would be blind.

Small tremors continued to ripple through her after the last of the freezing pain faded. She was left weak and frightened.

It took raw courage to force her hands away from her eyes. To open her lids.

Terror gripped her then. There was only gray nothingness everywhere she looked.

She was blind to the hands only inches away from her face. To her kneeling form.

Her heart thundered in her ears, as if to reassure her it still beat. Panic threatened to engulf her.

She fought it off and was rewarded with an awareness of movement. The mist pulsed to the rapid beat of her heart as she looked at the place she knew her wrists were.

Strands of gray emerged in a fine weave that captured and defined the shape of her fingers, her hands, her arms, the rest of her— as if she were encased in a spider's web.

Gray gave way to color, blended so all that remained visible from those initial strands was a thin line leading downward—like John's cable leash. Only, she understood intuitively that the thread she saw led back to her physical body—because she was alive, her soul her own.

Aisling glanced up at Felipe and Ilka. She saw the web overlay until she blinked and it was colored in, leaving only the threads leading to their physical bodies visible. She knew she had only to touch them, to sever those links—

And, as if following her thoughts, the deep voice of the old shaman said, "It's your birthright. Use it to do what must be done."

Aisling rose to her feet. She dared to look at him. He appeared exactly as he had before.

Elena's brother and those who stood outside the circle were pure spirit, transparent and nearly formless until she willed herself to see them in the same way she'd always seen them. And they appeared— torn and riddled with bullets, most of them bound to unseen entities by silken threads, souls bartered for protection, or sold while living and claimed in death.

She couldn't ask Zurael to do what she herself was unwilling to do—though she knew he was willing to kill Felipe and Ilka, had even promised as much in the library when they'd stumbled upon the picture in the newspaper and had names to go with the faces of the man and woman in red. But she refused to ask it of him. This was her task. Her burden.

"Is Peter Germaine your only partner?" she asked, her voice shaky as she grasped the cords tethering their spirits to their physical bodies.

Their eyebrows drew together in puzzlement over her odd behavior. She saw a flicker of uneasiness appear in Felipe's eyes, only to disappear under oily slyness. "We've told you quite a bit about what we can offer you. But you've yet to tell us exactly what you have to offer us."

A hard buffeting by the spirit winds warned Aisling she was running out of time. She didn't respond to Felipe's comment. Instead she looked down at the thin gray strands of silken thread she held.

She intended to break them. It was in her mind to do it. But before she could act, they blackened between her fingers, dissolved into nothingness with a sensation that had her mind flashing back to the instant when she'd touched her downed assailant in the workroom, when he opened his eyes and stared in horror at something unseen as his spirit left his body and entered the ghostlands. She'd wanted him dead, willed it as she fought him—and now she suspected it was her touch that killed him, and not striking his head against the edge of the workbench as she'd believed.

Movement in front of her tore Aisling from her thoughts. Freed from the tether of their physical bodies, Felipe and Ilka were no longer held immobile, trapped in the ghost fog.

They didn't yet understand what had happened to them. Their expressions told Aisling as much, the way their eyes held the same predatory intensity as when they'd glided toward the bay window where she and Zurael stood.

She stepped back involuntarily, and their smiles widened. "It's a shame you didn't strike a better bargain while you could," Ilka purred, stepping forward, their audience still unseen.

Aisling retreated farther, to the edge of the circle. Ilka and Felipe moved apart, thinking to trap her between them, heedless of the boundaries defining their safety.

Their ignorance was short-lived.

John's eyes flashed with glittering triumph when Felipe's foot broke the plane of the circle and the truth was revealed. For the first time, Aisling saw true terror on Felipe's and Ilka's faces.

Those gathered surged forward, their glee and satisfaction like a living, breathing thing. They reached in hungry vengeance, using hands and teeth to rip into flesh and muscle and organ tissue. They meted out a punishment that could last for eternity, filled the air with screams that were carried on the spirit winds as Aisling was swept from the ghostlands.

Seventeen

ZURAEL caught Aisling before she crumpled to the ground. He swung her into his arms, took the few steps necessary to reach the bed. The coldness of her skin alarmed him, and he hurried to undo his shirt so he could cuddle her against him, warm her with Djinn fire.

She smiled, and it touched every part of him, reached his heart and completely encased it. "It's done?" he asked, though the corpses on the floor seemed to answer the question.

"There's one more. Peter Germaine. He was here that night."

"I remember him."

Zurael pressed his lips to hers, shared the breath that was Djinn spirit.

The raw feelings of helplessness he'd experienced while she was in the spiritlands with Felipe and Ilka faded with Aisling in his arms.

In his time with her he'd gained a new appreciation for those pledged to the House of the Raven, and the ones who loved them. If the human ghostlands were a dangerous place, then the spirit birthplace of the Djinn would be no less harrowing. He didn't envy those whose task it was to guide the Djinn back for rebirth.

He deepened the kiss and moaned when her tongue greeted his with a warm slide of heat against heat. Fierce emotion swelled in his chest and he pulled her more tightly against him. He felt so close to her—spirit entwined with spirit—as if they were one being forced to live in separate bodies and unable to find completion unless they were together.

"Aisling," he whispered when he lifted his mouth, allowed her to take a breath that wasn't his.

He lost himself in eyes that were an endless blue sky, a deep ocean pool. When her lips parted and she glanced down shyly, suddenly appearing more vulnerable, his heart raced in anticipation of hearing her name what was between them.

"I—" she started, only to stiffen and turn in his arms, her skin chilling against his.

Protectiveness surged through Zurael. He put Aisling in the center of the bed before rising to his feet. With barely a flicker of thought, clear fingernails became black demon talons.

The corpses stood. Felipe's blank, dead eyes slowly filled, revealing amusement along with a hint of cruelty and madness. Ilka's held the nothingness of a zombie.

What had been Felipe laughed with John's voice and touched his neck. His gaze flicked over Zurael, dismissed him in favor of Aisling. "Another deadly pet, beautiful? And I was hoping . . . Well I'm sure I can amuse myself elsewhere before I'm forced to leave." He tilted his head toward Ilka. In a stage whisper he said, "Now she's *dead* weight, which is a shame, but I'll make sure she's taken care of."

John grabbed Ilka's arm, then noticed the studded baton at his feet. He bent down and scooped it up.

"A toy. How fun! Using it on Ilka won't be the same since she's not really with us, but it's the thought that counts, and I will enjoy the thought."

At the doorway he patted the clothing until he found the key to the room and slipped it into the dead bolt. "I'd suggest you stay here, enjoy your pet. You'll know when we're gone for good."

Demon talons became clear fingernails with John's departure. Zurael locked the door and returned to the bed. The driving energy to protect gave way to the pulsing desire to possess when Aisling's firm breasts and hardened nipples pressed against his chest. Except for the soft leather pouch containing her fetishes, she was still naked from the waist up.

The image of her turning, allowing others to see her—the memory of Felipe and Ilka touching her, even briefly, even though it had been necessary—drove all rational thought from Zurael's mind. She belonged to him.

Zurael stripped her with possessive hands, knowing that the only way to eradicate all vestiges of another's touch, of another's glance, was to give in to the hunger riding him with primitive intensity. He shed his own clothing without ever lifting his mouth from her mouth, her neck, her breasts.

Aisling trembled in eagerness beneath him. Opened for him so that when he settled his weight on her, his cock found wet heat and swollen, parted folds.

Her willing submission buffered the rawness of his lust, kept him from rutting like a feral creature. His thighs bunched with the effort to remain still, to savor the ecstasy of being inside her as his tongue mated with hers.

He shuddered when she freed his hair from its braid and it draped over them in a sensual curtain. He did the same to hers and was enthralled by the sight of Aisling's honey-gold locks entwined with the raven-black of his.

Zurael rolled to his back, taking her with him. He luxuriated in the silky feel of her skin and hair against his flesh. Grew more aroused when her mouth claimed his in a sultry kiss as she bathed his cock in hot, throbbing arousal.

His hands roved over her body, palmed her breasts and buttocks.

He swallowed her moans of pleasure and arched off the mattress when she began rocking, rubbing her clit against his abdomen, fucking herself on his cock with excruciating slowness.

It was too much, the raw pleasure more than he could bear. He put Aisling underneath him again, and this time he didn't fight the savage urge, the frenzied need to couple with her, to take her body and soul, and reinforce his claim to her heart.

Afterward he held her, buried his face in the gold of her hair as she clung to him in exhausted sleep. He traced the delicate line of her spine, contemplated the future and what he might say to The Prince, to Malahel of the House of the Spider, and Iyar of the House of the Raven.

He would die for Aisling. The realization should have filled him with terror. Instead it brought only determination to finish what needed to be done so he could fight for a future with her.

Zurael's thoughts strayed to the Hall of History, to Jetrel, the first of The Prince's sons, the one who had turned his back on the House of the Serpent and chosen to live among the alien god's creations instead of the Djinn. Idly he picked up a lock of Aisling's hair, finally understanding what had driven Jetrel to make such a choice.

The sun-shaped amulet glowed at her wrist. His attention was drawn for a moment to the amulet pouch. In his mind's eye, Zurael saw the tapestries in the House of the Spider, the erotic images of intertwined humans, angels and Djinn. And for the first time, he wondered if the Djinn might reclaim the land that was once theirs through alliance instead of bloodshed.

Noise beyond the door drew Zurael from his contemplations. Shouts of "Vote! Vote! Vote!" pulsed through Sinners like an electric current.

Zurael eased away from Aisling. She didn't stir as he dressed, didn't wake when he dressed her in case they needed to leave quickly.

He slipped from the room and locked the door behind him. The halls were empty, but the buzz of conversation told him those on the second floor were gathered at the front, where bay windows provided a view every bit as good as the one on the ground floor.

Anticipation clung to the air, rose and fell like a beast inhaling and exhaling. Zurael braided his hair as he walked.

There was a ripple of excitement as he reached the front rooms. Dressed and semi-dressed men and women crowded forward, murmured and whispered, their voices running together.

He stepped closer, not bothering to listen to their words. He didn't take pleasure in what he saw on the street beneath him. But there was a savage satisfaction in watching as werewolves and feral dogs tore apart the abandoned corpses of Felipe and Ilka Glass.

THEY emerged from the locked room shortly after dawn. In the gray light Aisling saw the thin tracery of lines that defined the boundaries of the physical self and contained the spirit in every person she looked at—save for Zurael.

She refused to believe he was soulless, settled instead on the explanation that because he could become formless, his spirit wasn't contained the way a human's was.

But even letting the weblike lines fade from sight and leaving Sinners didn't obliterate the terrible certainty that all it would take was a touch, coupled with a thought, and the gossamer strands she could see when she willed it would blacken and dissolve into nothingness, separating soul from body.

She wanted a shower and breakfast, a chance to come to terms with the events in the spiritlands, with the horrible gift of her birthright. But when they rounded the corner onto her street, Elena was waiting for them, pacing next to her chauffeured car.

"She might be able to help us get to Peter Germaine," Aisling said, balling her hands into fists, willing herself forward.

Elena was tapping her foot impatiently by the time they got to her. Her gaze shifted back and forth between Aisling and Zurael, until finally settling on Aisling. "I need to speak with you, privately."

A step took her to the car. She opened the door. When Aisling hesitated, Elena said, "If you no longer want my business, then you can give me back the silver pieces."

Sweat broke out on Aisling's skin despite the chill of the early morning air. Her stomach tensed with worry as the conversation with Father Ursu played out in her mind. She would need those coins to find a safe place to stay.

Instinct rebelled against getting in the car with Elena, but reason dictated. The engine was off and Zurael was close.

Aisling slid onto the backseat. Elena followed, closing the door behind her.

Automatic locks engaged. The driver started the car and pulled away from the curb.

"Where are we going?" Aisling asked, fighting the panic welling up inside her by telling herself Zurael could easily follow them by taking another form.

Elena shifted restlessly in the seat, fidgeted. She played with the rings on her fingers and the bracelets on her wrists, reminding Aisling of the junkies she sometimes encountered in the spiritlands.

"I overheard Bishop Routledge telling Luther you went into The Barrens and because of it the Church incurred a heavy debt to the guard. Were you looking for the man who sold Ghost to me the night I was taken from Sinners?"

"He's dead," Aisling said but didn't reveal the Ghost seller's connection to the Church, that the brands on his hands were given to him for consorting with demons. "Was Luther's brother, Peter, at Sinners the night you were taken?"

Elena snorted. "You've met him?"

"No. I saw him there, the day you visited and hired me. Later I found out who he was."

"Hypocritical zealot. He claims visiting the clubs is part of his job as deputy police chief and Church liaison. But it's the only time I've ever seen his cock pressing against the front of his pants. He's particularly fond of visiting rooms where the women are tied and gagged. I've met plenty of men like him. He believes women are inferior and weak, but at the same time sees them as seductresses who lead men astray.

"Peter despises me. He claims Luther will wind up in hell because of his affair with me—as if Luther hasn't had plenty of other lovers besides that cold, religious bitch he's married to. Peter would think it divine justice if I was sacrificed to the devil. But he wasn't at Sinners the night I was Ghosting. And he hasn't got the balls to act anyway. Peter never does any dirty work himself. He's convinced Judgment Day is right around the corner and he doesn't want to taint his soul."

Aisling looked down at her own hands. She'd killed with them. And at her feet lay even more bodies. The burden of their deaths weighed heavily on her.

Death drapes you like a billowing cloak, Raisa had said as she stared at the tea leaves. *It writhes at your feet and twines around you like a nest of serpents, so your touch becomes its harbinger.*

Yet as Aisling remembered those who'd come for Felipe and Ilka in the ghostlands, she realized she didn't fear for her soul as she once had. The ability to rive spirit from flesh might be her terrifying and unwanted demon birthright, but if those she touched were claimed by dark places that could be labeled hell, it was a result of the choices they'd made in their lives.

The car entered into the red zone. They drove through an area containing sex shops and brothels where prostitutes lounged naked behind windows. They passed the street where the row of Victorians lined either side, then began traveling along a wall that stretched for so many blocks Aisling lost count of them.

"This is The Maze," Elena said. "There are cameras set up all through it, with feeds to some of the betting clubs. Convicted criminals are offered a chance to run it in order to escape a tattoo or death sentence. Others run it for money."

Aisling's hand went to her amulet pouch. "What's in The Maze?"

Elena shrugged. "I don't know. I imagine it depends on what can be captured or purchased. I've never been there or to the betting clubs connected to it. Gambling on blood sports doesn't appeal to me."

The car slowed to a stop in front of a house set well apart and secluded from its neighbors. "I want you to meet an acquaintance," Elena said.

"Who?"

"Does it matter? I hired you and so far I've gotten nothing for my money."

The chauffeur opened the door and Elena slid out. She scowled impatiently at Aisling, began worrying her rings and bracelets again.

"Would you prefer to return the silver coins *and* the paper money I gave you? I'm perfectly capable of taking the matter to court."

Aisling shivered. Her stomach knotted with tension. She understood the game Elena was playing, but she had no choice but to participate.

Uneasiness settled on her as she left the car. Her spirits were lifted only a little bit by the warm breeze that swirled around her, smelling of the desert.

Elena didn't knock when she reached the front door. She stepped inside, seemed to care only about whether or not Aisling was following her.

The furniture was functional, the walls left bare. The sound of their footsteps traveled in front of them down the hallway. At the end of it a heavy door was propped open.

Warm air flowed past Aisling's arms. Elena stepped through the doorway first. Aisling followed.

A flash of red was the only warning Aisling had of a trap snapping shut. She saw the statuette from Javier's shop just as arterial spray from Elena's throat jetted onto the tile flooring and Javier began chanting.

Before Aisling could react, Javier's assistant was behind her with a knife, the blood-slick blade pressed to Aisling's neck preventing speech or movement.

Horror, regret, an agony of love pounded through Aisling as Zurael shimmered into sight, a band of sigils forming like a collar around his neck.

He struggled, naked except for flowing, nearly transparent trousers. His face contorted and his throat worked as if he screamed, though no sound emerged.

The chanting didn't stop until Zurael stood motionless, covered in sweat, muscles rippling and breath short. His eyes burned with the same terrible rage and hatred she'd seen the night she summoned him.

"A crude way of binding a demon by your standards, beautiful Aisling, but effective," Javier said.

She opened her mouth only to have the knife's blade draw blood. Javier shook his head. "I'm afraid I can't allow you to speak until I'm certain we understand one another. Aubrey *will* kill you if you struggle or attempt to summon help. I'm hopeful it won't come to that. As I said during our all too brief lunch, I believe we can be very good together. And I'm content to share nothing more than a working relationship with you. In fact, at some point in the future, I'll even be willing to let you have your lover back."

Aisling forced her body to relax. She willed her heart to slow. Fought the panic that too easily scattered her thoughts.

She became aware of the fetish pouch hidden under her shirt. It felt as though icy shards pierced the soft leather and burrowed into her skin.

The crystal amulet representing the being she now thought was her father grew heavy, making her remember the day she'd found it, when Aziel named her most powerful protector and told her he wasn't bound by the spiritlands. She could call upon him with a thought and pay whatever price he demanded—except Zurael was helpless and he'd already named her father his enemy.

As the cold radiating from the crystal filled Aisling's chest, clar-ity came and brought hope. She thought of the horrifying birthright she'd gained when she forced Felipe and Ilka into the spiritlands, and the beginnings of a plan formed.

Her mind calmed. She saw Aubrey's arm, held high to keep the knife in its deadly position, a tanned limb covered in silken meta-physical strands of gray.

It would only take a touch. A thought. But despite the knife in Aubrey's hand, she wasn't the greatest threat. Aisling met Zurael's eyes and saw the helpless rage in them, knew that with a command, he would become Javier's weapon against her.

She exhaled on a shaky sigh, and Javier nodded. "I believe you can ease up just a bit, Aubrey. At the moment we have more than enough blood for our purposes."

Aubrey relaxed her grip. Blood trickled down Aisling's neck, her own and Elena's.

Javier glanced down at the circle around him, then over at where Elena lay in a pool of blood, the jets of her arterial spray having trig-gered and powered a larger circle, the one used to trap Zurael until he was bound.

"It's quite ironic, really. The Church—operating under the erro-neous assumption they own me and therefore I can't possibly have anything to do with the dramatic increase in black magic ceremonies—whispered in my ear that I should make it known there'd be financial compensation if the mayor's little Jezebel ended up as a sacrificial lamb on a certain night." Javier chuckled. "Their plan *was* clever in some ways. Dear Luther coughed up the money to have you brought to Oakland, so their interest in you wasn't obvious. Father Ursu was probably beside himself with joy when he caught a glimpse of your aura. I did warn you about his special talent. No doubt he was expect-ing it to be a waste of time, but people with your gift, and who might be considered disposable, aren't that easy to come by.

"And Elena? I hope you don't feel sorry for her, Aisling. Raisa spotted her leaving your house the other day and unwittingly told me about it, thinking it harmless gossip. It piqued my curiosity, as you can imagine.

"Elena was never really interested in learning why she was taken from Sinners. It took all of three minutes in her presence to figure out she wanted to make a deal with whoever was creating Ghost, form a partnership where she offered the services of her captive shamaness for guided tours into the spiritlands. It took another minute to convince her you'd figured out how to make Ghost. And by our fifth moment together, I'd sold her on the idea that you could be *persuaded* to cooperate if she only brought you here.

"It's a shame I can't risk letting you speak, Aisling. Unlike the vast majority of magic practitioners, I'm not in love with the sound of my own voice. But perhaps we'll break the monologue up a bit by letting your demon talk. I'm curious. Beyond curious actually. I'm fascinated. And envious."

Javier stepped to the boundary of the small protective circle he was in. His hands slid from the folds of his black robe. One of them was wrapped with white strips of cloth, dotted where blood had seeped through.

"Where to begin?" he asked, steepling his hands so the fingertips rested on his lips. "A name would be appropriate. I don't need it with this particular entrapment spell, but I know just how much demons hate giving up their names."

He touched a band of sigils circling his wrist. The forms were the same as those around Zurael's neck. "Give me your name."

Aisling ached as she watched Zurael fight the command. Sweat beaded on his temples, rolled down his cheeks and made her aware of the tears on her own face. What tiny bit of hope she'd held that he might be stronger than the spell binding him faded when he said, "Zurael en Caym."

"An interesting name. I have volumes upon volumes of texts naming demons, and yours doesn't resemble any of them. What type of entity are you?"

Zurael struggled against answering. The night Aisling called his name on the spirit winds, he'd seethed and raged, known true terror for the first time in his life. He would have killed her without a second thought. But now he realized how gentle her summons was, how much of his own will he'd retained compared to the compulsion of Javier's spell.

He fought to remain silent. But the answer formed over and over, looped through his mind, growing louder and louder.

Javier grew impatient and asked a second time. Then a third.

Zurael became disassociated from his physical self. He became a spectator, watching as his lips parted and the words left his mouth. "I am Djinn."

His eyes met Aisling's and his heart wept at the sight of her tears, the guilt and anguish he read in her face.

Javier's eyebrows drew together. "The word is vaguely familiar. I'm sure I've run across it." He shrugged and tilted his head to the side. "Time enough to explore it later. What I'm interested in seeing is your true demon form. By all accounts you made quick work slaughtering my students. And then there are rumors Aisling was ejected from Sinners along with her companion—you, I suppose—which would explain the werewolf carcasses and the fact she lived through the experience. Show me what you look like."

Because he was in his truest form, Zurael felt no compulsion to change. But he took on the demon image, hoped to be able to use the sharp talons and deadly tail to free Aisling.

If she broke the larger circle, the one containing him, it might free him from the entrapment spell. And freed, he could kill Javier without the fear of becoming *ifrit*.

"Impressive," Javier said. "Can the Djinn take possession of a human body?"

"No," Zurael said, conserving his strength by not forcing Javier to repeat the question for a second and third time.

"Too bad. I'm curious. How did Aisling summon you?"

Zurael fought against answering this. He didn't want to reveal anything about her. But in the end he couldn't prevent himself from betraying her. "She called my name on the spirit winds."

"How is that possible?"

She is deeply connected to the ghostlands. She was born of them and can call the spirit winds at will.

Malahel en Raum's words rang in Zurael's mind. They grew louder and louder, until, with a third repetition of the question, he couldn't contain them any longer.

Excitement lit Javier's eyes. He hesitated only a second before leaving the small protective circle he was in and going to a table draped with a black cloth. He leaned down and pulled a wire cage from underneath, where it had been hidden by the dark material.

Aisling gasped despite the blade pressed to her throat. A fresh wave of fury swallowed Zurael at the sight of her pet, his fur matted with blood, one front paw tucked against his chest, unable to bear weight.

Javier lifted his bandaged hand and made a show of studying it. "Strangely enough, Aisling, despite an amazing collection of witches' shadow books, not a single healing potion or spell has worked on the wounds I sustained capturing your ferret. I hadn't intended to leave your house in such a state of destruction, but it hardly matters. You'll be moving in with me. Think of it as a get acquainted period as we begin working together."

He retrieved a gunlike weapon from underneath the table. Zurael didn't immediately recognize it, but Aisling's whimper of distress transmitted her horror and anguish at the sight of it.

Javier pressed the end of the barrel against the open mesh of the cage and pulled the trigger. A dart connected to thin wire struck Aziel. He jerked, cried, convulsed as electric charges pulsed into him until Javier released the trigger, leaving Aziel lying on his side, still except for his rapid breathing.

A fury unlike any Zurael had ever known filled him. He fought the entrapment spell until he was panting as hard as Aziel.

Blood poured from Aisling's neck where she'd tried to get to her pet. Javier shook his head. "This won't do at all."

He made a show of adjusting the settings on the gun. "If you force me to pull the trigger, Aisling, it will most likely kill your pet. Do not speak unless I specifically ask you a question. Do not move unless I tell you to."

Javier glanced at his assistant. "Aubrey, go ahead and release her."

Aubrey stepped away from Aisling, keeping the knife in front of her as if she felt vulnerable without her hostage. Zurael would have struck willingly, but wasn't given a choice. Javier said, "Kill Aubrey," and he did in a quick slash of tail and talons.

It was the instant Aisling should have rushed toward Javier and touched him before he could command Zurael to stop her—but she couldn't do it. Love for Aziel held her in place and the opportunity was lost in a spray of blood and crack of bone.

"I hate to waste a promising and very willing student," Javier said, "but I'm afraid that given the circumstances it was unavoidable. Students can learn *too* much. Now then, Zurael, I want you to take Aubrey's position behind Aisling. There's no need for you to bother with a knife. Your talons against her jugular should be sufficient."

It took three commands. But in the end Zurael complied.

Familiar heat swamped her as he held her back to his chest. The sharp tips of his nails pressed to her throat and she shivered with real fear—as she had the first time she'd felt them on her skin—and not the erotic fear she'd experienced since then.

"Make her bleed," Javier said, not bothering to pause before issuing the command twice more to force Zurael into obedience.

Aisling stiffened. Tears flowed freely down her face as sharp talons dug into her, sending rivulets of blood trailing down her neck.

"That's enough," Javier said, apparently satisfied that despite having once belonged to her, Zurael was now completely under his command.

Javier used his bandaged hand to pull the black sheet off what

Aisling thought was a table, but now saw was an altar. A clay tablet lay on top of it, next to a rectangular urn placed on its side.

She could feel shock ripple through Zurael. She could feel him fighting to release her, and though she couldn't be positive, she thought it was the sight of the tablet that caused his reaction, and not the urn.

Javier stood the urn up. It was covered in sigils. He pulled a stopper out and set it on the altar. "I'll admit, I haven't had much success in confining demons. For most of us they're extremely dangerous to summon in the first place, much less order into a containment vessel. And then of course, there's the risk of offending whatever demon lord they call master. But given Zurael's apparent devotion to you . . . well, I'm feeling good about my chances of being successful. Bring her closer."

Aisling barely glanced at the altar. Her attention went to Aziel.

Fresh blood was smeared across the metal floor of the cage. His breathing had steadied, but his eyes remained closed.

She wanted to weep at the sight of him. Instead she curled her hands into fists, readied herself to act when the chance presented itself.

"I'm almost embarrassed to share this with you, Aisling," Javier said. "And I suspect your skills, perhaps coupled with the application of Ghost, will make me feel as though I've wasted years of my life—and quite a few of my students' lives—trying to gather all the missing pieces of this tablet and translate it into something useful.

"Lately I've been so sure that a little tweak here, an educated guess there, and the incantation would work. Unfortunately all I've ended up with are empty bodies and, more recently, slaughtered students who brought me unwelcome attention from their wealthy families."

Aisling glanced at the tablet. It was old, broken, still missing small sections. An empty shape at the bottom captured her attention. Her thoughts flashed to Tamara's dead lover, his hand inches away from a flat piece of stone with writing etched on it, its shape the same as the one in front of her.

Some of the recovered pieces fit together tightly. Others crumbled at the edges, distorting the symbols or leaving blank spaces.

Vague memories stirred as she scanned the text. Ancestral memories perhaps, though some of the curves and shapes reminded her of those Zurael had drawn in the dirt. A cold shiver slid down her spine when she came to the sigils she did recognize, the ones she'd seen painted on Elena and later on Nicholas.

Javier ran his fingers over a line of text. "I won't bore you with all the details of how I've acquired the missing pieces over the years, but as you can see the tablet is ancient. In fact if you believe some of what's written in the moldy tomes the Church has in its possession, it was given to an elite priesthood by God himself, much like the commandments were handed to Moses.

"Instead of laws though, what's inscribed on the tablet gave mankind—or at least those deemed worthy by the priesthood—dominion over demons and other spirit beings. It's ironic when you think about all the heretics and witches and black magic practitioners who have been burned at the stake or otherwise killed by the Church and its religious predecessors. Most of them were working with faulty, weak spells and incantations, developed by man, while the Church once had in its possession god-given instructions. But I digress . . ."

He turned slightly, shifting his focus to the cage at his feet. "If she attempts to summon help, Zurael, kill her."

Javier pulled the Taser barb from Aziel with a jerk of his arm. The ferret cried, tried to stand, fell to his side again.

"Good," Javier said, putting the gun on the floor, then unlatching the cage. He waited a minute before reaching in to pull Aziel out by the scruff of the neck. "I asked you a question over lunch, Aisling, but you declined to answer. Perhaps you'll reconsider now and confirm what I already know is true. Could you summon a spirit and require it to possess the body of someone foolish enough to Ghost?"

Fear for Aziel churned in her stomach. Nightmare images from her first trip to Sinners crowded in. "Yes."

"Excellent. See, we're already starting to work well together. Now for a tougher question. Can you summon a spirit and require it to possess someone who is dead?"

Aisling's throat closed in on itself as she remembered John's voice coming from Felipe's corpse. Her heart thundered in her ears. She shook her head. Lying.

"Wrong answer, I think," Javier said. "And truthfully, you're of little use to me if you can't do that. Ghost is difficult to obtain, and there's always the possibility it'll wear off at an inopportune moment or become unavailable."

From the folds of his robe Javier retrieved an athame. And as quickly as Aubrey had slit Elena's throat, he did the same to Aziel.

"Prove you can be useful to me," Javier said, dropping Aziel's carcass onto the altar. "Bring your pet back to life or fill his physical shell with another entity."

Aisling shook with grief and rage.

Her throat burned.

Her heart felt as though it had been ripped from her body.

Even the knowledge that Aziel had died before, when he wore other bodies, didn't lessen the anguish of having witnessed *this* death, of knowing he'd suffered.

Through tear-filled eyes she saw the spiderweb strands crisscrossing Javier's face and hands. She forced aside the wild pain crashing through her heart.

"I have to touch him," Aisling said, the words barely a whisper. "And unless you want Zurael's spirit to take over Aziel's body, he can't touch me while I do it."

Javier's eyes turned to black ice. "Is she telling the truth, Zurael?"

"I don't know."

Javier hesitated a moment. He studied Aisling closely, then finally nodded. "Release her. But my earlier command stands. If she tries to summon help, kill her."

A shaky breath escaped from Aisling when Zurael's deadly talons dropped away from her neck. She took an unsteady step forward, kept her head down and tried not to broadcast her intentions.

Javier backed away from the altar. The athame remained in his hand, as if, like Aubrey, he felt vulnerable without a hostage in front of him.

Aisling blinked away tears and tried to appear as if her only focus were her dead pet. She was small and Javier was armed, confident not only in his personal strength but at having Zurael under his command. He never expected a physical attack, hadn't thought to command Zurael to prevent anything but a cry for help.

With each step Aisling reinforced the desire for Javier's death, just as with each swing of the owl fetish in her workroom, she'd desperately wanted her assailant to perish.

When she was close enough she lunged forward, and felt the slash of the athame blade across her palm as he instinctively defended himself. But if anything, the gift of her blood only ensured that his soul was delivered to those whose names she called upon in the spiritlands.

As soon as she touched him, his eyes widened in disbelief. They filled with horror in the instant she felt his soul part from his body, cut through cleanly like a scythe through wheat.

Raw emotion surged through Zurael as the entrapment spell dispersed. He reached Aisling before Javier's corpse hit the floor, took her in his arms and held her as she gave in to the anguish of losing Aziel.

"Aisling," he whispered, eyes burning as he pressed kisses to her wet cheeks, her lips, to the places on her neck where his talons had pierced her skin.

Fear for her, the fury and terror of being enslaved and forced to hurt her, to watch helplessly as she was hurt—all of it paled in comparison to the wrenching agony of witnessing her heartbreak and knowing he had to leave her.

He had to take the tablet and return to his father's kingdom. It wasn't just his honor at stake, but a future with her.

His chest grew tight with worry and fear. The task she'd accepted in the spiritlands wasn't complete. Peter Germaine still lived.

Against his chest her sobs gave way to tremors of pain, to shuddering gasps. He rubbed his cheek against her hair, told himself she was safe at the moment and he wouldn't be gone long.

"Aziel will come back," Aisling whispered against his chest, repeating it several more times, each time with more certainty, as if saying it would make it so. She pulled away then, lifted a face ravaged by sorrow, and Zurael found her exquisitely beautiful, utterly compelling in her vulnerability.

He brought her hands to his mouth, pressed a kiss to her palms in silent acknowledgment of what she'd done, saved them both. He understood now her silence since returning from the spiritlands after taking Felipe and Ilka there, could guess what had happened, what terrible price she'd paid for a gift she wouldn't welcome.

"I need to leave, Aisling," he said, and was barely able to endure the pain slicing through his heart when tears formed in her eyes.

She exhaled a ragged breath and gave a slight nod of understanding. "You want the tablet."

He leaned in, kissed the tears away. "I want you, Aisling, only you. If I hadn't promised to return to the Djinn as soon as I gained possession of the tablet, then I wouldn't leave you, not even for a moment."

His lips took possession of hers. His tongue sought hers, spoke of the things he hadn't yet put into words, the emotions she elicited, what she'd come to mean to him.

"I'll return to you," he said when the kiss ended.

Every instinct fought leaving her. But honor and duty demanded it.

He pulled away, turned to the altar where Aziel's lifeless body lay and felt a renewed surge of fury. The sting of failure.

Zurael gathered the tablet pieces. And when it was done, he kissed Aisling again, promised again, "I'll return to you," then gave up his physical form and went back to a place that was no longer home.

Silence settled around Aisling, heavy and thick, like the numbness making it hard to think, to know what to do next. Slowly she became aware of the metallic smell of blood clinging to the air, the death stench of voided bodies.

Elena. Aubrey. Javier.

Aziel.

The tears started flowing again. She wouldn't leave him here with the others.

Aisling picked him up, intending to escape the house. But as she stepped past Elena, she felt the phantom prick of Aziel's claws in her shoulder, the warm imagined brush of his tail against her cheek, as if even in death he served as her guide—reminding her of the promise she'd made to Sinead in exchange for being led to where Nicholas was bound to the altar.

It wouldn't wait. As dangerous as it was to travel to the spirit-lands in this house where magic had been raised by human sacrifice, Aisling knew the longer she waited, the more treacherous it would become to locate Elena and reunite her with Sinead. Even so, she might have delayed performing the task, convinced herself that with no one to stand guard over her physical shell, it would be better to wait, perhaps seek shelter with the Wainwright witches until Zurael returned and Peter Germaine was dead. But the heavy feel of the crystal amulet in her fetish pouch, the cold still radiating from it—so different than Zurael's heat—made her feel as if the being it represented was aware of her plight and stood ready to protect her.

She left the room where the corpses lay as they'd fallen. The house had the quiet, empty feel of abandonment.

It was in the red zone. She wondered if that would protect her from being arrested or if she should step forward and claim to be a victim before the bodies were discovered. Elena's driver could testify she hadn't come willingly.

Aisling pushed her worries aside for later, for after she'd paid her debt. She slipped into a small room, an office with a door that locked. She knelt on the floor without ceremony and fixed the name of her most powerful protector in her mind, though she didn't summon him as she slipped into the gray world of the spiritlands.

Eighteen

THE elaborately carved door to the House of the Spider opened. The same male Djinn wearing the simple white trousers of a student bowed low and stepped back, out of the way. "Welcome, Prince Zurael en Caym of the House of the Serpent. You honor us with your presence."

Zurael entered and found Malahel en Raum waiting for him. She was once again dressed in the gray concealing robes of a desert traveler, with little showing except for eyes so dark they appeared black.

"You were successful, I see."

He gave her the tablet, anxious to be rid of it, anxious to leave. Despite all the arguments he'd fashioned and his plans for making Malahel en Raum and Iyar en Batrael his allies, he felt a desperate, urgent need to return to Aisling.

"The human female who summoned you is dead?" Malahel asked.

Even the question sent a spasm of pain through his heart. "No. She isn't an enemy to the Djinn. I won't allow her to be harmed."

Spider black eyes bore into him. "She's enslaved you."

He stiffened, glanced away, and saw again the wall tapestries with their carnal depictions of intertwined humans, angels and Djinn. And rather than deny Malahel's claim, he said, "I am not bound to her in the way you imply."

The arrival of Iyar en Batrael forestalled whatever Malahel might say. He stepped into the room from one of the many hallways leading off it, his golden eyes gleaming against his dark face.

"Did the female have a chance to learn what was written on the tablet?"

Every muscle in Zurael's body tensed. In his mind's eye he saw Aisling kneeling in the dirt after they'd left the occult shop, easily duplicating the Djinn text he'd written in the dirt. He saw her standing next to Javier's altar, scanning the tablet, effortlessly committing it to memory.

"She saw the tablet but killed the human who possessed it. She freed me from his demon spell and made no effort to stop me from returning home with it in my possession."

Zurael met their eyes, let them read his determination, his intentions, reminded them with the force of his will that he was a prince of the House of the Serpent. "She isn't an enemy to the Djinn. I won't allow her to be harmed."

They offered him nothing. Neither alliance nor open disagreement, and he didn't linger.

Aisling was alone. Unprotected. Physically weakened and suffering emotionally over the loss of Aziel.

Zurael sought out The Prince. But when his father wouldn't grant him an audience, he turned away from his father's house and hurried toward the sigil-covered gate that led to the world once belonging to the Djinn.

Few could pass through it without The Prince's permission. Zurael would have preferred to gain it, to warn his father that he would lose a son if he sent an assassin to Aisling.

Miizan en Rumjal, his father's advisor, stood at the gate. He wore the scorpion of his house on his neck, though in the Djinn's prison kingdom it wasn't necessary.

"The Prince sent me," Miizan said. "I am to remind you that *his* words are still law here and he hasn't changed the ones he spoke to you last. Unless summoned, you may leave the Kingdom of the Djinn only once.

"He gave me no further instructions, but I will issue a warning. The House of the Scorpion is aware of your return. We are aware of the threat posed by the female who summoned you. We know she still lives and you wish her to remain alive. None from my house has yet been sent to her. But if you break The Prince's law and return to her, we will finish what you did not."

Miizan glanced at the gate, then transported away without saying anything more, leaving the pathway back to Aisling unguarded.

Zurael wanted to rage. He wanted to gather the sand around him in a seething mass and roar through the desert. The raw helplessness and fury filling him equaled what he'd felt when he was trapped and bound by Javier's spell.

Aisling. He ached for her, feared for her. Hated being away from her.

Zurael turned from the gate. Fresh determination surged through him. He would force his way in to see his father if necessary.

A swirl of air preceded the energy signature that was Irial. The Raven prince took form. His teeth flashed white in a savage smile. Green eyes burned with intensity. "So the game plays out. A prince of Serpents becomes the pawn to be sacrificed for a child of mud. I'd find the situation more amusing if I didn't suspect a similar fate waited for me."

AISLING felt changed, different. Whether it was gaining her birthright on her last visit or the culmination of her experiences since being brought to Oakland, she didn't know. But as the spirit winds swirled around her in greeting, whispered to her, she felt a confidence she'd never experienced before, and knew that as long as Elena hadn't entered one of the places of power in the spiritlands, then she could easily find her.

But it wasn't Elena's name Aisling spoke. It was Aziel's. She dared what she wouldn't have before, and the gray nothingness parted to reveal a man.

Confusion crowded in with her first glimpse of him. He was Irial and yet he wasn't. Instead of a stylized raven tattooed on his cheek, black wings and outstretched claws spread across his chest. And unlike the demon image she'd seen when she summoned Irial, Aziel was naked save for sheer trousers like the ones Zurael appeared in when Javier's spell forced him to take a form.

Understanding dawned. "You're Djinn," she said, feeling awkward, strangely shy now that Aziel was a man.

Aziel smiled and it flooded her with warmth and familiar comfort. He closed the distance between them and took her face in his hands, pressed a kiss to her forehead—touched her in the spiritlands, where few ever did.

His thumbs brushed away tears she didn't realize were falling. "You've always loved me well, Aisling. And because of you there's hope for others of my kind. A final lesson."

He stepped back. In the blink of an eye a robed stranger stood where Aziel had been, a black-haired man with sharp, unfamiliar features. She tried to see him as she'd seen the dead circling Felipe and Ilka, expected to see him as a pure spirit, transparent and nearly formless, perhaps bound by silken threads to unseen beings. Instead she saw a knotted mass, two entities tangled together so thoroughly their physical forms fluctuated between robed stranger and Djinn image.

"The Djinn are the children of Earth," Aziel said. "We existed long before the alien god arrived with his army of angels. He thought to enslave us, to give us over to his children of mud as familiars. I killed the sorcerer who bound me and now our spirits are joined. This is what it means to become *ifrit*. It is a Djinn's worst nightmare, what we fear even more than being bound, to become *ifrit*, soul-tainted, to have our names no longer spoken, to know we will never step foot in the kingdom carved out deep in the spiritlands where the Djinn wait for a chance to reclaim what was once ours.

"In the beginning, as humans mark it, the alien god tried to make an example of one of us. He forced The Prince into the image both Zurael and Irial have shown you, then named him demon. We were the first to be called by that name, but the beings to come after, the ones created by the children of the mud, they are the true demons."

"And my father?"

Aziel leaned in and pressed another kiss to her forehead. A love that had existed from her earliest memory flowed down the bond they shared, came with his thoughts. *Elena waits. I'll see her to Sinead. Leave this place.* And Aisling was given no choice as the spirit winds swept in.

She rose from where she knelt in the small locked office, still cradling what had been Aziel but no longer was. The sight of the ferret brought a fresh wave of sadness, not for his death this time, but for his loss from her life.

A final lesson.

He wouldn't come to her again.

Aisling swallowed hard. She wondered if Zurael would return—or if once he was among his own kind, free from the horror of being bound by Javier, he would decide against coming back.

Child of mud. He'd called her that more than once. He'd made no secret of what he thought about humans.

Not all humans, a small internal voice whispered in her mind.

She felt his absence acutely. Had expected him to be back by now.

Aisling unlocked the door and stepped into the hallway. Movement had her turning. Her breath caught in fear when she saw Elena's driver come out of the room at the end of the hall. He was crossing himself, mumbling to himself, his fingers tight around a short club.

His eyes widened when he saw her. He stopped and took a step backward then quickly recovered. "I knew Elena was bad news the first time I drove her. You look like you've lived through a nightmare, but that's not surprising. The red zone is the devil's playground."

The driver hurried toward her. "Time to get out of here," he said, and Aisling relaxed, felt almost faint with relief.

At the car he opened the door for her. But before she could get in, pain screamed through her as the club struck her head. Blackness overtook her before she could speak a name on the spirit winds.

ZURAEL let a prince's training serve him. Irial might enjoy baiting him, but his arrival at the gate wouldn't be for that sole purpose.

"Did you know she summoned me?" Irial asked.

"Yes."

"I would have killed her. I tried to get to her but her circle held."

"Aisling told me as much. She told me you chose to help her."

"Yes." Irial cocked his head. This time his smile was masculine and appreciative. "She is alluring. In more ways than one. I can see how you came to ignore my advice. You continued to couple with the little shamaness. You shared breath and spirit. Now she's like a potent drug coursing through your bloodstream and commanding your cock. And if I'm correct, she'll soon cost you a kingdom. But you were meant to be enslaved by her. And what we stand to gain— Did she tell you her pet showed himself to me?"

At the mention of the ferret, Zurael gave up trying to parse through Irial's other words. A fist tightened on his heart at Aisling's loss and her grief. "She told me you saw Aziel."

"Is that the name you know him by?"

Zurael stilled. "You know him by another?"

"I know him for what he is." Irial moved closer, as if afraid to speak the word too loudly. "*Ifrit.*"

Cold fear blossomed in Zurael's chest. Horror made worse by having so recently been bound to Javier. "You're sure?"

Irial stroked the stylized raven on his cheek. "I'm sure. It's the work of my house to keep the books bearing the names of those who've been lost, to grieve over each Djinn whose spirit we will never guide back for rebirth. He was once of my house, that much I know. And if I were to guess? For some, a father's love never dies."

Zurael heard the ring of truth in Irial's words, remembered feeling like he was ensnared, caught in a spider's web with Aisling, by powerful, unseen forces. "You see your father's hand in this?"

"Not only his hand, but The Prince's and Malahel's."

Unbidden, Zurael saw himself standing in the Hall of History with The Prince, the two of them in front of the mural of Jetrel—the son whose loss was a deep scar on his father's heart. "What game do they play?"

Irial laughed. "A good question. And since I am as much a pawn as you, I'll make the move expected of me. Did you know there is a way for the Djinn to willingly bind themselves to a human? To join souls so that both are equally enslaved and neither becomes the other's familiar?"

Zurael's heart beat so loudly that the only words he could form in the midst of its roar were "Tell me."

"Your desperation doesn't bode well for my own chances of avoiding an entanglement. If you do this thing, Zurael, I doubt you'll be able to pass through the gate and return to this place. It *will* cost you a kingdom. Do you really want the shamaness enough to pay such a high price?"

"Yes."

Irial touched the stylized raven on his cheek again, one that took on significance as he seldom wore it, just as Zurael rarely displayed the mark of his house and the nature of his spirit when he was in the

Kingdom of the Djinn. There was no need to. Its appearance was optional—unlike when he was in the world now held by humans.

"Share breath and will your soul into her keeping," Irial said. "And now I'll tell you how I came to learn it was possible. Then you'll know why I believe The Prince and Malahel have their hands in this game, too."

Zurael felt hope rise in his chest. "I'm listening."

Irial said, "When I told my father about the figurine you'd seen in the occult shop, he sent me to the library of our house to research the matter further. Oddly enough, a book I'd thought there couldn't be found, and so he arranged for me to use the library in the House of the Spider.

"While I was in the Spider's library, I was shown a collection of books that might hold the information I was after, then left unattended. A Spider's account of history is not the same as a Raven's or Serpent's. I was curious, as I imagined they knew I would be, and so I browsed those in the section I'd been given free rein to explore."

Green eyes grew somber. "There was a tale of The Prince's first son, the one whose name is no longer found in The Book of the Djinn. By the Spider's account, he came to their house seeking a way to bind himself to the human woman he loved above all others. He wanted to extend her life beyond the few years the children of mud possess, even if it meant shortening his own.

"There was no summoning in those days. There were no incantations forcing us to a human's will. The Djinn who could be taken alive were fitted with spelled bands and given to the children of mud as if they were animals. No knowledge existed of what it meant to be *ifrit* because no one had yet experienced the horror the Prince's first son would soon know." Irial shook his head. "The Prince's words were law then, just as they are now. His thoughts aren't written in the Spider's account of history. What is written is that The Prince forbade them from sharing the knowledge of how a Djinn could bind himself to a human. And in the end his son was lost in a way none of us could have conceived—and in a way that could have been avoided if he'd already been bound to the woman."

Zurael's mind raced with the implications. It was no coincidence that Irial stumbled upon the story of Jetrel—and played the part of pawn by sharing it. It was no coincidence he himself had been sent for the tablet.

His thoughts spun to his visit to the House of the Spider, to the words he'd spoken and Malahel's response.

The House of the Scorpion is full of assassins capable of doing what you ask.

What you say is true, but none of them was summoned as you were. None of them was brought to the House of the Spider by their destinies.

A raven and a spider, a serpent and an *ifrit*? What game did they play?

Unbidden, the image of Aisling's circle of fetishes came to him— a raven, a spider, a serpent and a bear linked by her blood. Why would the Djinn seek an alliance with a human who could summon by speaking a name on the spirit winds? One whose spirit guardian was *ifrit*?

The answer came in a rush that left him breathless. Excitement rose and crested, fell sharply when he thought he must be wrong. And yet he couldn't stop himself from saying, "If Aisling can summon an *ifrit*, what is to say another couldn't decipher the tablet and undo the curse creating one? That in working together, a shamaness and a sorceress couldn't find and free those whose names we can no longer speak?"

"Your thoughts mirror mine—and why I suspect a child of mud will be my fate. Such a plan would appeal to my father, and yours, as well as to Malahel—though whether or not they thought we would stop to figure it out will remain an unanswered question until this plays out."

Pain and worry slid through Zurael. He rubbed at the place over his heart. "She has an enemy still alive. If we're right, why have I been forbidden to return to her?"

"Unless summoned. Weren't those the words I overheard Miizan say?"

Hope flared in Zurael then died as quickly. How well he remembered Aisling's fear-shadowed eyes when he warned her against summoning him. How easily he remembered the guilt and anguish he'd read in them when Javier had bound him. "She won't call my name on the spirit winds."

"Perhaps not," Irial said. "Or perhaps she'll be given a choice as you've been given."

Zurael looked at the gate separating his world from Aisling's and saw a test instead of a barrier—a delicate weave of threads leading up to this moment in time. A son who dishonored his father couldn't be trusted. A love that wasn't strong enough to bridge the gap between Djinn and child of mud couldn't be fostered. She would summon him or there would be no future for the two of them.

CONSCIOUSNESS returned slowly, with a disorienting swirl of sensation and vision. Nausea threatened. It washed over Aisling and brought a wild panic that she'd choke on her own vomit and die before she could force it down.

She was bound to a chair, hands and feet made useless. Gagged tightly, savagely, as if whoever had tied her was terrified she might speak.

A small, heavy table was placed in front of the chair. The hammer resting on top of it seemed out of place, sinister, threatening.

Slowly the tiny piles of crushed bone came into focus, the broken onyx pentacle, the shattered stone—her fetish pouch tossed to the floor. Too late she realized Elena's chauffeured car probably belonged to Luther Germaine, and the driver, by association, was Peter's as well.

As if thinking about Peter Germaine had conjured him, he claimed the chair on the other side of the table. "I've gone to quite a bit of trouble to arrange for your death, but you've managed to avoid it. The man I spared from the fate of a third strike and hasty execution in exchange for paying you a visit, was found dead. The guardsmen, who tend to get carried away and turn searches into hunts, failed to find you in The Barrens, after Father Ursu was made aware of your failure to catch the bus and return home.

"The Church is wrong in compromising. My brother and the rest of them are mistaken if they think by forcing the humans who've been touched by the devil into one area of town they can limit their influence and keep them from taking over and turning God's attention away from us once and for all. Your kind is a disease that will spread until no place on Earth is free of it. You're a filthy perversion of what God intended when he created us."

Peter reached into his pocket. When his hand emerged, it held a familiar, casketlike container. His eyes filled with rapture as he stroked the thin metal. "I don't understand why you've been chosen to serve a higher power, but you have been. It's not my place to question the divine. If you're to be the tool that will open the gates of hell and flood this world with demons in order to bring about the apocalypse and Final Judgment, then so be it."

He opened the container and dipped his fingers into the gray substance. A malevolent presence swept in, this one more powerful than any Aisling had ever encountered in the spiritlands.

She recoiled when Peter leaned across the table, hand outstretched. She mentally summoned the only being not limited by the boundaries of the ghostlands—her father, though the price for calling his name would be high.

He arrived like a bolt of lightning, illuminating the room with blinding white and filling it with mindless, instinctive terror. Angel wings extended in full glory, his sword lifted and fell, meting out swift, uncompromising justice marked by a scream that continued long past Peter's death, as if vengeance followed the Ghost pathway deep into the spiritlands where it originated.

When he turned and looked at her, it took all of Aisling's courage not to tremble and cower in his presence. Her breath came hard and fast. Her heart raced and memories of the angel in The Barrens crowded in, merged with the vision of the being that stood before her.

His sword arm extended toward her and a whimper escaped despite her resolve to show only bravery. She jerked when the sword's tip touched the ropes, and cold lashed at her wrists before her bindings fell away, shattered as though the fibers were made of thin strands of ice.

He freed her ankles the same way, then knelt before she could stand, trapping her in the chair with the sheer force of his presence.

The sword disappeared from his hand and he leaned forward, gently untied the gag and pulled it away. Their eyes met, held. And Aisling was lost in a silent, endless darkness filled with a glittering galaxy of stars.

He called her back from the place that held her transfixed by saying, "You've done well. You've accomplished all I hoped you would. You've become what I dreamed you might be when your mother met my price."

Sharp pain slid past Aisling's ribs and into her heart. It replaced the dull ache that had never completely disappeared over being abandoned, left on a doorstep as an infant. Somehow it was worse knowing she was the end result of a ghostland bargain, and yet she couldn't stop herself from asking, "Who is she?"

"What does it matter? She chose a vampire's life."

He stood, elegant wings resettling as he offered his hand.

Aisling took it, allowed him to pull her to her feet. When he released her, she fought the urge to sink to her knees, to duck her head in the presence of his terrible beauty. She made herself meet his eyes again, and though her voice was little more than a shaky whisper, she still managed to ask, "And the price I owe you?"

"I will finish what needs to be done here first, then we will discuss what my aid has cost you."

Massive wings spread out to form a shield around her. He lifted his arms, and two gleaming swords appeared in his hands. A crack of thunder sounding in the room was her only warning. Then bolt after bolt of lightning struck, ripped through the house as if pulled from the sky and directed by an angel's wrath.

Flames erupted around them, destroying any evidence of her presence or Peter Germaine's death. Waves of shimmering heat were held at bay by a coldness deeper than any Aisling had ever known.

Only when the ceiling and walls began falling did he lower his arms. He tucked her against him in a surprisingly protective gesture.

Blinding white filled her vision. And when it cleared, she was standing amid the familiar destruction of her own living room.

"Summon your Djinn," her father said and Aisling knew he meant Zurael. Her gaze strayed to her wrist, where the sun-shaped amulet she'd gotten from Levanna Wainwright still rested against her skin.

Her father's fingers circled her wrist so the golden sun was caught between his flesh and hers. "Your Djinn means so much to you? That you'd risk my wrath even after witnessing only a fraction of what I'm capable of?"

"He means that much to me," Aisling said, knowing she would let her father sever the cords binding spirit to physical body and take her into the spiritlands with him before she'd betray Zurael.

"Your courage pleases me. But take care you don't become overconfident. The charm won't work on the higher hosts. The sight of it is reason enough for them to strike you down."

He changed his grip, stroked his thumb over the tiny sun. "A struggle is brewing, not unlike the one fought at the dawn of human creation. There are angels who would openly claim humans as their mates and acknowledge the children they've already created. But there are plenty who patrol this world and view its inhabitants as little more than a captive experiment. Who consider lying with humans a sacrilege, and the children of such unions abominations.

There was a time in the past when cities were razed and entire populations slaughtered to wipe out any trace of angel blood among those created from mud."

"And now?" Aisling asked, shivering as she remembered the look the angel in The Barrens had given her, the way he'd spat the word *abomination* at her. She'd thought he saw her as part demon, or cursed her for being with Zurael, but given her father's revelation she wondered if he'd sensed her angel heritage.

"Now is the time for building alliances, for strengthening them with blood ties."

Aisling experienced a stab of pain to echo the one she'd felt when she learned her mother had carried her for gain. This was her father's reason for her birth. "You want to use me to form an alliance with the Djinn."

He released her wrist. "It is one possible use. But there are others."

They might have been discussing what to plant in the fields, which animals to breed and which to sell or slaughter—the practical decisions of farming. She blinked back tears, refused to let him hurt her with his coldness. With his failure to acknowledge even her name. She swallowed her pride, her pain, thought instead of Aziel, whose voice held such longing when he spoke of the Djinn, of Zurael, who'd come to mean so much to her.

Aisling's hands curled into fists. She met her father's eyes boldly. "What will you do if I summon him?"

The sword appeared in her father's hand from nowhere. The sight of it made Aisling's breath grow short and her lungs fill with ice, but she stood her ground.

Approval shone in her father's face. "Aisling," he said, and the sound of her name was a symphony, a beautiful chorus that brought tears to her eyes along with a terrible knowledge.

His voice was as much a weapon as his sword. With it he could offer praise so glorious she might do anything to bask in it. Or he could deliver tortured visions of damnation so horrible her mind might shatter.

When the effects of his voice faded, he said, "You owe a debt, but I won't take your free will as part of my price. This moment has long been in the making. It's no accident Aziel has been your companion since birth. Summon The Prince's son. You are willing to risk my wrath and surrender your soul in order to protect him; give him the chance to show he returns your feelings, that he is willing to give up a kingdom for you."

A hundred different images crowded in. A hundred remembered touches.

Hope warred with fear.

Memories competed.

Zurael's fury over being summoned the first time. The promise of retribution she'd seen in his eyes. His acknowledgment later that he'd come to kill her.

Rest easy, child of mud. You're safe from me unless you summon me again.

His gentleness. His protectiveness and possessiveness. The way he'd kissed away her tears before leaving with the tablet.

I want you, Aisling, only you. If I hadn't promised to return to the Djinn as soon as I gained possession of the tablet, then I wouldn't leave you, not even for a moment.

Aisling's hand went to the base of her throat in an unconscious gesture, seeking the familiar comfort of her fetishes, only to be reminded by their absence that they'd been destroyed. Once, their loss would have left her feeling uncertain, frightened by her gift, but now she knew better who she was, what purpose her life might serve.

Her father stood in front of her, offering her the very future she'd barely let herself dream of, one with Zurael. It wasn't a trap. It was a test. And she would rather risk summoning Zurael and seeing hate in his eyes than to never know what would have happened if only she'd had the courage to believe in herself and in him.

"I'll summon him," she said, thinking her father meant to take her into the ghostlands when he positioned her so she stood with her back inches away from his chest.

Instead he lifted his arm and it was as though his sword cut through an unseen barrier separating her world from his. The spirit winds swept in, circled and swirled, waited to do her bidding.

"Zurael. Serpent heir. Son of the one who is The Prince. I summon you to me," Aisling said, and this time she could feel the winds carry her words deep into the spiritlands.

He arrived bare-chested, wearing flowing trousers and looking every inch the heir to a kingdom. Aisling's heart leapt at the sight of him, rejoiced at the hunger in his eyes as they roved over her, as if the angel at her back, the one he'd once called an enemy, didn't exist. As if he welcomed her summons.

The sword in her father's hand disappeared, and with it the entrance into the spiritlands. "You will stay in this world and join with my daughter?"

Zurael's attention went to the being that stood behind her, and Aisling stilled, felt her pulse throb at the base of her throat. She was afraid hatred would flare in his eyes, suspicion; instead there was only steely resolve. "You and my father have accomplished what you set out to do. But don't think you'll use us as pawns again. Aisling is mine and I won't be easily parted from her."

"I would expect no less from The Prince's son." Her father stepped away, taking his icy chill with him. "Finish it so I may bear witness that the first of the alliances has been sealed."

Zurael pulled Aisling into his embrace and shuddered with pleasure at once again having her in his arms. He'd been surprised by the sight of the angel, but not shocked, not after Irial's revelations, not after glimpsing the depth of the game his father and the others played.

He should have guessed what Aisling was, seen the proof of it in the caress of angel-red stones against the angelite blue of hers when he visited the House of the Spider. But even had he known it, he would have been helpless against her. She'd enslaved him, enthralled him from the first with her gentle spirit and indomitable courage.

He would give up a kingdom for her. He would give up his soul for her.

"Bind your life to mine, Aisling, take my spirit into your keeping so we can live and love in this world and beyond."

"Yes," she whispered, and he pressed his mouth to hers, moaned when she parted her lips and tangled her tongue with his in heated welcome.

His cock thickened, urged him to meld the physical with the spiritual. And he promised himself he would as soon as the angel was gone, knew that whenever he coupled with Aisling, whether it was a tender joining or a primitive claiming, it would always be a melding of two souls into one.

He gave her his breath, his spirit. Willed himself into her keeping as if she were one of the vessels used to bind the Djinn of old. He felt the connection between them deepen, as if gossamer strands joined to form an elaborate spiderweb holding both of their spirits at its center.

Desire flared between them, hot and fierce. Her body was soft against his, her small tremors of need nearly his undoing.

Reluctantly he ended the kiss and pulled away. He turned his head to find he and Aisling were alone in the room.

Her gasp drew his attention to her arm, to the coiled serpent inked around her wrist, worn like the bracelet he'd become when they'd been cast into the spiritlands together. He glanced at his own arm and saw only tanned skin where once he'd worn the mark of his house.

It was done then. But unlike the first time she'd called for him on the spirit winds, he felt no fury. He felt only joy that she knew his name.

Aisling laughed when Zurael picked her up and carried her toward the bedroom. She unbound his braid as he walked, reveled in the way his face tightened and his eyes grew molten at her touch.

They needed to talk. About what they'd learned. Where they'd live. The dangers facing them. But for the moment, for always, her happiness would be found in a Djinn's arms.

ABOUT THE AUTHOR

Jory Strong has been writing since childhood and has never outgrown being a daydreamer. When she's not hunched over her computer, lost in the muse and conjuring up new heroes and heroines, she can usually be found reading, riding her horses or hiking with her dogs.

She has won numerous awards for her writing. She lives in California with her husband and a menagerie of pets. Visit her website at www.jorystrong.com.